STRANGE LIGHT
LER MAHIA

by

Yvette Oloo

Enquiries can be sent to yvette@yvetteslight.com

ISBN:
Paperback: 979-8-9907477-0-8
Hardcover: 979-8-9907477-1-5
Ebook: 979-8-9907477-2-2

Book Cover by Sylvia Oloo.
Map Illustrations by Yvette Oloo.
Book Edited by Nzisa Kattambo and Beryl Wasambo (CammyBree).
Design Layout by Sylvia Oloo.

Book written in the year 2022 and published in the year 2024.
First published in 2024 by Spinkly Creations Limited.

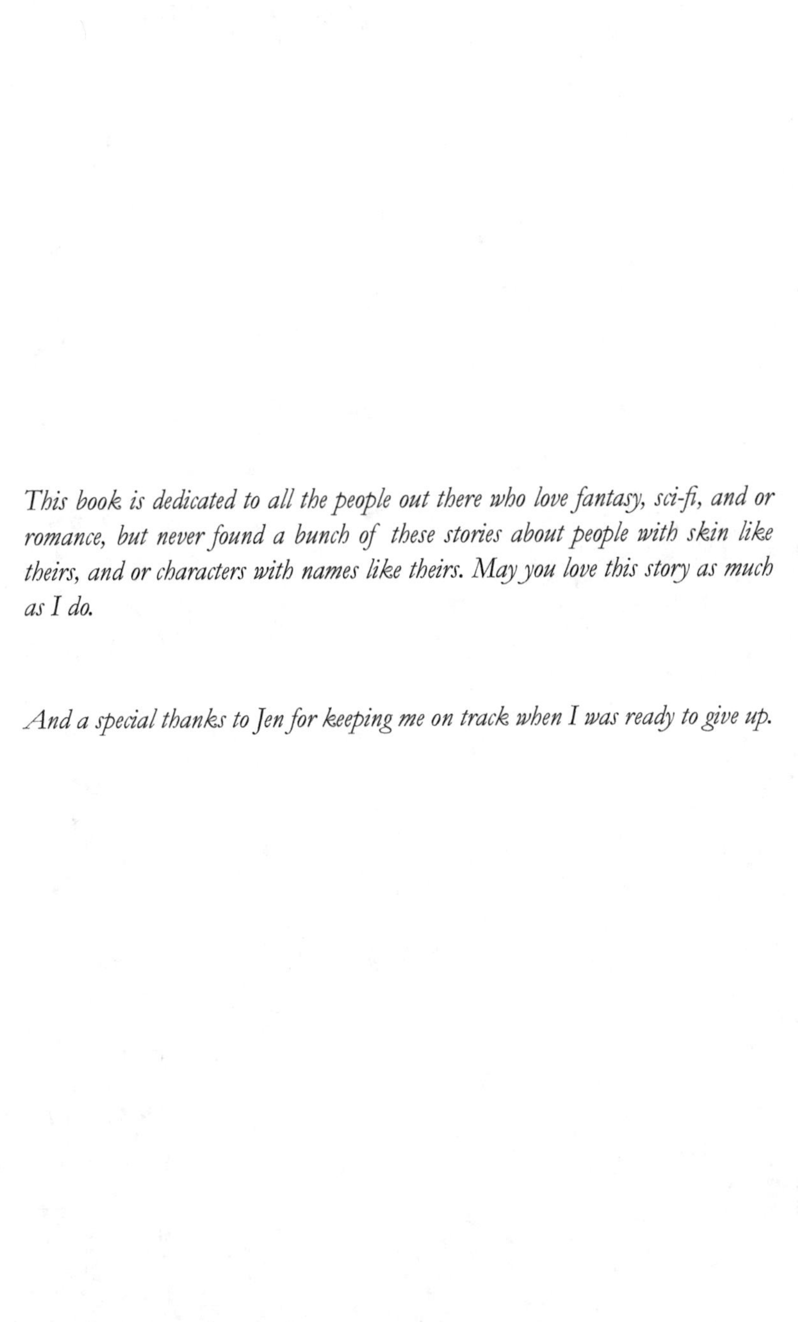

This book is dedicated to all the people out there who love fantasy, sci-fi, and or romance, but never found a bunch of these stories about people with skin like theirs, and or characters with names like theirs. May you love this story as much as I do.

And a special thanks to Jen for keeping me on track when I was ready to give up.

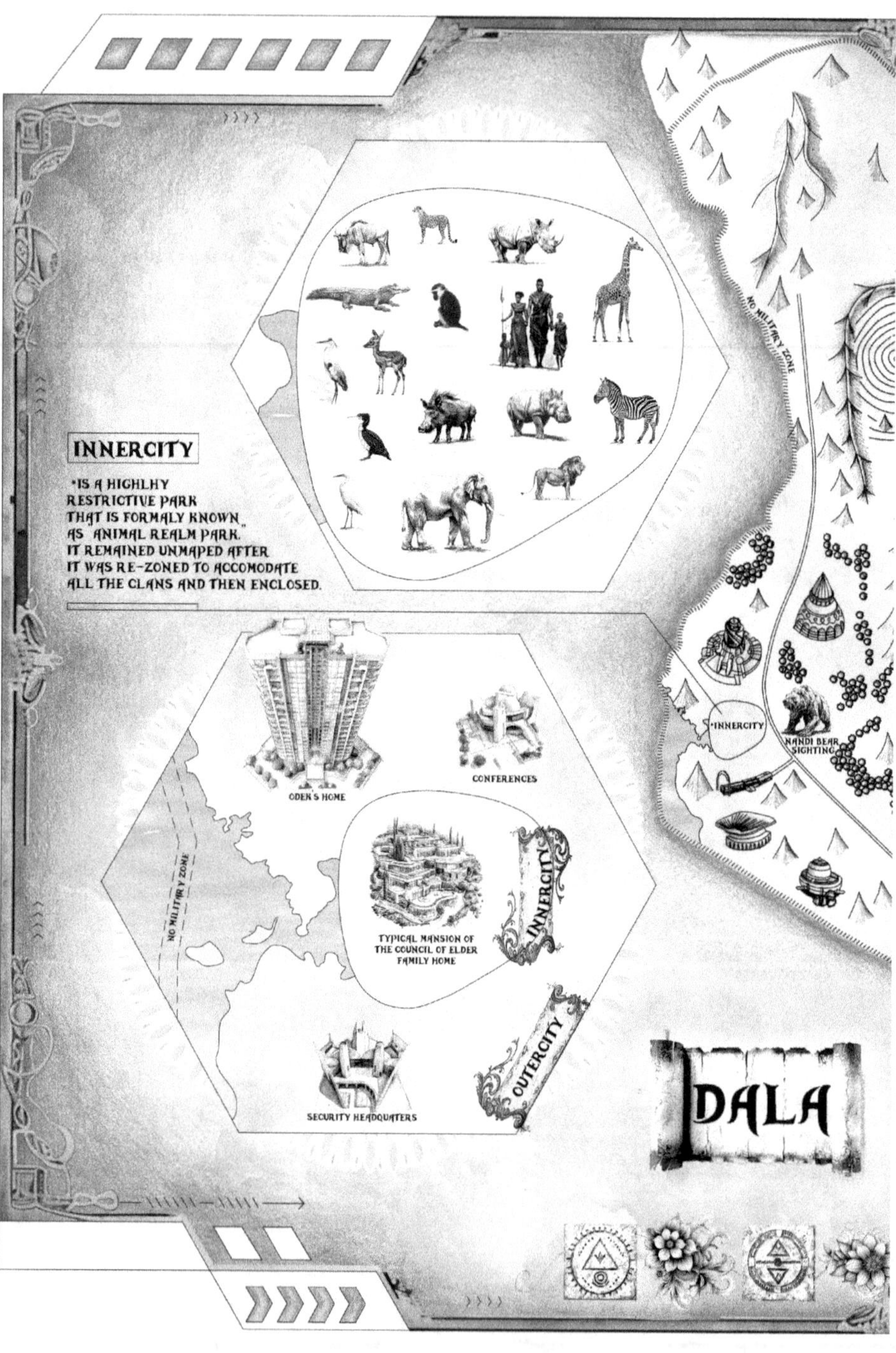

INNERCITY

*IS A HIGHLHY
RESTRICTIVE PARK
THAT IS FORMALY KNOWN
AS ANIMAL REALM PARK.
IT REMAINED UNMAPED AFTER
IT WAS RE-ZONED TO ACCOMODATE
ALL THE CLANS AND THEN ENCLOSED.

ODEN'S HOME
CONFERENCES
TYPICAL MANSION OF
THE COUNCIL OF ELDER
FAMILY HOME
SECURITY HEADQUATERS
INNERCITY
OUTERCITY
NO MILITARY ZONE
NO MILITARY ZONE
*INNERCITY
NANDI BEAR SIGHTING
DALA

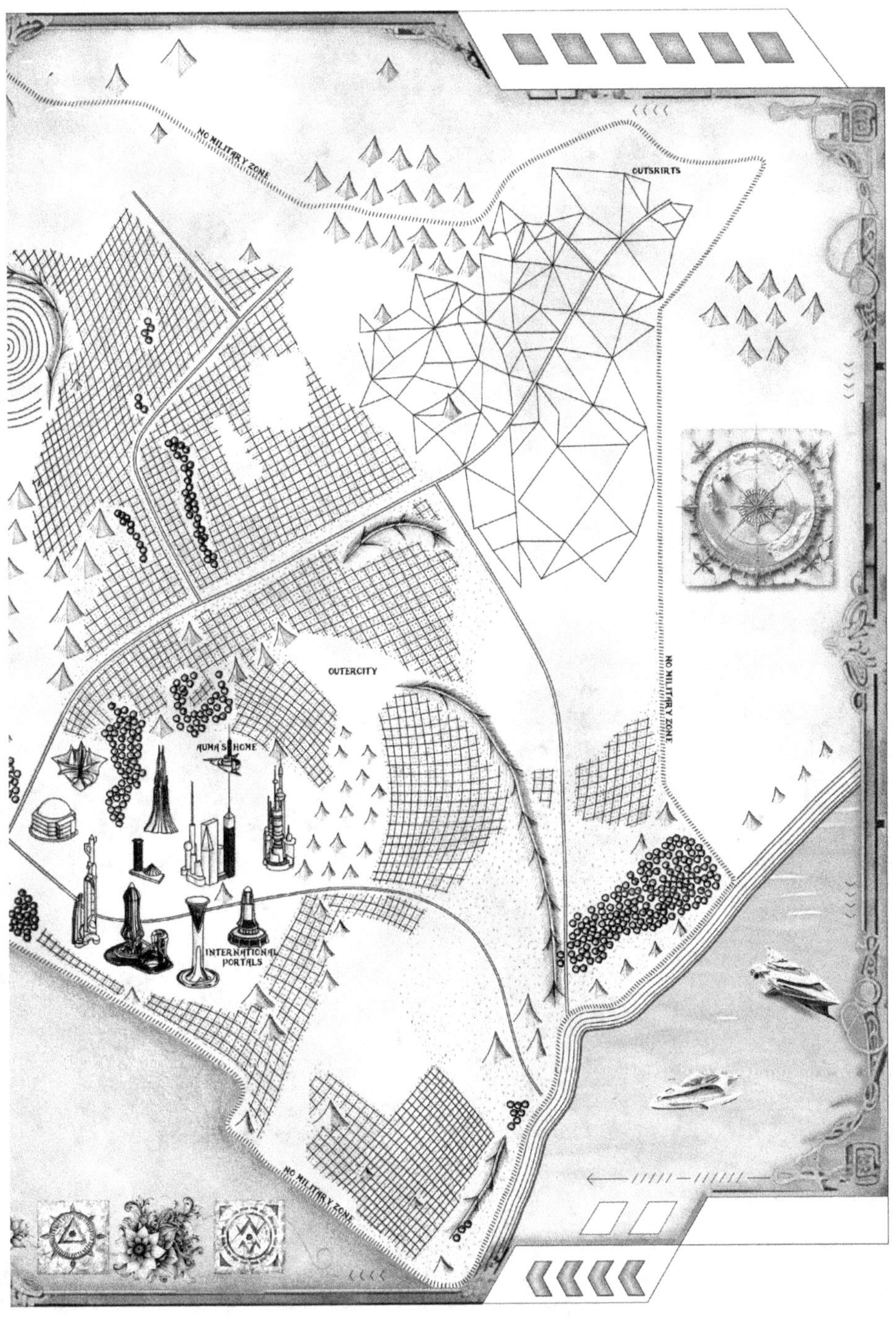

NO MILITARY ZONE
OUTSKIRTS
NO MILITARY ZONE
OUTERCITY
AUMA'S HOME
INTERNATIONAL PORTALS
NO MILITARY ZONE

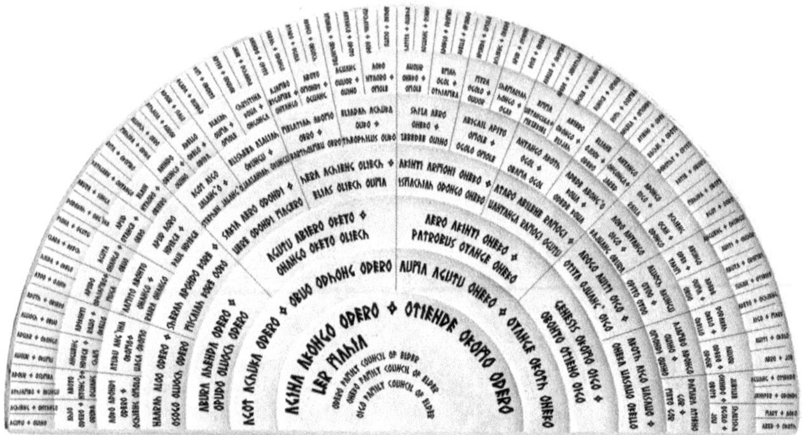

THE ODERO FAMILY TREE
THERE ARE FOURTY TWO COUNCIL OF ELDER FAMILIES. ONLY THE ODERO FAMILY HAVE THE ABILITY TO BECOME SUPREME ELDERS. WHEN POWER IS GRANTED BY THE ELDERS.

THE OKELO FAMILY SYMBOL
THE OKELO FAMILY OF THE RAWERE CLAN USE THIS FAMILY SYMBOL. (THE COUNCIL OF ELDERS IN OBUO'S FAMILY TREE.)

THE ONEKO FAMILY SYMBOL
THE ONEKO FAMILY OF THE KALKADA CLAN USE THIS FAMILY SYMBOL.

THE OIGO FAMILY SYMBOL
THE OIGO FAMILY OF THE KARUOTH CLAN USE THIS FAMILY SYMBOL.

THE ODERO FAMILY SYMBOL
THE ODERO FAMILY OF THE KAGER CLAN USE THIS FAMILY SYMBOL.

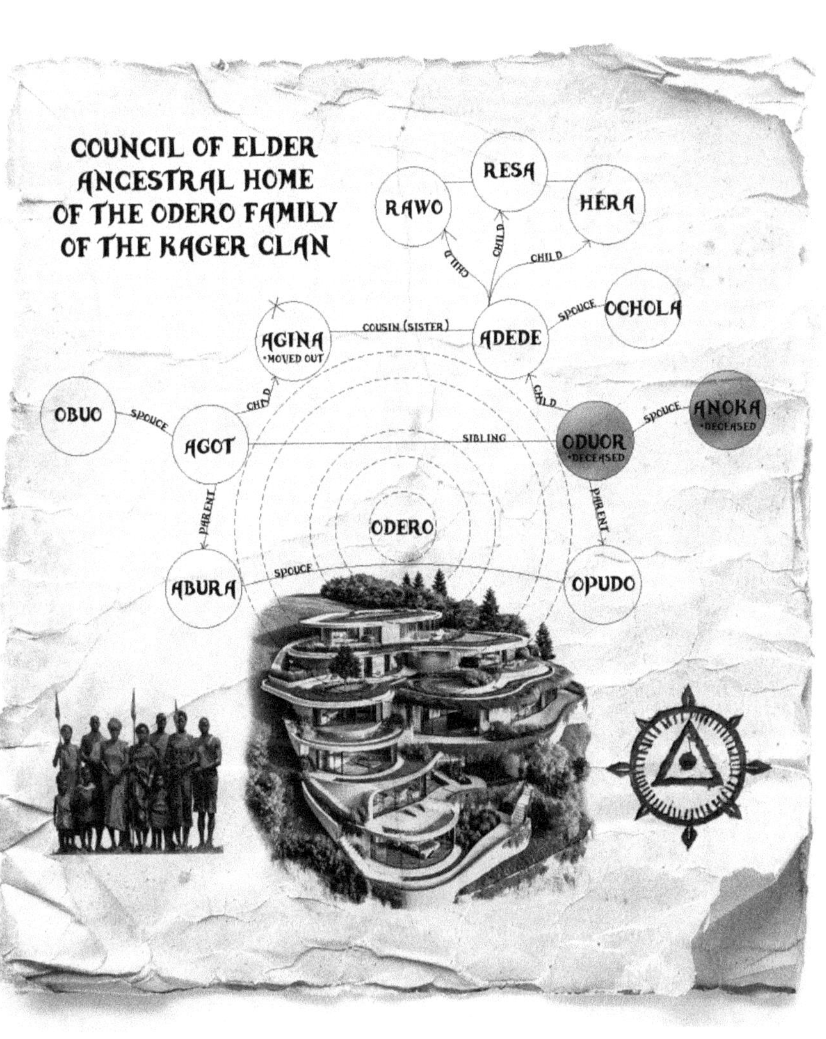

COUNCIL OF ELDER
ANCESTRAL HOME
OF THE ODERO FAMILY
OF THE KAGER CLAN
RESA
RAWO
HERA
CHILD
CHILD
CHILD
AGINA
•MOVED OUT
COUSIN (SISTER)
ADEDE
SPOUCE
OCHOLA
OBUO
SPOUCE
AGOT
CHILD
CHILD
SIBLING
ODUOR
•DECEASED
SPOUCE
ANOKA
•DECEASED
ODERO
PARENT
PARENT
ABURA
SPOUCE
OPUDO

CONTENTS

PART 1

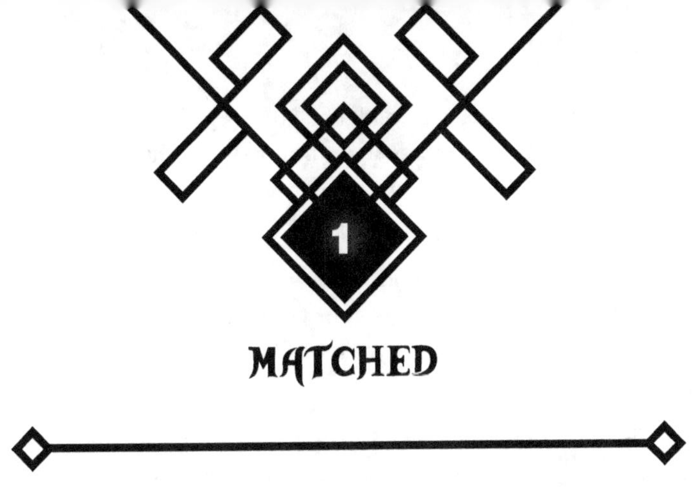

MATCHED

SHE SAT ON A branch in the middle of the tree. One leg hanging down swinging back and forth. At the same time, she lightly hugged her other leg, her foot flat, and anchored on the branch.

Her back lazily rested against the bark of the Markhamia lutea tree trunk. From her seated position, an opening formed by the tree leaves framed the sunset. Unfocused, she watched the sunset, feeling a deep sense of peace.

Relaxing among the trees in this cosy natural nook, surrounded by the soothing scents and sounds of the forest, while she witnessed the beauty of the sunset, was undoubtedly her favourite way to unwind. The downtime had become her cherished ritual.

It was probably nostalgia; Agina Akongo Odero had come to the same spot since she was a young child. An adventurer taking a pause. She felt like the tree knew her and had witnessed her becoming throughout life. The tree was like a landmark in her timeline, since it had been there for centuries, unmoving as the people and seasons went past.

When she first spotted the tree, she stared up in awe, thinking it was magical. It was unusually big for its species like someone had intentionally planted it and used magic to accelerate its growth. As a child, she would sometimes imagine it was a tree spirit that once lived as a deity.

In Agina's right hand, she had her spear twirling it between her fingers in a well-practised fidgeting motion, something she had done repeatedly over the years. She had carried the same spear since she was a child.

It was customary to choose one's spear when you were 7 years old or older and to carry it with you if your family was a part of the council of elders. It was not just a symbol of power; it showed you were always ready to protect others.

But Agina's spear was different; it wasn't just a spear. It was her com. A com was used to communicate, search, and operate applications; it was basically a portable computer and phone that came in various forms. The chosen form varied depending on the user of the com.

It suddenly lit up, reflecting a soft glowing light against her supple milk chocolate skin that had been kissed by the setting sun, startling Agina. She instinctively sat upright, but her afro got caught on the tree bark.

She jerked backwards in pain and dropped her spear, hearing it crash against leaves and branches before it landed on the ground with a loud thud. She half moaned in agony and reached over her head with both hands to untangle her hair.

Her hair had an extremely coarse texture and was tightly coiled. Though it was elastic, it was fragile and shrunk by seventy-five percent when it was wet. It always seemed to have a mind of its own, refusing to lay down when she wanted it to lay down, and refusing to puff up when she wanted to wear it up.

It was a battle she often fought with her tree. Once she managed to release her hair, Agina called out, "Arise." Her spear rose off the ground, weaving through the branches before steadily landing in her outstretched hand.

She had not been expecting to get any notifications from her com since she programmed it not to interrupt her during this time. Clearly, this notification had to have been different and coded to override all commands.

She called out, "Projector", as she held out her palm, holding the spear between her thumb and pointer finger. The spear projected the notification on her palm. What she saw had her almost fall down the tree. She steadied herself and took a deep grounding breath. Closing her eyes, she said to herself, "Okay. Agina Akongo, you cannot be freaking out about this now! Get yourself together!"

She took a few more deep breaths and felt herself begin to calm down. She finally opened her eyes when she felt calmer. She had felt a surge of so many emotions at the same time. Fear. Nervousness. Excitement. Anticipation. Worry. Denial. Relief.

She tried to stay open and present while she brought her focus back to the notification floating in her palm. She found herself in a long pause. "I haven't even opened it yet," she spoke out loud to herself as she took another deep breath and tapped the projection.

The notification expanded as it went into the application and opened the message. It was from True Match: an application that matches you with your life partner. It could also be used to find a date.

After her divorce, she had tried going on a few dates with people the application matched her with. However, the dates did not go well. She had made the intention clear that she just wanted to date, but she was not ready for that either.

She eventually decided to instruct True Match to only notify her when she got a suitable match for a life partner in her area. Years had passed since she had input the instructions, so it was not weird that she had completely forgotten about the application.

True Match was an intuitive program that matched people. Because the data was based on your experiences through life, you did not need to enter your personal information. All you needed to do was let it know you were open to dating or marriage, and input how far you were willing to relocate. Because people couldn't lie about who they were as easily, it had a very high success rate in meaningful and fulfilling relationships.

She felt her heart rate pick up again. She hadn't realised she had such a deep irrational fear, like a child afraid of monsters in the dark. She was terrified. One part of the message jumped out to her, so much so, that she could not even focus enough to read the entire message.

It was like the words had disappeared into a blur, but she could still see the part that was written: ninety-eight percent match. It seemed to become larger and overbearing as she looked at it. She froze again in panic. She couldn't bring herself to remember to calm down.

Somewhere in the depths of her, she could hear herself call out a name. It sounded like it was far away and muffled with something. She couldn't distinguish the name. It seemed to get louder and louder, and clearer.

But before she could discern the name her heart wanted to bring forward, she snapped back to present awareness. She focused on her breathing once again and calmed herself down. She hadn't even realised she was holding her breath.

Agina looked at the picture of the person she had been matched with. He looked familiar, but she couldn't quite remember where she knew him from. He was Otiende Okomo Oneko. She slid her finger on the projection as she read the rest of the message.

There was nothing other than the information that they both wanted a life partner and they both lived in the Innercity. Why was the rest of his information missing? She couldn't figure out why the application matched them!

In the past, matches she received listed more information on common interests and why they were a fit. It also included other random information. Also, everyone she dated, including her ex-wife was physically female bodies.

Though she was attracted to all types, she had not yet dated a man. Wasn't the selection based on past experiences? If it had known this, why had it only shown her females in the past? What has changed? Be that as it may, here it was, without an explanation, telling her that this was her match.

REASON TO RESIST

IT WAS STARTING to get dark since the sun had continued its descent, obviously uninterested in her crisis. Time didn't stand still, waiting for you to figure things out. The sun's orange flame painted everything black in silhouette. The shadows waited to engulf everything in darkness once the sun hid away. She would have started to climb down the tree, but she decided to stay a little longer and unpack what she was experiencing.

Maybe there was no information on him because he didn't use technology. If he didn't have a digital social presence, what would she find if she searched his name? He can't have been among the people who decided to contribute to society anonymously: only being known by a number.

The application had previously matched her with such anonymous citizens. Though they didn't have their name or picture in the application, their interests were listed. Why was Otiende such a mysterious person?

She searched his name, and it all began to make sense. He was popular, a celebrity. There were so many pictures and videos of him, articles, and a greatly loved digital social presence. There were even published biographies.

The amount of information was so overwhelming that she changed her mind and decided not to read any information. "Urg!!!" she yelled out loud as she buried her face in the palm of her hand.

She couldn't help but tell herself it was a joke. How were they compatible? Wasn't the app supposed to know her? The last thing she would ever want to do is date such a globally popular celebrity. Maybe the application left out his interests because she should have known who he was. How did she not know who he was if he was in the Innercity?

But her family didn't just live in the Innercity where the use of technology was avoided and to an extent seen as taboo, her family followed traditions. Though she embraced technology, a lot of her values were similar to the values of her family. So, she didn't use technology to follow other people's lives or do unnecessary activities.

She'll have to ask him about his interests and how he wants to be viewed and identified, rather than depending on the database to tell her who he is. It was a major part of her belief system to see people through their own eyes rather than how others saw them or how they were classified.

She exited the search engine and re-read all the information in True Match:

Name: Otiende Okomo Oneko. Age: 42.

The information was too minimal. The amount of information on the person she just searched, in comparison to the information in the application, were complete opposites.

But his face was the same. The same eyes that seemed to speak of a deep story with laughter. Shadow pockets around the curves of his eyes and lashes adding mystery to the serious gaze he held. His nose transitioned perfectly from narrow to wide, giving a sense of pride that was probably from the angle from which he took the photo, rather than him sticking up his nose to look down on someone. His full lips were at the borderline of telling the lie that they perked up because he had just blown you a kiss. This was the face of Otiende.

It looked so surreal next to her face that was childlike. A playful glow in her eyes that were thankfully topped with lashes that were erotic enough to make her look like an adult. Her rounded nose was surrounded by her cheeks which probably only looked that way because she had a fullhearted smile like a child that showed most of their teeth.

With his model pose, he looked serious, and with her puckish pose, she looked jovial. Maybe it was supposed to be an opposites attract thing. Almost managing to convince herself the match was an error, she finally climbed down the tree.

She had the urge to contact her cousin Adede Adhiambo Odero to let her know she was running a little late, but she probably wouldn't see the message. Her cousin's com might as well not exist. Adede fully lived her life the old way; she avoided using technology.

If Agina was truly in a hurry, she would have adjusted her spear into a hoverboard, mounted it and jetted out to her family's house. She needed to touch the tree on the climb down, and she needed to walk so that the intentional use of her senses could clear her mind and help her remain grounded. She also needed some time to process the information, so she walked off the trail.

It was a hill she knew well, this area was right in the middle of the Innercity. The Outercity surrounded it. It was easy to forget that the Innercity was isolated and could not be viewed from the outside. It was digitally masked to look like it was enclosed behind a great wall. The noise from the Innercity and Outercity were kept separate, along with everything else: the Intention was that the Innercity and Outercity never interact, so much so, that they might as well be parallel universes.

She heard her voice before she could see her, "Agina!" Adede's braided hair bounced as she ran up to her with a huge smile on her face.

Agina quickly put down her spear on a side table.

They embraced in a huge hug rocking side to side, then let go while still holding each other's arms.

"You are late. What happened? I know you won't miss your time in that tree. So, something happened after," Adede said, slightly tilting her head to the side and looking at her inquisitively. Adede knew her too well.

Agina laughed out loud and replied, "Yeah. I was there. I missed part of the sunset though. I got a message that distracted me."

"Message? What message? You don't usually get messages when you're in that zone," Adede said, emphasising the word *zone*.

"Yeah. This one was different. It's True Match. I have a life partner match. *Ninety-eight percent* match," Agina said, rolling her eyes and emphasising the ninety-eight percent.

"Ninety-eight percent!" Adede gasped in surprise. Even Adede, who rarely used technology knew It was rare to get such a high percentage.

"Ninety-eight percent!" Adede repeated and pulled Agina in for another hug. When she let go, she looked at Agina's face.

"What's wrong? Something is off. Who is she?" Adede rattled off, "What's wrong with the woman you were matched with?" She had a look of concern.

"Nothing is wrong. I think I just… am not ready. I haven't thought about dating let alone being married in so long. I'll show you," she said as she held Adede's hand and walked her over to the sofa.

It was a large sofa. The seat was deeper by one of the armrests, letting you either sit backless or stretch out your legs like you would on an L-shaped sofa. The pillows and the throw were blue.

The colour blue always seemed to remind her of her ex-wife who obsessively loved the colour. A memory of her quickly flashed before she forced it away to where she wanted it to remain vaulted. Then she refocused like she never missed a beat.

They sat cross-legged on the sofa, side by side. Agina held out both

her index fingers and thumbs, using them to form the opposite corners of an invisible rectangular frame. She called out, "Screen one," and the invisible frame between her fingers turned into a tangible translucent screen.

She used her index finger to navigate through the screen display, pausing when she opened the message from True Match. Reading through it again, she scrolled through to the rest of the message. Agina then turned to face Adede and handed her the screen.

She silently watched her as the emotions visibly shifted on her cousin's face. "I would have never imagined you with a celebrity," Adede said absentmindedly.

"You... You know who he is?" Agina stuttered in surprise.

"Not really. His family are huge celebrities. Since I don't go to the Outercity like you do, I only focus on people from the Innercity. I thought we all knew them. Even though people don't usually see them, the Oneko family are so popular that they often come up in elder conversations."

"But... how? I don't remember them at all, even from conversations." Agina was completely sure she would never have forgotten someone like that if she had heard of him before.

"Well, sometimes you behave like you are allergic to people. Add that to how you look more like you are possessed when you are too engrossed in your work. Nothing other than work matters to you. I doubt you would remember anyone that doesn't concern you." Agina remained silent since she could not argue with facts. "Come to think of it, I don't know if anyone in the Innercity would really know who they are. I hear they stay hidden and go everywhere with bodyguards. And they spend more time in the Outercity. Like they actually live there." A wrinkle appeared between Adede's eyebrows as she shared her thoughts.

"Humpf. You know more than I do. This feels like a blind date. Even if there isn't this celebrity-complication, I'll still have to take it really slow. I am not ready for a committed relationship. I have grown content with just me," Agina said, slouching backwards till her back was lying flat on the sofa.

"Did you set up a date with him yet?"

"No. I haven't yet taken it in. He didn't reach out to me either. Hopefully, he doesn't expect someone who is excited about him and doesn't mind a slower pace." She pouted as she spoke, clearly unable to shake off her prejudice against celebrities.

Often when people were matched by True Match, they got married within a month because they fully trusted the application's success rates.

"Screen off," Agina called out, feeling flustered. The screen promptly disappeared.

"I can't believe it! I'm excited. You must be so excited," Adede applauded. She could not stop herself from hugging Agina.

"Part of me is excited. No, that's the wrong word. Curious. But I'd rather not share this news yet. Especially with Mom. It feels wrong."

She couldn't help but feel like she was already engaged, and worse, in an arranged marriage with someone she didn't even know.

"Okay. Let's get going before they come looking for us," Agina said as she stood up.

UNEXPECTED RESULT

EARLIER THAT DAY, he sat on the open deck watching the sunset. Otiende Okomo hugged one knee, his bare foot against the wood. His other leg was outstretched. His dark espresso skin looked highlighted against the dark mvule wood floor. The sunset cast an orange light on his skin, making it look slightly like it glowed.

Otiende found that he now loved nights when he could just be home and wasn't at another event. He usually enjoyed the socialite events because he liked to interact with other people, even though they often were people he was not close to. He was the kind of person who had deep friendships with a few people he had known for a long time; not a person that kept an entourage they took to places.

Otiende's life had finally reached a sense of calm, so he felt like it was time for a change. He didn't make it a point to watch the sunset, but it felt fitting today. The sunset reminded him of new beginnings; another chapter closing.

"A new beginning," he said out loud as he took out his com. He downloaded True Match and filled out the questionnaire. The questions were much simpler and fewer than he thought. He had heard it was a simple application, but he didn't expect it to take seconds to complete.

Immediately, it returned a response. He straightened his leg and sat straight up, his heart beating faster. "Her! Why is it her? Out of all the people in the world. That's not possible. It has to be a mistake!" He wanted to be happy, feeling a tag of emotions.

But all that kept playing in his mind was the words he had hypnotised himself with over and over again, "She is not attracted to you. It will never work." He wondered to himself how the app made choices, and how it would know what you liked.

He scrolled through the information provided. She had a lot of interests and information about what she did. Some of them looked familiar. He was curious to see what his profile had said about him, considering most of the information that was published or believed by the public was not true. But his profile barely had any information:

Name: Otiende Okomo Oneko. Age: 42.

Was he unable to read his information? He got frustrated and flung the com beside him. It landed with a loud thud echoing on the wood.

He got lost in the memories of Agina as he watched the sunset, feeling a warmth inside him that he was sure wasn't from the sun's warm embrace. He hadn't thought he would be with her.

There was a seed that he knew had grown inside him a long time ago. But he buried those feelings. He had waited this long to finally decide to get married. But why did it feel like he had waited for her? Like it was always supposed to be her from the start. A ninety-eight percent match! Even if he liked her back then, he had not imagined they were that compatible.

He had kept his feelings a secret, to the extent that it felt like it was a secret that he kept from himself. Hidden in the depths of him like it was constantly on the run from a laser beam that would annihilate it the moment it showed up. He had run from these feelings and kept trying to hide from them.

He wanted to be glad and message her right away through True Match. But what if the application had made a mistake? What if she didn't want to be with him? He sighed. He would just have to wait for her to message first. That's how he would know if she was interested.

In the end, burying those feelings had just slowed down the inevitable. What had been planted had now risen from the surface like a wild weed adapted to a harsh environment. All he could do was think about her.

A week quickly went by, yet Agina still hadn't sent him a message. He sighed and walked closer to the edge of the roof. The roof was entirely covered in grass. The large houses in the Innercity were mostly built like this.

Mansions that were curved into the side of the hill, surrounded by trees. It looked magnificent if you looked at it directly from the front, with high ceilings, and the walls almost entirely made from glass.

However, the second floor was not entirely on top of the first floor: when you looked at it from the side, you could see it was strategically staggered like a stair hugging the hill. From the front you could not tell it was a flat roof covered in grass, it looked like the floors stacked perfectly on top of each other.

The extensiveness of the mansions could never truly be seen. When you approached the house from the back all you would see was the grass and landscaping on the roof. The only indication that a house existed was a gutter at the edge of the roof often done in stone.

He stopped right before the gutter, his hands in his pocket, looking out into the scenery. He could get a scenic view of the lake at the bottom of the hill when he stood there. Otiende stood there lost in thought when he got a notification.

Usually, he wouldn't be so eager to look at his notifications, but the anticipation had made him jittery. He found himself quickly taking out his com and looking at it. It was her! He hurriedly opened up the message.

Hi Otiende. I'd like to meet and chat. Probably start off with setting expectations. How about tea downtown this weekend?

He couldn't believe it. He was nervous and excited at the same time! So, was it real? He shook his head, a slight grin at the corner of his mouth. He paused for a while before he looked at his com and replied.

Hi Agina. Sure, I would like that. Chai Place is suitable. We could meet there on Sunday at 10.00 am.

He couldn't help but keep staring at the com, waiting for her reply. When he thought about it, he wondered if he had replied too fast. He had struggled to convince himself that True Match had made a mistake.

He even researched it and how it works. After all that, he found no evidence they ever made mistakes. Moreover, he discovered just how rare it was to get a ninety-eight percent match. But since the inner workings of the app were a mystery, and it was the first time it had not generated information on a user's interests, his doubt remained.

Her week-long silence left him with his thoughts of her but nothing to do, so he found himself dysregulated all week. Having gotten her reply a week later, he knew it was a sign she was not eager to marry him.

She had also suggested tea which was a short time commitment and casual. After a short time passed, she replied.

Great. I look forward to becoming acquainted.

He wasn't sure what to think when he read it. What could she possibly mean by: "acquainted"? Was she being too formal because she had forgotten him? She had addressed him by his given name. Or was it because of the circumstances in which they would meet? He ran a lot of possibilities through his mind before he sighed and finally replied.

I look forward to meeting you too.

UNLOADING DOUBTS

HAD HE MISTAKEN her for another person? He was sure it was the same Agina. It was her picture. He had kept a closer eye on her than he would ever admit. Like a child looking through the window of a store, at a toy they could never be allowed to touch, noticing when it was moved even the slightest inch. Yet pretending that they had no interest in it. Maybe it's because it had been so many years since they had met in person that she forgot. He had only been 15 years old then.

Either way, he was sure she was keeping distant. It could be that she felt awkward because of the way they parted, or that she didn't want to marry him. He had never had so many mixed emotions.

He went back into his house and changed into his running clothes. The night air was always cooler when it got dark, so it was a good time for a run.

He kept very few employees and rarely interacted with them to avoid the scandals that just seemed to follow him. Despite the size of his house, he didn't have any employees there. The house took care of itself. Since the house was unoccupied when he left for his run, the house went to sleep as he left.

Most of the systems of his home were automated and personally programmed by him. He ran along his usual path that had motion-censored lighting. He broke into a sprint before he gradually slowed down.

His mind finally seemed to calm down after the reality set in that he was going to have to start from the beginning, like meeting her for the first time. He also decided to let her set the pace. If he had waited this long, he certainly did not need to start rushing things. Waiting a little more would not hurt.

After taking a shower he used his portal to go to his friend's house in the Outercity. The buildings in the Outercity could not be as large and often housed several families on their multiple floors. He arrived directly at his friend's home from the portal.

They were close friends, so he had the clearance to come through his friend's portal. He looked around the brightly decorated entry hall with comfortable furnishing before calling out to Odek Oero Omondi and walking towards the dining room through a door.

"OT!!" said Odek, as they both arrived in the dining room at the same time. Odek took off a mitten from his hand and they clasped their hands together, bumped shoulders, and then hugged while maintaining some space between their torsos, patting the back twice.

"How are you? You seem to be in good spirits today. You almost look more excited than you were a week ago. You must have heard the good news," Odek said, looking at him with a clear look of amusement like he was just a step away from laughing at a hilarious joke.

"Is it that obvious? I feel like I have been holding my breath all week!" He hadn't fully realised how happy he was to hear from her because he still had doubts.

Odek laughed before replying, "All this time I have known you, you only get excited when you are creating some new project or competing. You have never been excited about your relationships... This one is indeed different. You must have just heard from her."

"She sent me a message a few hours ago. We are meeting Sunday. She wants to do tea." He ran his fingers through his hair, feeling a tinge of embarrassment. His hair had a coarse texture and a tight curl pattern that made it perfect for being held in the artfully crafted hairstyle he liked. It was parted several ways, and some of these parts faded in a tapered haircut that got shorter as it got closer to his hairline. Some parts were braided; the three strands twisting into patterns that waved through his head. Other parts were left undone, showing off the length of his dense curls. It came together neatly and beautifully like a sculpted piece of art.

"That's great! You were so worried it was just a mistake. Her interest in men was something you didn't know about after all." Odek tilted his head and raised his eyebrows.

"I'm sure... Sigh. There is a lot I don't know about her. I don't even think she remembers me." He felt a pain deep inside when he said it out loud. He didn't want to think that she had forgotten him.

"Now that would be surprising. People either love you or hate you. And they never forget you. You always leave a strong impression." Odek pointed at him as he said the last statement and then began to set out the food.

"Not with Agina. I always felt like she saw who I was and accepted me without being overly drawn to me." Otiende joined in helping him set the table.

"You have to admit that after you last saw each other, your life broke into chaos. How many girls have obsessed over you since then?" Odek asked, laughing out loud and slapping Otiende on the shoulder. "Let's not even include the stalkers!" he added.

Otiende ran his hand through his uniquely styled hair again and replied, "Yeah. Let's not mention them. It's a good thing there has been peace for a long time. I wouldn't have wanted to start a relationship with a mess going on. No one deserves that, especially not Agina."

"I hope it stays that way. For someone who is always trying to run or hide from trouble, trouble sure has a way of finding you," Odek said, as he squinted his eyes.

"The stars have all aligned for us to be together. And if fate won't allow it to happen peacefully, I am going to write a program that will!"

The two laughed out loud sitting together on the dining table as they had dinner, chatting late into the night. Odek's wife and children had been out visiting family, so it was just the two friends on the table. Odek was a wonderful cook, so the table had been set with several homemade dishes that they savoured as they spent time together.

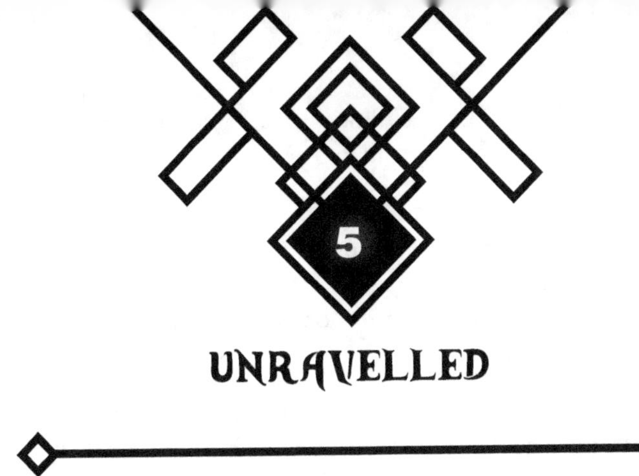

UNRAVELLED

THE SOUND OF people's voices seemed to blend as several conversations happened at the same time. Every seat in the room was occupied while others stood around in small groups.

Agina's family never failed to find a reason to gather. They especially liked to gather on Sundays. Not everyone came every Sunday but because their family was so large, it always felt cramped in her family's mansion.

Their family had lived on this land for hundreds of generations. Even though the land was typically passed down through the men, this tradition was different for the council of elders. Power and land were passed down through the women.

However, Agina had married a woman in the Outercity, given up her title and passed it on to her cousin Adede. Though she still called Adede her cousin, she had been adopted into her family when Agina was 7 years old, making her more like a sister.

Agina was now divorced and back in the Innercity, yet she still refused to claim back her title. Agina was the last remaining descendant of Supreme Elders who could inherit magical powers: the powers were usually passed through the first-born female in her family.

These ancient magical powers had not been seen in the world for over one thousand years, so considering Agina's unwavering resistance, her mother became less persistent about her title. The chance Agina would get magical powers was almost impossible, but her mother still hoped the lineage would not end with Agina.

Agina and Adede walked arm in arm circling their other cousins, uncles and aunts. They joined some of the conversations as they walked but didn't linger. Agina still had her spear in hand, but she carried it around so often that it looked natural and graceful, never looking out of place.

They stopped by the playroom next, but just peeked into the room, to avoid being encircled by all the children who would invite them for a game. They finally walked into the living room they often met in. "I have to leave soon, but I'll be back later. I'm sure everyone will still be here," Agina said, reluctant to let go of Adede.

"I am actually surprised you showed up today. I thought you would be preoccupied with getting ready for your first date with your *perfect match*!" Adede said, emphasising the words *"perfect match"* with a melodic tune.

"What date? What perfect match?" Agot Achuka Odero's voice came from behind them.

"Mom!" they said in unison, turning around slowly.

"I didn't see you there. Did you or Dad need any help?" asked Agina trying to change the topic.

"I knew I would find the two of you in here, so I came to look for the both of you. Now what match is this you are talking about?"

Agina and Adede looked at each other before Agina responded in an innocent voice, "I can't help you today. I have a meeting with someone. Perhaps you know him, Otiende Oneko?"

Agot was about to protest again but stopped herself when she realised she had been answered. She stood silent for a while without changing her expression.

"I thought you might at least know his family?" Agina said like a question, with a hint of disappointment in her voice, waiting for a reaction.

"You don't remember him, do you?" she asked, her eyes softening as she sympathised with Agina.

"The two of you were inseparable every time you met. You were just kids then and only knew him by his nickname: OT. He never came to conferences with his parents so you wouldn't have known his family name."

"OT?" Agina whispered, the sound getting stuck in her throat.

The memories came flooding back. All the times they met at the conferences. She shook her head. She turned to look at Adede. The look on Adede's face showed she hadn't known either. Agina shook her head again.

"It's been so many years. His parents are both elders who abandoned their titles, so OT is one of a kind; a pure-blood elder. They still get all the invitations. We don't abandon our own. Like I always tell you, you cannot quit what is in your blood. But he, like his parents and you, won't show up. So, I know that even if you asked others, you would never have made the connection."

Agina shook her head again. She wasn't sure what to make of the information she got. She certainly couldn't simply process the information.

"This is all too much," she finally managed to say, feeling overwhelmed.

"We'll talk later. Don't discuss while I'm gone," she said, giving Adede a warning look. Agina gave each of them a hug and left.

She walked into the city through the portal, feeling ridiculous, feeling lost, and sure she was moving like a zombie. She automatically moved her feet, autopilot taking her forward through memory; she had no awareness of anything she passed.

Should she have remembered him? It was such a long time ago. They probably connected deeply in the conferences because he was the only one there who didn't condemn technology's influence or shy away from it. If anything, he introduced her to the wonderful world of technology. She never turned back since.

She looked at the way she was dressed. *Casual enough*, she thought, looking down at her jumpsuit again, with a split leg, formed by her pants-leg-style that was wrapped, rather than stitched. The top of the set was off-shoulder on her left. The Kanga pattern accentuated her curves, so maybe it was too much.

Obviously, she had her spear not just because it was customary to carry it with her; she really loved it. It was the one tradition she didn't give up when she gave up her title. Its spearhead was made from carbon steel, unlike the rest of it. The entire spear was adaptable, being able to change in shape and size since it housed her com.

She took a deep breath and then made her way into the building that housed Chai Place. It was not on the ground floor, so she had to take another portal to get into its entry hall.

It was a place she had been to several times before. It always played relaxing smooth piano jazz music. People visited it regularly and seemed to talk in hushed tones; the noise level was low despite the number of conversations going on at the same time.

The room complimented the usual ambience with gentle low-hanging lights. Other than regular table seating, there were several sofa seating areas, with several fluffy pillows, and bar stools at the counter where the people didn't just talk with the company they met; they also talked with the tea sommelier.

She walked into the cafe expecting to search for him, but he was the first person she spotted, like a magnet drew her eyes to him, pulling her into a world where just the two of them existed. He seemed to have been lost in thought, playing with a straw in his hand.

She had seen a picture of him, but he looked more enthralling in person. Maybe it was playing with the straw that made him look more youthful; his features were softer, and she could see his younger self in his face. Thinking about his younger self made a warmth bloom in the pit of her stomach, a soft, comforting sensation that flourished as it radiated through her body.

How had that 15-year-old grown into this man that made her feel… Wait!… What on earth was that sensation she was feeling in her body? How could he of all people rouse sexual desire in her body when she was sure it was long gone after she had stopped dedicating her life to no one but the woman she loved?

She felt her heart beat faster. It couldn't be because she was nervous! She felt a weird excitement in her, like she was a teenager with a crush again; hoping he would spot her and fall madly in love, while also scared to be spotted because she was gawking and imagining him doing indecent things to her.

Her imagination was running wild with romance stories, picturing what was going to happen when he saw her. She had long forgotten the speech she had prepared to gently turn down the celebrity. Her defence had completely gone up in smoke. She felt like she had melted.

Her thoughts only seemed to want to take her straight into his arms, making her even more excited, which in turn made her thoughts wilder. What was she imagining!? Love? What if it's just sexual attraction?

It has to be infatuation, she told herself, forcing away the current thought of him being so taken by her that he had shamelessly pinned her to the table while he spoke of love in her ear and gently touched her face.

She finally seemed to form thoughts other than how he was going to react if he fell in love with her. Unfortunately, the new thoughts that flooded her mind were of her past marriage, knocking the excitement right out of her. The pain was enough to bring her to tears, that she had to force the thoughts away, or else she would end up being a mess.

Luckily, Otiende was distracting enough; her thoughts easily drifted back to how handsome he was when she looked at him. Instead of the excitement, her guard was now up again. A wall built high, created to never be taken down.

She wasn't going to repeat the mistake of fooling herself into believing love could fix anything. She was going to remain cautious, give him a chance, but allow herself to leave if things couldn't be fixed. Just looking at him had diminished her need to have one foot out the door. Now she was truly going to give it a try, with both feet, a way out still there just in case she needed it.

She walked over to him, and he still didn't break out of his daze. When he finally spotted her, she had almost arrived at his table. He put down the straw and stood up, holding out his hand.

He wore a sleeveless button-up shirt with a leather-like glowing fabric on his collar and down the buttons. His precise fit dress pants were in the same white colour as his shirt, tucked into his high-top shoes that looked like they were heavy but comfortable. The soles of the shoes glowed in the same blue as his collar. His arms were muscular, and he had several buttons undone, revealing a peek at a hairless muscular chest.

"Agina," he said, as she put her hand in his for a handshake. She felt an electric sensation that generated from where their skin made contact, that ran through her body straight to her core. Luckily, he didn't linger on the handshake. What on earth was this that he was making her feel?

She wasn't expecting to have this reaction, so she stood silent as they looked into each other's eyes. It was like time stood still as she searched his eyes, looking like she would find an answer that would tell her why he invoked such a strong reaction in her.

Even if time seemed to stand still, sensations were wildly running through her body. The raving sensations were everything but still. She became acutely aware of her breath, each inhale and exhale, stirring an energy that was building in the air.

She finally managed to find her words and found herself saying, "Let's sit." She had said it more to herself to break herself out of the trance he seemed to put her in.

He sat back in his chair, and she sat across from him, then she set her spear beside her. She hadn't taken her eyes off of him yet. She wanted to blame it on just finding out who he was, but in all honesty, he was breathtakingly handsome.

He sat in his chair with a slouch, but he had such an air of confidence that it looked like the straight backrest should bow to him and curve to match the curvature of his slouch. He was about to reach for the straw again when she gently whispered, "OT. I found you."

She had been remembering how she always found him in the conferences, hiding away. She would say that every time she found him like they were playing hide and seek. She had said it subconsciously. It was his reaction that made her realise she said it out loud.

She could see him ease like he was melting, though his posture was already relaxed. She felt like he finally really looked into her eyes as he sat up straight and balanced, somehow managing to look even more relaxed with such a proper posture.

RECONNECTED

OTIENDE SMILED AND said, "I am glad it's you who found me."

She was pleasantly perplexed when she heard his voice. Was his voice always so alluring? She didn't remember his voice being so deep and calming. It was a voice that vibrated deeply but still sounded so smooth like it was born from a bass string instrument. It was the kind of voice you heard over the radio from a host, or on a commercial.

"What have you been doing in hiding all these years? I must admit I didn't keep up with any of it and I only found out on my way here that Otiende and OT are one and the same. You'll have to catch me up!"

She was now also smiling as she looked at him in awe. Looking at his face as if seeing him for the first time; the face she remembered was there, but it wasn't really there. Just the feeling was familiar. But she would never forget those lashes. The way they moved like they were telling their own story was still the same phenomenon. Everything else looked older or more mature.

What she didn't know was that others who were not his close friends would say he didn't open up much. Though she wasn't a close friend by definition, he had a history with her, and she had seen a part of his personality others didn't get to see. So, of course, he opened up and accepted the invitation, talking for a long while about what he's been through in the past years.

  **STRANGE LIGHT: Ler Mahia**

As he talked about the relationships, work, his projects, and the competitions he won, she would naturally find herself gesturing and exclaiming, asking questions now and then. It was different from the well-practised body language she often had to show when she was in the role of a diplomat. Somehow hearing about what he had been up to was gratifying and warmed her heart. Listening to him was as natural as a reflex she always had.

"People have never ceased to misunderstand you," she said absentmindedly when he was done updating her. Coming back to focus she looked at him. "What did you always say when I told you: you can't hide from them forever?" she asked, shaking her head.

"Then I'll run as fast as I can. No one can outrun me!" replied Otiende as they both burst out laughing. Then he added a compliment, "You are a natural mediator. Even then you saw both sides clearly."

"It's their fault for not taking the time to understand such talent and a brilliant mind," she said, leaning her head forward in emphasis. Their banter came back naturally.

His eyebrows shifted as he said, "Actually, it's you who has a brilliant mind and creative talent. You see things others don't. I followed your work. It's simply genius."

Agina blushed at the compliment, feeling her face burning. "Thank you. You know, if you think about it, my career all started with us: the conversations and what you showed me."

"Seriously, I haven't met anyone with a mind like yours. We complement each other perfectly. I'm glad to get to know you again. A new beginning." He grinned at her, looking at her like she was captivating.

"Now you are just flattering me too much. With all the people you have met as the face of our technological world... that compliment is too much," she said, shaking her head.

She felt like she wanted to hide. But with the way he gazed at her and the sincerity in his voice... There was nowhere for her to hide.

He took her hand in his and said, "It is the truth."

She felt the energy through his touch again. Looking at him now, she felt like she could see their future together. She still felt like she didn't know him. But he was familiar, and it felt comfortable. She might not end up with the simple uncommitted life she planned; plus with what she now knew about Otiende, it was going to be enigmatic. However, she was open to it.

"How about we order something to drink?" she asked, not trusting herself to say anything else and trying to redirect him so he would let go. She thought he looked a little reluctant as he let go of her hand.

They were still in the Innercity, so only some services were provided by people. They entered the order themselves on a screen they pulled up from the centre of the table. He put in his order first, then switched it to her side so she could enter her order.

"After our conversation, I feel we need to start over. Even though we only met at the conferences, I had no idea you were an elder till my mom mentioned it. I avoided being an elder so much that there is a probability she would have gotten me to stay away from you if she mentioned you were an elder." She paused and looked away before she continued, "...I can't help but run away from elder stuff. But then again, you were my person. I would probably have said: look at OT, he is an elder and he uses technology all the time. That's why she probably didn't say it... If I knew it would have grown into a dangerous influence on our people." She clasped her hands together and put her elbows on the table, looking at him as the realisation sunk in.

"The fact that I was an elder was something everyone wanted to deny. I am not like everyone else. For them, it's easier if I am their famous superstar. A superstar can be different. An elder shouldn't be like me." He shook his head.

"Hmm. I felt different and wanted to stay away. They knew I was different. But being an elder was still constantly pushed to me. I am the last one." She spoke with sarcastic pride on the last statement.

"As time passes and we get to know each other, I look forward to defining who we are, irrespective of what others say."

She nodded her head.

"So, Hello. I am Agina Akongo Odero of the Kager clan. Nice to meet you," she said, as they both stood up. She took her spear to give the gestured greeting as it was done with a spear: holding the spear in her right hand she brought her other hand over it, her left palm facing her, and positioned it over the hand that held the spear. It was swift like a salute over the chest. Then she lowered her left hand and put the hand that was holding the spear close to her heart, crossing her arm over her chest.

"Hello. I am Otiende Okomo Oneko of the Kalkada clan. Nice to meet you," he said, returning the gesture as it was done in the same way without a spear: before him, he held one hand over the other, a short distance away from his body and just below his face. His right hand was in a fist, his left palm faced him, and was positioned over his right hand that was in a fist. It was also swift like a salute over the chest. Then he lowered his left hand and put his right hand in a fist over his heart, crossing his chest with his arm. The gesture, whether done with or without a spear, meant that you welcomed the person not just with your words but with your heart.

They both sat down again, and she set down her spear. Just then their drinks arrived. The waiter put the drinks and food on their table and left. The teacups and pot were clear glass, showing Otiende's orange-brown tea and her purple-brown tea. The food was served in a rotating tiered dish. There was a selection of dainty pastries and desserts, and finger sandwiches.

LIFE–CHANGING WORDS

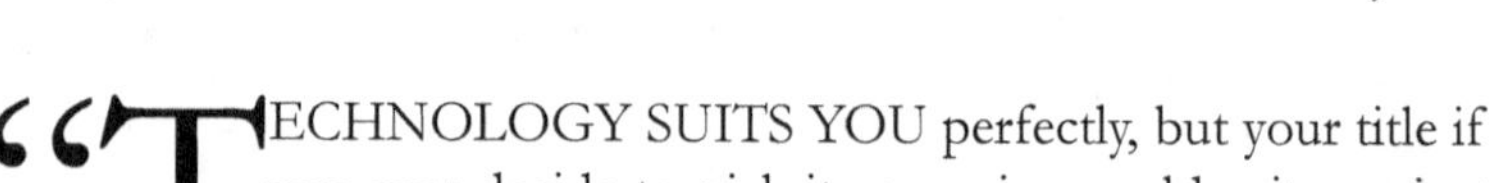

"**T**ECHNOLOGY SUITS YOU perfectly, but your title if you ever decide to pick it up again, would suit you just as well. You should never have to choose one over the other. You belong to both worlds."

She looked into his eyes as he spoke those words. There was something about the sincerity she felt when he spoke those words that made her hair stand on edge. It gave her a sense of coming into awareness at her core.

"You should say the same for yourself. You gave up your title too, your whole family did," she said. Though judging from what he just said, she knew it was something he was already deeply aware of.

"In the end, we still serve our people whether in the Innercity or the Outercity. We serve them all the same."

"My title was lost when I got married. I haven't even had the thought of taking it back. I knew what I was giving up then. So, I let it go." There was a pain in her voice when she mentioned getting married.

She did not have the intention of getting divorced but in the long run, it was the best decision for both of them. It was a pain she would carry with her forever. It hit her at any point, for various reasons.

She knew he sensed an unspoken story by the change in his expression. He asked, "Are you ready to talk about what happened?"

She looked down to create a pause in time like she did when she was faced with a question that was difficult to answer. She took a sip of her tea, to lengthen the time it took before she replied, extending the pause. Bringing intentionality to the forefront, she was fully aware of her sense of taste. She used the taste of the tea to connect to a stillness she responded more consciously through. Her core told her she was not ready for the conversation.

After she was done looking internally for a response, she looked up at him and said, "Maybe another time. Some things can wait. I would like our relationship to go slow." She changed the course of the conversation. "As much as I tell you, you need to stop running, I know you run because your stance is strong, and they don't understand and try to change you. Running is how you stand firm. But for me, standing firm is what I struggle with. Even when it looks like I am making firm choices, I am just running. I'm still learning to be firm. So, I need time."

He nodded his head before saying, "Of Course. However much time you need. I will wait. Knowing it's you, I can be more patient. Having you back in my life is enough."

"I trust it's as you said, OT, I know you will stay firm and wait. If I ask you to wait a few years on the marriage, can you honour that?"

"I give you my word Agina." He moved his head up and down.

"Let's wait on getting intimate too. Not waiting until we get married, I just need time. I don't want to be tangled because of sex." Her eyebrows were wrung with worry. She felt like the desire to have sex with him was already too strong.

"I give you my word Agina," Otiende easily accepted, not opposing the conditions she put forth.

They went over some expectations on how often they would speak, message each other, how often they would meet, and other relationship matters, agreeing on ideals. They also went over when they would get married and other expectations and preferences.

Then Otiende asked her about what she had been up to and he listened earnestly as she spoke, validating her as she spoke with his gestures and responses.

They had not noticed how much time had gone by. Late into the day they finally stood to leave.

"Were we the only ones in the cafe?" Agina asked, noticing as she looked around.

"I reserved the whole place. It's the only way I can meet in public without having my bodyguards right beside me. It's not that I can't handle myself. They are there, mostly to stop people from approaching. It also helps avoid legal disputes."

"Oh." That is all Agina managed to say. She somehow forgot that he was a celebrity.

"It's fine most of the time," he added when he noticed the look of concern on her face.

She nodded as they walked towards the portal, her scepticism about him being a celebrity returning.

"Here. Let me get you clearance to go to any portal you like, to and from here."

"That's not necessary..." she began to opt out, but with a swipe of his card and a few clicks he had already managed to get her the authorisation.

Getting authorisation through the proper channel would have taken weeks to get a response. That's why she didn't apply for approval to places unless she visited them often.

"Can you go anywhere with portals?" she asked, amazed at how simple it was.

"All public places in the Innercity and Outercity. Advantages of being... What were your words again?... *The face of our technological world,*" he replied with pride.

"Must be why I never ran into you all these years." When she first looked him up, she had doubted there was a celebrity who lived in the Innercity; she hadn't understood how he didn't run into people all the time.

He smirked as he said, "It is great for avoiding people!" They both laughed.

She gave the gestured greeting again and he also gestured the response. She used the gesture more so to avoid shaking his hand before she stepped into the portal and left.

ALTERED

SOMEHOW THE ENTIRE day had passed. How had she not felt hungry? It was already half past four in the afternoon. They both had not eaten or drunk much. She had told Adede she would be back, and she knew exactly what her family would currently be doing to prepare dinner, but she went home instead.

She had a lot to process, and she didn't feel ready for the conversation she knew she would need to have with Adede and her mother. As soon as she walked out of her portal, her house sensed her state of being and began to play relaxing music.

She took off her shoes and put them away in her shoe cabinet. Agina chose not to set her spear in its holder where it connected to the system of the house. Connecting it enabled her to make calls or use a computer from anywhere in her home.

Instead, she went into the house with the spear. Her home was located close to her family as was with most people who lived on their ancestral land. But unlike most, it was a small house.

She felt the size was better for her because she didn't invite her family over. Families generally liked to gather, so she would visit them as opposed to having them over. The house had a lot of technology infused with it. Most of which she had invented herself. Her family felt uncomfortable there because, to them, it seemed like the house was alive and unnatural.

Her friends who were not uncomfortable around technology tended not to come either because the space was so attuned to Agina, that it felt more like her private bedroom that was deeply personal, rather than a home. To them, being there was like an invasion of privacy.

Besides, people from the Outercity were not able to enter the Innercity. Aside from her family, most of the people she interacted with on a daily basis were from the Outercity.

Initially, she had designed her home like her cocoon; a place to transition and hide after her divorce.

Except for her entry hall and bathroom, the rest of her home was open including her bedroom. If someone else was present, she was able to digitally screen off certain areas as needed.

Likewise, she could also completely open up the side of the home that wasn't tucked into the hill, giving completely unobstructed circulation. It provided her with more open space.

She looked around her home, remembering that she had both worlds together. It was how her life should be, not split like she felt.

Like most homes, it had a high ceiling, but it was more so because her bed was suspended on a platform, appearing like it was on a floating balcony. So her bedroom wasn't quite a mezzanine floor.

The floor underneath her bed platform was sunk beneath the floor. Pillows and cushions made the sunken space look more like a sofa that was built-in below the floor.

The rest of her space was open, defined by her furniture; a sofa in her living room, and a dining table and chair set in her dining room.

The wall across from her giant glass doors wall, was all built-in cabinetry that was built high up to meet the ceiling. Her kitchen cabinetry and counter were next to the dining room along that wall.

She went over to the sunken seating nook and lay down on the pillows, her hands and legs outstretched, her spear still in her hand. She realised that she was no longer wondering about why they were compatible.

She smiled uncontrollably, looking up at the bottom of the platform. It was a painting she did herself; it looked like a starry night on one side, transitioning into a clear sky with a few clouds on the other side.

She always liked to believe the world had so much more than what we could see, so when all the lights were out you could see mystical creatures and spirits roaming the sky of her painting.

She felt like she had completed a cycle and was starting a new cycle. A new beginning. She was content.

She felt a need to release energy in her body, shedding the thoughts that had held her back, to enable herself to truly feel the joy of reconnecting with him. So, she got up and went to her exercise area. It was a space without furniture between the sunken seating nook and the glass doors.

Before she began the body movement, she stood on a particular spot, rocking back and forth as the floor adjusted its firmness. When it was as firm as an exercise mat, she stopped rocking and walked into the middle of the clear space.

As her home switched the music to a more upbeat song, she began to stretch into different poses with her spear in hand. Some of the poses were fighting stances. Some were part of an elegant dance. The rest were just her feeling the energy in her body and expressing it.

She continued as the songs changed, moving to the beat, feeling the release of energy flowing through her body. She finally stopped when she felt more relaxed, and the music transitioned to a meditative song.

As she walked over to the glass door, it automatically slid fully open, and she walked out onto the deck. She also had an open area outdoors where she exercised.

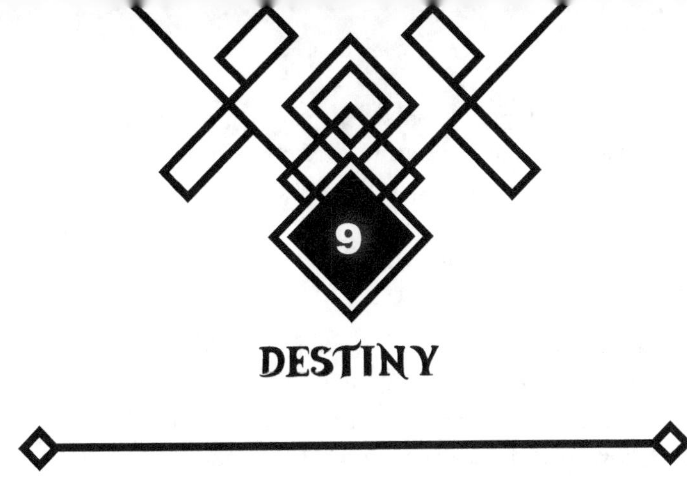

DESTINY

S HE WALKED OVER to the side that was more like an outdoor living area picked out her traditional stool, Kom Nyaluo, and then walked back to the exercise area.

She positioned the stool in the middle of the clear space and sat on it balanced with her back straight. She then crossed her legs at the ankles, with her palms face up, resting her hands on her knees. She gently closed her eyes. Her spear was in her right hand, between her thumb and pointer finger.

What came to her was the statement Otiende said, *"You should never have to choose one over the other. You belong to both worlds."* She had struggled to believe it since she never felt like others fully accepted it.

She felt that meeting him again had been good for her. In her circle, the two worlds tended to be clearly separated and she felt stuck in the middle, having to choose. Maybe it was because she shifted between the Innercity and Outercity during the weekdays. The places were so different that it felt like switching personalities to function alongside others, every time she crossed over.

In her home, she didn't have to choose. Before she had her home, she felt even more separated in two. She was most comfortable when she had both.

"Both worlds," she said out loud as if testing the words. She went into meditation, letting the thoughts pass by, deciding to let them go.

She cleared her mind. Then she began chanting to herself an old ceremonial chant she had learnt, since it was fitting for the moment: saying the words made her feel like she was calling for power and strength. She changed the words slightly and added her part to it, so it would speak more in alignment with her soul that she had just acknowledged.

As if in response she heard a voice, ancient within her, asking if she accepted the power. Without hesitation, she replied that she did. In that moment she held the unwavering view that she belonged to both worlds. She finally felt a deep internal balance.

Agina repeated the chant she created. She felt an energy rise in her like a power within, and she exclaimed out loud like she was declaring to the world: **I command nature and technology. Both worlds are mine.**

Her eyes were still closed when she went into a visualisation. She felt like she was having an out-of-body experience, existing more in an infinite space that looked like the galaxy. Where a power as infinite as the space broke free from within her, lighting the infinite space with a blinding light.

In that feeling of expansion, she could still sense what was around her. The little things were part of the infinite space, but also weren't the space; she could sense everything as a whole, while still maintaining the ability to define it as the leaves on the trees, the birds in the trees, the insects flying, the dirt at the foot of the tree, feeling every particle of soil. etc.

When the visualisation ended, she opened her eyes. The first thing Agina noticed was her spear felt different. She wasn't sure what was different. She could sense it, almost in the same way she could sense everything when she was visualising power coming from within her. It was unlike sensing an inanimate object or something that had life; it was a newfound sense.

She looked at the spear, and then noticed tattoos on her arm. It didn't make any sense. She examined the tattoos, lifting her arms and noticing that they were on both arms and extended across her skin to her torso.

She peeked under her clothes and concluded that it probably covered everywhere except the palms of her hands and the soles of her feet. Worried and intrigued, she ran into the house and looked in the mirror. She was relieved it didn't cover her face down to part of her cleavage, but it crawled up the back of her neck, probably continuing up and covering her scalp.

She looked at the pattern again, admiring it. It reminded her of ancient tattoos her ancestors wore. It was beautiful. It looked like something she would have designed herself. Then she suddenly remembered the visualisation and what she was chanting… What the heck had she been chanting?

She replayed it in her head. What ceremony was that chant from? She went into a panic. She was no longer present, no longer just observing, nor aware of the moment. As thoughts began to swirl in her head, the wind began to blow.

The house began to play a song that usually helped her calm down and a screen projection came up showing search results. The results showed Supreme Elder Initiations where her ancestors were granted magical powers. She reflected upon the chant she modified: balancing the old and the new, where both their traditions and technology would thrive.

What had she just done? Power? She had called forth… What responsibility had she just taken on? She began to cry. Her thoughts swirled as the wind picked up. She heard thunder. She was panicking even if she knew she needed to stay calm.

Though she hadn't bothered to learn anything about the powers of Supreme Elders, she was certain her thoughts and her power was connected, affecting the weather. She could feel the broken boundary where laws and anything normal were shuttered, breached and connected through this power. In the visualisation, she thought she had only imagined feeling powerful.

It became clear to her that her spear showed her search result because she had thought of the question: *what ceremony was that chant from?* She looked at her spear again and had a better awareness of what was different about it.

She had always known nature is connected, that it was a synchronicity where we are all one. But now she also had a sense of connection to all things electronic; she could sense the networks and all signals; she could sense their performance and when they were processing tasks; she could sense the flow of electricity and she could influence how all these things worked.

She decided to test it out. She let go of the spear and as expected it hovered over towards the entry hall, the house opened the door, and the spear went in. Then the door closed behind it. She didn't go to check. She knew it went where she thought it should return to.

She was feeling too overwhelmed, like a heavy weight was placed on her chest. She wiped the tears that had wet her face. The tears didn't go on, like they had sunk in her, adding to the weight. She suddenly couldn't cry or feel anything anymore.

She went to the kitchen and picked out something to eat. When she was almost finished, she ate as she walked up to her bed, finishing it just before she took off her clothes and threw them to the side.

She sunk into her bed, angrily pulled the covers over her body and fell into a deep slumber, the weight of what just happened pulling her into extreme exhaustion.

WHAT MAGIC BROUGHT

OT: Agina, are you okay? I know about your powers. There is a problem I need to talk to you about. Meet me here as soon as you can: Portal data attached.

So much has happened. But I think I'll be alright. Leaving now to head to you.

OT: Okay. I'll see you soon.

-End of text messages-

S HE WALKED THROUGH the portal to find herself in a large entry hall. It was the first of its kind she had ever seen. It had a mix of traditional decor and modern decor. A few of the decor pieces were technology-based, but overall, the room was in the traditional style.

The decor did not look particularly expensive, but you could tell a lot of money was spent. Perhaps it was the size of the room and the grand staircase that looked like first-class steps only dignified people elegantly ascended or descended.

Before she could look around in amazement Otiende walked into the room. She wanted to run into his arms, seeking comfort she knew she would find. She just felt like he would understand how she felt about the mess she got herself in.

But she stopped herself when she took a look at him. He was wearing a suit that was closer to the classic suit with a tailcoat jacket. The grayscale pattern on the jacket is what made it look modern. He wore a collared white shirt that had several buttons undone. Realistically, she didn't just want his comfort. She wanted more. Being in his arms was not a good idea.

"Hi, Agina. Come this way."

"Hi OT, I am really confused about what is going on. How did you find out?" she asked, feeling perplexed. She opted to walk beside him, avoiding his touch as he gestured what way to go.

"I'll show you. Technology has a way of finding things out. Unfortunately, sometimes it tells these things to the wrong people." He seemed deep in thought as he kept facing forward.

They walked into a room that was filled with several large monitors. She could tell that the monitors could come together to make a giant screen. She wasn't sure if she discovered this because of her powers. Sensing technology was new to her, but it occurred so naturally that it all just passed, like her thoughts.

"I work here sometimes. I can help you more in the Outercity but you're safer in the Innercity. The council will trust and protect you no matter what. This is our territory that no one else can step into."

As he spoke, he was looking at the monitor and opening the file he wanted to show her. He gestured with his hand to control the computer.

"This is what was recorded last night," he said, as a video began to play of Agina rising into the sky with her tattoos glowing in an orange light. Like she was frozen in her disposition, she had her spear in her right hand and she was holding the seating pose she adopted while seated on her stool. Her eyes were closed.

When she stopped rising, she tilted her head to the sky. Her entire body suddenly lit into a blue light that was sent out into the sky like a light beam. The light beam lasted a few seconds before the video stopped.

Then another video played. It seemed that there was a missing part and it continued with Agina's face forward. Shortly after the video started, she began her descent back to the ground, disappearing into the trees.

"That's impossible," Agina denied, having watched the whole video in disbelief. It was like watching what had happened in her mind from outside her body. She thought about where and when the video could have been taken. In response, the date and the time appeared with a location on the screen.

She wondered who could have seen the video and the information also showed up on the screen, giving a detailed explanation of who they were. Otiende was about to explain, but he watched in awe as the information came up on the screen, and then looked at Agina.

She shook her head. "I thought it all happened in my mind. I can't seem to stop my thoughts from making things happen. I have never felt so out of control." She turned to look at him, a look of worry and confusion on her face.

He put an arm around her shoulder, hugging her from the side. Rubbing her arm in comfort. She found herself relaxing, like it was a dose of exactly what she needed. When she felt more at ease, he let her go and said, "I still have more to show you."

He gestured again and another video played. The video showed what happened not long ago when she went to work in the Outercity, hoping to distract herself using her current project. It showed her walking out of the portal in her studio lobby, but in a second, retreating back through the portal.

"I slowed down the part where you returned through the portal. You moved so fast that you can't clearly be seen when it plays in real-time." As the video of the lobby continued to play in slow motion, masked people pounced into view and stabbed into the empty space she had occupied, one of them showing an obvious sign of frustration for having missed their death strike.

"I knew I had to leave immediately. I was not sure why, but I knew I had to listen to the internal warning," she spoke absentmindedly, remembering what had happened. She knew it wasn't simply because she freaked out at the last second and didn't want to face the people she worked with, but she couldn't pinpoint why she suddenly needed to leave.

"I am glad they didn't harm you. I don't know why they want to kill you but there's one more thing I want to show you that might have something to do with it." He carefully looked at her, like he wasn't sure what to make of everything.

He gestured again. This time a video didn't play but it was a series of news reports. A worldwide blackout happened yesterday, which lasted for a second and also took out all the electricity's backup systems.

But what was strange was that everything, whether powered by fuel, batteries, solar, gas, wind, water, or everything that needed to be powered, went completely dead for about a second. Most people didn't notice the point when it happened.

But the aftermath was noticeable, especially with devices and machines, because after they shut down they had to manually be restarted if they didn't have the ability to restart on their own when left in the on position. It happened around the whole world at the exact same time, including satellites that were orbiting around the earth.

Unfortunately, this caused various forms of damage either directly, or indirectly through a ripple effect. Moreover, some people were injured or killed, either directly or indirectly by the devices and machines shutting down.

The speculation was that it was a weapon of some sort, or that it was aliens. The stories ranged with all kinds of explanations, the absurd stories sounding just as believable. What was clear and consistent was that it was more powerful than anything they had ever known.

"Everyone wants to know what was powerful enough to cause it. Your light triggered the suspicion of people who have always watched us. The digital mask around the Innercity turned off. Even though it was such a short time, people were able to see the Innercity for the first time. Anyone could have seen the light. However, they could only have known it was you if they had this video." He still had that careful look on his face, like there wasn't a judgment or a conclusion.

She reached a revelation as she remembered the names of the people who had the video. She didn't know them. Otiende was probably able to tell who should or shouldn't have the video. He was an integral part of their security.

"These spies that have always watched us… we always thought they couldn't get information from the Innercity. This proves we were wrong. To make matters worse, you are now under surveillance. There is a channel open to the public where anyone who knows where to look can watch and track you. Your place of work and everywhere you frequent are under constant watch. They are getting away with it because they view you as a threat.

For now, you are safe in the Innercity; the barrier and encryption that was built when the Innercity was enclosed will keep them from tracking or watching you. For now, they can't get into the Innercity. This is where I wanted to help. We need to manage and eliminate the problems." There was a deep determination in his eyes as he spoke. Nothing would have been able to wiggle out of his gaze without agreeing to his help.

"I used to think the Innercity was like a cage, a bunker built for survival and protection that just kept people separate. Ironically, it is what is protecting me. Sigh. Over a thousand years and it just had to be me. I wasn't even consciously aware I was calling for this power. I was just thinking about the balance of the old and new, which isn't even what the powers are supposed to be about. I feel so wronged." It was all too much; she hadn't stopped feeling overwhelmed. She turned her head to look away from him.

"We'll figure something out," he said, coming to stand in front of where she had turned to, looking her in the eyes. It made her feel reassured.

They spent the rest of the day putting together a plan. It felt like old times, like he had never left. Their synergy was the same. Even though, there was a sense of urgency and their experience was greater.

CLEANSING

OT: Sorry. I'm letting you know in advance that I am going to violate our decision on texting. Texting morning messages and night messages won't work when stuff keeps coming up. Different circumstances call for different measures. Even if you just left, I wanted to message you to wish you the best. Sticker attached.

No worries. I am fine with that. I get it. Nothing could have predicted how things have ended up. Thanks! Sticker attached

-End of text messages-

SHE SAT IN her tree in the same pose she usually relaxed into. She watched the sunset, thinking about how much things had changed since she got that notification from True Match. One thing was clear: There was no going back.

"Set well for me to get blessings," she said as a sunset enchantment in her native language.

The way things have turned out will be better for everyone else. But what about her? Moving forward felt like a death of self. Yet she could only move forward. Can she still say fate is cruel when in turn, the thing that is crushing the freedom she fought for is bringing good to others?

No matter what she had experienced there was always another sunset. Even when the weather didn't allow her to see the sunset. It was still there. There was a part of her that would always be there every day.

Even if it felt like a lie, to now turn to this life she had viscerally rejected, what could she do? When now, her presence felt like a lie with the distinctive tattoos on her skin? Why had she fought so hard to end up here?

She connected to this part within her that was as sure as a sunset. Closing her eyes, she connected beyond her, to this stillness that never changes within all things. She could feel how movement surrounded this stillness, rising from the stillness and coming back to rest.

At that moment she knew what she needed to release. Like it would in the composition of a song where certain sounds faded off, so a focus could be created to accentuate an instrument or vocals. This combination of silence and sound, giving the song its unique makeup. She found that part in her that needed to fade off and be silenced, and let it go.

Since she was still connected to the stillness in everything when she did the internal cleansing; it released all the toxins in the air, the plants, the ground and the water; clearing away.

Also, she was connected to electronics, so she found herself scanning and detecting malicious software that had corrupted or threatened networks, their security systems and other programs; narrowing down how they had stolen the video, and removing these infections. The cleanse restored their technology and strengthened it so it would not be vulnerable in the future.

It somehow felt like she was orchestrating music, but bringing sound to a silence. Finding what did not need to be there and putting it out of existence.

Having done that, she felt stronger, opening her eyes. She knew a long life's journey was ahead of her, but she couldn't worry about what tomorrow would bring. She climbed down from the tree, and with her spear in her hand, went over to her family's home. It was time to face them.

Her family's homes on their ancestral land were the only homes she ever walked into through the front door. Because of the way land was divided in the Innercity, it was a known custom that you could only move freely between your own family's homes on the same ancestral land. It was a modified ancient agreement that avoided conflict between clans.

When they needed to cross into others' ancestral land, they used a portal which was often built in every house, no matter how close the house was. Because of this, even if someone somehow managed to come into the Innercity, they wouldn't be able to easily find their way around. It would be like walking through a forest without trails that connected everything, and every section was a closed pocket.

The Innercity was never mapped to protect the wildlife and their natural habitat. Part of the reason why people and technology were limited was to protect and preserve nature. Because it was a highly restrictive preservation area, even other countries that knew of its existence, knew they were not allowed to disrupt it.

When she walked in her family's front door, Adede and her mother were already there like they were waiting for her. The looks they had on their faces told her they had questions. But now there was something else she would have to face first. She put her spear down then gave them both a hug.

"Were you really just waiting for me?" asked Agina in disbelief. They were always too nosy about Agina's life, discussing it like it was their own life.

"If you didn't show up, I would have come looking for you!" said Adede.

"As if you would ever. You would probably run the moment the house tried to interact with you," she laughed, replying to Adede.

"I am fine. Okay. I just... Had a situation yesterday," she continued to say, pulling up her sleeves and showing her arms.

Agot gasped out loud in shock, holding her chest with her right hand

and covering her open mouth with her left hand. Adede just stared in surprise. "You were granted power?" Agot asked as tears started to run down her face.

She then gave Agina a long hug as she said, "I'm sorry honey. We never did the ceremony for you. I honestly never thought it was possible. We all tried before you. All these years, it never worked. I even tried it several times and it never worked."

Agina could do nothing but return the hug. Before yesterday she could understand the burden of carrying a dormant power that hadn't been seen in over one thousand years. Adede also had tears silently running down her face.

"I am happy for you," Agot said, finally letting go and wiping her tears. You could almost see a burden had been lifted off of her. Adede gave her a hug too, congratulating her.

"We have to tell our Dana. She's in the dining room," said Adede.

They walked over to the dining room, asking her questions as they went along. The dining room was open and had a really large table that sat twenty-six people. When the rest of the family gathered the table looked too small because they didn't fit most of the time. The open setting helped because more people would sit close by on the kitchen island or in the living room.

Abura Ahenda Odero was blessing the food that was set on the table. You could see the resemblance between the three of them when they were together, Agina, Agot and Abura had the same rounded nose and small face that made Abura look youthful even in her old age, and the four of them had the same lashes, passed through generations. Their eyes were somewhat different, but they looked like they had bought the same set of lashes.

They silently waited for Abura to finish. "Dana," Agina said when Abura was done, as she gave her grandmother a hug. It was their native way of saying grandmother.

"Let me look at you," she said, looking at Agina then pulling up her sleeves and taking her arms to examine them.

She couldn't have possibly heard their conversation, but her grandmother was that way. She always either sensed things or she already knew because someone else had told her.

"The council called for a meeting tomorrow. Agina has to attend. They didn't say what it was about but it's also mandatory for elders to be there. I knew something had to have happened, because Agina's presence has never been mandatory. The council took a lot of effort to send out invitations to all council members who are or aren't elders," Abura said, thoughtfully.

She turned Agina around. The tattoos on her neck were hard to hide because they continued onto her scalp. There was certainly no way the tattoos had just been created without first shaving Agina's head. It was the evidence that magic had created the tattoos.

"This is a great honour," she said, bowing to Agina.

"Dana, don't bow. That is too much for me." She couldn't wrap her head around how she should let her elder do something like that.

"It's the natural order. You may do things differently, but the council doesn't. We follow our traditions. And we rarely change traditions. We take pride in keeping our culture alive. The Innercity keeps the culture and nature alive," Abura said, brushing away her concern. "Now power has been given to you. Over one thousand years and the power wasn't given to us. It chose you. So, know that if you change things, the council will support you." Her grandmother always spoke slowly and had great wisdom. She was the head of the home; their warm but stern leader who commanded to be listened to just by her presence.

"Sigh. I know I always say things should be different. But I had no intention to change things. I just wanted it to be different for me. My title was something I didn't want. So, I definitely don't want this. This all started when I met OT yesterday and... It just reminded me of how I wanted and loved technology and our traditions. Both. Not separated." She felt exposed as she spoke; it was a feeling like she was naked but had been required to be naked without an alternate choice.

"Sigh. No matter how much we tried to separate you and OT, the two of you were inseparable. By the time you finally separated, it was too late. Your ideology had already formed. And now you found each other again." Abura gave her a slight smile, the laugh lines that had formed as she aged becoming more exaggerated.

"I only met him because we were matched by True Match." She couldn't help but look down when she said it. She was blushing, and it wasn't just her face that was burning.

"So, it was technology that brought the two of you together. Maybe he was always meant to be in your life just as you feel technology was always meant to be in your life."

Agina still couldn't look up. If anything, she was now blushing even more. Just yesterday she had been thinking about ways to turn down the celebrity she had been matched with. She still had not adapted to the idea of marrying Otiende, her childhood friend.

"Let's have dinner then. Let the children and everyone else know we are ready," she said, turning to direct her attention back to the table. Once she turned it was like a signal that the conversation was over. Respect for these non-verbal cues was common in their culture.

Once everyone had gathered, they walked over to their seats. Adede wanted her to change her sitting position because their hierarchy had changed but Agina declined. She knew her mother and Adede had so many questions they still wanted to ask and that there was still so much that was left unsaid, but that conversation would have to wait till later.

 ◆ **STRANGE LIGHT:** *Ler Mahia*

INITIATION

OT: I want to come to the meeting just to see your face when everyone bows to you. Don't cringe!

If only you wanted to see it bad enough that it changed your mind about coming with me.

OT: My parents and I also received the invitation. We are not initiated elders so they cannot make us come, even if it is mandatory for all elders to be there. It's better this way. I don't want to have to talk about us yet. They will wonder why I am with you. I would never go there as an elder.

I know. I didn't even want to talk to my family about us yet.

OT: Meet me at the same place tomorrow. Embrace the moment. You will do great!

-End of text messages-

AGINA LOOKED AROUND the council's grand hall. The room was plain in its decoration and was a meeting room with tables at all seating rows. She had not been in this room yet. She only came into the building during the conferences when she was younger.

What made the room look elaborate was the council members that had gathered in the hall. All the elders had their spears, so you could tell them apart amongst the crowd. The initiated elders sat in the front in a half circle. Being seated made their spears look longer because the spears had an average height of 1.80 metres.

Some of the elders were dressed more extravagantly than others. But no matter how they were dressed, they looked like royalty, all of them having been born into their titles. Most of the initiated elders were from Agot's generation. Few were from Abura's generation or Agina's generation.

They represented the people in their lineage, and they did a good job at it. It was almost unheard of that people felt like they lived an unfulfilled life in the Innercity. This was part because it was important to follow your passion.

Few like Agina and The Oneko family had passions they pursued outside the Innercity. Otiende's parents were quite rare because they became popular outside the Innercity. Otiende was one of a kind because he was also a global sensation.

Agina, Abura and Adede sat with the other council members. Agina wore a flowing backless goddess dress in an Ankara print. A slit on her dress showed her tattooed leg, as she sat cross legged. Agina always held grace that easily tipped to sexual glamour.

At this point everyone had seen her tattoos. Most people reacted in shock, and everyone was talking amongst themselves. Her family remained silent. Including Agot. Everyone now knew why the meeting had been called so suddenly.

Agina couldn't help but think of Otiende and how he would stick out in the room, just like he always did around the people of the Innercity when they were younger. The way he dressed looked more like he was right out of a global fashion magazine.

One thing that Otiende and all the elders had was that air or royalty that wasn't arrogant. It was a presence that was felt even without his title. If he dressed like them, he would look like he belonged.

They were all born leaders. But she couldn't see Otiende dressed like everyone else in the room.

Drums began to play a beat, and everyone became silent. It seemed to mark the start of the meeting. The meeting must have started as usual because everyone seemed to follow invisible ques.

It was always this way with the council. People knew what to do because they learnt it at some point. It was passed down and strictly followed. They were not laws, and they were not written down, but it was how things were done.

Agina noted that the meeting was being held in their native language. The initiated elders took turns speaking, knowing what order to follow. They announced who they were and who they represented. They then moved onto the topic of Agina.

Agina was called to step forward. She had her spear in her hand and her dress was trailing behind her as she purposely walked forward. Her flowing dress seemed to do a graceful dance around her as she walked. She stopped in the middle of the half circle and stood before everyone else.

Spear in hand she did the gestured greeting. The elders and everyone else returned the greeting, all the elders holding their spears in their hands. The initiated elders then all bowed by bending slightly as everyone else got on one knee to give a bow.

"We stand here today, and we call our ancestors to witness that we acknowledge the favour you received, when you were granted the magic of your ancestor; the great magician Gor Mahia." The oldest initiated elder was the one who spoke.

Because Agina now had an acute sense of awareness, she could feel the change in the room. She knew her ancestors were arriving. She could somewhat sense the spirits joining them. She felt the hairs on the back of her neck stand up.

She remembered what her grandmother had told her to say earlier that day. She couldn't help but feel like she should have paid more attention to what elders did. Maybe then she would never have gotten herself into this situation. She would never have said the chant. And most of all, she would never have to fake it. She felt unworthy in front of her ancestors.

"Rise and witness the name I have been found worthy to be granted," she said, and they began to raise their heads and stand up. The name she was bestowed was tattooed on her back. The tattoos were not just patterns, they told a story, sometimes with images or words.

It was hard to pretend when she could sense her ancestors there. She had listened to what she was supposed to do and say today, but she had never had the intention to follow through with things for the rest of her life. She did not want to be a Supreme Elder.

At that moment she decided to be frank about things from the beginning. She already knew what she wanted to do instead. She just didn't think she would say it at this moment. She gathered her resolve.

In doing so, her ancestors' presence became clear. She could now see their faces. She looked around at them as she turned to face everyone else, her back to the initiated elders in the half circle. Her resolve was unwavering even if she caught the looks of hope and admiration on the faces of her family.

"I am **Ler Mahia**," she said, announcing it to the world and her ancestors. "Ler Mahia" meant: strange light.

She could see from the hand that held her spear that her tattoos were glowing. She got a nod of acknowledgment from the ancestors. She could somehow see them all. See them even if they were beyond the walls. She could see all their faces no matter how far they were. She turned around and faced the initiated elders.

"Supreme Elder, our Ler Mahia, Agina Akongo. From this day forth we serve under you. You are our chosen leader, supreme above us all," said the same elder as they all bowed down again.

"Rise," Agina said. Giving them a moment to get up and come to the realisation that she was about to do something different. It was not

what they expected to hear or do. So, everyone was quick to catch on to Agina making a change.

"I cannot undo who I am. My actions in the past might be seen as me trying to undo who I am. But I have already come to this point. I was granted this power for acknowledging who I am and for my desire to bring balance to this world. Not because I wanted to be your Supreme Elder."

She needed a second to gather her resolve again when she saw the look on her mother's face. She knew her mother probably feared the worst and thought she was going to renounce her title.

As she grew up, she avoided the responsibility of being an elder and finally gave up her title when she got married and moved to the Outercity. If her mother had not kept pressuring her, she probably would have done the same thing Otiende did and given it up when she was 16.

"I will only accept that you have initiated me as The Supreme Elder if you accept that this will be an inactive role I perform, and that you will all maintain your current roles as the initiated elders, leading beside me as equals. Maintaining balance is my priority and the oath I took to get this power. My powers are more suitable for restoring the imbalance where it has plagued outside our barrier. Do you accept?" Agina asked, then bowed her head.

"We accept," they all said in unison, bowing again. She figured they accepted it like a command they were given. That their hearts were much more rigid and slow to change. But she was sure that with time, things would change. Agina raised her head and then asked them to rise.

If things had gone as planned, Agina would have been given a seat in front of the initiated elders, like a queen's throne, and all the initiated elders would have stepped down to sit amongst the other members of the council, but instead, they hurriedly prepared a similar extra seat where she sat at the centre of the curved table among the initiated elders.

They then went on with their meeting as they maintained their current roles, discussing matters that concerned Agina; they had looked for her to lead but she explained how she was inactive.

When Agina heard the briefing about the blackout, and spies, including how Otiende would handle the matter. Agina now understood why Adede had said Otiende came up in conversations. Though he was not actively there, she inferred that he helped with the technological stuff and security. He had an active role. Hence, they always had something to talk about when it came to Otiende.

Elders were terribly good at keeping secrets. If Adede had spent all this time at council meetings and had never discovered that Otiende was an elder, it was definitely because they did not want people to know.

They proposed a celebration of Agina's power, immediately following the conferences, since she hadn't got her power during a Supreme Elder initiation ceremony. They were grand ceremonies where anyone could gather. Powers were typically granted during these ceremonies as people stood in witness. It was the first time power had been granted outside the ceremony, leave alone granted with no witnesses.

They had to rush to acknowledge and initiate her by holding the meeting. As a consensus they had hoped they could at least arrange a public celebration for those who weren't members of the council. It was nowhere near the same as witnessing the powers arrive, so they wanted to make it the grandest ceremony they could manage.

Everything about her getting her power was not traditional and they were forced to find alternate ways. The conversation went on for a long while because it took some time to agree on what they should do.

This is why people rarely managed to make appeals to the council. They were rigid and took a very long time to agree on changes. However, since it was a celebration and most of them liked celebrations, it made the decision-making process easier.

WELCOME HOME

AGINA CAME THROUGH the portal and found him waiting. She couldn't help but admire the entry hall again. "Supreme Elder, our Ler Mahia, Agina Akongo," he said, giving her a bow. She burst out laughing, and he laughed too, moving closer to her.

"Why do I struggle with this stuff? Even nature has its order, it knows where it stands, and it accepts what it was created to do. You should applaud me for not cringing when they bowed! How can someone get used to that?" She kept her gaze low, embarrassed by just the thought.

"I knew you would be amazing," he said, taking her hand in his and giving it a gentle squeeze of encouragement.

She met his eyes. Laughter was still in his eyes, but she felt he was being sincere. He let go of her hand and they stood looking into each other's eyes for a moment. She could still feel the warmth and gentleness from his hands.

They turned away awkwardly and began to walk to the studio. There was a sense they needed to do something else but couldn't. They were both reluctant to continue on, but just standing and staring at each other was becoming too much.

She remembered he had complimented her, so she awkwardly tried to continue the conversation as they walked, "Thank you. Things have really taken a turn, haven't they? We meant to meet again for a date on Saturday, but now all this happened. Now instead, the extended family is meeting this weekend to celebrate. And I am here instead of my studio. Not to mention, we have been meeting every day."

"I have such luck to get to work with you. And... I have good news. Take a look," he said, gesturing for her to go towards the screens.

They stood side by side, a distance in front of the screens, as he gestured for the screen to open a file. A report was displayed on the screen.

"We managed to trace the people who tried to attack you. They were arrested but they are not talking. We are avoiding forcefully extracting information from them because it's harmful. We suspect that even if we extracted the information we wouldn't find anything useful. We try to remain humane. Today, once we confirm everything in my lab is secure and successfully create the protective encryption, we can go into the Outercity tomorrow to conclude the project," he said, turning to look at her.

"That is good news," Agina said, holding one hand in the other hand and tucking it under her chin. "I have practised using my power to secretly open portals, like we discussed. I should be able to manage now. Let's create a simulation to test it. When we get to your lab tomorrow, we should be better able to simulate the plan and analyse it for weaknesses."

So, they spent some time simulating the plan.

"That was great! You're ready. Tomorrow, we should meet here first, then go through my portal. It should be safer that way. My bodyguards will meet us on the other side," he said, as he turned off the equipment they had been using.

Looking around, she said, "I heard you always use bodyguards but I haven't met them yet. Is this place also reserved for you today?"

"Not exactly," he said with a grin. "This is actually my home. No-one knows where this place is. It's a secret that I currently live in the Innercity. I don't bring people over. Even my family haven't been here yet," he said as he was leaning over towards her, then straightened and continued. "I have so many homes and I move a lot, so they haven't been to all my homes. My studio is actually my home office that I use when I don't want to go into the Outercity. I don't need bodyguards here because this place is... hidden. Otherwise, when I am in my other homes, I use bodyguards," he said, smugly crossing his hands. He was too pleased with himself, like he had just divulged the most interesting gossip.

"How did you manage to get all this working in here?" she asked, gesturing towards the equipment in the room.

"I could barely get my house to function without having to get through so many hoops with just the power, then I had to invent with getting a network to work through the home. And I have a tiny home!" she said in admiration.

"I can show you around and explain how everything works," he offered, showing her which way to go. "But it might take a while," he said as they walked side by side. "We can start with this room." As he explained she listened.

14

THE BEGINNING

THEY WALKED FROM room to room, entering some rooms and just walking by others. It was much larger than her family's mansion and that was part of how he had managed to get so much energy to power up his technology.

She was quite fascinated by how he had managed to pull it off. The entry hall had given the impression of a luxury hotel lobby. Taking a closer look at it when he showed her around made it look less hotel like with his family photos and memorabilia on display. It was a beautiful and well-maintained house.

The tour ended at his favourite deck. The one he said he often used. He pointed out that it was where he first installed the True Match application that brought her back into his life. They stood there for a while looking out into the view.

"It's amazing how you put all this together OT," she said looking out into the distance, lost in thought.

"The way you love technology and how you understand it, and are good at it, is outstanding. If you had pursued it academically you would actually beat even the greats that we have." He turned to look at her and continued, "But it's balance for you, isn't it. Just enough to make things better."

"It's how I saw it the first time you showed it to me. It was like magic. Do you remember the flying Nandi Bear," she said, turning to look at Otiende, a gentle smile on her lips.

"Yes. I still remember it all. Not everyone in my group was giving me a hard time about being different and playing on my com. But those who were giving me a hard time were not being nice at all. So, I went out on my own," he recalled, sounding distant as he travelled through the memory.

Thirty-four years ago…

At the conferences, the children were grouped according to their age. Otiende and Agina would not have been in the same group, nor been close enough to meet. All the same, that day was Agina's first conference and the beginning of their meetings at conferences.

She was supposed to be with the 3–5-year-old children, but she didn't even get there. Some of the older kids had decided to find Otiende after he went out on his own. They asked Agot if she had seen Otiende. But she hadn't seen him.

"We never find him every time no matter how much we look. They need to stop being mean to him," said one of the children as they ran off.

"Mom, why were they being mean?" Agina turned up to look at her mother, demanding an answer like she had been insulted, the look on her face sullen.

"Sometimes people are just mean. They don't need a reason, honey." Agot braced herself for it. She knew it was coming. It always came when her voice was like that. The determination that she had never managed to move even the slightest bit.

"But Mom we have to find him."

That was how she never made it to her group. She refused to do anything else but find him. So Agot was forced to agree. Agina wandered around silently, a look of determination and stubbornness on her face.

Legend has it that after Agina was born, Agot's eyes became stern and never changed back. It was said that this happened because she became so accustomed to scolding Agina. No matter what, Agina always seemed to win against her.

Agina ploughed on. Every now and then she would stop as though in thought then take off in a particular direction. Agot had tried to change Agina's mind a few times, then eventually gave up. Finally, Agina disappeared behind a stack of folded tables in a narrow storage room gaped with a large door, and didn't come back out.

The heavy doors to the room had been left wide open. The room appeared to be fully packed with conference room furniture. Agina crawled between the folded legs to find a large void space in the back where Otiende was seated facing away from her.

"I found you!" she said happily.

"Go away. I'm not coming out," he said without looking to see who it was.

But Agina wasn't going to give up. She came up to sit beside him instead. "I'm your friend. I stay here too," she retorted, refusing to budge.

Otiende stopped playing on his com for a moment and looked at Agina. He had every intention to be mean so he would scare her away, but he changed his mind.

Maybe it was the look of determination on her face, or maybe it was a realisation that he didn't like it when people were mean to him. But either way, he changed his mind. In the end, "fine" was all he said.

"Agina?" came Agot's voice through the tables.

"I found my friend. He won't come out. Mom, look I'm being a nice friend and stay here," she replied. You could hear the sense of pride in her voice.

"Agina, you can't stay there all day. I'm going to give you some time to come out." But Agina wouldn't leave or respond.

Agot tried to convince Otiende to leave but he didn't want to leave either, even if his hiding spot had been found. He just remained silent.

For a moment shuffling could be heard like Agot was trying to come in to drag Agina out herself. Or perhaps she was trying to move the tables.

She then let out a grumble in frustration. "I'll be back," she said as she walked off.

"What are you doing?" Agina asked Otiende.

"Playing a game."

"Why?"

"I like playing games. They are interesting."

"I like to colour," she said, taking out her backpack.

She took out her colouring book and some colours and started colouring a drawing of the Nandi Bear. They sat that way for a long while. One colouring and the other playing on his com. At some point, Agot came back with what seemed to be reinforcements but none of them could free them nor get them to come out. It was more risky to try to move the towering furniture that was stacked high and had become interlocked. The furniture was not rolling like it should.

"Mom. I'm colouring." That is all she managed to get out of Agina. Having learnt that hiding was a pattern Otiende used to cope, she couldn't help but be frustrated that Agina was accidentally pulled into his attempt to sort himself out by literally creating a boundary to regulate his emotions. So, Agot left to attend to the matters of the council. Someone was left behind to keep an eye on the children.

"Look. I finished!" Agina said, proudly showing Otiende her colouring. Otiende stopped playing and looked to see the drawing Agina was showing him.

"Cool. It has wings?" He turned to look at her as he asked, meeting her eyes that seemed to gleam. They were squinted slightly as she smiled as though she was trying to show all her teeth.

"Mom add wings. I told her it has to have wings," she joyfully explained.

"Can I show you something even cooler?" he asked. He couldn't help but be compelled by her joy.

Agina nodded her head.

He got back on his com and after a short while, took the drawing and pointed at it with his com. The com looked like it was supposed to take a picture but instead, the Nandi Bear came to life.

Agina squealed with excitement, laughing in amazement. "Can I have it?"

"Wait. Let me make it bigger." He projected it into a physical hologram that was the size of a large dog.

She got even more excited about her drawing coming to life, playing with the hologram. The Nandi Bear was a cryptid creature that originated in their country and had several stories written or spoken about it.

Indeed, they stayed there the whole day. The person who was left to keep an eye on them could only report to Agot that there was a lot of laughter. Agot had shown up regularly to stay updated on Agina's wellbeing.

At some point, Agina fell asleep cradling the flying Nandi Bear's hologram in her arms, with her head on Otiende's lap. Otiende continued to play games as she slept peacefully.

They truly did become friends that day, exchanging snacks and having conversations. Agina was even escorted to the bathroom only after she was given a promise to be brought right back. She didn't want to leave him, but it wasn't because she was being stubborn.

Even at a young age, she was the type of person who cared about others. She wanted to be his friend and keep him company. At that age, she had also already decided that she didn't like the council activities. So, spending time with Otiende was where she preferred to be.

Otiende knew when the conference was going to end. Being someone who regimentedly followed a schedule, he managed the time perfectly, emerging with Agina just before Agot showed up.

Back to the present time…

"After all these years I still have it in my com," Otiende said, as he smiled and leaned forward slightly.

"Really?" said Agina in surprise, her eyes widening.

Otiende took out his com and projected the hologram. Agina walked over to the hologram in excitement. "It really is like magic. It was the two worlds coming together! I couldn't have had a better first experience with technology," she said grinning and glancing over at Otiende.

"Thank you for showing me that," she said, feeling overwhelmed with gratitude.

She sat cross-legged on the deck and the flying Nandi Bear came to play with her. Otiende sat close by on the deck across from them, watching them play. The joy on her face was enough to brighten anyone's day.

Occasionally it would run over to him, and he would play with it, then it would go back to her. Eventually, it cuddled in her arms like it did when she used to sleep. Otiende moved over and sat beside her, and they watched the sunset together.

LOSING SIGHT 1

THE NEXT MORNING, she arrived to find him waiting for her in his entry hall.

"Hi Agina"

"Hi OT"

He reached out his hand and she shook it. It was an awkward handshake, considering their past. But it was a boundary she knew she didn't want to push. Less physical contact with him was better. Even if he had let go, she could still feel the heat of his hand.

She knew that he felt it too because of the way he always reacted like he had to forcefully stop himself from lingering. He couldn't help but lightly touch her by gently brushing against her when they were close. He often reached out, lightly tapping or nudging her in a playful teasing manner.

Judging by the look on his face, he sometimes surprised himself when he reached out. Otiende was always bold, he never had the shyness to stop his actions. So it wasn't shyness, he was limiting himself by reaching a little bit to remain appropriate. It was the boundary she set.

"Are you ready?" he asked.

She nodded her head. He set the location and went in first. Then she followed behind him. Usually, even when she was intending to be fully covered, she dressed in the Innercity fashion when she went to the Outercity. She had custom traditional themed clothes. However, today, she chose to wear something closer to the fashion of the Outercity.

Maybe she chose the outfit because she was meeting people for the first time today, and she already felt awkward for accidentally accessing ancient powers that she didn't mean to summon. So, she was avoiding standing out, and especially avoiding calling attention to her culture. The outfit also covered her tattoos.

In her full-body suit, she didn't look that different from everyone around. However, she had overlooked the exclusivity that she was with Otiende. To make things worse, she just happened to be wearing the same green that he was wearing, and she had arrived with him. So, she immediately became a focal point of interest.

She could feel her pictures being taken. She tried to convince herself it was Otiende's picture they were after: he was standing so close that air couldn't have existed between them. But she could sense how they adjusted the cameras to focus on her.

They hadn't shared the circumstances of how they met or reunited with anyone except for family and friends. So, she wondered if he would manage to stay formal. He introduced the bodyguards first, stating their names. But didn't tell them her name or who she was. Then they began to walk.

The bodyguards were going to be following them around for the day. The people around seemed to be arriving for the day's work. Were they all just nosy colleagues? He said he usually needed bodyguards everywhere he went, so he must have needed them at work too. Were his colleagues fans too? She thought to herself in awe.

He gestured and they walked side by side to where they would be working. The bodyguards followed closely but at a distance. His lab was a large room, similar to where she worked, but much different in its setup, since Agina worked as an inventor.

There was different equipment around the room, but most of the room was left empty. Especially a large area in the centre of the room. There were screens around the room, connected via wires to various equipment, and a large floor-to-ceiling screen without any equipment in front of it.

Everyone in the team was introduced to her and once again he didn't state her name or who she was. She was briefed on what they would all be doing, and shown the equipment they would be working with.

They then proceeded to simulate their plan. She felt the emotions in simulations more deeply today. Maybe it felt more realistic because the equipment was more advanced. Luckily, she had already tried it several times, so she was quick to react to worst-case scenarios.

During their lunch break, Agina and Otiende sat together in the breakroom, while their bodyguards stood outside the door. They spoke about how the plan was going and what they thought they could do to make it better.

Agina suggested bringing in one of her colleagues to take a look. He was what she called an expert at destroying things. Otiende agreed it would be worth having him take a look, without giving it much thought.

Agina reached over her head to her back and pulled out her spear. It seemed to appear out of nowhere, but she had been carrying it, concealed on her back. Now that she had powers, she was able to send and receive messages without having to take it out, but it was more natural for her to use her com this way.

She sent him a message and he agreed to take a look right away, not wanting to waste any time. He loved to destroy things and was very curious, so he often came across as a mad scientist.

Because he didn't have access to the portal they came through, he had to go through the building's security clearance. Agina put away her spear and waited as he got cleared through the security. After some time, her colleague Tony was escorted into the room.

She noticed Otiende had somehow moved closer to her, but she didn't remember when. They went over the plan and as Agina suspected, he had a more permanent way of destroying the surveillance system, making it almost impossible to set up again.

They spent the rest of the day re-adjusting the plan. Tony had only just heard of Agina's power after he arrived at the lab, so he was extremely curious. Agina and Otiende were sitting together talking about unrelated tech stuff when Tony approached to ask about her powers.

"So, what can you really do?" he asked, leaning in as if speaking about a secret. But he never managed to get too close. Two of the bodyguards immediately stepped in and moved him away, startling Agina.

She had forgotten the bodyguards were there. Now she understood what Otiende meant when he said the bodyguards mostly just made sure no-one came too close to him. Now that she thought about it, Otiende hadn't left her side for most of the day. Did he ever let anyone else come close to him?

She couldn't imagine why he would constantly need to keep people away. However, when she recalled what Otiende had said when they met at the cafe, it made sense that he didn't want people coming close. Did he really live his life isolated from everyone?

She found herself wondering what it would be like if he didn't have his bodyguards. Bodyguards seemed to have solved the problem he had. It's only in the past few years that he had them consistently follow him. It is also within that time that he finally lived in peace.

"It's okay. He's fine. He's my colleague," she said to the bodyguards. The bodyguards looked at Otiende, then retreated only after he gave them a nod. Agina got the impression that colleagues had been a part of the problem in the past. Despite their retreat, Tony didn't dare come closer again.

"Sorry. I've had people try and attack me at our studio. Luckily, I managed to get away, so they are here to protect me. To answer your question, I haven't figured out my powers yet. My focus has been on this project; taking down their surveillance system," Agina said to Tony.

She wondered if he knew Otiende was a celebrity and that those were actually his bodyguards. Scientists generally did not keep up with society unless it was a social problem they needed to fix. At least that's how it was for her and the people she had worked with.

"Yes. Yes… Such luck. Over a thousand years and now you have it… We are at about the end of the day. I'll go check on things one last time." He waved to the both of them and went to look over the equipment.

"I trust things are okay here. We should also conclude our day. Let's go," Otiende said, getting up as he held her arm and immediately let go after she stood. They left the lab, walking as though they were in their own world, and nobody could break up the space between them.

This time he gestured for her to go through the portal first and then he followed. When they got to the other side, they stood looking at each other.

Looking at her longingly, he said, "You should get some rest. I'll see you tomorrow."

"Yeah. I'll see you tomorrow," she replied.

He reached out to shake her hand and she shook it. He let go reluctantly. They stood staring at each other for a short while before she reluctantly went through the portal and went home. Once she was on the other side, she stood looking at her hand for a while then sighed before she headed to her tree.

She took her spear out from its conceal carrier and walked with it in her hand. When she reached the tree, she didn't climb up it right away. She knew it had wisdom acquired from all it had seen and she felt like somehow, she could learn from it.

She closed her eyes and she listened and felt. There was something extraordinary about how nature co-existed and how energy flowed through it. Each holding its own space but connected. She listened and took note of what it felt like. She wanted to remember that feeling tomorrow. That feeling of being in balance.

16

LOSING SIGHT 2

Agina♥: Did you fall asleep yet? Sorry for texting so late. I'm too nervous to sleep, even though I know I need to get some rest for tomorrow.

Do you want to talk about it? Can I give you a call?

Agina♥: Yes. I would like that if I'm not troubling you.

-End of text messages-

H E FOUND HIMSELF feeling nervous. He trusted Agina but he found himself wanting to protect her. What if something went wrong? She could protect the world and defend herself, but who was there to watch her back?

He had to calm himself down. He didn't want her to sense that he was nervous after the long conversation they had when he called last night. Even before she got her powers, she was always good at reading his emotions. He looked at the time. If he went for a sprint, he could probably run it off and do a quick breakfast instead of sitting down to eat.

Otiende quickly changed into his running clothes and ran on his track. He took a shower after running a few laps then ate a breakfast bar as he got dressed. He ended up in different clothes than he intended.

He wore another suit with a long tailcoat. The suit looked more modern with the collar standing differently and the buttons going diagonal instead of down. Something about the way certain parts had a geometric print was similar to Ankara style fashion. He thought she might appreciate it.

He was now feeling much more relaxed and present in his body. Just as he walked into the entry hall, he heard the alert that Agina was arriving.

She walked into the portal much different from yesterday. He found himself staring in astonishment. She had on a sleeveless dress today. It was the first time he was clearly seeing her tattoos. She had a brass bracelet on her left upper arm paired with a wide brass necklace and large matching earrings. Her makeup was also shining brass.

He wondered about the tattoos. The tattoos on her arm turned and twisted, part shapes, part flowing and organic, looking like a representation of what she was: both worlds. He would have also liked to see her name that she was bestowed and the story that the tattoos told. But her back was covered. The tattoos were not black, so they contrasted well against her dark skin.

Today she had her hair pulled up. He had seen her neck, so he knew the tattoos rose up the back of her neck. With her hair up, it must have been clearer that the tattoos were on her scalp. He thought about how a crown would look on her. It would suit her perfectly.

Her spear was not concealed today. She held it with her usual air of confidence. For anyone else it would look like it was inconvenient to carry, but for her, it was natural. She had never used it in combat, but she was well trained in yielding a spear.

Today she showed up looking like a Supreme Elder, holding her spear. He decided he liked to see her this way. He felt a sense of pride and gratitude for witnessing this side of her. Her confidence was radiant; she always gave this sense that she knew what she was doing, even when she admitted that she was clueless.

She stood, also looking at him. He could tell she was just standing there because she was not sure how to greet him. It was a hesitant pause. They were already moving at a pace faster than they had agreed on, texting and calling often and seeing each other every day.

They felt the need to move on to something else and go with the flow, but it would rush things. He knew she still wanted to take things slow. One thing he was certain about was that he did not want to slow things further than they were now.

"You look beautiful," he finally managed to say. There were many other compliments he wanted to say, but he held them back, along with his desires. He needed to keep his mind from wandering down the sensual path it was going so he began to silently recite complex formulas. It was the best way to distract himself, because she looked elegant and alluring in her dress.

"Thank you. It felt appropriate for today. My changing-the-world-today outfit!" she said, pumping her fist in the air to show a sign of strength.

He widely grinned, then said "Even without your powers, you were still changing the world. Changing my world at least!"

They both laughed.

"Are you ready?" he asked.

She turned to face the portal. He stood beside her, facing the portal too. He subconsciously found himself reaching for her hand. He couldn't say what always overcame him, but he would just find himself naturally seeking her. He was never that touchy with people.

When he intertwined his pinky finger with hers, she held his hand. He could feel her determination, so he knew she would be okay. She took a deep breath in and spoke, holding resolve, "I am ready."

They let go of each other and he went in first. He nodded at the bodyguards and turned, just as she came through the portal. He could still feel the heat of her hand and wanted to hold her hand again. But it was not the right time.

He was glad they had previously secured the area to make sure people's cameras and speakers on their com, including any other cameras or speakers, could not be used to spy on them.

They had to constantly maintain security measures and encrypt everything in her location, every time she came to the Innercity. They had also encrypted his lab. There was a surveillance system that had been set to find Agina wherever she was, using all available cameras and sound. If they had not done this, they would have been at risk with such a larger number of cameras on them.

She said hello to the bodyguards. Because she dressed differently today and people were not used to seeing council members holding a spear, they immediately got people's attention. Their pictures were being taken repeatedly and people were discussing amongst themselves.

It was a rare occurrence to have people leave the Innercity. While Otiende and Agina left regularly for work, they didn't attract people's attention at their respective workplaces: their colleagues were used to them. Most people were not even aware Otiende was from the Innercity.

In all honesty, people always took pictures of Otiende, so in that regard, it was different because it was more than the regular attention he got at work; the pictures or videos taken never stopped. It felt like he had run into a group of his beige O_ts.

His fans were called O_ts, pronounced: oats. His mild-reacting fans who were usually in the technology sector were brown O_ts. They were the yin passive energy. While his over-reacting fans who were usually energised were white O_ts. They were the yang energy associated with activity. The beige O_ts were somewhere in between.

Part of it was because of her spear. He knew they didn't have an awkward reaction to Agina's spear; she was somewhat of a diplomat, she should have witnessed these kinds of reactions in the past when she travelled outside the Innercity. He knew she hated the attention. He was glad they were not out in public where fans could ambush them.

The other part was because he had shown up with her in his lab for the second day in a row. He made it a point to avoid people. When he showed up with someone it was always for a specific event and most of the time, the collaboration was announced in advance. His social life was carefully planned and his schedule was often shared. When it was a surprise appearance, it had only involved someone well known in the entertainment industry to create an impactful reaction.

Similar to yesterday, there was a similarity in the patterns they wore, they almost seemed to contrast old and new styles as they walked to the lab, leaving the people with cameras behind in the lobby. It gave him a feeling of nostalgia when he remembered how they dressed this way in the past; they always seemed to contrast.

LOSING SIGHT 3

MORE THAN ANYTHING, he wanted the day to go smoothly. Everything had already been set up and checked before they arrived. Agina took her position and gave a nod, then they began. She closed her eyes, and it appeared like nothing had changed.

But their screens seemed to come alive, displaying information at a rapid rate. He had watched her in a simulation and run tests on a smaller scale, so this was nothing new. However, it was still amazing to watch.

The pace quickened and the information was so fast it couldn't be read. The incoming information suddenly stopped as portals opened. She lifted up her arms and held them outstretched beside her, and then the screens continued displaying information at an even faster pace.

Metallic spheres the size of tennis balls began to hover then shot into the portals at lightning speed. The information on the screen stopped, and a warning was displayed. He didn't read the warning, because he was too engrossed in watching Agina.

Tony walked towards one of the portals to examine it. Otiende's focus was on Agina's glowing tattoos. It was like a light had been lit inside her and the tattoos were a window letting out the light. The light this time around was an orange, soft and gentle light. It was not like the bright light he saw when she first got her powers which shot a light beam into space.

     STRANGE LIGHT: Ler Mahia

She held up her hands in front of her, grasping her spear with both hands. The warning sign displayed on the screen disappeared. At that same moment, Tony went into the portal. Agina's eyes were still closed. She didn't seem to have realised Tony had stepped into the portal.

Her tattoos stopped glowing and she brought her hands back down, closing the portals. Otiende stood, unable to process what had just happened. He expected Agina to reopen the portal Tony had gone into.

The situation had gone differently than they had planned. None of them had expected Tony to enter the portal but he went in the second before it closed. Coming out of shock Otiende suddenly realised he needed to do something fast.

"Agina!" Otiende said, trying to get her attention. But she hadn't opened her eyes yet, she was still rapidly processing something. The screen was displaying information at the fastest speed since they began. He could see that she had a look of concern, and the screen displayed a search entry that returned the result: location unknown.

She finally opened her eyes. "What happened to Tony?" she asked confoundedly.

The team was typing vigorously, trying to process all the information that had been showing up on the screens. Otiende was supervising so he was the only one who watched it all happen. One after another, his staff looked up, realising that something had gone horribly wrong.

In honesty, it had happened too fast for him to react. He also wasn't close enough to physically do anything. He knew how fast Agina could react, but even she was caught off guard by the situation.

He walked towards Agina not sure what to say. "He went into one of the portals. Is it possible to reopen it?"

"That was my intention but…" She turned and pointed at the large screen.

Otiende hadn't really managed to see all the information because it had been appearing too fast. There was a warning against reopening and entering the portal because the radiation levels there were too high.

But the greater concern that the computer displayed was that once Tony entered the portal, he was immediately teleported to an unknown location. They had no intention to engage, but now that they were holding Tony hostage they would have to initiate contact. But even so, it was unclear who they would need to engage to negotiate his release.

The portals and spheres had been masked by Agina, and Agina had the task to override all the defence systems. As far as he knew they had otherwise been undetected in all the other portals they opened in other parts of the world.

Since she had not planned on having anyone go through, nothing could have been done about Tony being discovered and teleported. She could bend technology to her will. Not people. People will always be unpredictable no matter what actions you prepare for.

"That was never part of the plan. What got over him? Why would he go in?" she asked, a look of distress on her face. She could not understand why he had done that despite knowing how dangerous it was.

He started to feel a breeze that was steadily getting stronger. He thought it was strange and also realised that the temperature had dropped significantly. So, it could only mean one thing.

"I don't know Agina. Maybe we should leave and let them work on a plan to rescue him."

"I can't just leave. I already left him in there!" she said in distress, her voice raised, as the wind burst out in intensity, causing lighter objects to fly around.

"Right. I need to calm down," she said sarcastically.

The power started flickering. Then he saw what looked like lightning. He knew it wasn't a good idea, but he decided to give her a hug. She seemed surprised at first. It had been so long since they hugged. He really missed her. Missed the closeness and familiarity they had.

The feeling of holding her was overwhelming him with feelings of warmth and unprocessed emotions.

She gave in and returned the hug. Melting into him as she pulled him closer. It felt like so many emotions he had been holding onto finally got relieved, flowing out from a hidden place where they had remained stagnant. He felt like he finally met Agina again. The way she felt in his arms made it feel real that his Agina was back in his life to stay.

The hug seemed to calm her down since everything went back to normal. But they stayed in the hug much longer, holding each other tight, like they were afraid to let go. He was taller than her so he could see past her head. He saw everyone pretending not to watch them, but he could do nothing about it now. He had already crossed that boundary. Plus he had crossed that boundary in front of his staff and bodyguards.

When he held her like this he felt like he could protect her. He didn't feel so helpless anymore. He rubbed her back for a while then he let her go. "Let's leave. Okay? We will do everything we can to find him," he gently said, like he was soothing her.

He knew that she felt helpless but there was nothing she could do at the moment. So, they left.

SUPPORTIVE

"COME THIS WAY," he said, cautiously holding her hand and leading her to the deck. He sat on the floor and invited her to sit beside him. She slowly sat, laying her spear beside her.

"It wasn't your fault Agina," he said, turning his torso to look at her.

After a long pause, she said, "I know but it still feels like I should have done something. It made me realise that as fast as technology can get and as fast as I can get, my reaction speed can only be human. I was able to do all that across the world in such a short time because technology works at technology's speed. I only had to tell it what to do…Technology can solve technology. But what can solve a human problem?"

She turned her head to look at him. "How did I know how to save myself when I was attacked? Are my instincts only good for self-protection?" Even though she had calmed down there was still a hint of distress in her voice.

"Nature doesn't need to be told what to do. It follows its own path even when we alter it. Even good plans can be useless against it. Destruction is part of its cycle. We just accept the destruction more readily when it comes to nature because we understand it's out of our control with its own purpose. Our acceptance of destruction is quite different when technology malfunctions or when people make choices." Otiende did not like seeing her like that. The Agina he knew was always strong.

As he finished saying that he saw a hen appear, followed by her chicks. He got up and picked up one of the chicks and put it in Agina's hands, before sitting beside her again. As per tradition, he neither ate chicken nor eggs, but he had free range chickens.

She gently massaged back and forth with her fingers, ruffling its feathers. "It's so cute!" she said, a smile on her face. She petted it for a while. It seemed to help her with what she was going through internally.

As much as he wanted to make her feel better and never see her looking distressed, she would have to be the one to work through her feelings. Their relationship would never work if it was his job to make her happy. Or vice versa.

So, he could only offer helpful things to support her as she worked through her feelings. She began a conversation about him having chickens in his home since he wasn't supposed to eat them, then talked about other things. Later, they had lunch together on his outdoor dining table on his deck and spent the afternoon talking.

At the end of the day, they both stood in front of the portal staring at each other. The awkwardness between them had disappeared. He reached out and held both of her hands in his, the spear hovering when she let it go. It was always like she was one with her spear so he felt like it was natural that with her powers, she could now control it with her mind.

"When will we meet each other again?" he asked, squeezing her hands.

"I would like to try and get some resemblance to normal. So now that the surveillance is down, I'll go to work this week. Let's meet in a week, next Saturday."

"Alright. I'll keep you updated on what we find."

"Sorry for leaving a mess of things," she said, looking awkwardly.

"That's okay. We knew it would leave us a lot of work. We expected to clean up. I want to leave you with a few bodyguards. I usually don't have as many as we have had these past few days. It was better that way in case we split up. I won't take no for an answer. They will meet you in the Outercity when you get through the portal to your studio."

He heard her sigh in frustration. "OT, I don't know if I can get used to that." Her whole demeanour seemed to frown.

"They are really good at not getting in the way. You will not even notice they are around. There might be other people out there trying to harm you. We probably upset more people by shutting down the surveillance system. Not only that but we corrupted their systems completely. They will only become more daring. The bodyguards will also be able to sweep the place before you get there, to make sure you are not spied on or targeted." He had to make his concerns clear. She opposed so much about celebrities but the bodyguards were about more than his lifestyle.

"Argh! Fine! I give in. I have never had to use my spear on anyone. I trust its defences and attacks, but that might still be better. Especially if it's not a one-on-one fight," she unwillingly accepted, avoiding his eyes.

"Okay. I'll see you Saturday. Enjoy the celebration with your family. I'm sure they are happy you got your powers."

He gently squeezed her hands again and then let her go. She took her spear and left through the portal.

He stood looking at the portal. He couldn't help but think of the time she wouldn't have to leave. His home felt so empty when she was gone. It had been just him in the home for so long. Now once again, he was left with the thoughts of her.

He thought of how he had started developing feelings for her. He honestly was not sure when it happened. He wondered how much different things would have been now if he had not shut down the feelings. He was usually bold. Why had he been so helpless with Agina in the past?

But things had already gotten this way. There was no use thinking about what would have happened. What he did know was that they needed to have a conversation about his feelings. He wanted to be open and honest. So, what he had to think about was how to tell her.

19

LETTING IT OUT

ER ROUTINE ENDED in almost the same way every day. So she had just watched the sunset and was on the way to her family's house. She found herself thinking about Otiende and how their lives would be if they lived together.

They both lived alone now, and their homes were more like a place for them to unwind and escape. But there was a difference. Her home was designed around her. It really was a home for one; she had dinner with her family almost every day so she didn't feel isolated.

In contrast, his home and even the furnishings were made for a large family. The concept was like her family's home; meant to be multi-generational. But it was just him there and he hadn't had people over.

Being the first one to experience his home made her feel like it was a place that was meant just for him. It didn't feel like empty halls and rooms waiting to be filled. It felt more like an open space for him to truly be himself. He intentionally isolated himself.

When she got married to Chloe, they lived in the Outercity. So, while she was married, she never saw her family as often. Coming into the Innercity was impossible for Chloe. There were Innercity restrictions on who could be granted access: you must have been born in the Innercity to be able to enter it.

At the time she was married, Agina felt like she was isolated. It was something she avoided naming and addressing. Agina had truly wanted Chloe to be enough and to be her new family. But in the end, it wasn't fair to give her the role of replacing her entire family.

"Agina. Good. You're here. I could use your help," said Obuo Odhong Odero. Agina's father had on gardening gloves and a cap. Like Otiende he was tall, but he was more slender. He was known to be someone who was always smiling and who could make anyone feel better.

He took off the gloves, but he was also holding shears, so his hands became more occupied. She went over to hug him then paused before giving him a hug from the side.

"What can I help with?" she asked, looking around. She had come to meet her father first because after reuniting with Otiende, she had been progressively avoiding the rest of her family. She currently was not in the mood to see them.

"We need to harvest food so we can feed everyone at the celebration. I should get the rest to help."

"No. It's fine. I got powers now," she said, waving her hands proudly. "I might as well use them for something," she continued, still wanting to avoid seeing them.

"Ah. Yes, you do," he said suddenly becoming cheerful. "There is lots to do. You will be just perfect for this," he said, leading her deeper into the garden.

Their garden was vertical. Most gardens were done this way to save space. It wasn't technologically advanced like the other gardens in the Outercity because Obuo liked to be hands-on with his garden. It was his passion.

The more advanced gardens, particularly in the Outercity, planted, watered, fertilised and harvested themselves using technology. The technology even checked for diseases and pests, whether the garden was indoors in a controlled environment, or outdoors.

She sensed which vegetables were ripe. She knew that he would only have manual tools, so she used the spear to cut. She created an updraft to levitate the vegetables she had cut into the basket.

She moved faster and faster as she went. Her spear appeared to have become invisible. Agina always liked to try things in different ways and experiment, so she enjoyed the process of figuring out the most effective method of harvest.

She was glad that she was able to help her father, it kept her distracted. Though she was still feeling guilty that Tony disappeared, focusing on the plants had taken her mind off things. In five minutes, she had harvested everything that they needed, filling several baskets. It was work that would have taken several people and a long time to finish.

"Your powers naturally suit you. I know you will do well," he said after watching in awe, placing a hand on her shoulder.

"I am not so sure about that after what happened earlier today. My colleague disappeared into a portal I opened. He can't be found. How?... If even my moment, when I received power, brought death?" Her voice began to waver as she spoke.

Obuo stayed silent for a moment.

"I see how that is really difficult for you. You're good at seeing the grey; seeing things that others don't. But it seems that because life is involved, you are feeling lost. You're going to need time to give yourself the grace. Give yourself permission to not get it right." Her father always knew the right thing to say.

She felt like she needed to cry. She had avoided elder leadership her entire life. Even before she knew what it meant to lead. But because she accidentally gained powers, she had to do something about it by becoming the Supreme Elder. Also, she had been so confident about love but failed, and now had to face love all over again with Otiende. Ever since her divorce, she wanted to hide away, truly feeling like a disgrace. She became afraid of messing things up, doubting her choices. Yet all she seemed to do was mess up.

Even if she chose to run from it all, having powers had already pushed her out of her comfort zone. So whether she liked it or not, she was now taking on a lot of responsibility at a fast pace because of how things were ending up. She hadn't yet gone through the grieving process of losing the life she thought she should have. She was so worried about so many things that she didn't even grieve for the lives of all the people who were lost because of her.

"I just... I just..." Tears started rolling down her face.

"Sigh. Agina. You don't always have to be strong. Holding in your emotions isn't good for you. You were born into this. At birth, you had a role that had so much responsibility. It's okay to not choose a path that chose you. I want you to know that you are already enough. You don't need to fit into anything else. Don't you see it? You got your power by just acknowledging who you already are," he said as he hugged her.

"Look, if you are not feeling up to the celebration, we don't have to have it. Okay?" Obuo said, speaking tenderly.

"Thanks, Dad. I think I'll just go back home now but be back tomorrow for the celebration. I have had too much today."

When Agina got home she did what she had been holding off on; she cried. Because her powers were still very much connected to her emotions, it rained. And it didn't just rain; It poured.

20

AN UPDATE

e-bot... Project the call.

~*Hi Agina. How are you doing?*

~Terrible! How has it not even been a week? OT, too many things have gone wrong in such a short time!

~*It's going to take time to adjust to everything. You are doing great. Do you want to talk about what happened?*

~I was pranked. I was startled. Then my instinct kicked in. So what happened was, without even touching her, I pushed my aunt across the room. She was fine... I doubt she will ever try to jump-scare me again. But that wasn't the worst part...

~*Okay. I am glad she is fine. What was it? What else happened?*

~The push made her knock over a candle. It would have started a fire… but I was faster and put it out.

~*Wow. Almost started a fire... Calm down and give yourself more credit. Don't forget that even if you start a fire, you have the power to put out fires. Your victories will eventually stand out stronger. Mistakes cannot be avoided.*

~Yeah. Mistakes. I have been a mess all week. I don't know when I will get myself under control. Our ancestors were lucky to have each other when they had powers. I am the only one. Everything is passed down by word of mouth. So, I can't even do research. I have to wait as my family slowly recounts what they were told or worse still, it's whatever they remembered.

~*I understand this frustration. In the past, I thought about writing a book about our traditions. I trust you will manage with what your family shares. You are great at figuring stuff out… What about your project? How has it been going back to work?*

~It's weird. Everything feels different. The good thing is, I have been able to make better progress with everything I was working on. With powers, I can speed things up and see more options.

~*That is good news. Things will only get better from here. Think of this as a learning curve.*

~Yeah. I think things will get better the more I learn. Especially when I am out of this adjustment phase. Honestly, I have been enjoying a large part of it all.

~*That's good. I'm glad to hear that. I have an update to show you. Your bodyguards will bring you to my lab when you are ready. They will help set up your studio's portal so you can get here directly.*

~Okay. I can go there now.

~*Okay. I'll see you soon.*

-End of call-

SHE WALKED INTO the lab to find him standing at a computer. He looked up just as they arrived. "Agina," he said, gesturing for her to join him. The bodyguards she came with seemed to disperse immediately. He squeezed her hand in encouragement saying, "This could either be good news or bad news."

She couldn't help but feel a sense of dread. He turned his attention back to the computer, letting her hand go.

"I doubt you found him. You would have let me know immediately. What information did you find?" she asked, still feeling the warmth of his hand and resisting the urge to look at her hand.

"You are right about that. After analysing the information, it seems that he did not intentionally walk into the portal. His mind or functioning was hijacked. He was being controlled when he made the decision to go in. He did however initially walk over to the portal on his own will. Unfortunately, this put him in the range of their frequency of control."

"That room was really strange. It was abnormally out of balance. It would make sense that their technology can even control a person's thoughts. Technology shouldn't be able to do such things. I did what I could by restoring the balance. But even so, I still couldn't save him."

She could feel that her emotions and powers were synchronising again. She paused and did a short mindfulness practice. Tapping into each of her senses. She started by just focusing on touch. Then she focused on sight, taste, smell then hearing. It brought her a sense of stillness. It helped her align herself.

"We have several people working on it. We'll figure something out. Our technology has always been different so sometimes it's like working with apples and oranges. But it's not a concern, we work with their systems and know them well."

"OT. I do trust you," she said turning her body to face him and grabbing his arm.

"It's them I can never trust. You didn't feel what I felt. Even with this power it was resisting my command because it came from a human. I had to bypass that by getting its kind to speak to it. Am I making sense? These powers don't make sense to me. I just... feel," she spoke intensely.

Realising that she had a tight grip on his arm, she let him go.

"Yes. You're making sense. I apologise for not seeing the bigger picture: that your concern stems from understanding the situation at a deeper level." She could see him searching her eyes like he was trying to understand her.

"No. I can't blame you. My emotions have been all over the place. Normally I'm centred. I haven't taken the time to communicate what I am experiencing. I trust my inner guidance. I just don't understand what it's communicating. So, my lack of understanding is showing up in all types of ways." She wanted to look away and hide from his gaze, but she had already done enough damage.

"Your inner wisdom is powerful. I have seen the outcome of what it has shown you. But still, I must apologise. I am sorry," he said, taking her hand and holding it between both his hands.

They stood looking at each other. She wanted to resist further but seeing that he had already apologised twice, she doubted her resistance would get her anywhere.

"Okay. Okay. I accept."

Somehow, they had moved closer to each other, closing the space between them. She couldn't remember if she had moved or if he had moved. All the same, she was looking up at him, so close that she could kiss him.

"You think about balance a lot. Don't you? It all started with people wanting to be stronger, faster, smarter, good looking, but some people just never knew where to stop. Our country, Dala, was lucky because before things became a mess, we opted out of becoming their pawn by isolating ourselves. We evolved without becoming like them, who have become either partially or completely manufactured. You are right about the odds of the situation. We don't have the force to go against them, but we will live on. We have always figured ourselves out," he said, filling the answers he felt he knew. He touched her hair, affectionately pushing it back.

"Yes. We'll figure this out our way. The Dala way. People around the world figured out how to restore peace, solve the crisis of food, and other victories. But civilizations are built by improving on what we already have or inventing better. So, technology can only evolve. In places like that, where Tony is trapped, it can only become more intrusive and inhumane as it evolves," she said, crossing her arms over her chest.

"We are creating another way of finding him that aligns better with our systems. It will take longer, and we are pressed for time. But it's our best option. We can't beat them at their game. Since we are forced to play, we'll play it our way," he said like he had been challenged.

"Mmm."

"All in good time. I'll let you know if anything else comes up. Do you want to get back home through my portal or go back to your studio?" he asked as he held her arm, then let go.

"I think I am done for the day. I'll go home through your portal." She felt like the day had been draining enough.

"Okay. I'll escort you back," he said, nodding to the bodyguards.

They walked to the portal followed by the bodyguards. He let her go through first, to his home's portal then he followed. When they were both through, they stood facing each other.

"I'll see you Saturday. We can meet at The Mpandaji park."

"I love going to Mpandaji Park! It's one of my favourite ways to experience nature," she said, her eyes brightening as she smiled.

"I enjoy it too. I look forward to experiencing it with you," he said in his deep vibrating tone, making the hairs on the back of her neck tingle. Ever so often, when he spoke in a soft tone it played with her nerves.

She knew she was blushing. She felt like she had just drunk something hot that rushed through her face and she couldn't stop herself from smiling. The last thing she wanted to do at that moment was touch him.

Since her spear was concealed, she did the gestured greeting without her spear as a goodbye. He returned the gesture and they both said goodnight before she went home through the portal. She knew it was obvious she was escaping, but she needed to save herself.

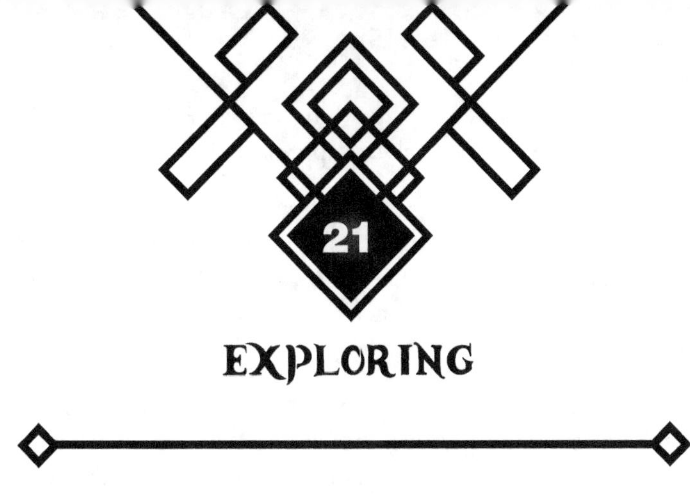

EXPLORING

THE INNERCITY WAS a hilly place. Some places had more elevation changes than others, rolling down into a vast lake. It was a place where you could see breathtaking views that mesmerised you and made you have a deep sense of gratitude.

Tucked deep within these hills in an uncrowded area separated from the animals and people, lay The Mpandaji Park. Veined with trails through its hills, plus through its flat areas that were easy to hike.

What set the park apart from the Innercity's rolling hills was its obstacle courses. Some of which were elevated off the ground between the trees of its forest. What's more, the structures were completely open, even in spaces like their office and portal.

She went through the portal a little early and found that he was already there. There usually were not a lot of people in the park so there was hardly anyone around. Two people she did not recognise were standing next to Otiende.

He introduced them to her. They were going to be their bodyguards for the day, but they wouldn't need to follow them around closely. She wondered if people's reaction in the Innercity was still to be wary of him, like they did when he was a child or if everyone had forgotten to be afraid because of his fame.

There must have been people in the Innercity who did not recognise him. She knew that in the Outercity there was a split between the people who loved him and hated him, but regardless he needed to avoid both. Since they both always approached him.

"Let's get started," he said, reaching for her hand. They walked into the park holding hands. This was not the first time she had done this. She had held his hand often when they were children, and as children they had hugged when they met or said goodbye. But now it was different.

They didn't have any intentions then. Now, having her hand in his, sent tingling sensations through her. She felt more connected to him as she felt the warmth of his grip; his hand seemed to embrace her in more than one way.

"Which way do you want to climb?" he asked, stopping at the intersection where most of the trails began.

"We can go this way. The climb is more challenging, and it has some extraordinary views," she said pointing to a trail that seemed to disappear up into the hill as it rounded a corner.

"Yes. I would like to take some pictures along the way."

"I wanted to take pictures as well. How about I take a video and you take pictures? I can do it all hands-free now," she said as she sent her spear ahead of them. It hung suspended in the air like it was being yielded by a ghost.

"Tell me you still have those old pictures and videos we took. I still can't believe you kept my flying Nandi Bear all this time," she said, turning to smile at him.

"I still have them. You have had your spear all this time. Don't you have old memories too?" he asked, smiling back at her.

"You are right. I probably do. We should take a look at them sometime."

They went to put on the climbing gear and then started on the trail. She went ahead of him and though she was perfectly capable, he would still occasionally offer her a hand.

They stopped along the way several times to take pictures. They took pictures of each other and pictures together. When they arrived at the end of the trail they sat on a rock and watched the view.

"It's really beautiful today. It's hard to believe the sun is surging today so it's too hot for others outside our barrier. They can't really be outside without protection. On days like this, I am glad we are enclosed in the Innercity and protected from it all. We can be outside at a park," he said, staring absentmindedly into the sky.

"Yes. Out there we are the ones who always have to stay protected. I still find myself wondering if we are at a disadvantage. We haven't evolved to the conditions outside the barrier. Even the people of Dala in the Outercity naturally evolved. You know... OT, at least some of our people are okay out there... Because our DNA is different, we have to constantly preserve it. What I wonder is if it really has any use other than keeping us in a box like we are preserved museum exhibits?" This was a question that often bothered her. Her eyebrows were furrowed deeply like they had been wrung tight, never to be released.

"I don't know... Have you decided what you would like to do with your power? With technology, we've talked extensively. Do you have an idea of the organic direction you would like to go? What about the natural side of things?" he asked as he leaned back, supporting his weight on his hands.

"I don't know yet. Nature has a way of trying to evolve and create balance. Here the balance tips in favour of nature. Out there I haven't explored nature as much because I can't directly come into contact with it; we are limited because we need to stay preserved. I want to explore what is out there first. Not just the pretty parts I saw as a tourist," she said, turning to look back at him.

"Yes. And sometimes limits are good," he said, as he stared into her eyes.

Judging by the way he said it and looked at her, she wasn't sure if he had meant it in reply to what she said or if he was talking about something else. He took a picture of the view and leaned over to show it to her.

She looked, but she was too absent-minded to see the picture. She noticed how he was so close. He had said something, but she didn't hear it. She was holding her breath and hyper-aware of his presence. "Agina?" he pressed, turning to look at her just as she turned to look at him.

They both sat there looking into each other's eyes. She wanted to kiss him, but she couldn't bring herself to do it. She noticed that he was also holding back the desire to kiss her. She could see it in the way his eyes hungered but the feeling was trapped, seen in subtle motions like how his lips tightened.

He was so close she could feel his breath on her face. She had already asked him to wait, and he was doing just that, being so obedient. She was the one who hadn't been ready and had long forgotten about marriage when the message from True Match just dropped into her spear.

But after all that had happened between them since they reconnected. Considering that it was Otiende, her childhood friend. Was she ready for at least a kiss that she truly desired to give? Why was she hoping he would cross the line and kiss her?

"Agina?" he whispered. She could hear a different question in his voice this time. His eyes were warming like they were cooking the question: do you love me? She knew her expression had been giving away what she desired. Recovering mindfulness, she began to panic and quickly got up.

"Yeah. W- We should get going," she said, rubbing her hands together as if dusting them off. Then put them in her pocket. She didn't trust herself to do anything but want him, so she took the cowardly way out. All she could do was try to get away and hide. He almost looked like he was relieved as he got up and gestured for her to lead the way.

She hooked herself onto the zip line and accelerated down the metal cable after jumping off its platform. She always loved this part, the adrenaline rush. It gave her the sensation of quickly falling through the air; Thrusting forward like she was flying, with the wind against her face; gravity pulling her faster and faster, like there was nothing that could stop her.

When she got to the bottom she landed onto the platform, unhooked herself, and then turned to watch Otiende follow behind her. Watching someone else always felt different. It always looked like the person would never be able to stop; like they would crush into the end. Watching it brought fear. Experiencing it brought excitement. As expected, he also reached the platform and unhooked himself.

They came back up the mountain using a different path. The slope was gentler, but it had challenging raised obstacle courses along the way. When they got to the end they stood on the obstacle course platform, enjoying the view.

The platform was elevated in the trees. Its wooden planks seemed to hug the tree. On one side it looked out to the trees below that carpeted the hill. On its other side, adjacent to the course they just came through, were stairs. The steps were few in comparison to their height above ground since they landed at a high point on the side of the hill.

"It really is beautiful up here," he said, his eyes beholding their surroundings. There was something really relaxing about nature.

"Yeah. The best part is the feeling when you zip line down. It's amazing. It just truly feels free. Like nothing can hold you back. The only way is forward." She reflected, reliving the moment in her head.

Leaning towards her, he took a picture of them, and then they both looked at it. She turned to look at him, but he kept looking at the picture. She found herself looking at his lips and wondering what it would feel like if she kissed them. Wondering if they were going to feel gentle or unwavering like he was.

Noticing she was distracted again, he turned to look at her. It felt like the world around them was fading. As their eyes locked, time seemed to slow down, creating a time capsule of intimacy where only the two of them existed. It seemed to shield her from all the worry and fear she had.

With his face so close once again, the feeling of being free and not holding back came back to her. How could she hold back when her inner voice was her guide, and she already knew what she wanted to do? Wasn't she a free spirit that listened to her inner voice?

Then she reacted, closing her eyes, she leaned up to kiss him. Their lips touched, the mere brush of their lips causing a gentle spark to dance along her lips and twirl down her body.

Her heart beat faster, raising in volume. Was that his heartbeat that she heard; their heartbeats had synchronised in rhythm. Their breaths had also mingled, colliding and intertwining into a warm flow. It was as if the universe acknowledged them coming together.

In her body, tenderness surged through her, like the delicate flutter of butterfly wings against a summer breeze. Then their lips parted after the light kiss, a pause like she had confirmed what his lips were like: soft and gentle.

She looked at his lips briefly before closing her eyes again. Then she met his lips again, confirming and exploring. He didn't react at first, allowing her to take her time. Then he responded, sending electricity rushing through her body. In the end, they both needed air; they parted looking into each other's eyes, an eternal flame awakened.

"Agina. Are you sure about this?" he asked, holding her chin with his fingers. She slowly nodded then said yes, feeling flush. He smiled and then went in for another kiss before she changed her mind. He held her face, leaning down as she put her arms around his neck, reaching up to close the space between them.

This time when their lips met, it was fiery. A desire they had both been holding back on was ignited and burning wildly. With their heads tilted, their lips spoke words they would never be able to describe.

She pulled him in closer, her lips opening slightly. His tongue slipped inside her mouth, gentle but demanding. Calling for her to bring her feelings forward. She felt her knees give in as he deepened the kiss.

Just when she felt like her heart was about to explode, they parted. She could see the fire burning in his eyes, like a ravenous beast that had just been jolted from a deep slumber. Just his gaze was felt all over her body.

"Um. You should get down," he said, looking part amused and part shy.

She hadn't noticed she had been slightly suspended in the air. She let go of him, but she was still suspended like her heart that had taken flight. She closed her eyes and grounded herself, slowly descending back to the ground.

"Come... We are not done yet," he said as he led her off the platform, holding her hand. She followed him as he took the stairs to the ground and led her off the trail.

She silently followed, intrigued by where he was leading her, feeling a sense of excitement, not just from the mystery but excitement from where their skin made contact. She felt a nervous exhilaration from holding his hand like she was a teenager again. After trekking for a while, he stopped.

GIVING IN

"WE ARE HERE," he announced.

Where was here? They seemed to be in the middle of nowhere. Then he led her further ahead. They arrived on a small platform that had a blanket with a traditional pattern on it. There was a basket in one of the corners and four unlit torches upright in the four corners.

"I brought dinner," he said pointing at the basket. "I hope you can stay longer," he said looking at her with a mischievous smile.

She felt like her heart was about to jump out of her chest. There was only one answer she could give. She never thought he would have prepared such an ending to their date.

She remembered Adede saying he was often seen as cold and aloof because he was straightforward and his parents were celebrities. But now that she thought more about it, when they were children, other than his family, she was the only one in the Innercity who interacted with him.

Where did people's opinions come from? Were those just assumptions made about him? She didn't want to make assumptions about him. But even if she knew how warm and gentle he was, how could she ever have imagined he could be romantic?

"What did you have planned?" she asked, her voice almost sounding like a whisper.

He moved closer to her. "I had planned to watch the sunset with you and have dinner together. But now I also want to kiss you," he said in his deep electrifying voice. The gentle reverberating sound of his voice sometimes made his words sound more exciting.

The expressed desire caused tingles in her belly that shot electricity up her spine.

"I want..." she said and then swallowed.

She was about to say that she wanted to kiss him too but realised that was not the question.

"I'll stay longer," she said instead.

"What was it that you wanted?" he asked, a daring grin on his lips.

She smiled, finding her gaze dropping to his lips.

"I want to kiss you."

As the words left her lips, she felt like molten heat flowed through her body, releasing a flood of energy in her. Heat rushed to her cheeks.

"Then kiss me," he said, inviting her to do what she desired.

She knew those words were the okay he was looking for. That he wanted her to be sure about what she did. When they met at the cafe, she had expressed that she had wanted to wait longer before she kissed him or became intimate with him.

She knew he would immediately step back if she changed her mind. But she was sure, this was what she wanted. She put her hands behind his neck and head and drew him closer.

When her lips met his, it was like her lips would never part. She put her arms around his neck and gave herself what she desired. He kissed her back, taking what he had wanted now that she had offered it.

Their lips caressed, their tongues explored the depths of each other, and they sucked on each other's lips, drawing in the sweetness of each other. They kissed this way for a while, crossing the bridge to a different kind of friendship.

They reluctantly parted just as the sun began to descend. They sat on the blanket and watched the sunset together. Occasionally, they would chat as the sun set, enjoying where they were at the moment.

When the sun had set, he lit the four torches. He then took out the dinner and came back to sit beside her.

It was mesmerising looking at his face in the dancing flames, as she listened to the fire cracking over the night sounds. He was like a dark-on-dark canvas painting, defined by the shadows. The shifting light revealed mysteries of his face you didn't quite see when it was light.

She wanted to see what mysteries she would find exploring the shadows of his face. She touched his face with her fingertips, gently feeling the side of his face. She stopped under his chin and said as if she was in a trance, "Your face is like perfectly sculpted art. Meaning behind it. Too open to interpretation. You're handsome."

She kissed him on his cheek then continued, "They might interpret you wrong. But that… They haven't got wrong. You are very handsome," she said with a grin. Then she kissed him, stopping the response that was just about to leave his lips.

As she kissed him, she knew she had to intently stop herself. Her body was calling for more. She knew it wasn't yet time to go there. She had somehow managed to not answer the call. They were going to get married eventually, and some foundations were better built before creating the bond that sex created.

After the kiss, they remained close; their faces almost touching, lingering like an echo. A smile across his face and hers. He affectionately rubbed his nose against hers, looking playfully into her eyes.

As their noses gently grazed against each other, a shared energy passed between them like a silent conversation. The tender gesture created a new intimate connection as their breaths exhaled, the warm air gently caressing against the other's cheek.

With their faces still near after the gesture, she closed her eyes as he brought his forehead to touch hers. It felt like an embrace of their minds and spirit. There was a sense of vulnerability as if they were exposing their innermost thoughts and feelings to each other.

As their foreheads touched, the gentle pressure made her feel supported. She could feel the subtle temperature variation of their skin, a comforting warmth where she found solace in his presence.

Then she opened her eyes when his forehead parted. He rubbed her nose with his again. His lashes seemed to move slowly as they blinked, painting shadows on his face.

They might still be the same lashes, she remembered, but now there was something more they held. They didn't feel the same when she looked at them, especially when she was this close.

"You are beautiful," he said with a smile, then turned to look up at the night sky. She followed his lead, looking up at the vast sky.

The sky was filled with stars, like dust made of light was scattered across it. Their twinkling made them look like they were layered in more than three dimensions. Watching the stars was always lovely, but watching the stars with him was spellbinding.

LOOSENING UP

S HE HAD YET to unpack all the lessons from her marriage, leading up to her divorce. They weighed heavily on her heart. The more she thought about it, the more it seemed to confuse her. It haunted her like a ghost, more so when she thought about making the right decision for her and Otiende.

Thinking about why she had to stop herself when they kissed and why she could not have sex with him sank her mood. She had been having a good time with him. She just wanted to spend time with him and enjoy what it felt like. So instead, she turned her attention to the food; any form of distraction was welcome. For such a small sized basket he had managed to get a variety of foods.

"What are all these? I don't think I have had some of these before," she said, gesturing widely at the food.

"I haven't had some of them before either, so we get to experience them for the first time together. It's also a good way to discover what the other likes."

Her stomach fluttered when she heard him mention discovering what the other likes. She wondered what he would like. What thrills Otiende? How does he want to be treated?

They started with the ones they hadn't tried before. They would close their eyes and try three at a time, then decide which ones they liked best out of the three. There was something thrilling about feeding him bite-size pieces with a fork and watching the reaction on his face. Sometimes she just couldn't help but burst out laughing.

When he was done with three, she would take a turn, closing her eyes and consciously experiencing the taste. There was anticipation as she waited for him to put the food in her mouth, then just experiencing what the food felt like in her mouth.

She would sit perfectly still, her mouth hanging open in wait for the food, her heart beating fast in a rhythm that frequently moved that fast when she was around him. She found more excitement in wondering what exactly he was doing while her eyes were closed, imagining the expression on his face.

They took turns this way, until everything had been explored. When they were done, they talked about what they liked including what wasn't in the basket that day. Time ran late into the night as they slowly ate their dinner. They did a lot more talking and laughing, so the dinner took a long time.

Otiende put everything back in the basket and folded the blanket when they were done. "Someone's going to pick these up. Let's go back," he said as he stood up and took one last look around.

"We can take them back. No need to bother anyone else," she said reaching for the basket.

"It's not a bother. They already know to come and pick it up. I wouldn't want them to come all this way for no reason. Since people don't use technology out here, we can't just change the plan. Even with the zip line it's still a long way down and I want to experience the night view with you. The stars are beautiful tonight," he said, stopping her from taking the basket along. He took it from her hands and placed it back down.

"I haven't been in this park in the dark. I didn't know it was possible. Do they stay open this late?" she asked, wondering if it was the people who worked there that would pick it up.

"Not this late. Being a celebrity has its advantages. It's also the reason for a lot of hate; possessing too many privileges. I don't use these privileges often, but for you I will buy the stars to spend more time with you," he said, and then kissed her cheek like he was making her a promise.

"OT! Not too much," she said and lightly traced her thumb over his lips. It had also been a statement to herself.

"I haven't even gone all out yet! When I look into your eyes, I know I would have married you already. It's time I should have had with you. That lost time also belongs to us. Time knows no bounds. Realistically, we can tell time has passed because of change that happens. So even if events happen later. It's still the same time. That's why I wait. Regardless of now or later. That time is ours to have." He always knew what to say.

She felt her heart beat faster, she wanted to give him her all but she really didn't want to rush things, then end up repeating the same mistakes. Would he still love her later, or would he also just speak of words of love and change when he found a reason to move on?

She knew Otiende was not a repeat of Chloe, and it wasn't fair to make that comparison, but there was still too much she didn't know about him to rush into intimacy. It was the sexual bond she had with Chloe that tangled her and crumbled her belief in love.

He had two long-term relationships in the past but they both came to an end because of people who would rather not see him succeed. They might end up the same way, not because of how good or bad their relationship is. But because of other people's bad intentions. How would she be able to handle that?

Weren't there stories about them already? She never kept up with stories, but she was aware their pictures had been taken when they went to the Outercity. He was too popular for those pictures to not have become a story. She didn't dare try and find out. They had not been discreet this whole time. Moreover, Otiende was just the kind of guy who would never deny things if information about their relationship went public; he wasn't just straightforward, he was honest.

"Even later, no matter what, I will still struggle with receiving. This power I have can command nature and technology. People see it as an even greater power than what our ancestors had over a thousand years ago. They marvel at what I could possibly do. Yet I still can't bear receiving a bow from the council or anyone else for that matter. Humble works better for me. Okay. No need for stars. Today was enough. I really liked today. I don't know if I can do your version of all out. But... If I ever feel the need for us to go all out, I shall let you know. I'm nice. I won't crush all your dreams to buy me the stars," she said, patting his chest like she was consoling a child.

"But Agina, I had all these wonderful plans of how I was going to treat you like a queen. Even buy you a crown. Can you at least consider the crown? I thought of the design already," he said with an exaggerated pout.

"No!" she said laughing.

"I can only try and ask... As you wish."

He reached into the basket and took out a light for their walk down the mountain. After turning the light on, he put out the torches.

"Let me take that off your hands," she said as she took the light. She let it go and it remained suspended. She liked to play around with technology, using it how it was not meant to be used now that she had powers.

"Now I can just focus on you," he said with a huge grin.

They slowly made their way down. When they got back to where they had gone off trail, they took more pictures. Agina used her spear to light their night shots, taking pictures transformed by the sparkling stars and glowing moon.

The mystery created by the shadows and strategically placed low light made the night shots unique. They spent quite some time experimenting and loving the outcome of their pictures.

When they were done with the photographs, they zip-lined down to where their day started. They took off their climbing gear and returned them. As they walked towards the portal, she only remembered the bodyguards when she spotted them and wondered what they had been doing the whole day. She hadn't noticed them the entire time.

Agina and Otiende lingered, standing in front of the portal. They both didn't seem to want to end the day. The portal was outside in the open and it looked fairy-tale-like, held up by flowering live vines that were as thick as her forearms. The park was beautiful, but more so today, it looked like the portal would transport you to a place far away where there was a happily ever after. The lighting at the portal hung like string lights, creating more of an enchanted look.

"I want to work on something else with you. I'd like to come up with a way to prevent being cyber harassed. I don't think I can manage any of the stuff you put up with. Especially now that we are like this," she said, reaching up to kiss him on the cheek.

"I'd like that too. We can meet in my home studio," he said and gently touched her hair.

"I'll see you Monday," she said as they hugged.

She liked the way he fit in her arms. It felt more natural to part this way. It was a comforting feeling that was warming. This time it was not like the awkward goodbyes from before. They held onto each other longer than they probably should have, before they went their separate ways.

COMPROMISE

Agina♥: OT, I forgot to mention that I will need to rely on your help more with this. I am not sure how the digital social space functions for myself, let alone for celebrities. I don't have much of a digital social presence.

I got you. No need to worry. You can count on me. I already figured as much. Here is a perfect meme. It's me beside you, coming to the rescue. Image attached.

Agina♥: That's so funny. I love it. It's fitting. I think we would make a great rescue team.

-End of text messages-

HE STARTED BRAINSTORMING ideas for their new project on his own. He didn't see things like she did, finding links where they didn't seem to exist. But he was well aware of how things worked, and how stories ended up becoming viral.

He found himself wondering what he could have done differently to avoid all the things that had ended up happening to his relationships.

Could he have tried harder? Would it even have made a difference? His partners were the ones who gave up on him. Or rather, gave up against the madness of the large fanbase. Since he could remember, there were always people who had a problem with him. It was the reason why he had met Agina; he had been hiding from people who had a problem with him.

He didn't want to change who he was because of these people, so when he was younger, he could only hide to stay true to himself. Over time, he learnt different ways to deal with people, but it was not fair to have to ask anyone, much less Agina, to endure what he had endured.

He heard the alert that Agina had arrived. He knew she could find her way, but he went to meet her.

She was wearing something sleeveless again today. Her tattoos truly were a work of art and were stunning. They had an elegance that reminded him of the ceremonial henna tattoos other cultures wore during weddings.

He could also see her legs today. Her legs seemed to be longer, with the way they were framed by her dress; she was wearing a dress that was short and tight, but it had another layer that didn't fully wrap around. From the back it probably looked like a gown whose length flowed all the way to the ground.

She had what he would call the perfect female body and her clothes today accentuated it. The layers made her waist look smaller. The way she usually dressed was fashionable. Her clothes clearly always had a traditional print, but it was not traditional dress.

They met halfway on the way to his studio.

"Agina."

"OT."

They gently called each other's names as they embraced in a long hug. He liked to hear her say his name, somehow it sounded better when she said it. Only people he knew from his childhood and his parents called him OT.

The way he felt when she was present, when she was close, when she kissed him... He knew his love for her had grown significantly. He just couldn't stop himself from unravelling what he had tried to bury inside. He was madly in love with her.

His feelings were so strong that he couldn't tell if he had ever stopped loving her. It was his fault for deciding it was something he wanted to hide and resisted pursuing.

She smelled of jasmine. It was probably her soap, but he loved the scent on her. He imagined that she was the type of person who used natural organic products and wouldn't put on perfume. She cared about doing things naturally.

After they broke off the long embrace, they still held each other's arms. He looked into her eyes knowing he would never get tired of seeing into her soul. She was so full and expansive. She shifted her hands and gently pulled him down to kiss him.

He liked the way she tasted; she was always sweet. But it probably had nothing to do with his taste buds. They kissed slowly for a while. Once he started, he found himself diving deep into her. A place where time stood still, and it was just them. A place where she had never left, and she would never leave. It was like a conversation between their souls.

"We are supposed to be working," she said, having parted from the kiss and speaking into his shirt where she had buried her head.

He smiled at the adorable behaviour. He didn't want to see her so helpless, it was a subtle seduction, but he was probably even more helpless. What he wanted to do was carry her into his bedroom.

"I started us off with some preliminary ideas. So, we are actually ahead with work," he said, running his fingers through the curls of her afro.

She lifted her head from his shirt and looked up at him. "Were you trying to cheat so you can sneak in more playtime? I can't tell. You are also passionate about projects that are meaningful to you," she said, squinting one eye and looking at him inquisitively.

"Sneaking in playtime sounds much better and romantic. Except I also want to protect you. We can automate all tech to defend you from attacks. But just being with you in public leaves you vulnerable to a different kind of attack you have no defence against." He was smiling but he didn't think it hid his fear. His tone was too formal.

"I really don't understand your fandom. Or should I say anti-fandom? Shouldn't you be protected as well?" she asked in disbelief, catching on to his fear. Her jaw went slightly slack as she searched his eyes. Her long lashes curtained her bewilderment.

"My parents chose to be entertainers. We had these discussions often. They wanted to protect me. It's not that they didn't care." His gaze softened as if he was peering into a distant memory.

"But in the end, you can't control people's choices and thoughts. At least we don't. After seeing what happened to Tony, it seems people do control others' thoughts." He shook his head in disbelief, then continued. "My parents found it best to teach me strength and good character. Instead of keeping me from it, they chose to prepare me for it."

There was a subtle shift in his posture, as if he was figuratively stepping back in defence. "But sometimes people just feel challenged to push harder when they see you're not backing down. Trying to stop it might make it worse. Even when I was young, not just at the conferences, it wouldn't matter how you convinced others to treat me."

He spoke slowly, as if carefully selecting each word, trying to convey the depth of his emotions. "But at the same time, I don't have to just stand there and take it. So, I would walk away, hide, not look at these stories, or just turn all the devices off. I practised my right to choose what was in front of me."

"Trying to stop something that is already travelling at full speed is hard. It needs great force. It would be more like a vicious attack to counter everything. Stopping something before it is in motion is easy. We can stop this for you, such that it never exists," he disclosed, trying to help her understand his experiences and why he had arrived at his choices.

He hugged her, holding her tight. He just wanted this moment wrapping her in his arms to last forever; her, safe in his arms. He wanted to forget people wanted to kill her. He wanted to forget his crazy stans. He just wanted it all to go away.

"I never thought about this back then, but your childhood was difficult, wasn't it? I just saw who you were. OT. My friend. I didn't even bother to find out who your family was. If it mattered to you, you would have told me. Right?" She was looking at him again. It was like those eyes questioned his soul and he couldn't escape without answering her.

"I had been experiencing it long before you came along. You were the best part of it all. You saw me. That was enough."

She hugged him even tighter than they had hugged before. It was comforting to hug her. He felt a lot of the tension in his body melt away. He was confident this was what he wanted to protect.

"Let me protect you OT. We can slow the momentum. Maybe one day it will even stop. I can't comfortably protect myself while I leave you in that mess. Say you will let me protect you," she pleaded with him.

He could feel the vibration as she spoke because she was still hugging him tight. He wanted to protest but then he remembered how stubborn Agina was when she made up her mind; he realised it would make no difference. What could he possibly do when she asked that way? Like she was pleading with him.

It made him want to kneel and offer her the world; anything in the world no matter what he had to do to get it! Then he thought of another idea. If he was going to compromise, he needed her to do that too.

"Fine. You can protect me. If you will spend more time with me. The two of us together, not meeting because of some project. I like seeing you every day."

He could feel her freeze. He knew he was holding his breath, waiting for her response or any reaction. Time seemed to have stood still.

All he could hear was his heartbeat which seemed to get louder and louder. Then she finally came back to life again.

She loosened the hug and rubbed his back as she spoke, looking at him, "You can have more time."

He felt relieved at her reply. He couldn't stop himself from asking. Because of Agina's character the worst that could happen is saying no.

She kissed him on the cheek and then said as she looked into his eyes, "We both get what we want. But we have more work to do now. We didn't even make it into your studio." She shook her head as she said the last statement, a slight grin on her face. She said it but the look in her eyes said she would rather keep kissing him.

"Yes. We can have time together after work. Work first," he said as he smiled, pleased with himself.

They finally continued, walking towards the studio holding hands.

BUTTERFLY EFFECT 1

THEY WORKED WELL together. He had a different understanding than she did, and they were able to integrate their ideas seamlessly. He couldn't help but remember the first project they worked on: her spear.

Thirty years ago…

He arrived on the first day of the conference as usual. Before he went in, Otiende's uncle Osano Omolo Oigo stopped to have a conversation with Otiende.

That day Otiende was wearing all silver with lines that ran through his clothes. The lines were lit up and looked like they were externally circulating some sort of glowing fluid through his body. He also had a helmet over his head. Because of the way the clothes fit, seeming to be one piece with the helmet and his shoes, he looked more like he was a robot.

"OT, why don't you take off the helmet? The kids here aren't used to it. Even the kids in the Outercity might not be used to it. You know these clothes are more in style with the kids you meet when you travel abroad with your Mom and Dad because that's the only place you get these clothes," Osano said, as he bent over to lower his eye level.

"I like it. I'm not taking it off. Mom said I can wear what I want," he stubbornly said.

No one was able to see Otiende's face, but his voice was firm and even, like he was giving a formal complaint.

"Why do you say you want to come to these conferences every time, when you hide most of the time? People are already saying I am forcing you and today you won't even show your face."

Otiende was silent. You could clearly see the frustration on Osano's face.

"Sigh. This is my brother's fault. You are all the same way. You care for the culture and where you come from, but you have a weird way of showing you care!" he said relaxing his facial expression.

"You probably like to come because you have a friend now. You leave here very happy every time. I could just arrange for you and Agina to meet. You don't have to keep going in there to get bullied and then run off," said Osano, straightening his back to stand tall. He wasn't usually good with children to begin with, but he was good with Otiende. Unfortunately, when Otiende got like this no one could move him.

"This is my choice. I have never asked her to come. That is her choice. Let her be."

If Agina was seen to be stubborn, Otiende was impossible. Because he was worse.

"I'll take my leave then. I'll see you when it's over," said Otiende, exiting like fabric tumbling over the cliff with the wind, never to be seen again. He walked into the room where his group was meeting. He didn't even wait for Osano's response. So, Osano just shook his head as he watched his nephew go in.

He could hear the reactions of the other kids in the room. You would think they would be used to Otiende by now, but they just seemed to drift further and further away. As the years went by, they saw him as more and more different. Except for Agina.

It was a mystery how she always found him. No one else was able to find him even once. Even when they searched the whole day. Osano even tried to stay behind a few times and follow him, to see where he went. But he was too fast, and could wiggle out of any situation; he always lost track of him.

He was right. No one ever told her to go look. If anything, they diligently tried to stop her. You would think she would forget such things as a young child. Especially when they had just met. They avoided mentioning him so she wouldn't go look.

They tried to convince her she shouldn't go whenever she decided to go looking for him. But it was hopeless. The only thing they would have done is restrain them both. Restrain one so that they don't run, and then restrain the other so they wouldn't go looking.

But they were both like little activists, so taking away such a right to movement would have been worse. Though they were young they were just as relentless and assertive as activists who will NOT be silenced.

They could do nothing but let it happen. They tried to get rid of all the places they could hide but he found a different place to hide every time. How could there be so many hiding spots?

After some time, they decided it didn't harm anyone. They were no longer followed, and they didn't try to find them anymore. They didn't need someone to keep an eye on things either. Perhaps they felt guilty about not being able to stop the other children from bullying Otiende.

Because of the way others treated him, Otiende tended to be cold and distant. Agina on the other hand was friendly and always got along with people. As much as people would like to see their interactions and see how oil and water seemed to mix, it was never seen.

Osano could only want to protect his nephew but was left to walk away as the sounds in the room faded away with the distance.

In the room Otiende went and took a seat as others gasped and cursed, moving away from him.

The room was one of the many conference rooms in the building. Up front, it had two steps up to a platform where a large table stood with a computer on it. In the rest of the space, there were several long tables with swivelling chairs along one edge, a seat placed every two metres or so.

The long tables were set up in two u shapes with an inner smaller u and a larger outer u. There was a large screen on the wall and a smaller screen and microphone were at every chair. When the other children had moved away, they either abandoned their chairs or rolled away.

Their tutor and her assistant tried to get everyone to calm down, but you could see panic in their faces. Most people in the Innercity had never left the confinement of the walls their entire lives. Furthermore, right in front of them had suddenly shown up someone who was taboo. How much of him was him, and how much was technology?

After the room was silent enough the tutor said, "Why don't we say hi? You all know who this is. We have already talked about how we are going to behave today."

"Why do we all have to be the ones that change? He is only one person. He can leave those dark spirits where he came from."

Some children cheered at that statement a boy had made. It was clearly inciting others to be rowdy. When the adults finally got the room silent enough, the tutor added, "He was born here. He is one of us. Now say hi so we can move on to the next thing."

Otiende just sat in silence. One of the other children who had always tried to advocate for Otiende started: "Hi Otiende. Don't mind them."

She hadn't moved away like the others, so she was a short distance away. A few seconds later the word [Hi] was digitally projected in front of Otiende.

There was an even worse reaction around the room. Even the ones who hadn't moved away were frightened. Was it really Otiende or

   **STRANGE LIGHT: Ler Mahia**

was it a robot? It wouldn't have been as bad if the children had not thought this type of technology was evil.

They were convinced that he was the bad spirit they had been warned against. They were like a religious child meeting a demon and being instructed to be friendly towards it. The tutor couldn't seem to calm the children down.

"Why don't you turn that off Otiende? And maybe let them see your face," the tutor said, projecting her voice over the noise. She was forced to project her voice to be heard even though she had been standing close to him; the room had been too noisy.

But what she said seemed to rile them up even more. They might as well have been a mob going on a witch hunt, considering the things that they said, their body language, and the way they looked at him.

Otiende had already felt discouraged when he got in, so it was the reason why he sat in silence from the beginning. He hadn't planned to just sit there quietly. Considering he didn't want to talk anymore; he used his speech projector instead. [Forget it] was digitally projected in front of him before he got up and ran away.

"Wait!" The tutor called after him and tried to grab his hand. But he managed to dodge and ran without looking back. That was the shortest time he had ever stayed in the group. Usually, he would endure a little longer, but it tended to go more or less the same way.

When he stopped running, he got into an empty room and closed the door behind him. He hadn't been in the room long before the door opened and Agina walked in. She ran over and hugged him.

"OT. I found you," she said after breaking from the hug.

26

BUTTERFLY EFFECT 2

S HE WALKED PAST him and sank into one of the swivelling conference room chairs. It rolled backwards slightly with the force of being occupied. She then took off her backpack and pushed it onto the conference room table.

It was easy to think that she had known where to meet him or that she had seen him go in. But there was no such thing. Usually, when Agina was asked how she always found him, she said she just knew.

He was still standing, out of breath, wondering to himself how she had such luck and wondering if he should have hidden somewhere else. But he was tired from running and felt like he needed to rest. He liked the space he had found.

"This hiding place is not so much like the other hiding places. I like it. It's more you. It's more like an open place to be alone," she said, gesturing that it was a large open room.

Because it was one of the larger meeting rooms that sat hundreds of people, it would normally have been used by the council at the conferences. But it was the opening day of the conferences. So, everyone was in one meeting.

Otiende finally seemed to snap out of his thoughts. He digitally projected the words, [You don't have to stay. I will be fine.] as he crossed his hands.

"Yes. But I want to stay. That is so cool. Come. Don't just stand. I want to see it," she said, gesturing for him to come.

"How do you always find me?" he asked, walking towards her.

She shrugged her shoulders. "Maybe I have an internal tracker or some type of powerful magic that only finds you. How cool would that be? Then I'd always have a friend," Agina said, leaning forward. With the excitement on her face, she looked more like she was letting him know he had won something.

"Finding me is boring. You need to do more cool stuff." He turned his head to the side as if to shrug her off. His tone was very dismissive but that did not deter Agina.

"Cool stuff is that helmet. How would I find it without finding you first? So, wouldn't that mean finding you is cool? What else does it do? Show me!"

She could always pull him in with that question. He gave in and did a full demonstration. She couldn't have been more excited.

"How am I supposed to do stuff as cool as that? The only way I can get to do stuff that is cool is to make it. There is nothing cool in all of the Innercity! If I couldn't go adventuring outside the house, I would go nuts," she said, lazily throwing her body back in defeat.

"You have been outside the Innercity. Don't you ever bring anything back?" he asked, genuinely surprised.

"As if I would dare. Have you met my Mom? Right. You have met my Mom. Do you know my Mom? She would never let me. Negative energies and evil spirits. You know?" she said, gesturing her hands wildly to demonstrate evil spirits, with a look of slight disgust and disappointment on her face.

"Yeah. I have had enough of that today. I just got this outfit. I like it. So, I wanted to wear it." He crossed his hands and sat next to her, sinking into the chair with the heavy feeling he was carrying.

He digitally projected the words: [It's pretty cool.]

"How does that work?" she excitedly asked, perking up in her seat.

"You have been outside the country. Right? This tech is different. It's not like the stuff we have in Dala." He went on to talk for a long time, explaining how it worked. He expounded on everything that could be explained down to the minute details.

"You are so lucky. My Mom has a com that she now hides. She was not letting me have it again after she found me with it. I live in a technology-dead zone. But even before she found me with it, you couldn't put coms on the dining table. On the table! What is the reason behind that? It won't poison the food. But do you know what she will allow on the table? A spear. A spear! It touches the floor like one thousand times. I should get a com that looks like a spear. Then put it on the table without letting her know it's a com," Agina said as she burst out laughing.

"Can you imagine the look on her face?" she asked between laughter.

Otiende still had the helmet on his face, but he had changed the mode so that the helmet was transparent. Even though it was transparent, it was coloured silver, so it made his face look eerie. You could see him laughing silently. They were laughing so hard.

When they had finally stopped laughing, he said. "Now you absolutely have to get a com that looks like a spear."

"But OT. Where would I get such a thing? I would have to make one."

"Let's make you one then."

That conversation turned into how they were going to make her a com that wasn't just a spear but was many other things. It wasn't just going to be her secret prank. It was cool. It was technology. It was Agina's first com. It was also her way out of her technology dead zone.

Otiende had his com with him, so they contacted some people and arranged everything. Over the rest of the days at the conferences, if someone had happened to walk in on them, they would have been surprised to see the setup Otiende's com had given rise to.

He might as well have had a portable lab with him. It had everything they needed to design the spear that was a com. They focused on it for the rest of the days they were at the conference, and it was delivered to Agina when it was done.

For a long time, no one knew what Agina's spear really was, but her mother or no one else could protest against Agina following their tradition: When elders reach the age of 7, they can take up a spear, showing their dedication to protect and serve their people.

Considering Agina usually showed no interest in anything that was related to the council, they happily held a large formal ceremony to initiate her into spear yielding. They believed she had finally found something she liked about being an elder.

FOR LOVE

Back to the present time…

AGINA AND OTIENDE had exhausted all the possibilities, analysing and running some simulations. They decided to test the program protecting Otiende from digital social harm first, to see if they really could get the program to act more like an immune system that evolved to protect itself.

They set it to only target new information and report what it had done. They didn't intend their final system to send reports, it was supposed to be a discreet program that always lives in the tech spaces, invisible and untraceable.

Agina used her power to run it across the world. Otiende noted that her tattoos only light up sometimes, like when she extended her bandwidth to use her power across the world. She let it run for a few minutes as she collected the reports, then pulled the program back.

It was amazing how there were already pictures of the two of them in so many digital spaces. He had not expected that there would also be pictures of the time they met in Chai Place or The Mpandaji Park. It confirmed that there was too much room for things to go wrong and they needed everything about their digital presence to be more controlled. Luckily, they had not yet gone viral.

The report found loopholes and suggested ways to improve its effectiveness. They used the report to adjust the program. It was easier to create these types of programs because Agina only needed to tell it what needed to be done in theory, without having to write the program.

"Somehow the program feels like energy I cultivated or a life force I created, that is being let out… Makes sense why our people see these things like spirits; the program seems to have a life of its own with a vibrant energy.

Can we send it out together in a better way? Like create a ritual or something and thank it. I want it to know it was created out of a place of love. And that its work is light."

He didn't know what to make of her statement about love. But he knew it was not the time to bring up how they felt about each other. He knew that he could not bring it up anytime soon either. She seemed to be terrified by the subject. He will have to leave the opening that led into the conversation about how they felt, even if he knew that he loved her and wanted to let her know.

"I would like that. I'll do it with you," he replied, appreciating her take on things; she didn't just give it thought, she put her heart into it.

"You might be more tech-oriented but I know you won't disappoint me and tell me you have no ceremonial stuff. What do you have?" she asked like she was daring him to say something different.

"Come. Let's see what you would like to use," he said as he took her hand and led her out of the room.

They entered what looked like a meditation room, then he led her to another room at the back that seemed to have no windows. He didn't turn any lights on, but the room lit up as soon as they walked in.

"Definitely not disappointing!" She gasped as she looked around the room. There were so many items on display that it looked more like a store than a museum.

She pulled him into her arms and kissed him. This kiss felt different. It was driven by a spur of joy that came from within her heart. Not yearning. Not wanting. It was pure joy. It filled him in ways he didn't know was possible. When he kissed her back, he knew it came from a different place within him too.

She parted their lips, putting her hand on his chest as she asked. "What do you think you want to use? You have made me so happy. Let's find some things and make this up."

You could see the joy in her eyes. He wanted to stare into those eyes forever. But she let him go and started picking up some items. He picked some things too.

"Shield, flywhisk, headdress and drums. Of course, dancing shall be done," she said.

She put on some accessories and put some on him too. Some of the accessories they put on were instruments that jingled as you moved.

"Paint my face first," she said, handing him white face paint.

"What do you want me to paint?"

"It doesn't matter. We are making it up. For us."

He paused then drew a heart on her cheeks. He felt like his hands were trembling slightly. The warmth of her cheeks was stirring thoughts he knew he shouldn't be having at that moment.

"Your turn," he said, handing her the paint.

"What did you draw?"

"Hearts"

"Perfect. I'll draw hearts too."

She looked up at him and paused for a while, then after turning his head to the side, drew on his cheeks. He could feel the warmth of her hands on his face and the cold paint as it was slowly applied to his face. She looked into his eyes again before she put away the paint.

She attached feathers that were on a leather band to both of his shoulders and then put the headdress on his head. The headdress had long, large, ostrich feathers, but felt light on his head. She stood back and looked at the results then took off the headdress.

"Let's go outside. This won't fit through that door when you are wearing it. I also want to bring the Abu. You can play it as I am sending off the program," Agina said as she took off her shoes and picked up all that she had chosen. He also took off his shoes.

"You will launch it from outside?" he asked, picking up the items he had pulled out to use.

She looked thoughtfully, then said, "Yeah. It's ready to go. Sending it is all in my head anyway. Let's start with you on the shield and me with my spear as we dance. Then just dancing. Then you on the drums and me with the fly whisk. Then the Abu as I send it. You will have to find some music to play up till you are on the drums. It will just be the sound of your drumming while I am on the fly whisk, then just the sound of your Abu."

Holding what they had gathered in their hands, they began to walk out.

"Okay. Any singing?" He turned to look at her as he asked.

"I don't know what to sing. If you think of anything to sing just jump in and sing. If I think of anything I will jump in too."

They arrived at his deck and set everything up. She put the headdress on him, and he put a headdress on her. His headdress was grand and went along with the feathers on his shoulders. Hers was small, it was just fabric wrapped tightly.

They searched through some songs, before they found a song they both liked. It was more like a traditional song in their native language.

"Ready?" he asked, placing his hand on her shoulder.

"Yes," she replied, then stepped back.

They began their ritual, smiles across their faces. They hadn't rehearsed but considering they both knew traditional dance; it was easy for them to coordinate.

As the music played, they moved around the deck, both following a circular pattern. Most of their movement was in the feet, moving the left foot, then the right. They also moved their shoulders, Otiende moving his shoulders more exaggeratedly. Agina moved her waist more.

She held the spear midway, its spearhead facing down while she held it at an angle. She would thrust the spear higher to the beat, then bring it back down, maintaining its angle. He would push the shield forward and back to the beat. They mainly danced like this but used other dances.

Then they put down the shield and spear. Now that their hands were free, they swayed their hands left and right to the beat, Agina's hands flowing more smoothly, and Otiende's hands moving more sharply.

They would dip their heads every now and then as they faced each other. Then standing side by side they moved like they were giving a double high five on the left in sync with the beat, then the same double high five on the right in sync with the beat. Then circle the deck again, dancing with their palms together, his right palm on her left palm.

When the song was over, he picked up the drum without missing a beat. Playing as he continued to move his shoulders. He hit the top of the drum and occasionally hit the side of the drum using drumsticks.

Agina moved around the deck a lot more, flicking the fly whisk as she danced, sometimes swinging it up in the air like she was waving it around. She moved her waist more vigorously, then got on her knees, continuing to move her shoulders and waist.

When the final part came, Agina put down the fly whisk and closed her eyes. He stopped drumming and played the Abu, its distinct sound sounding more like a whistle, but resonating deep like a horn. The sound was amplified because it is an instrument created by using beeswax to stick several gourds together, then securing the bond by tying it with the bark of the Grewia tree.

Otiende had seen her use her power several times before, but it was still mesmerising to watch. Her tattoos glowed as she rose up. He hadn't seen her rise up before; other than the time he watched it in the video. Could he include the time they first kissed? He thought as he smiled to himself.

He found his heart racing as she went higher and higher up into the sky. It was somewhat frightening, but he kept playing the instrument. She stopped somewhere above all the trees and gracefully spun around with her arms wide open.

Then she brought her hands together as if in prayer as she descended back to the ground. When she landed back safely on the deck he stopped playing. He was relieved but he could still feel his heart racing.

She opened her eyes and came toward him. He put down the Abu and then walked towards her.

"It's done," she said as they hugged. She seemed to be amazingly calm, so it helped him calm down.

"Do you want to go back in and check on anything?" he awkwardly asked, not sure what to do next.

"No. It's invisible. It should not be found. So, there is nothing to check. I should always be able to find it with my powers if I really needed to. That's the only way to find the programs."

He still wasn't sure how her powers worked but it seemed to have no bounds. Everyone should probably be glad it was Agina who ended up with the powers; she had the purest heart he knew. If it was a person seeking power, they could have easily conquered the world.

28

FALLING APART

H E PICKED A song that was slower with a strong beat. Dances originating from their country were more upbeat, requiring a lot of movement; whether it is moving the shoulders, the waist and hips, or footwork. So, their beats tended to be strong. Unlike the song they chose earlier, it was modern with traditional influences.

"Join me in this dance," he said as he held out his hand and started the song.

She put her hand in his and they began to dance with their arms outstretched as he continued to hold her hand. They watched each other dance as they moved their bodies and feet to the beat. She had a smile across her face and would occasionally look down like she was shy.

He brought her arm up causing them to step closer, then let go of her hand while they danced more vigorously at the chorus.

When the chorus was over, he held his hand out again and taking her hand in his, he turned her around. They continued to dance as he felt like he had cradled her in his space, but there was still distance between them. Towards the end they danced closer while he held her waist. He didn't want to forget any second of the dance. It gave him a feeling he had never felt while dancing with someone before.

Dancing was a huge part of their culture so most of them not only enjoyed dancing, but also knew how to dance well. He had to admit she was really good, especially at twisting her waist. It made him want to try a more seductive dance with her. He would have loved to keep dancing with her, but he didn't think he would be able to keep holding himself back.

When the song came to an end, he hugged her from behind. "You are a good dancer," he said close to her ear, before he let her go.

She laughed. "No. You're a professional dancer. You're really good. I still remember the dances you showed me though I've never seen your professional work."

"I really like that about you. You have seen me through our experiences together. Not what is out there, and you still get it. You get it better than they do."

"I don't know. There is so much about you out there that it makes me feel like I don't know you," she said, avoiding his gaze.

"I get where you are coming from. But I honestly feel like you are the only one who knows me. Even when you were just 3, I felt understood. Now, I still feel the same way. Besides, what do you value more?" he asked, trying to hold her with his gaze she couldn't fully avoid.

"The experiences I have with you are more valuable. You have a point," she said, looking up at him like she felt reassured.

"Now can we have time together?" he asked with a look of mischief on his face.

She laughed then said, "First we put away all these things."

"Then time together?"

She laughed again. "Yes. Then time together."

He began to pick up what they had previously brought outside. She picked up some things too. He took off his headdress and they walked back into the house as he said "I was thinking. Dinner. I usually have dinner with my friend on Monday. Not every Monday but I was supposed to meet him for dinner today. I want to go over with you. Introduce you to him."

"You already want me to meet your friends?" she asked in shock, glancing back as they were walking.

"Is it too fast? I know we are not engaged but we were matched and have already decided when to get married." He hadn't thought it would be a problem, but now that she questioned him, he realised they were not even engaged and there were still some things they had not discussed.

"For a slow timeline, the meeting should happen in at least three months. It should even be up to five months."

They arrived in the display room, and she turned to look at him and continued talking. "It's only been two weeks," she said in a matter-of-fact way.

"I know. But he's a childhood friend. I met him before I met you. Our parents were friends first. They also lived in the Outercity. I used to talk about you all those years ago. So, it feels like he's always known about you. Agina, I have known you for more than two weeks," he said, feeling defensive and completely thrown off.

She sat on a Kom Nyaluo, deep in thought. He did not want to interrupt her thought process. He had already ruined things by saying the wrong thing.

"Our situation is rather complicated. Logically, we started the timeline two weeks ago. Then what about my parents who have already met you? I have also met your uncle and his husband and your Dana. What about our history? Because I can't pretend to know nothing about you. If we start from the beginning, so much has changed since then. We still don't know each other well enough to say we have known each other for thirty-four years, because of the gap. Let's make a timeline that isn't bound to anything. Okay? And what about our engagement? Because are we engaged or not? Our marriage is at the end of this timeline in three years," Agina said in a daze.

Her words made him feel uncomfortable and exposed. He should talk to her. She seemed to have not fully returned from her thoughts before she got lost in them again. It was almost like she was thinking out loud. He returned the items in his hands, then took what she had in her hands and returned them too.

The direction of her gaze was fixed as she seemed deep in thought and stared into space in silence. Or maybe she was staring at the leather apron that was decorated in blue, while she thought about something else. He couldn't tell. Was he imagining she was looking at the blue apron intently? He couldn't think of why, so he guessed she was just staring.

He took another stool and sat in front of her, their knees almost touching, and then he held both of her hands in his hands. "Agina…" he said, then rubbed her palms with his fingers. She felt warm and soft.

"Agina. If it's too much for you, I understand. We just never talked about friends when we set our boundaries and expectations. I have already passed the limit we set for when we would see and text each other and I asked for more time." He felt like he'd just lost something. It made him nervous, scared even. He wanted to reverse time and not ask the question about meeting his friend.

"It's not you. It's her," she said, almost in a whisper, while she was pointing to the blue decorated apron with her head, like it was a person she was pointing out.

He rubbed her hands again. Wherever she had got lost, he knew he wasn't going to be the one who would pull her out. He hadn't expected things to turn out this way. Tears started to fall from her eyes.

"Sorry. After all this time I still cry about her. It's the little things like the colour blue that just push in these thoughts that sometimes leave me vulnerable," she said, taking her hand away to rub her eyes. She whipped the tears away more aggressively than she needed to.

"I'll go with you. I just… We do need to talk about this timeline." Her voice broke like she was trying hard to hold herself together.

He got up and pulled her up into his arms, hugging her. He hated to see her like that and felt so helpless.

"We have time to talk later. Cry if you need to. I'll just silently be here." He held her tightly as she silently cried. Sniffling every now and then.

When he held her this way, he understood why a longer timeline would work better for them. Old memories would always come up; things that were unresolved. But it wasn't the timeline he was pushing against. He just wanted to see her more often and introduce her to Odek since he had planned to go there. He wanted her to understand that.

"Come. You don't need to apologise for feeling," he said, as he took her hand and led her out of the room.

He wanted to take her back outside so she could stay there for a while and see the sunset, but it had unexpectedly started raining. So, he sat down on the L-shaped sofa and pulled her down to sit with him. They were both still barefoot and still had face paint from their ritual.

They sat on the edge of the L such that their feet were up on the sofa with their legs intertwined and he was holding her in his arms. He stayed holding her, wrapping himself around her. He wasn't surprised she was still crying. It had been difficult for her to just leave it all behind and move on.

When she seemed to have finally stopped crying, he called her name, but she didn't answer. Had she fallen asleep? Her breathing was steady and even. He got up from under her and lay her down, then went and found a blanket to cover her with.

He took a warm wet towel and wiped the paint and tears off her face. She was sleeping so peacefully that he didn't have the heart to wake her. After watching her for a while, he was sure she was not going to wake up since he had been wiping her. He left her a short note on a notetab.

I'll be in my room. There is food in the kitchen if you want to eat. The house will guide you or help you if you ask.

After talking to Odek on the phone, he had something to eat on his own and went to bed. He had not expected the day to end this way. There were conversations they would need to have.

HIS CONFESSION

SHE COULD SENSE something was different. Where was she? She was slowly waking up. She opened her eyes and looked around. Sleep was still clasping her senses in a viscous pool, slowing her awareness. She finally realised she was still in Otiende's home. She slowly sat up and looked around.

There was a note on the table. She read it and put it back down. *How had she fallen asleep?* She thought to herself. Thinking back to last night. She hadn't even realised she was mentally exhausted since Chloe was a constant weight on the back of her mind.

She had still been holding on to hope before Otiende showed up. Maybe now she could finally let go because she had a reason to let go. Thoughts of her always flung her in directions she couldn't predict, forcing her anywhere within a wide variety of emotions.

"You are up." Otiende's voice came from behind her.

She moved aside the plush blanket she was covered with, put on her shoes that had been placed beside the sofa, stood up and turned to face him.

"Yeah. I… Cried myself to sleep," she said with a look of embarrassment on her face.

"You doing okay?" She could have felt better if he was looking at her weirdly, but she could only feel embarrassed because he looked understanding and concerned when he asked.

"Yeah. I'm fine. Guess I needed to let that out," she said feeling awkward, suddenly not knowing what to do with her hands as she moved them randomly.

"I was about to go for a run. Do you want to eat something?" he asked as he walked towards her and hugged her.

"No. I should get going."

"Okay. We can meet here tomorrow after work. We'll bring up what needs to be discussed then." He paused as if giving her a chance to change her mind.

She nodded her head. "I'll see myself out."

He gave her another hug, rubbing her back. Then she left, feeling like something heavy had been poured into her body and weighed her down, making it hard to move or think.

There had been a lot to think about. She decided it would be a good time to properly talk about Chloe. The past two days felt like they had gone by slowly.

They had just sat down on the sofa. She sat cross-legged facing him and in the same way he sat with just one leg up, facing her. The sofa had sunk slightly with their weight. She could feel its soft fabric underneath her, and felt Otiende's knee that seemed to demand to make his presence known.

It felt like they were picking up where they had previously left off, considering the last time she was there she had cried and slept on the same sofa. The tension in the air indicated that it was going to be a serious discussion. She wanted to start the conversation by talking about her struggle to move on, but he started before she could.

"I need to tell you something that I have been hiding. From you.

From everyone. I'll need you to keep an open mind. I don't expect you to be okay with what I have done or to understand."

The words that were about to leave her lips completely disappeared. What could he possibly have to say? She looked into his eyes. She couldn't understand what emotion was there. He was waiting for a response from her.

She sighed. "I can't imagine what you could do. What do you need to say?"

"It all started when I was younger. I can't remember when exactly. Maybe I was 5. I wanted someone to play with. I wasn't patient then. So, I created a fake person. An anonymous citizen. They were like an invisible friend. A year younger than me.

My parents played along but they didn't realise that I had actually hacked the system and created a person. Digitally they were real in every way, but they didn't exist. This went on for years. I always wanted to stop. But I kept thinking about things that this person would do and, in a sense, lived this second life.

I even got them a job when I got older. At some point, I worked with you. Remember how back then you would work online to avoid more conflict with your parents, because they thought you were too young to work in the Outercity by yourself?" She slowly nodded when he paused, then listened in curiosity as he continued, "I hadn't intended to work specifically with you. But it felt good to connect again. Even if you didn't know who I was.

From then on, I worked with you on and off. I was just a colleague. Until we became friends again. This helped because we stayed in touch, even after you started working in the Outercity, and were no longer working online. Then... Sigh. I didn't even want to admit to myself what I was feeling. But I had feelings for you.

I was hesitant to approach you. Maybe because I didn't know what would happen if I revealed my identity after keeping it from you. Or maybe because you were still underage when it happened and I felt like those are feelings I shouldn't have.

Besides, I wasn't sure how you would fit in my life as Otiende the celebrity; I was highly motivated to keep moving forward, so I was always busy. Maybe the biggest reason was that I didn't get the sense you felt the same way about me. I was just a male friend.

Then you got married so suddenly. You were so happy. So, I couldn't say anything. We stayed friends. Then you got divorced. But I was in a relationship then. So, I could only support you as a friend as you went through the breakup.

Time passed. Gabriella's online harassment case was so bad that there was so much legal action that needed to happen. I decided this second life needed to die. If they investigated closely enough and found out, I would go to jail and possibly get a death sentence. So, I finally stopped. I lived a double life for thirty-three years. Not a single person knew until now, as I tell you this.

It wasn't all, deceiving you intentionally. I was too out of control to stop. Part of the fault was in my coping patterns: when I am hiding under this identity, I don't have to be anything else but myself. It's not an excuse. I just... I was young and I never stopped myself.

This means we haven't completely lost contact over the past twenty-seven years. You just didn't know you were speaking to me. I am sorry. I know it's a lot to process. I am not asking you to understand. I wanted you to know."

She sat motionless. How could two people's lives possibly get more complicated than they were!? He was her friend #1008.

She knew Otiende was smart. Watching him work these last two weeks was an observation confirming he was more like a hacker. But can a 5-year-old hack their system!? If it was him, she believed he could.

She just kept looking into his eyes. Like an answer would be there. Agina had never discovered what happened to #1008. She just stopped hearing from them. She never had the heart to confirm if they had died. She stubbornly continued to write to him for over a year, with no reply, before she finally stopped. But she would have never guessed it was him.

He had been in her life all this time and she didn't even know. When she thought about it, there was no reason why they couldn't have stayed in touch when he was 15 years old and he walked away twenty-seven years ago. By the time they parted, they both had a com, and their parents wouldn't have had trouble bringing them together.

She would love to blame it on the conferences, considering how every time they met, it was like something that shouldn't happen. They were supposed to be with different groups and most people there would have happily tied her up so she would not go looking for him.

But the blame was still on them. They were both stubborn enough to have managed to keep in touch. At that point, no one was monitoring their coms. Instead, they stubbornly chose to stay away.

She couldn't believe that he had abandoned her twice! If both times he had made that choice to not speak to her, wasn't it a possibility that he could choose to walk away from her at any point even if they got married? She didn't know if she had the heart to face such a rip. She had had enough pain when she lost him both times.

HER CONFESSION

WHAT AGINA HAD the hardest time moving past was that he had developed feelings for her even before she met Chloe. What kind of patience did he have to have, to just wait in silence, never telling her? Then he chose to discard those feelings because he wanted her to be happy, even if she was happy with someone else. But not only that, he had been the biggest supporter of their relationship. What was love anyway!?

The way he looked at her, and how he had touched her even before they kissed... She didn't need to ask him if he had feelings now. She had asked him for patience, asked him to wait and he just accepted. Now she was unsure. She was having a hard time holding back, so he must have it worse. Was she torturing him after he had waited for so long?

When she had fallen in love she didn't wait. Between the times she first met Chloe and got married, was less than a month. She was torn. Part of her wanted to shorten the time for him. He couldn't just be content.

She seemed to have a harder time holding back than he did because she cracked first. He always looked so composed, while getting married again was all new to her. She was never the type of person to hold back; she was out of character every time she stopped herself. Yet she came up with the crazy idea that for her healing, a longer timeline worked better. What should she do? She had a lot to work through.

Something broke in her. The defences she had unknowingly built into a fortress came crumbling down. She had only thought about what she wanted when she made those choices. How could she just keep him away now that the fortress had crumbled? For how long he had waited, she wanted to give him more. Needed to give him more, but she wasn't sure how.

Maybe that's why he was understanding about Chloe. He had known about her relationship at a personal level. He had been there for her when she went through the breakup. But there were some things he still didn't know that she hadn't told anyone.

He dropped such a bomb on her, but even with all that was just revealed today, it would still be the best time to bring it up. He took her hands in his. Holding them together. She was still looking into his eyes. It was like she would find an answer there. Find words to say to him.

Or maybe she just wanted to remember the person who was sitting in front of her now. Not the person she would marry in the future or the person he had been in the past. But the one in front of her. The one whose warmth she felt in her hands at the moment.

"I don't know what to say. I am glad you told me."

"You don't need to say anything. With what we had started talking about, I couldn't keep hiding it from you," he gently spoke, then kissed her left hand.

"I also need to say something that I don't want to hold back anymore..." she said, bracing herself.

He squeezed her hands. She continued "My marriage to Chloe really started to fall apart when it came to time for us to grow our family. I was supposed to have the procedure done so I could carry our child. I had said I was okay with it.

But I kept bringing up excuses to postpone it. Then on the day I had to go in, I couldn't go through with it, and I just ran. I came back to my parents' home. Told Chloe I needed some time. But then I couldn't bring myself to go back.

I thought I would be fine with the procedure. She didn't want to have kids right away, so I thought I had enough time to get ready. But in the end, I think I was too traditional. Too much technology was needed to make this child that will biologically be from both of us. It didn't matter who carried the child.

She knew I didn't leave. I just needed time. But too much time passed. I know it was my fault. But she filed for a divorce on the grounds that we had lived separated for so long. Then she found someone else on True Match.

It was her time to have children. That was her plan. It didn't matter if it was me or anyone else. Did being married for ten years mean nothing? Sigh. I think I have already told you about this. I still can't believe you are #1008. We talked about my life then and talked about the fate of such a child who will probably never be able to enter the Innercity.

After the divorce, I decided to move out of my parents' house and build the place I live in now. Long after the divorce, I finally went back to get my stuff. But when I saw her I... We secretly had a sexual relationship after our divorce. Her new wife knew we had had sex after they got married. But she wasn't aware of how often we met. It went on for a long time.

Their child knew me. But she didn't really know who I was. I wasn't there often. I shouldn't blame it on her, but Chloe was given an ultimatum: We become a polygamous family, or it stops. She was such a young child, but she said that her Mom loves me more than her Mom.

We did everything secretly, so her daughter should not have known. But it brought up a conversation about us. They were married with a child. What was I? Ultimately, something needed to change.

I had really tried my best to move on. Before all that started, I had already tried to date others and hopefully get past it all. But I just couldn't get over her.

She liked sex with me better, I hadn't wanted to let her go. For Chloe, it was the sex, and I knew it. We met for the wrong reasons. I know it wouldn't be right even if I had a good reason. Every time we met, I convinced myself it was the last time. But years just passed. Once the ultimatum came and it was clear what we did had an impact on their child, she finally cut me off.

I thought we loved each other from the start but it was more about her life's plan. For her, loving me fit her life's plan, till it didn't. She wanted a child I didn't give. For her, having sex was acceptable because it fulfilled her needs, till it wasn't acceptable. It impacted her child. I don't even know why I thought about what to choose with the ultimatum. She decided on her own.

It's been nine months since I heard from her or saw her. I might have been divorced for a long time. But we broke things off merely nine months ago. Actually, we never had that closure. She just went silent. I heard it from her wife.

It's also her wife who told me about the ultimatum. No matter how I look at it, we got divorced because of my traditional principles. Because I ran. Maybe the way she ended things was payback.

But I am still mad at her for how she ended the marriage, and for the court trial I had to go through. Just had someone drop off those divorce papers while I was at work. Like I haven't been in conversation with her the whole time. Then the way her lawyer portrayed me as such a horrible person.

I was clueless. It felt like a surprise attack; we talked almost every day with the exception of the time I stayed in our sacred circle. I know my time there was unusual. My mom was so surprised I managed to stay in the sacred circle that long without running water or electricity, where they build their houses out of mud and still wear beads instead of clothes.

But when I look back at it, I think she was mostly surprised that I was able to go along with their rituals and superstitions. Since they do things one hundred percent traditional and true to the post-colonial era with very few changes. But I really needed that retreat.

Maybe my guilt for running made me accept the invitations to meet Chloe over these years. Maybe it's why we would have sex for that long without actually having a meaningful conversation about us. Maybe it's knowing that I initiated the sex that first time I went back, because I missed her, turning her into an adulterer."

She was relieved she had said that much without crying. She didn't just feel emotional about Chloe, but these things made her feel like a bad person. She didn't think she could say more. It was his turn to just be silent and absorb what she had just said.

OUR STATUS

OTIENDE SQUEEZED AGINA'S hands again. She could see the information overload swimming in his eyes with nowhere to go. The things they just shared were not things that one could just absorb when one hears them. They both knew it.

For instance, even if she fully understood what he did, it was overwhelming when she tried to think about each and every thing she had said when she had spoken so to him as #1008 over the span of that seventeen-year friendship.

He interrupted her thoughts. "That's why your emotions are the way they are. I never intended to rush things and change the timeline. I made sure you were ok with us kissing. I just wanted to spend more time with you," he said apologetically, caressing her hand.

"I know," she said with a look of understanding.

"What happened is in the past now. We took this long to happen for a reason. It doesn't matter if we put the obstacles there ourselves. I don't believe in fate often. But this?... Us... It's fate. In fact, every time I find myself believing in fate, it's got something to do with you. We are a ninety eight percent match. But that two percent can still come between us. Anything can come between us if we let it. So, we must work through our issues. Okay?" he said, looking for her response even though it was obvious they both knew relationships can be difficult to navigate. They had both come today with the intention to reveal information, even if it wasn't an active problem, so that they could appropriately move forward.

"Mmm. Open, honest communication, that is oriented towards solving issues, while we ensure what's best for both of us. Let's discuss all this new information we just unloaded later. I can't comb through it now. We had other things to discuss about the timeline," she said, feeling tension all over her body.

"Yes. A longer timeline is still best. We know when we want to get married. I don't want to change that. So, I think the next thing to discuss is: are we engaged?" He spoke gently, his deep voice seeming to vibrate in rhythm like music.

He leaned in and lightly kissed her on the cheek. Then they put their foreheads together. "We need to officially get engaged," she said, speaking softly with her forehead still on his.

For some time, they both remained leaning in, with their foreheads touching, looking into each other's eyes. Then they both sat back up with their spines straight, relaxed and balanced.

"What did you have in mind?" she asked, subconsciously stroking his palm with her finger as he loosely held her hands.

"The conference is coming up soon. I think it would be good for you if we went together. I want to go with you. I would like to have an engagement ceremony the day before. We'll have a long engagement, but I think it's better that way," he cautiously replied, uncertain about whether she would agree or not. But they had already come this far, and their intentions were clear.

"It should be easy to get my family together for that. What about your family? It's done somewhat differently in our clans. We should coordinate what practices we want to perform." Rituals were usually the same in the Innercity with some differences in how different clans did their details. She spoke like there was certainty in what they would do next, but they just were not sure how to proceed, so it would make him feel more at ease. She saw how his body visibly relaxed when she spoke.

He hesitated before he began to speak, "With my parents it's uncertain. But I already asked them if they would be available that day if I were to plan something important. They'll get back to me when they know, if they can clear their schedule. With the rest of my family, it should be fairly easy. But… You mentioned practices in our clans. Were you thinking of having a traditional ceremony?" he asked, speaking with caution once again. She knew it was important to him that they didn't have any misunderstandings. Though she spoke the way she did, she tried to put everything on the table, so he wouldn't be so tense. They were both too tense. It needed to be a lighter conversation.

"Yes! We have less than three weeks to the conference but if we do the planning in the Outercity they can probably even get it all done in just a week. I am terrible at planning, so is it okay if I leave most of the planning to you?" He finally seemed to lighten up when she told him he could do the planning. It also made her feel more at ease.

"Yes, I am fine with that. You're only human after all. We all have weaknesses. Oh No! I forgot. You are a super-powered human," he jokingly said. They both laughed. Most of the tension was now gone.

"My emotions are currently my greatest weakness. I still can't get my happy, mad, sad, scared and hurt emotions to not affect the environment. Like it rains when I cry! One day I will learn how to manage it all," she said, rolling her eyes.

"Is that what the rain was about? I did think it was weird how it was raining so heavily when the skies were clear," he said, gesturing the visible description by moving his hand up and to the side, to emphasise what he said.

"Yeah. It would have been much better if I had intentionally called down rain. I don't have a training guide I can use to figure stuff out. I have no choice but to try and figure it out as I go. Because no one in my family has experienced this, they can only give info in the sequence they learnt. It's not according to what I need. They understand it less than I do. None of it makes sense; they are just stories, songs and poems," she said, shaking her head.

"Making it up is good. It's how you got the power in the first place," he said giving her a slight nod.

"True… I'll meet your friend on Monday. As for family, we can meet at the ceremony. Everyone else we can meet at the conferences or figure something else out," she said, trailing off to thoughts of who he needed to meet.

"This ceremony… You know what it means if we have a traditional ceremony, right? I want to make sure we have the same understanding. Did you think it through?" he spoke more cautiously than he had ever spoken, sounding scared, like his words could shutter the most impregnable surface.

"Honestly, I didn't think it through. But I can't see myself having any other type of ceremony. I just decided on it as we were speaking. This past day I could only think about how to tell you about Chloe. Now that I have, I think I can finally put it behind me and focus on us. So, let's have a traditional ceremony. Then we have the conferences," she said, then shrugged her shoulders. This was how she could give him more. She didn't want to hold any guilt for making him wait. The ceremony was a huge commitment. Plus going to the conferences was a big deal. She probably would have found a way to skip it all together. If it's what he wanted she would give it to him.

He interlaced his fingers with hers then brought their hands to the side of his face, rubbing her fingers against his cheek. He had a look on his face that she hadn't seen before. She felt compelled to agree to whatever he would say next. It was like a puppy pleading, but there was nothing puppy-like about Otiende.

"Let me go all out with our outfits at the conference." The way he said it almost sounded seductive. It sent shivers up her spine. How on earth could he make such a captivating voice sound even more captivating? Women have to be dropping at his feet just from hearing him speak. In fact, the same has to have happened for men and the others! There is no other way possible. How was there such a thing?

"I want to get our clothes custom-made, but not in Dala. I want to get them made abroad. They don't have to be elaborate; I just want matching outfits. Let the world see us together and let them know we are a force that is not in hiding," he said. There was almost a dare for the people against them to say something in that statement.

His thoughts seemed to shift as he tilted his head. He then added, "I put an end to #1008 four years ago. Maybe that's when I decided to stop hiding. I want them to see us and see that we are home. Not hiding from them."

"OT…" She paused and looked at him. She didn't want to admit that if he put his mind to it, he probably had the power to convince her to do anything. "It's fine if you keep me in the process." She could only give in.

"I will." His agreement was really quick.

He seemed happy about wanting to be involved. She decided that she liked seeing him happy. When she thought back to the time they spent together, he always seemed to be in a good mood. Maybe she was overthinking about having tortured him by making him wait when he had loved her for so long. How did people see him as aloof when she had never seen that side of him?

Was he usually in a good mood because he got excited about work? They were not always working. Maybe it was the topics they spoke about…

She decided to just let that thought go. He had already said several times that he was himself around her. Why should she now think about the things that were written or said about him?

However, he was to blame for having people think he was hiding. He had suddenly not shown up in the digital social space after they reconnected. It was not just his fans who had been wondering what happened to him.

They spent the rest of the night talking about their engagement ceremony. To some extent, she was worried about leaving him to plan things. His world as a global superstar was so different from hers, but she figured it would be okay if she knew what he was planning. After dinner, they continued talking late into the night.

A CHALLENGE

S HE MET OTIENDE early that Saturday morning. They had on full protective body suits that included a helmet because they were leaving the country for the day. Four bodyguards were accompanying them.

They had to wear these protective clothes to maintain controlled conditions. If they were exposed, they wouldn't be able to get back into the Innercity. Both their outfits fit like gloves and looked like they were made of leather or some similar fabric.

But they were not just regular fabric, they maintained certain variables like the temperature. Their helmets were their central control. As they looked around it would tell them not just the conditions in their suit, but give them an analysis of their outside conditions.

The first stop they made was to prepare their outfits. They could have had the outfits created without having to go there in person, but it was a good excuse for them to pay a visit and travel together; Otiende knew the store owner well.

All the while, Otiende led the way. He had done all the preparations. He often bought his clothes abroad ever since he was a child. It had been his style since she met him. The place they went to didn't have clothes on display. Instead, they had large screens you could browse through, or filter a search.

The store had designated areas with the option of testing clothes on your hologram or trying them in person. They walked through the store and went into a room in the back. The walls of the room displayed various fashion designs and there were a few clothes on realistic-looking mannequins.

They met the designer in this studio. They sat across from each other on lush armchairs with a tall backrest. They talked for a while before discussing what they needed.

"Such beauty! Are you sure I cannot convince you to model for me?" The designer was too excited to see Agina. "The world has been deprived by not having access to the people of Dala if they truly are anything like the two of you or his parents," said the man across from them with long silver hair neatly coiffed to reveal a thoughtful face.

"Pierre, the world wanted more than they could have so we made that choice. But I know you mean well. I feel honoured to meet you and wear your designs," said Agina.

"Oui. Oui. No harm intended. Otiende is the best person I have worked with. The honour is mine to meet his wife. I am humbled to design your outfits. Who would have thought such a power couple could be formed!"

Pierre showed them their holograms with all the outfits he had designed. They walked around the holograms as they discussed the outfits and concepts. They accepted the designs after making some adjustments.

"I am ecstatic to have done the work for you. It is my first time designing something with traditional Dala influences."

"As promised, we will send you pictures from the day of the conferences. But remember my warning, you can only post them on your website or else the privacy settings will not allow it. These pictures will be heavily guarded." Otiende said, and then they said their goodbyes.

They then left to have their date. On the way out they ran into one of Otiende's fans. The bodyguards stopped them before they could come anywhere near. "Otiende! Love your work! It's such an honour to run into you. I am glad you look alright," they said, then eyed Agina like understanding had washed over them. Otiende and Agina were holding hands.

"Thank you," Otiende replied, before quickly leaving. His voice had been changed by the helmet; he sounded different.

"How did they know it's you?" she asked after they got into a shuttle. Their outfits were encrypted, stopping people from identifying them. In that country, outfits that concealed people's faces gave some sort of identifying information.

"The problem with O_ts is that a couple of them are involved in the kind of work I do. So, they have the ability to hack systems and are good at identifying my body form. When they see a suit that has a person's identity hidden or masked, it's a challenge they cannot drop. No matter how careful I am with everything, there is always that one person who finds out. They love to let me know they found out. That's why they approach me. The only good thing about brown O_ts is that they don't let others know they found me. They leave others to solve the challenge themselves. It's the white O_ts I worry about. They are relentless," he said, his eyes furrowed.

"You are probably the worst of them all, when have you ever given up on a challenge? Like attracts like," she said, while smiling, intending to tease him.

"Like? Have you forgotten we are a ninety eight percent match? I have one challenge at the moment," he said, then took off his helmet. He closed the space between them and then took off her helmet. He knew the shuttle was perfectly conditioned for them to stay with their helmets off.

"OT!" Whatever protest she was about to make was stopped by his lips.

They were in a shuttle with the bodyguards, so it felt like they were kissing in front of an audience. She wanted to push him away. However, she couldn't resist the feeling of his lips, so they kissed passionately, failing to realise when they had stopped.

The bodyguards could only wait. They didn't dare to stop their boss. If they opened the door when they had their helmets off it would compromise the both of them. It was the one oath or rule that no one had ever broken since the Innercity was built.

If you accidentally became compromised, then you could never return. The portals into the Innercity could detect what a person had been exposed to at a micro level, just like it could detect your DNA even before you attempted to go through the portal.

At its scale, the Innercity was the only place left on the planet where nature had been preserved, including the animals and the people. Their DNA had not evolved in any way and they were maintained in their manufactured natural habitat.

Most people in other countries didn't know it existed. Not because it was a secret but because it was in Dala; the country that no one had cared about and intentionally turned their backs on. Some people even went to the extreme to try and erase them by rewriting history. Making it seem like they did not exist. So how could the new generations know?

Those who remembered them just knew they were poor people who secluded themselves years ago and were lucky to have survived, figuring out their own technological advances to further develop themselves. In all honesty, people were forced to stay away because it was against the law to go to Dala or to help it in any way. So, they choose to do nothing.

The fact that no one in the Innercity had been exposed yet was because most people didn't leave the Innercity to avoid the risk of accidentally getting exposed. So, it further isolated the people and their culture, making them an unknown mystery.

Everyone outside the Innercity who didn't know about how the Innercity worked, knew Otiende couldn't be exposed but they mistakenly thought it was because he had an immunity disease. It was left this way because it was better for public relations. Moreover, almost all people thought Otiende and his parents were from another country because they had multiple citizenship.

BUILDING A FANTASY

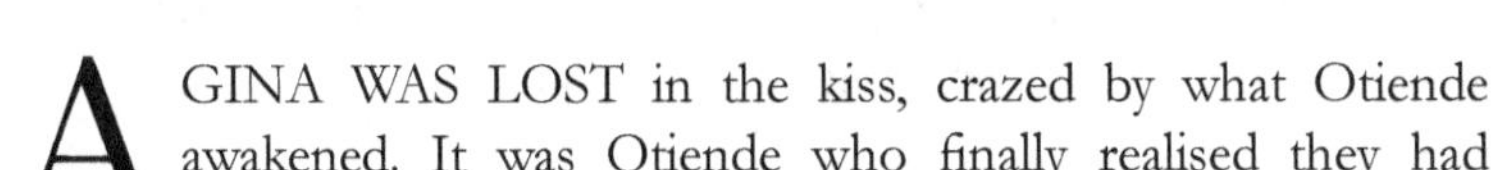

AGINA WAS LOST in the kiss, crazed by what Otiende awakened. It was Otiende who finally realised they had arrived.

"Later," he reluctantly said as he pulled back, touching her jaw with his hand.

They put their helmets back on, covering Agina's face which was flush with longing and embarrassment, and then they went into the place which couldn't quite be called a building or an open area.

"This is the super builder. It builds anything you would like in seconds. Sometimes longer if the build is more complex, it's like a virtual space or a simulation but it's all physically there. Well, except for the people. The people are usually bots, but they look real.

It's advanced printing technology but the smells, touch, taste and sound are real. There are no tricks to your mind. You won't be able to tell the difference between what is real or printed because of the materials they use, printing the atomic structure. It's the largest one in the world. It works best if it builds one vision at a time so we will both need to alternate."

He took her hand and led her in. "Come. Let's build a fantasy."

"You know I am going to want to know how this all works," she said, looking at him with excitement.

He laughed. "Always. I used to spend time figuring out how things worked because I knew you would always ask. But we can talk about that when we are leaving." She was pleasantly surprised to hear that; she didn't know how much effort he had put into impressing her.

They went in and put on the equipment they needed.

"Where would you like to start?"

Because Agina had heard that it could build anything, what was on her mind was the impossible. Could it build the impossible? The vision she had was similar to the painting she did under the platform of her bed; spirits and mystical creatures. Particularly the ones who she believed lived in some type of parallel universe.

She couldn't help but believe in these things having grown up in a culture that often spoke about spirits and ancestors and had all sorts of rituals to communicate with and appease these spirits or creatures. Especially after her experiences of accidentally entering other dimensions when she was trying to learn how to create portals where she saw what was unknown, and her experience of seeing the ancestors when she was initiated.

That's how they came to stand amongst all kinds of spirits and creatures. "Can I interact with them?" She was like a child asking for permission to play with a dream toy.

"Yes. But be aware that it's meant to be realistic. So, if its nature is to be dangerous, it will try to harm you. They usually do not succeed in harming people because they are robots that will reset before that happens. But you could still get hurt."

She practically ran towards the closest one, with joy in her steps. They were still holding hands, so he was involuntarily tugged along. They were still wearing their helmets, but she could tell he was smiling. She went around introducing herself.

It wasn't all good though, some of them refused to acknowledge her, others communicated that she would have to prove her worth, and others tried to attack her but her reflexes were faster. Either way, if they attacked, they would disappear back to where they came from.

When she was done, she thanked them all, bowing to them and reciting her promise to protect the world. She had taken out her spear that she had been concealing on her back when she did this. Otiende also bowed when she bowed, only rising several moments after she rose.

"Time to build your fantasy," she said, turning to him. In a swift second, she retracted her spear and wore it concealed on her back. The carrier and the spear were both invisible.

He approached her while he said, "I am already living my fantasy." He held her in his arms. "I love spending time with you. The only thing I would probably do differently is not just travel the world like we are doing now. But travel to the stars and across time to an earth where we don't have to protect ourselves outside the Innercity, and…"

She felt it in her, what he was about to say. It was in the shift of his voice. That voice of his that felt like it gently spoke to all the nerves in her body, reaching more than her sense of hearing. But she asked anyway.

"And?"

"The moment when we make love is still a fantasy." She still wasn't ready to hear it. She felt herself go weak. Hadn't she known what he was going to say? She tried not to think of it. But it's something she thought about more often than she would ever admit.

Was it because knowing it was different from hearing it? What would it be like to touch him, and to explore his body? She had never been touched by a man. She found herself pulling him closer and holding him tight.

It was all she could manage to do because she felt weak, and she didn't think her legs would still work. She also didn't trust anything she would have said at that moment.

"I think about that moment and where it would be. When it will be. Don't worry. I know you're still not ready. But I can't stop myself from thinking about it," he said, rubbing her back.

At this moment it was a good thing they had helmets on. It was probably the only thing stopping them from fulfilling this fantasy. If their lips had touched at that moment, they probably would not have been able to stop at just that, despite where they were.

They were in their world just the two of them. The sound of a bird flying above broke them from their trance. It startled the both of them. They both looked up. They had been so engrossed in that moment that they hadn't realised their surroundings had changed.

They were now on a beach with palm trees, sand so clear it looked white, and water that was clear blue. There was a bed beside them with a canopy for shade. The fabric from the curtains was tied down to the poles, but it was still swaying to the wind.

She marvelled at the beauty before her eyes. It was really beautiful and romantic. There were what looked like paper lanterns placed on the ground, creating a walking trail. There were tables beside the bed with drinks in a tub of ice and some cut fruit. Towels were rolled and arranged on the bed.

The smell of the ocean was just as intense as she had experienced in real life, a saltiness, and dampness that was comforting. The sound of the waves crashing on the shore was soothing. It was paradise.

Several generations had not known war that affected the environment, but they had known an environment deeply affected by people hungry for development at the cost of the earth. The effects of their greed were everywhere.

Places like this just didn't exist anymore and if they did exist, they couldn't be in such places without being enclosed in protective garments or having some type of assistance with technology.

"Come. Let's walk on the beach," Otiende said, holding out his hand. As they walked, he told her about some of his other fantasy places. After their date last week, she was not surprised by how romantic these places were. He had thought about a variety of places.

"I wonder what the most common builds are? How does it really work?" she asked.

"We can probably go check the data," he suggested.

Their surroundings suddenly changed. It showed five different scenes of nature that didn't exist in their world anymore.

"You asked it, didn't you?" he wondered, realising that she had probably used her powers.

"Sorry. I didn't mean to. I still can't fully control it," she said, feeling embarrassed.

"It's fine. You don't need to apologise. Do you still want me to explain, or did you figure out how it works?" he asked, putting an arm around her shoulders and rubbing her arm.

"You may explain," she said, with a look of intrigue and excitement. She liked to hear Otiende explain how things worked.

34

FANTASY BECOMES REALITY

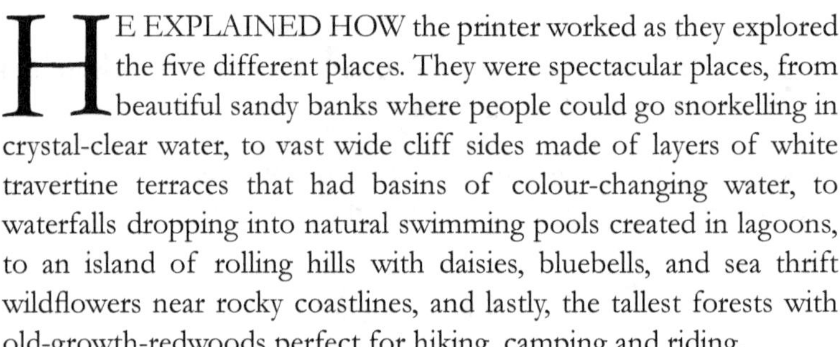

HE EXPLAINED HOW the printer worked as they explored the five different places. They were spectacular places, from beautiful sandy banks where people could go snorkelling in crystal-clear water, to vast wide cliff sides made of layers of white travertine terraces that had basins of colour-changing water, to waterfalls dropping into natural swimming pools created in lagoons, to an island of rolling hills with daisies, bluebells, and sea thrift wildflowers near rocky coastlines, and lastly, the tallest forests with old-growth-redwoods perfect for hiking, camping and riding.

"I wonder if I can do something similar with my powers. But something that will stay permanently. Do you know where I can find plants?" she asked, turning to look at Otiende.

"No. But we can find out. Your com or my com?" he asked, reaching into his pocket.

"Your com."

Before he even took it out it was already showing them where they could go. Using the shuttle, they followed the directions and got the plants, then went to the most appropriate place where they could leave a permanent installation without causing trouble. While they had been on the way, they had talked about what they would create and how they could adapt it.

"This is crazy! I don't even know if it will work," she said, looking at the place that they chose. It was a place they had not planned to go to so more people were walking around than they would have liked.

If a crowd formed because they drew attention it would be difficult for the bodyguards to manage. However, they expected the build to go quickly so they were willing to take the risk.

"For this, crazy is good," he responded.

"Time to deconstruct and construct," she said as she spun her finger around causing a stone to look like it had disappeared, then it slowly reappeared as a mini statue. After that short test, she was sure it would work. She looked at Otiende and nodded.

"You're ready?" she asked.

"Yeah. Let's do this."

Agina walked into the abandoned space that should have been a park. As she walked it looked like the space was quickly disappearing. As Agina continued to walk the ground also disappeared, leaving her walking in the air, looking like she was walking across an abyss.

The park reappeared as she kept walking, starting from the bottom. It was a complete transformation into a space that was a mini paradise location. She closed her eyes and kept walking as it came to completion.

The plants that they had brought had become a part of the park. She adapted the park in such a way that it would not need maintenance and it would be able to sustain itself. Because she used the same concept as the superbuilder, anyone who watched would easily think that they had just created an illusion.

There were lots of flowers in the park, with a walkway, arched by climbing flowers. A water feature with falling water, fully grown trees shading scattered areas, a partially separated natural playground with slides set in mini hills, swings hanging from trees, and a crafted natural surrounding to climb and explore.

"We should leave," urgently said one of the bodyguards.

Otiende quickly followed Agina into the park. She could feel that someone was coming towards her, so she stopped walking and turned around. When she opened her eyes, she saw Otiende rushing to her.

She rushed to join him. When they met, he took her hand, and they rushed out together. She wished they could have stayed longer but they didn't want to draw attention to themselves. She was glad they could at least say they were the first ones in the newly renovated park.

They hurried back to the shuttle and left, leaving behind some confused bystanders. As expected, pictures of them leaving the park while holding hands were taken. They didn't know if it was because they were recognised or if it was because they had just walked out of a park that came to life.

"We will be back to see it on another day. Let's go get something to eat," said Otiende after they were safely back in the shuttle.

She was glad they were both able to take off their helmets. Where they ate had to be carefully chosen so they would be able to take off their helmets while they ate. They ordered their food using the digital menu and waited until their food was delivered.

It was almost as if the food came from above because the food travelled over people's heads on mobilised dinnerware. This time the restaurant was not void of people, but they were seated in a private room isolated from everyone.

The room was large enough to host a small party with a table for sixteen. But it was set with a table for two. One of the walls was completely covered by a window, letting in light and giving them a view of a well-designed garden.

They spoke comfortably, seated across from each other. But they also had moments where they would look at each other as they ate in silence.

They talked about their travel experiences. Though they had both started travelling at a young age they had seen things differently.

Agot liked to travel, so she took Agina with her whenever she could. But she was given the talk about technology and how it can be bad or evil almost on a daily basis. She rarely heard about other things like warnings about drugs or safe sex. Technology was not going to ruin Agot's daughter!

As they talked about it Agina realised how much of her life had been influenced by her mother and her beliefs; her culture's beliefs. Technically speaking, Otiende's family was at the same level as her family even if they had more popularity and material things.

Otiende had been given the freedom to embrace technology wholeheartedly. His ethics could be seen in the way he worked, and it was a huge part of what made him popular. For him, technology wasn't a place to proceed with caution. It was a place to play while maintaining an awareness of the dangers.

Putting it simply, Agina had been in a playground with padding and a helmet, with someone constantly telling her to watch out. While Otiende had been told the dangers in the playground in advance and then he was free to explore, making his own choices on how much risk he was going to take.

The way he had explored other countries with his parents was such a contrast. Agina understood more and more his parents' decision to not always try and protect him. Otiende made choices that were his. He had autonomy.

Agina was like that some of the time. Those were times when she was most powerful. Too often, she had had someone telling her what choice to make. Because of this, she easily ended up in uncertainty when there was no one to tell her what choice to make.

She had some awareness of this. Hearing the two experiences spoken in contrast this way, helped her be fully aware of where her uncertainty was rooted. It's not that people were expected to always know things, it was more about the capability to make choices and stick to them, without being stopped by fear.

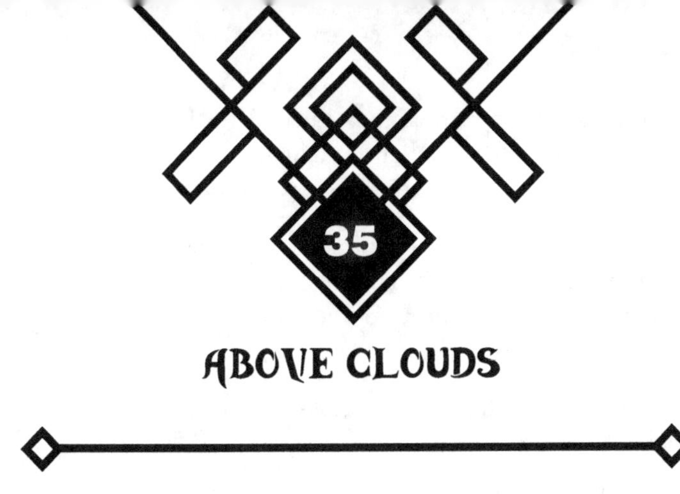

ABOVE CLOUDS

THEY HAD ALREADY arrived late for lunch and considering they had taken such a long time talking, they left several hours later. She was surprised to see that a crowd of people had gathered outside the restaurant when they left.

At a time like this, she appreciated Dala and how they had portals inside buildings as their way to get around. Other countries had portals too, but they didn't have a complete system like they did. It probably also helped that Dala was a small country, so they didn't need to move many people at the same time.

She could feel a shift in Otiende's body language as he held her closer. They waited briefly while the bodyguards did crowd control. The security guards of the building seemed to have handled the crowd after struggling for some time. For the first time, Agina found herself wondering if they had enough bodyguards.

These must be white O_ts. The type of fans that made Agina's skin crawl because of the way they idolised him. The joy on some of their faces was so apparent, others were even in tears. The security guards had managed to stop their screaming.

Most people just took pictures or videos and greeted him, others would yell out random statements of admiration, while others held signs. The bodyguards made sure no one came too close.

They walked arm in arm as they hurried to the shuttle that had been waiting for them. Otiende held his hand up, occasionally turning it left and right other than waving, he remained silent.

She knew it was something she would never get used to, but it was his world, and she was now in it. They had their helmets on so she knew these pictures would manage to get posted in some digital spaces where the risk was low.

"We have one more stop," he said as he took off his helmet. She took off her helmet too.

"Are you okay? I hadn't expected such a crowd. We had not planned to go public yet," he said, looking at her with concern.

"I am fine. Judging from what we already found, they still haven't figured out who I am. You heard what they were shouting. I think all the mystery and your silence is stirring up O_ts," she nervously said, as she fidgeted with her helmet before she put it down beside her.

"Sigh. If you really are okay, then can I change the topic?" he asked as he lifted her head with two fingers under her chin.

Before she could reply he had already taken her lips in his, giving them love. She held the back of his head, feeling her way through his thick hair to his scalp and rubbing his part-braided hair. She became more relaxed, her worries forgotten. The shuttle ride once again became the place where they passionately kissed.

And once again, they were too distracted to notice they had arrived. The bodyguards who worked with Otiende had worked with him a long time. Some of them had even worked for Otiende's parents when they used to travel together. So, they have known him longer.

But this was a part of him they hadn't gotten to see. In the past, he had been discreet with such affection.

Once again, they could only wait for him to finish. This time they waited even longer until he finally noticed they had stopped. She reorganised his hair then they put on their helmets and went inside.

"This is the highest lookout point in the city. The sunset is beautiful from here," he explained.

Agina couldn't express in words what it was about the sunset that drew her in. It was like a daily ritual for her. She made it a point not to miss it unless the sky was just too overcast to see anything. Even when she lived in the Outercity with Chloe, she still made it a point to watch the sunset.

The lookout point had jutting boxes that had transparent walls, floors and a ceiling. It was like being in a glass box that was open on one side. They stood in their box with him standing behind her, holding her in his arms. They had taken off their helmets only after getting in the box. She had also put down her spear that she had concealed on her back.

"It's beautiful up here. It's like standing above the clouds," said Agina.

"Yes. One of these days we should visit one of the floating cities. They also have stunning views."

"I would love that. The underwater cities also have amazing views."

"Yes! Let's travel the world together. Create new memories," said Otiende.

They watched the sunset in silence. When it was over, he kissed the side of her face. "The night view is beautiful. I like the lights. It's different in the Innercity when the lights go out because there, we have minimal lighting to be conscious of the animals," said Otiende.

"I love the lights. Especially watching them from afar. It feels like watching the heartbeat of a community. The sign that life is happening there or will happen there. It's the dots connecting the story, weaving our presence here. But if I were to choose. I would choose the darkness of Dala. Because then, when a light turns on or when a candle flickers, it's someone using their sense of sight at that particular moment, while everyone else rests and the nocturnal animals move about. They don't leave light on." She spoke as she stared into the distance, but her mind was elsewhere.

When it became dark, they didn't leave right away. They stayed that way for a while, watching. She turned to face him, looking at his face in the dark and noticing how the cool-coloured lights reflected on his skin. Especially the reflection of the lights gleaming in his eyes.

She couldn't help but be drawn to him. He slowly leaned in. As he got closer something happened to the air between them. It made her hold her breath. She could feel with all her senses how close he was getting. He leaned in closer and closer. She closed her eyes in anticipation.

She was very aware of her heart beating. It was beating so fast and seemed to be fighting harder because she had held her breath. He had stopped. She could feel him still lingering there. She opened her eyes.

To stare into those eyes when he was this close was flooding her with emotions, she was sure didn't have a name.

"Breathe. Or else I won't be able to take your breath away," he said so faintly it sounded like a gentle whispering song.

She couldn't see his lips, but she was sure it would be curved into that sly smile. His eyes were certainly curved in that way. She heard him and she knew what he was saying but she was still holding her breath.

How could she breathe when he was this close, and he just spoke to her in that gentle deep voice? She still wondered when his voice had changed. Or had she changed her thoughts about his voice? When she finally let go of that breath, it released with it desires she had been holding on to.

"Don't be silly," she barely said, sounding out of breath. It was meant to be a comeback but saying, it fell short, was an understatement. She instead sounded breathy and seductive. She gave into those desires and closed the distance between them, holding him by the back of his head and neck. She kissed him slowly and he returned the kiss in the same way, yielding to each other in a slow enchantment.

36

PROTECTING THEM

WHEN THEY FINALLY decided to leave, they put their helmets on and she concealed her spear again.

She thought this time they had been lucky, and no one had recognised him. They had preserved the whole place. But someone spotted him right before they went in the shuttle. They wildly called out his name as they waved.

"Agina," he called, turning to face her after they had settled in the shuttle and taken off their helmets.

Looking thoughtful, he spoke, "I've been thinking: do we want to keep spending time ironing the details for our ceremony with the planner, or don't you think we are at that point where we can let the planner handle the rest of the details? I think we can focus more on rehearsing."

He was used to having managers handle details. He also had an assistant who always made sure things were going as they should. She was getting exhausted by the questions about the event planning that seemed to keep coming, so she imagined the menial tasks were also draining on him and too time-consuming. He had wanted to spend more time with her but she was sure it was not what he had in mind. It was a good proposition, since they had already got most of the details of the ceremony taken care of.

"Let them handle things. It doesn't need to take up so much of our time anymore," she said, waving her hand nonchalantly.

"How is your family taking things? Are they being too much?" he asked, slightly leaning in towards her.

"I wouldn't doubt they are more excited about this ceremony than I am. Maybe it's because they couldn't be a part of my first wedding since it was a small modern wedding in the Outercity." She also leaned in slightly.

"How is your family taking things? I only met your uncles and your Dana. I remember them being laid back, but they were still animated. They must be excited too," she said, feeling out what she remembered.

"Would you doubt it? I have lived abroad for a long time and met all kinds of people. I can guarantee you that people of our culture love gatherings and ceremonies!"

They both laughed before he continued, "They are excited. Even my parents are excited and will be in the Innercity for more than two days. I don't remember the last time they stayed that long. They usually just pop in for dinner. If both of them aren't filming or promoting, one of them is supporting the other. They were less busy when I was a child."

"That's good. Traditions and ceremonies are good for bringing people together," she leaned back, feeling content.

"Yes. Since we are doing a traditional ceremony there are still steps to take till the dowry is paid when the last ceremony is done. There will be a lot of gatherings and rituals after this first ceremony is over. I look forward to the events. I am glad it turned out this way. I always felt like I missed out on a lot of traditions," he said with a smile, wrapping his arm around her shoulder.

They got out of the shuttle when they arrived at the international portals. They went through the security to go to the portals. Since

Agina was seven she always had the clearance to travel with her spear. She did not have to wear it concealed. So, she got through with her spear just fine.

When they were heading towards their portal, Agina suddenly felt her instincts sharpen in the same way they had when she was attacked at her studio. She wasn't sure what it was exactly but judging from her memory, she was sure she could sense an intent to kill.

Moving fast, she took out her spear and spun around to stand behind Otiende, holding her spear in an attacking stance. She had turned just in time to see someone in the distance aim a weapon towards her. Before he could do anything, he collapsed to the ground.

A handful of people around them also collapsed to the ground. Two people were still closing in on them, looking like they intended to attack. The bodyguards had shifted to a defensive stance with Agina and Otiende in the middle, finally realising something had gone terribly wrong.

"Stop them," she said to no one in particular. Otiende was the last to react, still looking to see what was going on.

Agina wasn't sure about what to do. Should she take them on? But her instinct had already taken over her thought process.

It was like she could see through everything, as she saw things right down to their atoms. She could see the composition, information, data and analysis from the technology. It was like everything was weaved together analysing and processing the situation. It all moved fast but she processed it faster.

As soon as she thought of what to do, it happened so fast that she was the only one who could follow what was happening. The weapons two of the portals security guards were carrying, withdrew themselves and aimed at the two people who were still rushing to them.

It was supposed to be a weapon that just bound them, but the moment the restraint came into contact with them, it also took them out as it bound them. The weapons stowed themselves before anyone even realised what had happened.

They stood that way as people were just beginning to realise something had happened. Agina felt the intent to kill reside, but her instincts were still sharp and focused. People who looked like security agents rushed to them to see what was going on.

First, they searched the fallen people. They took the weapons including the one who had already drawn their weapon. The two who were bound did not have weapons. They checked their pulses and confirmed they were all still alive. Then they turned their attention to them.

"What happened here?" asked the person who appeared to be their leader.

"I don't know. I should be the one asking you what happened. There were weapons beyond your security check. How could you let such a situation occur?" Like ice, Otiende replied. Agina got out of her attacking stance and stood beside Otiende as she concealed her spear.

"We need to detain you all for questioning." As their leader spoke his certainty seemed to disappear.

"That is unacceptable. Do you not know whom you are speaking to? We have diplomatic immunity, and we didn't do anything wrong. We shall be leaving for our country now since you are too incompetent to guarantee basic international portals security. Our safety in this country is not guaranteed." Ice seemed to frost over the agents with Otiende's words.

"We need to see your identification before you leave." They attempted to break out of the ice.

"That is unnecessary. We will send someone to follow up and get a report on your investigation. We expect your full cooperation." Otiende said as he turned to leave, leaving them ice cold, stranded on an isolated iceberg. The bodyguards followed, with Agina holding Otiende's hand.

"Wait. Sir?"

"Since you don't seem to know how to behave, it would be best if you don't try and stop us," Otiende said without stopping or turning to look back.

Two of the bodyguards went first, then Agina. Otiende went next and was followed by the other two bodyguards into the portal. Agina and Otiende hugged the moment they both went through.

"We are leaving for the Innercity. Thank you," Otiende said to the bodyguards as he held Agina. The bodyguards nodded. Then Agina went into the portal first followed by Otiende. When they got through to the entry hall of his home they hugged again, embracing each other for comfort for some time.

37

ALLEVIATING

"**Y**OU TOOK THEM out. Didn't you?" he asked, worry clouding him.

"Their own weapons took them out, not me. I influenced the weapons. It would have been no use to try and get information from them, and letting them speak would have been more problematic. At least that's what analysing the situation told me. I am glad you realised that and made leaving the priority," she said, feeling the weight of what happened hit her.

It had all happened so fast. Once she became more alert, there was so much information to process all at once, flashing past faster than it had when she was destroying the surveillance system. But she was the only one who could see it. The information was so tremendous that it had felt like she was hanging on to her life, while the information storm tried to pull her into a black hole to her death; The sheer amount of information swept through her like a tornado trying to carry everything in its path. She couldn't even feel fear at that moment. She could only react.

"Defending you is proving to be much more complex than I thought. Yet you got it done so efficiently. I will trust your defences then. You did well." There was a pain in his voice, like a child who had tried so hard but still lost. Praise, acceptance and defeat.

She thought about the confrontation with the agents. He did sound cold then. But he also sounded like he knew how to wiggle himself out of such situations. So, the agents could only let them go.

"Stay for a little bit. It's hard for me to see people come after you. If you had reacted any slower, you would have been dead. How are you feeling?" He was gentle once again, holding her arm. She could still sense his fear of having almost lost her.

She hadn't had the time to process things yet. She was still too hyper-focused, adrenaline still rushing through her. She would rather be with him than be by herself at the moment. No matter how you looked at it, it was hard to experience such a thing and not be affected.

"I'm... It feels... What do they want?" she could barely form words. She felt like she was sinking. She wasn't sure what to say. There were still so many unanswered questions.

"I don't know either. The thing about rising up, is that it gets you enemies. The higher you go, the stronger your enemies become. We can only prepare ourselves for whatever is coming. I will support you in whatever you decide is the best course of action. You're not alone in this. I'm always here for you." His words held her up like a plant support that didn't just keep plants stable so they didn't fall over, but it also protected the plant from the wind.

"Thank you. I would rather not be alone right now." She gave a half-hearted, saddened smile. She had never felt this vulnerable and utterly helpless in front of him.

They hugged for a while as they spoke.

"I know it's best if I take care of my own emotions. But you put me in a better mood. I like how you make me feel better," she said, trying to uplift him too while she remained in the hug.

"Why do you think every time all those years ago, I would first give you the option to leave? I'd find a different place to hide the next time, hoping you don't find me? I was trying to learn how to stand on my own and sort out the anger and hurt I felt. But I liked having you there. You also put me in a better mood. It's okay. I understand your need for dependence. I know what strength that gives, and I also know that it takes time to get there. At times, it takes isolation, but people are meant to live life together. So, I'm here now and I want to live life with you," he admitted, as he kept holding her in the embrace.

They parted from the long hug and looked into each other's eyes. She saw a lot of emotion in his eyes. She could see his struggle. She wanted not just this moment with him but moments that lasted forever. She wanted to be with him for the rest of her life. She felt tears running down her cheeks, falling without permission.

She was tired of feeling like she was fighting internally by trying so hard to be strong. They were both like this now. A life-threatening situation would put anyone's emotional state in turmoil, drawing tears from them that usually sink into dark depths, where they are meant to remain unreached. She reached up and wiped the tears that had started running down his cheeks with her thumb.

Then holding his face, she kissed him. Not because of the yearning she always had for him, but because she couldn't put to words what she felt, what she wanted: She wanted to live life with him, different from what she always had and knew. Even if it still terrified her and she didn't know what that would look like yet.

They left the entry hall and went into his living room, settling on his couch. They spent time together just holding each other. Their moment together was like watching clouds in the sky, moving as though the clouds were chasing each other. Or were the clouds separating? Where do the clouds start? Where do the clouds end?

Then the clouds cycle. When the clouds become the ocean, when they become waves moving as though one wave is chasing the other wave. Where do the waves start? Where do the waves end? Moments like this are the cycle in relationships. Partners are sometimes separate, sometimes together. But never entirely together. Where the connection starts and ends is uncertain. For this moment, they were partners helping each other.

"I hate the feeling that people are always coming after me. Wanting me to die. And it's because of their own assumptions." She was finally able to talk about it. They were still holding each other on the sofa in consolation.

He stroked her hair as he spoke, "I am sorry I didn't react fast enough. I froze. I couldn't do anything. But when I look back at it. What could I possibly have done but get you out of the situation? I want us to be able to live, not to always be hiding. That means sometimes we run into such people. Sigh. We can't control other people's intentions."

They had stopped crying some time ago, and he didn't look so defeated anymore, but he still reminded her of a puppy that had been scolded when it had been trying to be helpful.

"I am glad you were there," she said, interlacing her fingers with his. Then she continued to speak, "That was my instinct reacting. I don't know what I would have said. I wasn't fully controlling what I did, it just happened."

"I didn't expect our night to end that way. I can't speculate on what could have been. But other than that scare, I had a good time with you today," he said, then kissed her on the cheek.

"Yes. It was a beautiful day. Hopefully, we left a place that others could enjoy," she said, giving a weak smile.

"You did a great job with transforming the park. Maybe we could do that at some point, go around the world creating these slices of paradise." Their sombre mood had finally lifted.

She sat cross-legged and turned to face him. "I would like that. It's a good start before I figure out a master plan of what I need to do to create balance. Seeing how today went, I think we need to create a defence system for the Innercity and for Dala." She was silent for a while before adding, "Creating attack systems is complicated. Instead, we can create programs that cause their weapons to malfunction, lose power, or turn against themselves. Something that stops them without us needing weapons, like today. Our country hasn't seen war yet. I don't want them to bring an attack on us to force my choices and take away my intentions to restore balance. That was part of Dala's history. We didn't want to comply, so they isolated us to force us to join them. We lost a lot of people back then. But in the end, the people we lost are less than the casualties war brings. We can't let war begin. No matter what, I will not use weapons to attack them to make them stop," she said, feeling a sense of righteousness.

He looked into her eyes, showing a renewed sense of hope as he said, "That is a good idea. Your powers suit you. I don't think anyone could use your powers any better to do good."

38

RAGING FIRE

"I DOUBTED IT should have been me who got powers. Sometimes I still do. Then I realised I am my power, and my power is me. That's why it's tied to my thoughts and feelings," she said, her head shifting slightly in enlightenment as if she was re-examining something and noticing something new about it.

He gave her a light kiss then he said, "I never doubted it."

"Your resolve is impressive. How can you believe in me? I didn't know we would work. Despite the ninety-eight percent statistic and my belief in numbers. Even after my Mom told me you were OT. I don't think relationships work for me. And how am I supposed to believe I can be with a celebrity?" Her eyes widened as she looked in disbelief.

"Actually, I had my doubts about us working too. I thought we could at least have a friendship because we have that in our history," he said, shifting his eyebrows as he continued. "But if I look at your history, you were only interested in having female partners and you never showed any interest in me even when I was #1008 and didn't have a gender classification. Other people always said you were a flirt. But you never even once flirted with me." He tilted his head back slightly, which made him lower his gaze.

"Sigh. I am. I mean... It was a choice. First of all, being in this position of liking women particularly put me in a place where I had to draw strict boundaries to not flirt with my friends. So that's why

I didn't flirt with you. Second, I have never specifically said I was opposed to a partner who wasn't a woman. My mother also knew this. It was more like picking a type. I made this choice when I was younger because no matter what I genuinely liked out there, the people I physically met and I was drawn to were females. The rest of what I liked felt more like fantasies, rather than reality, because those feelings never progressed with anyone; they were people on screens I only fantasise about. When it's not experienced and it's just your imagination, no matter how beautiful it feels, it might as well just be a romance novel. I was idealistic, but I preferred reality. Because I experienced it physically, and those feelings grew whether we ended up together or not, it became my type. I trust what my body tells me. You are the first male I met that made me feel this way. So, you're the first male I ever kissed. I've never been with a male before," she revealed, feeling awkward about explaining herself. She had never tried to piece it together.

In reality, part of what stopped her from ripping off his clothes and passionately making love to him was that she was not sure what to do. She only had a rough idea of how things went in theory. It was a bridge she never thought she would cross. So, she never feasibly thought about what to do with a male body.

He looked into her eyes. She was still blushing. But she couldn't look down when he held her face in such a way. "It's okay. I'll show you. I am glad I am your first."

If she was blushing before, now she was on fire. She was convinced that she had also lit a fire in his eyes. Her stomach fluttered, sending fire up and down her spine. Even his hand that held her chin felt like it was on fire.

She leaned in closer. Or was he pulling her closer? She couldn't tell. They leaned closer. When their lips made contact it was like a fire had been ignited. She slowly closed her eyes, consumed by their passion. It was a fire that could only be put out with fire.

With every movement of their lips touching, it burned brighter and hotter. She wanted more. She opened her lips slightly. His tongue was like a wave of fire. Their movements were slow, but the fire was raging. His hands were rubbing her back.

She subconsciously moved her legs, placing them over his lap and inched closer to him. She was still seated on the sofa. It was just her legs that were over his lap.

Her arms had made their way around his neck. As the fire raged, she felt like her brain melted. A sound escaped from somewhere in the back of her throat. Did she just moan? He pulled away, but she still needed a minute to gain her composure.

"I won't be able to stop if you keep kissing me like that," he said, his breath sounding laboured.

Her eyes were still closed, she was lost too far in the moment to have returned. It was like her mind couldn't catch up. He almost sounded like he was out of breath. It was a warning that sounded more like a hint at a dare, with a cocky undertone. She took deep breaths to calm herself down. When she opened her eyes, he was smiling, looking at her in amusement. "OT?" she called, shaking her head.

"I know. I wasn't going to go there."

"You're making it hard for me."

"It's hard for me too."

"But I can't not kiss you."

"Me too. I want to kiss you all the time."

They had spoken rapidly to each other then they both burst out into laughter.

"I should go. I think I need a cold shower," she said, feeling overwhelmed as she ran her finger through her hair, and then let it go.

He nodded. "I'll walk you to the portal."

She had started to get carried away when kissing him. Everything in her body wanted to make love to him. She felt like she was burning for him. They left the couch and walked to his portal. She avoided touching him like he was a hot stove, she didn't trust herself to make body contact with him at the moment. They stood in front of the portal.

"I'll meet you here Monday," she nodded and quickly went in, not trusting herself to stay a second longer.

WELCOME ABODE

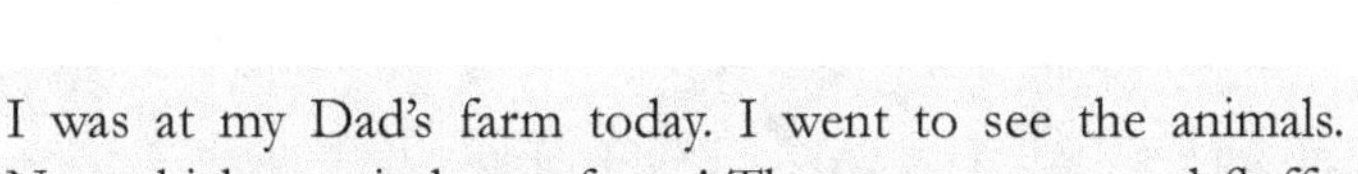

I was at my Dad's farm today. I went to see the animals. Now chicks remind me of you! They are so cute and fluffy. You were right. Chickens do make the place feel like home with their clucking, scratching the ground, pecking, hopping around, and the poop they leave everywhere.

OT: Hehe! The chicks here remind me of you too. Everything here reminds me of you. I am so glad I got this chance to get to know you. I am grateful to have you in my life again.

Me too. I never imagined running into you again.

-End of text messages-

INSIDE THE LAB smelled faintly of burnt dust from the equipment heating up. The constant sound of the cooling fans fading in and out as the air they moved kept the equipment's temperature steady. Their sounds ranged in volume despite their size, with the smallest computer sounding just as imposing. The windows filtered in sunlight, giving a soft light.

Agina and Otiende were at the screens working diligently. It wasn't hard for them to have distinct boundaries between work and what they had outside of work. They both took their work seriously.

But there was a difference from the last time they worked together in his lab around his staff: They were more comfortable around each other.

They were no longer pretending not to know each other so they no longer had the awkward interactions that came from the thoughts: I shouldn't-.

"We can stop here for the day," said Agina, stowing away the notetab she had been writing on.

"Yes, we've done enough for today. We should be able to conclude this tomorrow morning," agreed Otiende, signalling to his staff.

They both got up and walked out of the lab together. Even if they were not holding hands, no matter how you looked at it, they looked like a couple. The chemistry between them was visible to the naked eye.

"Actually, I need to go home first. I wanted to bring dessert. I made it myself," said Agina, the corners of her mouth moving up in a diagonal as she smiled in pride.

"It's a casual dinner. His wife and children usually spend time with their family and the two of us hang out. It's usually something simple. Bringing dessert might put him in an awkward position of wanting to have done more." His eyebrows were drawn together as he shared his concern.

"I can't just go empty-handed. It's our culture. I'll just pick it up then meet up with you," she said, remaining determined.

They arrived at the portal that they always used which was closest to his lab.

"Actually, let's not separate. We'll go to my place first to get it, then we can go to your place to leave from there," she said as she turned to face him.

As they were walking the bodyguards had been following from a distance, so it felt like it was just the two of them in front of the portal. He seemed to be seriously thinking about it. He had not been to her home yet. His curiosity was now peeked.

"We could do that," he said, glancing at the bodyguards and then looking back at her.

"Let's go then," she said, as she turned and went through first.

She waited on the other side as he came through. As soon as he came through it was like the house turned on. Almost every part of its interior lit up prompting for information to be put in, some with screens that had appeared, some integrated in, others appeared as hovering text. Even the floor had text that lit up, waiting to be set up. There was also a floating pyramid that appeared, that looked like it had a light sphere in its centre.

"Sorry. I forgot what this house is like when someone new comes in. It wants to know all your preferences. It already knows me well, so it doesn't react the same way with me. I can't fully turn it off without turning the whole house off, but I can ask most of it to prompt you later," she said, awkwardly looking around.

"It's like your spear. Hidden tech in plain sight. It suits you," he said, looking around. He marvelled at the sight of her house.

"Yeah. I really like my spear. So, I had the same concept in mind when I built it. People don't usually stay long. Which was my initial intention because I wanted to hide, and I was seeking comfort. But then I didn't have the heart to get rid of any of it. Instead, I added more stuff over the years. Being a creator, I can only think of things to create. The dessert is this way."

He followed her out of the entry hall. As they walked more parts came on. Her home was all open so there was just one room to walk into. She walked into the kitchen area. He followed her in as more things lit up.

"Are you sure you don't want me to postpone all the prompts?" she asked, starting to feel agitated. She hadn't seen her house this way. She always turned off the prompts as soon as people walked into the entry hall.

"No, it's ok. It's interesting seeing all the things you can customise. Agina, your home is more tech than my entire house combined. Well, maybe minus my studio. It definitely has more tech than my other homes. You can no longer say I am more tech-oriented than you are. You are surrounded by a lot of tech. It doesn't matter that it stays hidden."

He pulled her into his arms and gave her a light kiss on her cheek. They were suddenly interrupted by a voice. "Welcome. May I please familiarise myself with you?" They turned to find the pyramid had followed them and was hovering beside them. It was the main system of the house in its physical form.

"This house is really persistent. It's like a device setup, or an update prompt that doesn't stop till you do something. Unless you want to go around setting it up, I'll need to postpone it."

Suddenly all that had lit up went off and the pyramid disappeared. Seeing her home this way, it was hard to believe that its interior was not just ordinary items. She finally felt relaxed.

"Let me show you around. It's just this room though."

She held his hand, and they walked around as she explained everything to him, even demonstrating how her spear plugged in. She also showed him the bathroom. "It will take a lot longer to talk about the tech. I'll show it to you when we have more time. There's one more place I would like to show you."

She walked towards her deck and the door automatically opened. "This way," she said, stepping out into the deck that was tucked into the forest. Because her house was built later and not passed on, it was not in a clearing that had seen a lot of life with paths worn down by feet, as they experienced life. The trees surrounded it closely. Something was captivating about the aged trees that created a picturesque view.

They were nature's skyscrapers that freckled the sky with their leaves. They might not have been as tall as real skyscrapers, but they were majestic when you looked up past their knotted arms, as far as your head could reach. She led him in, the leaves crinkling into the forest floor.

"Your home is amazing. I like it," he said, giving it a last look as he followed her into the forest.

"Thank you. I haven't seen your other homes. You have too many. I thought they had more tech than your Innercity home. Most homes out there come loaded with tech."

The inner corners of his eyebrows angled up as he spoke. "They probably do if I consider their size. I grew up in the Outercity with my parents after they renounced their titles. So, I stayed there, then I bounced around different countries. I like to settle even if it's just for work. I only started living in the Innercity. Though I was done building it long before that: it was my escape place no one knew about. When I moved in, it wasn't just an escape anymore. It became home. Then I decided I wanted someone to share it with. But meeting people in the Innercity is… Needless to say, I installed True Match thinking I would have to move again. I told the application it could pair me with someone anywhere in the world. Our people don't use tech, so I wasn't expecting to be matched with someone in the Innercity. Where are we going to live when we get married? We have a matriarch. Right now, you are our leader. But you don't want to fully live the life of a Supreme Elder."

Her eyes were unengaged as her instinct led her forward. Deep in thought, she replied, "I don't know. When I renounced my title, everything was supposed to pass on to my cousin. The way I saw it, I permanently moved to the Outercity. Of course, my mother and everyone else said I could come back because it was my rightful place. But I… going back after we get married feels like living a lie. To live that life without tech is false. Because of the title I gave her, Adede lives there despite being married. You can't just give someone a title and then take it away. She's my cousin, but she's my sister. I know we give these titles to our men and then take them away, but that doesn't make it right. When I got this power, she wanted to step down. I wouldn't let her. So as a leader, I decided to change things. I figured the elders couldn't argue with me, seeing as to how they were all supposed to step down, and even if we led equally, they still treated me like I ranked above them. Even if it's a superior position I was born into, it's like one day I suddenly woke up the head of our country. I wasn't mentally ready. No matter how much I prepare now, I still can't live that life."

There was silence for a moment. Even the orchestra of birdsong stopped. He looked down at his shoes, their steps echoing on before he broke the silence. "If you feel that way then my home might be best. It's not built on ancestral land. It was built on private residential land. There are no ancestral homes there. The whole estate is going to solely belong to us. It's not as large as ancestral land because private properties don't have the purpose of housing a long lineage that passes down homes for generations. But it's enough for us. I got it since I gave up my title but still wanted to have a home in the Innercity."

40

GIVING IT UP

THE SMELL OF the forest surrounded them as the gentle breeze carried the fragrance; the decomposing parts of it hung silently in the background, while the organic smells melded together like a damp breath, joined by the smell of freshly broken branches under their feet.

The fracturing of the branches stopped as she stood for a moment in surprise. "It's a private residence!? On private land!! I didn't know those still existed. I thought we only had preserved land for wildlife and ancestral land for each clan. That means it's never been built on; there are no ancestors there! I know they didn't just give it to you and you couldn't have used tokens to buy it; so, it must have cost a fortune to buy. Housing is usually given or passed on. Even when it's newly built, the land is still given or passed on. So, money can still buy things in the Innercity!" She shook her head in disbelief.

"It was worth it," he said, smiling with pride. He was already a person that had an air of pride. It was a dignity earned from all his success. He raised his eyebrows and gave a slight nod.

"People without titles are lucky that they don't have to deal with these kinds of things. They can always find a place to go without pissing off their ancestors. I can't even count how many rituals I had to do, to jump through hoops, to be able to build on my own ancestral land. All that because I'm supposed to be living with my family!" She narrowed her eyes, shuddering at the memory.

"It has its pros and cons." He shrugged.

"Yes. It does. Your home will be best then. It's only going to get more complicated when we get married and have a child. If you take a look at what happened to you, your parents gave up their titles. You ended up with these two titles. Will our child have to take the titles that you gave up, or will they get the title that I gave up? They will probably get all three. Will it be a girl who ends up with powers and gets the Supreme Elder title? Will they want to rule as Supreme Elder: leader of all? This is why elders don't marry elders. Dealing with one title is enough. What are we supposed to do with three?" she asked, wrinkling her eyebrows. Just the thought made her nervous.

"We have time to think about it. Having children is still a long way from now. We'll cross that bridge when we get there. But first, I start by making love to you." His words made her feel shy. She felt even more shy when he pulled her into his arms then he kissed her cheek. Then luckily, they continued walking.

"We'll cross that bridge later… We are almost there," she echoed then stated, her focus distracted.

They walked a little further, and then she stopped. She looked at the tree she always climbed, placing her hand on its trunk, its cracks and wrinkles showing its age. It was a lightly coloured wood with a teak-brown.

It wasn't majestic in its height but anything along the hills could look tall from an angle. What they called a Siala tree was more popular for its yellow flowers and medicinal properties, rather than a forest tree with majestic height.

"This tree. I have climbed this tree for so many years, to watch the sunset."

"I remember you talking about it. It's a big tree to climb for a child!" He looked up at the branches with his eyebrows wrinkled in thought.

"When it comes to stuff like this, I used to think I am invincible." She walked to the other side of the tree. She tilted her head to look at him from behind the trunk, saying, "Climb it with me."

Before he could reply, she was on her way up in a well-practised movement. She stood on a branch gesturing for him to join her. He climbed up just as easily. He was athletic so it was not a problem for him.

"Sit first. I'll sit with you," she said.

He paused and looked at the branch they were standing on. Then he sat adjusting himself. He reached out his hand for her to join him. She sat in front of him.

"Closer," he said, adjusting himself again.

"Lean on me," he added.

He had sat with his legs on either side of the brunch. She adjusted herself and sat with one leg on the brunch, slightly bent and the other leg hanging on the side. She leaned into his chest. He put an arm around her, helping to hold her in place. She was facing the direction of the sun. He had to look around her head to see ahead of him, but he could now see the view when she leaned on him.

"I love this place," she said, feeling warm in her heart.

"It's your home. You don't have to give it up. I will move into your family home with you if you change your mind. Even if you change your mind much later," he said, stroking her hair.

"I know. But there are some things that you can't turn back from once you experience them. You've seen my home. That's me. There is no room for me in my family home." She looked down at her fingers wanting to twirl her spear in them, but her hands were empty. It was her fidgeting motion that she did with her shortened spear, as though she was twirling a baton.

"I lived most of my life outside. I didn't experience that kind of restriction in my home. But that's how my parents felt. For them it wasn't so much the technology they wanted, it was the lifestyle. They especially like to host guests or throw parties. An elder might have a lot of privileges, but their life is very restricted."

There was a long pause as she watched the sunset.

"Why did you give up your title? It seemed to be something you really wanted," she asked silently like she was afraid of interfering with the serene placidity of the forest.

"I got tired of asking to be accepted when the world out there didn't just accept me, but they would call out my name in admiration. You have seen what some O_ts are like. Besides, we have a matriarch. As men we lose our titles the moment a daughter is born, any reason really when a title gets passed on, or in death. Women keep their titles no matter what, even after death. We are just a supporting cast. We temporarily hold these titles; they don't belong to us. As a man, we are better off being born in a regular household, because then you can at least be the head of the household."

"You say we should cross the bridge of passing on titles when the time comes. But… I waited ten years, and I still couldn't cross that bridge of bearing Chloe's child. I always knew she wanted a child after she spent time focusing on her career.

We have both given up titles. There is a difficulty here in our history. That bridge will still be hard to cross when the time comes. It's better we figure it out now. Our child will have three titles passed on to them through us. This is the burden that we carry." She turned to look at him. A serious expression on her face.

"Then we should have three children. They can each get a title," he said with a straight face.

"Is it really that simple? How do we decide who gets what? Why are we so complicated?" she asked in frustration, turning forward and leaning into him.

"Not complicated. New. We'll make things up. But if you think about it, having three children works. The three of them can take up these titles. We can hold it for them until they are ready to be initiated.

If they don't want to take them up that's okay. They don't have to be born into these titles. Or they can hold all the titles from the moment they are born. Either way, they can stay with us. We are not on ancestral land. They will always have a place to go to. We'll be the land of... we can make up the name of our dynasty and kingdom."

"Three children is a lot. Can we even have one?" she was starting to feel pressured, finding herself worrying about everything. Elders tended to have smaller families because they held a lot of responsibility.

"I am fine with you changing your mind," he said with understanding.

"You're always saying that!" She turned to look at him, feeling some of the tension in her body disappear.

"Because I mean it. I want to live life with you. Don't feel pressure to do or be anything." He shook his head slightly, the corner of his lips curving in a smile.

"You know who tells me that? My father." Her mouth went slack, opening slightly.

"He is right."

"But I still feel like this."

She looked into his eyes, wanting to be understood. It was like she was pulled into a trance, "Do beautiful fantasies exist?" she asked, imagining an ideal world and getting drawn into his eyes.

"We created our fantasies. We just have to live them." He was giving her permission with his comforting eyes, which spoke another message.

"Live," she said before she kissed him.

She had no awareness of how she turned her body to face him. She stopped to take a breath, looked into his eyes, and then kissed him again. She was there but she wasn't really there. She was lost in him.

41

GETTING ACQUAINTED

"WE SHOULD GO. I'll get down after you," said Agina. She should lead him since she could navigate better in the familiar starlit forest with dense shadows, but she was not going to crawl over Otiende to climb down ahead of him.

He got down the tree and then waited for her below, as she followed. The moment she got close enough he lifted her by her waist and helped her down. As they walked back, they talked about their engagement ceremony.

She led the way, holding his hand. When they got back the glass door automatically opened as the light came on. As he followed, she walked into the kitchen and opened the oven.

She bent down and took out a basket. In it was the mandazi, wrapped in decorative food-grade kraft paper. She held up the traditional reed basket that had a lid and a handle, smiling as she said, "Mandazi."

A huge grin spread across his face. He crossed his hands as he spoke, "Okay. Maybe the desert was a good idea. I'd love to have some, and I think he would appreciate them."

She sat beside Otiende at the dining table in Odek's home. It was a naturally well-lit room with a large wooden dining set that sat eight people. Odek was sitting across from them. They talked for some time. He was now talking about how he met Otiende.

Odek was an expressive person; he moved his hands spiritedly as he talked, "Our parents were working together on a project. There was an event both our families were attending. This kid was dancing by himself like he didn't care. Probably because he was really good at dancing. He was like a star! Even the way he was dressed, he looked more like the host of this formal party. So confident. Then my mom told me to go make friends with him because I looked bored, and he looked like he was having fun. Of course, I didn't. I was too shy. But he clearly wasn't. He even had a crowd of people watching and cheering! He was that good at dancing even then. But it was a long party. Through the event, he always seemed to find ways to occupy himself. He made games out of nothing! When he was done dancing my mom brought me over and asked if he minded playing with me. He didn't say much but he did play with me. Thanks to him I had a good time at that party. I would say he actually went out of his way to make sure I was not bored. Our parents were friends and always kept in touch so that's how we stayed friends."

She felt Otiende's touch on the back of her hand. It didn't seem intentional, but their arms had come closer together. They both had their arms on the table. Reflexively her fingers found his, and stayed this way, her fingers brushing against his.

"I think you have heard how we met. We stayed out of touch for so long and then met under different circumstances," she said, turning to look at Otiende with a smile on her face. He smiled back, looking at her.

She brushed her fingers against his as she said, "It was fate. Or should I say it was a program?" They both laughed.

"Good for the both of you. OT was convinced the program got it wrong. But it was right after all." They both turned back to Odek as he spoke.

"How did you meet your wife?" asked Agina.

"I used the same program: True Match. I had suggested he use the program years ago when he wanted to get back to dating. He already knew about the program, even before I suggested it, but he waited this long to use it to find a partner."

Otiende and Agina looked at each other and smiled again.

Odek continued to speak, "He works with tech and uses tech all the time, and I don't. But he was absolutely convinced it was wrong. Up until that moment he has never doubted his tech!"

"That was my fault. He trusted me more. I hadn't shown interest in him, but I had shown interest in women. I was ideological at the time, and it felt more like true love when you find someone similar to your body. Because then, it's not about the instinct to reproduce; my mom might have put too much pressure on me to continue our line." As she said it was her fault, Otiende was shaking his head at her and putting his finger on his lips.

"Not your fault," Otiende said when she was done talking.

She laughed.

"So, what work do you do?" she asked, turning to Odek.

"I am a professional athlete. Most of the time I compete in running. OT has competed with me before in sponsored races. When he trains with me, he will train even harder than I do. I have never met someone with such determination," Odek said, speaking lively with expressive hand movements.

She continued to ask him about his interests and family. She talked a little about her family before the conversation turned to the engagement ceremony.

"That sounds like a lot. You have put so much more effort into it than my wedding!" Odek said, with one of his eyebrows pulled up as he tapped on the table with his finger.

"It's tradition," Agina and Otiende said at the same time then they both laughed.

Otiende gestured for her to speak. "By the time the Innercity barrier was built a lot of the traditions had already started to disappear or get modified. Traditionally there was a lot that was done in ceremonies and rituals, taking up to one year, for a traditional wedding to be completed. But we will be completing it in three years. This ceremony is one of the first steps. It's called Aiye. Once it is done, we would be considered married. But we are not truly married till the dowry is paid. We'll do this in a ceremony called Nyombo. On average, there are five weeks between the Aiye and Nyombo. Marriage had been modified when colonisation happened, and foreign religions became an influence. Aiye became more like an engagement ceremony, while a wedding ceremony would happen at a church where vows were exchanged. As you know sometimes the vows are not exchanged in a church. So that's why the ceremony is this elaborate and just as important. Essentially, it's like half of the wedding, so it's taken as seriously as a wedding. Both the Aiye and the Nyombo make up the wedding. Other traditions happen between the Aiye and Nyombo, but they have become less popular. All this is what used to happen before exchanging vows became a thing."

"That's interesting. I have learnt so much about traditions from OT. No one else knows these things. They only seem to exist in the Innercity," Odek said, looking deep in thought.

"That's a point I often make. In fact, the further you go from the Innercity, there are people who don't even know the Innercity exists, even if it's in their country," she said, looking glum.

Otiende took her hand and gently squeezed it.

"Sigh. I am glad he talks about these things," Agina said, feeling disheartened.

"He grew up here like me. But I think the traditions were always a part of him. So, he was always different. I wasn't surprised when he moved to the Innercity. Even O_ts who are nosy as ever don't know he is there. This place you both live in is such a mystery whether you know it exists or not." Odek moved his hands as he spoke.

"Such a world we live in…" she said, turning to look into Otiende's eyes, "Standing out in the Innercity and standing out in the Outercity. Only place you don't stand out is between. But there is nothing in between but a fence you find yourself on."

"I walk the fence with you. It's a place I would rather be," Otiende said in a daze. They sat staring into each other's eyes.

"I'm going to go get some fruit," Odek said, standing up and leaving.

When he got back, they were still looking into each other's eyes, and they were still holding hands.

"Really? You should just kiss," Odek said, putting the fruits on the table.

Otiende held her face with his other hand and kissed her. She had been staring into his eyes so intently that she could only kiss him back.

"And they really kissed!" Odek said, shaking his head and crossing his hands in mock anger.

"You should just get a room," Odek said in disbelief.

"We don't do that," said Otiende in response, as he smiled in mischief. "Don't say what you don't mean," he added with a daring grin.

Odek threw his hands up, "Okay. I give up. I did say you should kiss. I remember what it's like to fall in love. I wish you both the best." He pointed at Otiende as he spoke, "He's too easy to make fun of because he is always so direct."

"Tell me about your experience of falling in love," Agina said, directing the conversation back to Odek.

They talked about his relationship for a while. They also talked about Otiende, particularly the memories they shared. When they were done with dinner, he brought out the dessert she had brought.

"This is really good. I can't believe you made it yourself," said Odek as he bit into the fried triangles that were mostly made of flour.

"Not entirely by myself. There is always someone else in the kitchen at my family's house. I eat there every day. Or at least I used to before he waltzed into my life, taking my time for a spin. I usually don't cook at home. Or at least cook this type of stuff," said Agina.

"That's great that you can cook. That has to be the one thing that OT is not good at. I love to cook. When we meet for dinner, at least he gets a home-cooked meal," Odek said, gesturing his arms wide across the table.

"In my defence, cooking is not necessary. And I am not entirely helpless at cooking," said Otiende, leaning forward.

They all laughed.

42

DEFENCES UP

THE TWO CIRCULAR pillars with a crossbeam going across the top looked more like a door-opening that was an ancient relic, than a portal that was an advanced means of travel. The structure stood tall with ancient text wrapped around the material that looked like stone. If it was placed in the middle of the ruins left by ancient civilisations it would not look out of place.

But when Agina's portal was activated, the inscribed ancient text glowed in a cyan-blue light. What appeared like an empty door opening would then be occupied by a dark grey surface that appeared eerie and looked more like a black mirror because of the way the light reflected off it.

Its style did not match anything in her home, so it made it look more like a monument on display with the way it was placed. It was like the rest of her home, technology that was hidden.

Agina came through the portal to find Otiende waiting for her in his entry hall. They hugged, then he kissed her.

"Are you ready?" he asked in concern, holding her in his arms.

"I think so. This is a lot more nerve-wracking. It's easier when it feels like you are gambling with just your life. When it's the life of everyone in Dala, it's different. I didn't even have the heart to go through any more simulations even if they ended well." Agina's face was clouded with concern as she spoke. She had had to watch Dala be attacked countless times so they could test how the program saved people.

"I have worked in security for Dala for a long time. We will be fine. It's seeing your life on the edge that is more nerve-wracking. I can't bear it. I can't lose you now." He brushed his thumb on her cheek as he spoke.

They put their foreheads together with their eyes closed. "Let's not cry in the morning, Okay. Talking about deep emotions is not the best way to start the day. I need a minute. And I might need your support when I get there." She looked up at him. Then they hugged.

"Let me stay like this for a little bit," she said, speaking into his coat.

After standing wrapped in each other's arms for a while, they went through his portal. Everything was already prepared by the time they got there. Everyone took their positions, most of them in front of a screen.

Even if no portals were involved, anything could go wrong. Agina hesitated, closing her eyes. Then took a grounding breath. She knew she needed to be more grounded. But she could feel herself shaking, ever so slightly, out of nervousness. She held out her hand, and he was already on the way to her. The moment she held his hand she felt much better.

What she needed was an anchor to something that made her feel solid; he was that for her. With her eyes closed, she began. There was nothing noticeable as it happened. Just a tranquil peace and silence. After a short while she opened her eyes.

"It's done." A sense of peace could be felt in her presence as she made the statement. The process was different in her mind with everything she needed to do, her creation weaving in labyrinthine encryption and forming the complex program installation. Having their country's defence strengthened, gave her the room to feel safe enough to relax.

When she got home that Thursday evening, he was already in her entry hall, talking to the main system of the house. He had arrived earlier than her since she had allowed the portal to give him access even when she wasn't there. She let go of her spear and it made its way to its place where it connected to the house.

"Great. You started setting it up." She walked over to Otiende, and they kissed.

"What did you tell it when it asked how we are connected?" she wondered.

"Future husband." He had the largest grin when he spoke.

The floating pyramid moved further away from them and asked, "May I please scan your body?"

She stepped away from him. It started scanning him. It let out a blue light that surrounded him and a red laser light slowly scanned his body.

"You don't have to be fully set up. It's all voluntary." She watched it record every part of him as she spoke. It was an intensive scan because it helped her keep track of her health, letting her know if anything was concerning. He could have skipped the part.

"I know. It's time your house got to know someone else," he said, grinning at her with a warm smile that sent shivers through her.

When the scan was done, he walked over to her and held her in his arms as he continued the setup. When they were done adding him as a user to the main system the pyramid disappeared. They went on to the rest of the house.

Just the entrance hall had questions like: When you put away your coat or shoes should we clean them? The number of things that could be automated seemed endless. As Otiende put in his information, she would talk about what she preferred and how she had set it up in the system. It was a good way for them to get to know each other.

They took a break to watch the sunset on her tree, then got back to continue the setup.

"How do you get up there?" he asked, pointing to the bed.

"It lowers down. But not all the way. It's the only place that will always override anyone else's settings when I am here. But you should still set it because it will keep asking. Plus, there is always a possibility you will be here without me. It's probably better to show you first."

She walked towards it and stopped. She stood on the spot while stairs appeared, and the platform started to lower down. She began to climb the stairs while they were still appearing, and the platform was moving downward. By the time she got to the last step, the platform had stopped lowering.

Before the bed's platform lowered there was still enough headroom above and below the platform, with more headroom below the platform. When it lowered there was still enough headroom below and above the platform with more headroom above the platform.

There was only enough room for one person to comfortably walk around the bed, so she stepped aside and waited for him as he followed her up. She pointed as she spoke, "It can raise a railing around the edge of the platform, but I always keep it down. It will give you a warning if you step too close to the edge.

The steps will disappear if I am asleep or if I am not on the platform. There are other settings but let's set them up later. When you set it up you will see all the other options. We should have dinner."

He looked around with a look of awe as he said, "Yes. It took long enough to set up what we already finished. There is still much to set up. I like the view up here. Your home is beautiful."

"Not too strange? Even when the tech is hidden, people at least find the placement of my bed strange. But a bed really just has one purpose. It's not much of a functional space. I didn't want to hide it away either. It deserves a presence."

"Agina... a bed doesn't have just one purpose." He turned to her and said with a matter-of-fact tone, with a hint of suggestiveness in his eyes.

She blushed and looked away. How could he be thinking about that at this time? Or had she been out of a relationship for too long that it hadn't crossed her mind?

"It's not strange at all," he said, redirecting the conversation back, coming closer and putting an arm around her. "People have so many opinions about what they don't understand or about what is different. In fact, people have opinions about everything. I like your home a lot because it's where you just live your life as who you are. It's where the real Agina shows up."

"As persistent as my house is programmed to be about asking people to input their information, I never thought anyone would actually be added. It feels good to not feel so alone. We have walked this fence alone for too long. Now that we have crossed paths again, we can walk it together. I am so glad you came back into my life. And are here to stay." She looked at him like nothing else in the world mattered.

"Yes. I'm here." He stared at her so intently as he spoke. The look in his eyes shifted, making her feel like he was sensually touching her. The look in his eyes only got more intense making her feel like he was devouring her because he was starved.

Ducking from his arm she crossed over him, holding him by the waist and looking into his eyes as she passed, then stopped on his other side. She was now closer to the stairs. She put a hand on his shoulder as she said, "Come. Dinner."

She held his hand as she led him down the stairs, feeling the remnants of what was in his eyes pass through his hands to her body. The stairs and platform returned after they both got down. She felt like she had to make that escape from the bed. Thoughts had begun flooding into her mind. They were so close to the bed. Too close!

She had felt so comfortable with him in her home. They had been friends first, so her mind didn't always wander there. Until... her mind started wondering again.

They set the dining table together. It was a small round table that sat four people on soft cushioned seats. They choose to sit beside each other.

It was an easy prep dinner that didn't need to be cooked so he helped in the kitchen. She had already cooked some side dishes the day before at her family's house, she just heated it up. While she was there, she didn't hear the end of Adede's excitement about having him over for dinner.

She had to guide him a few times on what to do, holding his hand in hers as he chopped or mixed. Energy passed through them, stirring up the desires she was trying hard to ignore.

But she didn't trust herself to let the touch linger for too long; thanks to him, she had already been having thoughts about him. It was already too much to stand so close to him. The way her senses reacted made her too aware of their whirling desires.

So, she kept busy preparing the food. As they were making their dinner, they talked about his experience with cooking. He didn't seem to be as helpless as Odek had led her to believe.

The food was just about done. She gave it a taste, bringing a spoonful of food to her mouth.

"Can I try some?" he asked, standing so close behind her that their bodies almost touched, and his breath fell against her neck.

She slowly moved away and took another spoon, stuffing his mouth with a heaping spoon. He seemed to be well aware of the game he was playing, smiling naughtily as he slowly chewed.

When it was all done, they put the food on serving dishes. They took the food over to the table and sat down.

She sat cross-legged on her chair as she often did when she was at home. It brought her knee closer to him, making their seating position more intimate. The conversation about his cooking turned to talking about awkward or embarrassing experiences.

They were smiling and laughing the entire time, talking late into the night. They were old friends reunited. Their glances were more than a glance. There was a kindling sensation whenever they dared to briefly touch. Their hearts beat faster when their fingers connected. Their relationship grew every time they met.

NAUTICAL

OT: Why do I miss you when you are not around? The time spent with you doesn't feel like it's enough.

Yeah. I miss you too when you are gone. As much as we've been spending all this time together, being with you alone doesn't feel the same as how we have been meeting as a group for engagement prep.

OT: You are right. I look forward to finally spending the day with you. I think our next stop should be an underwater city. Which city would you like to visit?

Tekoa. I love it no matter how many times I have been there.

OT: I love Tekoa city too. I'll make arrangements.

Here is a place I want to take you to when we get there. Wear your swimsuit. It's a hidden gem. Location data attached.

OT: Okay. I'll put that at the end of our itinerary. It sounds exciting.

-End of text messages-

CITIES LIKE TEKOA were made to be tourist destinations. Their structure was anchored, unlike other underwater cities that floated. They were originally built to convince people that going underwater was better than going off-planet.

So, it was extravagant, self-sustaining, and solved a lot of issues such as constantly purifying the water. The moment Agina came through the portal she got excited. She loved the place. Tekoa's international portals were located in the area of the city that projected out from the ocean.

The roof of the room was transparent and retracted. So, it was like arriving in a large sports stadium that had its roof open. On that day the sun was not too hot in Tekoa. Though you likely wouldn't directly interact with the sun because most of the city was underwater; people often sunbathed in air-conditioned rooms underwater.

"Let's go under!" she said, holding his arm and happily pulling him along. They had on full-body suits again today. They were more colourful today but suits like that were less common in places like these where people often came to enjoy the sun or water.

What probably made them stand out even more is that they had six bodyguards with them today. They had a private self-tour of the place. Considering how many tourists were around, Agina was glad they were not drawing people's attention. She found herself loving the place more. People seemed to mind their own business.

Agina especially loved the part where they got to look out into the endless ocean, watching the fish swim along. Otiende stood behind her, holding her in his arms. They would spot different types of fish then name it and show the other where it was.

When they were standing under the transparent walkways the sun looked different from under the water. It almost looked like the sun had been melted and poured onto the surface of the ocean. The brilliant shining liquid sun, sending its brilliant rays down to the bottom of the ocean. But even in this liquid form, it was still too brilliant to look at directly. It lit the water making it look blue.

Otiende took off her helmet, then he took off his. There weren't any other people around. They took pictures against the blue background looking to see what fish they had managed to capture in the background.

"The fish don't notice we are here. They just live their lives. We are not that different: separated from the people outside our Innercity barrier. This indifference is the separation we have known. I used to like watching the fish when I was younger, doing all types of tricks to see if I could ever get the attention of a fish. But I never could," she said, touching the glass-like surface.

"Sigh. I spent most of my life outside that barrier. No matter how long you swim out there, whether you get people's attention or not, you are still you. A free spirit can't just stay within the walls when the vast ocean is out there. Having found you to venture out with makes life so much sweeter. You are not alone. But your spirit is free. Even I cannot bind you. You cannot lose that freedom." As he spoke, he took her hand and placed it on the glass-like surface, putting his hand on top of hers and interlacing his fingers with hers.

"The freedom is an illusion," she said, turning the palm of her hand and taking his hand in hers, interlacing their fingers once more.

"So, abandon the illusion and create a better reality. I trust with your power, it will come to you, what you must create."

She turned to look into his eyes. It was like looking into his soul. She couldn't help but to be pulled in. She reached up to kiss him. She felt such a deep connection with him that she couldn't quite explain.

Later, they put their helmets back on. As they walked on Agina noticed a digital board with Otiende's picture on it. She stopped to read it. Then turned to ask him, "One of your endorsements?"

"Yeah. These sorts of things are not common in Dala maybe because we don't have tourists. Or more so because we don't push products. However, when you are abroad you will easily spot one of mine in places I have recently been in. I performed my last event in this city not too long ago."

"What performance was it?"

A smile slowly spread across his face, and then he said, "Here, let me show you."

He took out his com and projected the video in three dimensions. The video began with him rising to the stage dressed in a sparkling suit as the beat developed. He then began to sing and dance to a large audience that were holding lights that synchronised.

He slid his feet back and forth in a sudden smooth rhythm. His upper body moving perfectly in rhythm with the music. You could tell he was a well-practised performer with the way he occupied the stage, moving from one side to the other in sync with the backup dancers, knowing how to engage the elated audience.

It was the first time she saw him performing. She didn't know much about these types of large-scale performances, but even with her little knowledge, she could tell it was a really good performance.

When the song was over, they showed the crowd applauding and screaming. She was surprised by how large the crowd was. She knew there was a large stadium in the city, but it was different to see it fully packed with people. It looked more like an organised swarm of ants when they panned through the audience from a distance.

He had done too much over the past years for her to possibly try and catch up with it all. With his character, he didn't expect anything from her. So, she hadn't bothered to look. He already felt uncomfortable with what he called forcing her to face his fans.

Agina recalled what Odek had said about Otiende already being like a star when he was younger. He had always been exposed to the entertainment industry and he had absorbed it. It was part of him.

"That is amazing. It looks like it comes so naturally to you." She wasn't sure what to say. What compliment could you give such a star who has the kind of fandom he has? He was probably used to hearing praises his whole life.

"Thanks. It was a lot of practice rather than talent." He appeared to be pleased enough with her comment.

"Will you continue acting and performing? You know, doing the things you used to do?" she asked cautiously. He spoke about their future together often, yet he never mentioned his plans for the entertainment industry.

"I don't know. Maybe at some point I'll come back to it. I've already given it forty two years of my life." That was his whole life he had given to entertainment, when he said it like that it sounded final.

They moved on from their tour to have lunch. The fish they served were freshly caught. The Innercity was originally a fishing community, so they often had fish served in this way with the head and tail not cut out.

Again, they took a long time talking over their lunch. It was the same when they left the restaurant: O_ts had gathered outside. Agina realised that he probably got spotted in restaurants more easily because he took his helmet off while he ate.

This crowd was a little harder for the security guards to manage because of the screaming white O_ts that pushed each other, just so they could take a look or get a picture. It made her very uneasy.

AQUATIC BLISS

THEY GOT INTO one of the pods in the transportation tubes and went off to Agina's location that she requested. The tubes networked through the city like veins transporting vital necessities and so much more. They arrived in the underwater caves that were not so far away from the city.

The caves were beautiful. The water in them was crystal blue, lit by sunlight from a hole at the top. The water right under the hole reflected the sun so brightly it almost looked like it was its own light source.

There were not as many tourists there. Before they could go any further, they were approached by someone who looked like he was a local. The bodyguards had intended to stop him, but Agina explained he was dropping off some gear that they would need.

"We are going to go diving. There is a place I want to show you that we can only get to by going under," Agina said to Otiende as she took the gear from the local and then thanked them.

They put on their diving gear and Otiende followed Agina into the water. Agina insisted that the bodyguards stay behind. Besides, she had only set up gear for two that adapted to their suits. Agina used a flashlight on her equipment at the front of her forehead to light the way.

After several turns and diving deeper and deeper, she finally came up to the chamber of a sea cave. It was pitch black except for the light she had and the light Otiende had. She swam along the water surface to a limestone rock and sat on it.

She took out a device and focused on it for a short while, pushing buttons, before she announced, "The best thing about places like this, is that it's the closest you can naturally get to a controlled environment where you don't have to cover up."

She took off her helmet to reveal a huge grin. "And with my powers, I can even cheat a little by purifying it further so we can have longer exposure."

She took off the gear and her suit and remained in a bathing suit. Following her lead, he also took off his gear and suit and remained in his bathing suit.

"That's brilliant that you found such a place. I never thought of that," he said, moving closer to her.

"I like to explore underground caves. I mostly come back here to test new experiments and theories. New caves are always more fun to explore. So, for fun, I go for adventures in new caves. I have been wondering if I can push this environment further with my powers... clear the water and air."

She lit the place with several lights above and below the water. The water now took on a luminous blue colour. It looked surreal, almost like a swimming pool lit at night. It wasn't a large cave, but it was big enough.

She reached out for his hand, wanting him to be a part of the process. After he held her hand, she closed her eyes and focused on the water and air. After purifying in this way for a long while she opened her eyes. She took the device and focused on it again, pushing buttons. "Perfectly clear now." She put the device down and got in the water as she said, "Come in."

The water was cold, but it was just how she needed it. She watched him come in the water. With his chest bare she could now see how muscular he was.

She hadn't known someone who was so confident about showing his body that they would wear their shirt with their abs peeking like he always did. Did he just live his life like it was a performance, like he was always ready for a photo shoot? He must spend a lot of time maintaining his body. It was an athlete's body. It didn't show that obviously when he was dressed because he was somewhat lean.

She focused so much on work that she associated with a small group of people. She usually surrounded herself with scientists who didn't care much about the way they look. The men in her family didn't care about such things either.

He joined her in the water. They swam beside each other, and swam back and forth. Splashing each other with water and laughing as they avoided the water. They were in their own hidden world like a secret between lovers, the ripples and sound they created unable to leave the sea cave.

They got out of the water and jumped back in from a flat rock shelf, jumping in with different forms, over and over again. They were not deep dives, just play as they frolicked. Occasionally he would hold her as they played in the water, even spinning her around. The way he made them twirl and dipped her into the water, made her laugh, a testament to her joy that filled the cave.

They also took pictures as they played, particularly underwater pictures and videos, making faces and taking pictures together.

They swam back around and got out of the water, pausing for a moment. They both stood at the top of the rock again. He held her in his arms from the back as they both looked out at the water and stalactites that hung like rock icicles.

"I really love this. There is something about being able to interact with nature that has been around for thousands of years. Just look at the way those stalactites hang. Slowly changing with the years passing. You're insightful. You're beautiful," he said, his gentle voice rising from the silence in its deep melody.

"Thank you. I know it's a privilege to always have our ideal environment in the Innercity. Created for us. But it's more special to find it untouched with features we don't have in the Innercity. So, I love secret little pockets like this. It wasn't perfect but I hope I did good by leaving it better than I found it. It just naturally maintained good enough levels."

With a sly grin on his lips, he leaned forward and said, "I was the one who used to find places to hide. Who thought you would find such a perfect hidden place." They both laughed.

She held his hand, and they jumped in together. She began to swim back then stopped where she could stand with her head and part of her shoulders outside the water. "Come here," she said to Otiende. He paddled his arms as he moved toward her.

"If we stay still enough you can see marine life in the water," she said looking intensely at the water. As she looked, she noticed tiny colourful fish swimming in the water. "Look!" she said excitedly pointing to them. But she startled them, so they swam away.

He laughed. "I like how you get excited about things. You become like a little kid and your face is already so cute. So, it makes you even cuter."

"No. Do not call me cute. I had enough of that when I was younger, so I declared the title sexy and embraced that identity fully. Don't call me cute," she complained, suddenly getting worked up.

He laughed even harder. "Is that why tomboy suddenly became the sexy girl that was provoking everyone on the playground whilst still somehow managing to be tomboy!" He continued laughing even harder.

"How did you even hear about that?! That happened after you left," she said defensively.

"Agina," he said trying to catch his breath, "I have family that were there. It was a big deal for those people who suddenly noticed you, but you wouldn't ever give them any time of the day. Only girls had a chance, and I heard your standards were so high. So even the girls were distraught."

"Is that what happened? I don't remember it that way. All I remember is constantly having to defend my identity… I pull off a damn good sexy," she declared, holding her head high.

"Yes. You do," he said, coming closer to her.

"You're really sexy," he said, too close to her ear at a slower pace, making his voice flow even more gently and do a dance with her nerves that she was not ready for. She was convinced he knew exactly what his voice did to her. Wasn't he an actor? Hadn't he also done voice acting?

She was too weak to say anything as he approached her face and put his lips on hers. She completely gave in to him. They kissed with a passion like they had been holding back the entire day. Under the water, their hands roamed. The skin-to-skin contact burning despite the cool water.

Agina could barely hold back. Sounds were escaping from her lips. Like a light brush stroke, her tongue found its way into his mouth. In a quick sweep, she found that she had been lifted and her legs were being held on either side of him.

Instinctively she wrapped her legs around him as they continued to kiss. She knew she had completely lost awareness of what was going on when he pulled away and tried to get her attention.

"Watch those hands. Or else even God won't be able to get me to stop," he said with the most daring and amused grin she had seen him show.

Those hands? She thought. What hands? What had her hands been doing? She suddenly realised where she had been caressing and pulled her hands out from his swimming jammers like she had just touched a hot stove.

She also let her legs loose, releasing him from the tight grip she had wrapped him in. But he was still holding her to his body, so she hadn't separated from him. She could feel that she was blushing. So, she instinctively looked down, only to find his eyes looking at her in amazement. So, she quickly turned away.

She felt mortified. When she realised he had not reacted yet and he was just watching her confusion, she said, "Sorry. We should leave."

"Agina. Look at me." She reluctantly looked at him. "Do you trust me?" He had a smirk on his face and didn't wait for her to reply before he continued, "I don't want to leave yet. You're going to kiss me again without losing your awareness. You can have control without using avoidance."

Her heart started beating faster. She knew there was fear in her eyes as she looked into his eyes. But he was right. Running away wasn't always the way to solve things.

"Trust yourself," he said, looking deep into her eyes.

"You're helping me dig my grave," she finally said.

"You are the heroine in this story. You have more control than you think you do. Just throw me in the grave instead. Kiss me. I want to be kissed by you." The tone in the last plea is what got her to finally give in. It knocked down whatever protest she had that was making her weary of proceeding. So, she cautiously kissed him. Then stopped to wearily look at him.

Still holding her he began to Walk toward shallower water, then he sat her on a rock as he remained in the water, looking up at her, with a smile pulling his mouth wider. He was standing between her legs, his arms around her waist. He stood this way just looking at her.

She didn't dare to say anything. She could see by the look in his eyes that he was not going to let her go anywhere. So, she just sat and avoided looking at him. Her curiosity kept drawing her eyes back to his eyes, but each time she would look away.

He held her face, looking at her gently, his smile wider. Now she couldn't avoid his gaze. She wasn't sure what she was so afraid of. All she could see was love in his eyes. She felt her heart beat faster as she looked at him.

She wasn't sure when exactly she had moved, but he had gently guided her face closer to his. He touched her nose with his, looking at her.

Her caution seemed to have escaped. Instead, she felt drawn to look at his eyes, watching them blink. Her awareness of him had grown so deep that she could see how his eyelashes moved in detail.

The way she registered their movement made her realise she was subconsciously accessing her power as she followed their motion. It was like it put her in a trance that helped her relax. He continued to look at her, bringing their foreheads together. He slowly closed his eyes and then opened them.

He appeared to find solace by just looking at her up close. The gentleness in his eyes made the tension ease from her body as she let him look at her with their foreheads together. He slowly closed his eyes and gently gave her a light kiss on her lips. Then opened his eyes to look at her again, with his forehead on hers.

They continued the moment with their forehead or nose, which was deeply intimate. It was like he patiently waited for her to readjust to his presence, till she had regained the comfort she felt around him. It was a valued intimate treasure achieved without them kissing.

PART 2

45

FAIRY TALE 1

THE WEEK WENT past fast. Throughout the week, Agina had been drowned in preparation and rehearsals, but after everyone parted, she always made time to talk to Otiende alone. She felt his presence lingering everywhere as she looked around.

She knew they had made the ceremony very elegant, but she was still taken aback by the result. As she looked around, she wondered if they had gone overboard.

It couldn't be helped that Agina had been swept away by the moment, excited to have a traditional wedding. She wasn't able to have one when she first got married. Moreover, the excitement of people around her was contagious.

She later realised every vendor they hired was excited to live out their dreams of servicing an elaborate wedding; they saw Agina as their Queen who was marrying Otiende, their beloved famous celebrity. In all their history there was no other prominent couple that held such power.

The setup was simple and absolutely gorgeous, but the vendors had overdelivered from what they asked. There probably had never been a ceremony in Dala put together this quickly that was this large and elaborate. It made their ability to influence and network more obvious.

The guest list seemed long, but it had been reduced by limiting it to family members. Traditionally it had been a ceremony for family members. Realistically this tradition had only been strictly followed to reduce the number of O_ts that were looking for an excuse to meet Otiende; it was a tradition that wasn't always followed.

As Agina looked around, she noted It was early in the morning and people were already moving about. The decorations had been designed in a colour theme of dark teal, bold orange and white. There were also traces of raspberry and dark red. The centrepieces were done with flowers and fruit in these colours, paired with complementing place-setting jewellery and elegant scented candles. The candles were placed in candle holders in a similar design as the place setting jewellery.

The tables were wooden, and the chairs they used were wooden with fabric cushions. They used formal place settings with polished silverware and white dinnerware. Each seat had different-sized wine glasses. The plates at each seat were layered and topped with napkins elaborately held together with the place-setting jewellery.

This extravagance wasn't Otiende being allowed to go over the top. His heights were high up. His parents' wedding had been even more expensive. This was Agina going over the top. For instance, she let them convince her that real custom crystal chandeliers with lights were a good idea.

The crystals didn't just hang down in a beautifully tiered chandelier, they threaded throughout the space in an intricate pattern, continuing between the tents and under the tents, refracting the morning sun and appearing to be gleaming. Because of their shape and arrangement, they still made a statement without refracting the light.

Otiende's family was always this way with material things so he would never have hesitated to spend money. He generally spent the most money in the family. Since they were bringing together the two families, it worked to bring down the level of his expenditure.

Agina stood, looking at the tables under the tents. Her favourite part of it all was the flowers, especially the flowers on the entrance centrepiece and the centrepiece placed behind her seat and Otiende's seat.

She had a thought about how she would like more flowers. Unexpectedly more flowers appeared under the tents, hanging among the dangling crystal lights and threaded string crystal lights. Flowers also appeared on everyone's seats.

She smiled to herself and intentionally added more flowers in other places then walked away feeling satisfied. She wondered if anyone would notice the change. The theme was still sparkly with the bold colours, but the added flowers made it look more like they had incorporated an enchanted garden.

As she was coming into the house Agot spotted her and approached her saying, "Come, let's have breakfast before it gets too crazy over here."

She followed her mother into the kitchen. The other kitchen was being used for the day's cooking so their open kitchen was not flooded with people. Their open kitchen was used more often because the family cooked together. It was open to their dining room and living room.

Today the dining and living room furniture had been taken out. The two rooms had been set up as a large lounging space with new matching sofas arranged in a large rectangle. It was where the discussions would be taking place. She sat on one of the empty stools around the large kitchen counter.

Her parents and grandparents, Adede and Adede's husband were also seated at the counter beside each other. She greeted them all like she usually would but there was a different atmosphere that day that felt somewhat like surface tension. They often said the house felt empty without her there, that it was where she belonged. However, she never felt like she fit among them.

Even now that she often had Otiende by her side, bringing him there would just be adding another person that didn't fit. Adede ended up being the one who brought up what was on everyone's mind, "So, you really are leaving?"

"Leaving? I had already left. I am getting engaged. I am not moving anywhere anytime soon. I love my little house." Her family was like this and she had not told them about moving into Otiende's home in the Innercity.

She went over to Adede and hugged her as she said, "We've spoken about this too many times already. You can't say you didn't see this coming. When I left, I didn't have the intention of coming back. So, when I returned, I moved into my own place. This is not my place anymore. But you are all still my family and I carry that with me no matter where I go." She stood with her arm around Adede's shoulder.

"Sigh. Sometimes I feel like we should have put in more effort to make you feel like you belonged. But that's in the past. With the way it started, I believe this was the only way it could have ended. Your destinies are intertwined. And these are your choices. We see that you're happy. We wish you the best," said Obuo, releasing part of the tension between everyone by redirecting the conversation. Her father always had a way of making her feel better.

"That's better. We are all excited about this. We have been enjoying these moments these past two and a half weeks since we announced we officially want to get engaged. Now is not the time to think about what would have been or to fixate on where I should live," Agina said, returning to her seat.

"Yes. Today is a happy day for you and for all of us. This subject should be dropped. We are at this point already. Let's speak of it no more," said Abura, somehow managing to sound excited even if she was being stern and assertive. Being the head of the household suited her well because everyone listened to her, but unfortunately, that role was progressively being handed to Agina. She didn't think it would be happening this soon if not for the engagement ceremony.

At that moment, Agina got a silent call on her com. She knew it was Otiende since she could use her com telepathically. She could ask devices to do things from the moment she got her powers. But it was recently that she figured out how to receive information from devices without asking.

Her facial expression and body language must have changed instantly because of the way she was being looked at by everyone. "Excuse me. I have to take this call," she said as she got up and hurriedly left the counter.

"Good morning," she answered the call without waiting to be excused by her family or before she put distance between them. She was also vaguely conscious that she had moved too fast for a human.

She noticed she sounded very excited to speak to him or was probably relieved that she had escaped the conversation.

"Good morning. Is it still crazy over there?" he replied.

"I think most of the chaos happened yesterday when they rushed to finish setting up the decor. I haven't been to the cook's kitchen, but I think that's where the chaos is. Luckily, I didn't have to watch any of the slaughtering or shedding of blood. Otherwise, I would have made an executive decision as a Supreme Elder to end this tradition for everyone for all eternity."

"So, I'm guessing you didn't have breakfast yet?"

"Not yet, I'll have some later but before people start to arrive." As she spoke, she made her way to an unoccupied room that was close by.

"How about over there? How are things?"

"It's strange being here at Dana's for the night and having my parents here. But it's been nice. Everyone else got back after dinner yesterday, so it was just us left. I was just about to go have breakfast. How are you feeling?"

"I am feeling good. Excited. A little nervous. How about you?"

"I'm glad. I like to see you happy. I know the nerves will pass, especially once things get exciting. As for me, I'm doing great. I woke up feeling really good today."

"Did you sleep well?"

"Yeah. I slept in my old bedroom. It brought up a lot of memories. like how I used to sleep here when we had conferences and Uncle Osano would come and pick me up. Now I am here again when the conferences are about to start, coming to our Aiye today. Somehow it feels like this place is related to you. Did you sleep well?"

"I had a hard time falling asleep. But I slept well eventually. I can't believe it's only been about a month since we reconnected."

"It feels like I have known you all this time, yet I still have so much to learn about you."

"Likewise. I look forward to getting to know even more about you." Both of them could not hide the excitement in their voices.

"I want to tell everyone how I feel about you. I want the world to know. You know how I feel about you Agina, right? That I have already fallen in love with you. You don't have to say anything back. It's enough for me that you choose to stay beside me."

She paused. There was silence at both their ends. Agina felt a strong connection towards Otiende, and she was physically attracted to him, but she didn't know if she loved him yet.

Her heart was racing, feeling like it was about to explode and keep expanding. All because she heard him say he was in love with her. It wasn't the first time he said it without saying the words: I love you.

"You understand how I feel. I appreciate you not rushing me. Today we will let them know how we feel through this celebration. We deal with the rest later by making our public appearance at the conferences."

FAIRY TALE 2

"" **A**GINA! AGINA!"

Agina had been talking to Otiende for about an hour. She rushed a goodbye and left the room, looking for Adede who had been calling out her name.

"Agina!!!"

"I'm coming!!" she yelled back. She found Adede in the hallway.

"Where did you disappear to?" she asked, wrapping an arm around Agina's arm, and walking beside her as she went towards the kitchen.

"I was on a call," Agina spoke, blushing with a huge grin across her face.

"Can't relate. We don't use coms much. We go see people. You should just conclude your marriage to him by accepting the dowry and get it over with. Then you can wake up beside each other and spend all day with him," said Adede, somewhat singing the last part as she dramatically gestured with her hand.

"But then I'd miss all the fun in dating. I haven't gone on a date for years. I want all the experiences!"

"What dating? You are already getting engaged today! In fact, it's not just an engagement, it's Aiye. You know traditionally it's like you're getting married in a few hours. It will be more like dating your spouse."

"Hush. Hush. Don't spoil my fun," Agina said, shaking her head.

"You know you want to," Adede said, teasingly shoving Agina with her hip, a knowing look on her face.

"But I am not ready for all of that yet," she sincerely said in a solemn tone. "I've been down this road before. This is important to me. For me truly connecting means time. Bonding means no sex. At least for now. Probably not for much longer because I won't last as many months as I thought I would. I need to connect in other ways first. Things are moving this fast because we connect so easily. Not because I am ready. Plus, this is *NOT* being done entirely like a traditional wedding. It's modified because we are concluding this at the end of three years. We need the time to get to know each other. Besides, traditionally I can live with him once the ceremony is over, if I choose to. You *all* need to stop treating this like we are getting married," she said, stretching out the sound of some of her words to add emphasis. "Traditional marriages don't take that long."

"Fine. Torture yourself all you want. Then keep coming to complain about how you are sexually frustrated."

"Torture! No, that's not torture. Torture is you all trying to convince me to change my mind about where I will live. Not only have I had to hear it for years, but now it's being shoved down my throat!"

"We really have been unfair to you," Adede said shifting to a sad expression as she spoke.

"Shhhh. We don't speak of it. Remember?" Agina whispered. They both laughed.

"You have to rush through your breakfast now. The elders are about to arrive to start the ceremony."

"I'm hurrying. I'm hurrying," she said as she began to eat.

Shortly after eating, they arrived at the entrance hall. Everyone was already there. Before they could even say a word, the elders began to arrive through the portal.

Three initiated elders came through the portal, standing before it. Because this marriage involved three council of elders' families, there were probably also three initiated elders at each of the other two council of elders' homes. Obuo's family were the only ones who were not council of elders, so they didn't need the portal ritual.

"Supreme Elder, our Ler Mahia, Agina Akongo. Good morning."

They used their spears to give the gestured greeting, then remained with their heads bowed as everyone else also bowed to Agina. Agina still hadn't gotten used to people greeting her in such a way, no matter how many times it happened after she got her powers.

It was especially awkward for her family who she grew up around to do such a thing. She wondered if she would ever get used to it as she looked throughout the room at her family who either had their heads lowered, or were down on one knee.

"Rise. Good morning," she said, the words feeling strange as they left her lips. They felt like something a queen should say, not her.

Moreover, she wasn't sure she could get used to the change in hierarchy. Everyone had to respect her decisions. They could only give advice. Maybe it wasn't so bad to have such responsibility suddenly placed on your shoulders when you wanted to change the world.

She always wanted to change a lot of things, but now that she was about to officially have Otiende by her side, she felt more confident. He was supportive of her, so it gave her more courage to speak up.

"Good morning Honourable Agot Achuka," spoke the oldest of the elders as the oldest usually spoke for the rest of the elders.

"Good morning Honourable Atieno Ayoo, Honourable Awiti Achieng, Honourable Agutu Aluoch. Thank you for proceeding over connecting our portals," Agot replied, also formally addressing them.

"It is an honour to serve our Supreme Elder," said Atieno

"Let us begin," said Agina as she gestured to the portal.

The portals in the council of elders' homes were a little different, not because they functioned differently, but because of the history they recorded.

In this case, the frame of the portal was much larger, and on it was the history of marriages and how the unions affected the titles.

At the top of the portal, a fan chart displayed the ten most recent generations. This half-circle chart featured concentric rings where each subsequent change appeared larger and resided in the inner circle. For instance, the second half-circle was split into halves, each representing a parent, while the third half-circle was divided into four sections for the grandparents, and so on.

The remaining vertical area of the portal exhibited names organised in rows and columns, forming a complex web that required instruction on how to follow the lineage since the sections changed in size and location, symbolising the lineage's progression across countless generations, making a linear arrangement impossible.

Currently, the centre of the fan chart above the portal has the names Agot and Obuo with the title underneath. It was the first time Agina was going to see the name-changing process, which was only witnessed by the family, every time the elder who was next in line to become an initiated elder, got married.

There had been a break in the ancient magical power that had been passed down. The last name that had the power underneath the title was over a thousand years ago. Before the powers were lost, every name before that up until Gor Mahia had magical power. The names of these chosen ones were coloured differently, gleaming in the light or dark like they were enchanted.

No one knew why the power stopped when it had previously continued on for millennia. There was probably a sense of relief for everyone to have the power show up again. A sense of pride. They had been like queens without their thrones for so long: unable to claim they were supreme above all.

Over the generations, an unspoken acceptance, that they had returned to the times before Gor Mahia, had grown. They had accepted that the gift that was passed was not infinite and it had run its course.

However, all Agina could feel was dread. She hoped the dread would pass once the discussions were over. She was glad she wouldn't be there while they talked. They began to gently drum the floor with their spears as the council of elders proceeded.

"Today with our ancestors as witnesses, we join in the first of our ceremonies for the union of Agina Akongo Odero and Otiende Okomo Oneko. Agina Akongo bears the power of Gor Mahia, commanding both nature and technology, entitling her to be our Supreme Elder granted the name Ler Mahia. The Council of Elder title of the Odero family of the Kager Clan, the Council of Elder title of the Oneko family of the Kalkada Clan, and the Council of Elder title of the Oigo family of the Karuoth Clan will be carried and passed on through this union. May your union be a marriage with happiness and may you be blessed with children," announced Atieno.

Everyone present started to cheer and ululate as Atieno entered a code and swiped a card. Everyone proceeded to drum the ground as loud as they could with their spears, and shook instruments that resembled a rattle.

Agina could also see the ancestors join in cheer and celebration. She wasn't sure how she felt about knowing that every time people had been calling ancestors to witness, they had been showing up, shifting from their spiritual dimension into the world she lived in.

Everyone began to sing and dance as they revolved around Agina in a loop. She stood in the middle as she danced and let them sing, allowing herself to be enveloped in their joy. They moved around her in a circle over and over again, as they all danced expressively.

As Agina and Otiende had suspected, all three titles had been passed on to them despite what they had previously denounced. The realisation sunk in that it wasn't like a magnet they could discard, but their titles were more like a compass, always returning to the North Pole.

A marriage was like a reset. It changed things. It was the reason why it was important to keep these records. Some of the records dated back to the time before their ancestors migrated to the land that became Dala; a time before countries as they are known today were formed.

It was the reason why elders had to learn ancient text; so, they could read the records on stone carvings or stone paintings, and papyrus. The pictures of these relics were displayed in their entrance hall; the original stone and papyrus were reserved and stored away. They needed to be able to accurately pass on information that had been written in this form.

Currently above the portal were Agina and Otiende's names along with Agina's power and the three titles. It was the longest text beneath any names in their history. Because all the text required more room, the concentric circles had all changed in size, becoming smaller as the centre became larger. Her name gleamed with that enchanted light that other magicians had. It was also historically the most amount of titles ever seen in a fan chart.

A different version of the same writing was probably in the Oneko family home and Oigo family home. It was like the three titles had merged, with their names being at the centre of all three portals. Usually, just families merge, not titles. For the Oneko family and the Oigo family, titles were merging once again.

She hadn't seen the moment the digital inscription happened. She was immersed in the celebration. She couldn't help but wonder how future generations would view their union; elders didn't usually marry elders. Would it be seen as something negative or positive?

The dancing and singing helped ease some of Agina's nerves. As the song concluded, the other elders from the other portals began to arrive. Once they had all stepped through, they greeted Agina in the same way.

"Connecting the four portals was successful. Your guests may now start to arrive," said Atieno.

"Please stay for our celebrations. I would like you all to attend the discussion," said Agina.

The elders all nodded. "As you wish, Supreme Elder," said Atieno. If any of them were surprised, they never showed it. They always seem to accept anything she says.

"Please show our guests their tent, then help them get settled for the discussions," said Agina, gesturing to her family. She still found it weird to speak like she was the head of the home, rather than her grandmother.

Everyone was anticipating what was going to happen in the discussion. They knew Agina was up to something because she had set up a tent with sofas and another separate tent with dining tables for the elders. She had also set up places for them to sit during the ceremony's discussion. When she was asked about it, she only gave a vague answer.

Agina found a way to slip past everyone into an unoccupied room to call Otiende. This time she projected a hologram of him into the room. They stood facing each other as they spoke. She spoke first.

"They accepted my invitation to stay. The rest is up to you."

"Good. Everyone is probably wondering what is going on. But they will have to accept how we will be sharing the responsibility."

"Do you think I should have told them why the elders are here?"

"I trust your decision."

"Thank you. And thank you for bearing this with me when I am supposed to carry it all on my own."

"It's best this way, not just for you but for our children. It will put less pressure on them to carry titles till they are older. And it's less pressure for us to have children right away. You made the right choice."

"We have already discussed this several times, but now it's happening. Now it's written over our portals. OT I..." No matter how she thought to say it, it didn't sound right. "This feels final. I am glad we can just live our lives now. Together."

"I want to hug you but I'm stuck over here." He lifted his hand. She also lifted her hand. They put their palms together.

"Do you feel that?" Agina sent a sensation through the hologram.

"Yes. That feels good. Can I feel it over here?" he asked, putting a finger over his lips.

"Let me try. Come closer." He slowly approached. "Closer. Here," she said, putting a finger over her lips.

She tilted her head up and the lips of the hologram touched hers. She sent the sensation to both sides, so she felt it too. It was a little bit of warmth with an ever-so-slight tingling sensation. He lingered for a little bit before separating from her.

"I'll kiss you later before it's over. I'll go first. Then you can find me." There was an understood hidden meaning he presented with that request.

"OT, that was such a long time ago that I used to look for you and I don't even know how I used to find you. What if I don't find you?"

"You always found me Agina. It's the biggest mystery."

"You just turned this into a challenge, didn't you?"

"I like a challenge. I also like to kiss you."

"I'll find you then. This time ask me to stay. You always told me I should leave."

"I always wanted you there. I didn't want you to feel like you had to stay."

"I always wanted to stay. We were friends. We are friends."

"I am lucky to be marrying my friend. I never dreamed I would find a love like this."

"Feels like this is how it should have been from the start. Like we should have stayed in touch. That's all in the past now, I will cherish these moments, not worrying about the past or future. It won't be simple, and our challenges will only increase. We have a lot happening in our lives at the moment. They say that the third time's a charm;

we've already parted ways twice before. This time, it feels permanent. This is it for us, right?"

"This is it. We won't separate again." They put their palms together again. A promise cinched and etched in their hearts.

They talked for a while, then they were interrupted by Otiende's alarm.

"I have to go get ready. I'll see you soon."

"See you soon."

She stood in the empty room for a moment, looking at the space where Otiende's hologram had been, and then she left the room.

FAIRY TALE 3

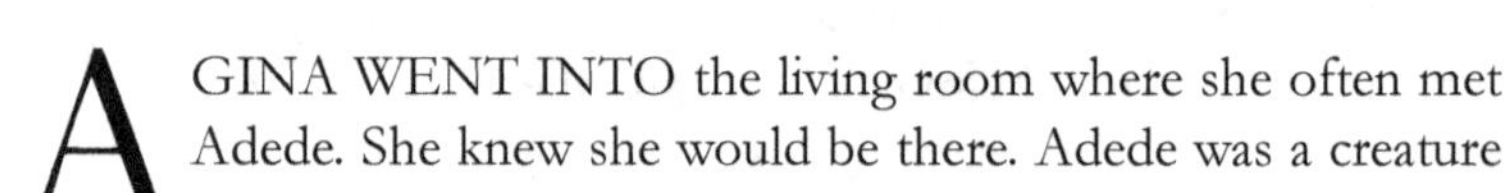

AGINA WENT INTO the living room where she often met Adede. She knew she would be there. Adede was a creature of habit. It's why being an elder came so naturally to her.

"There you are! I already went around looking for you and you were nowhere to be found. I just can't check every room, or go around screaming your name like this morning. *There are guests now,*" said Adede, then whispered her last statement, as she rushed to Agina.

"I was on a call." Agina shrugged her shoulders.

"I knew it was that again! Agina, it's your engagement day and you keep sneaking off to talk to him. For someone who managed to keep a com secret for years, it feels like a bit too much. You can resist using your com."

"You make it sound like I have ulterior motives or like I am not supposed to be talking to him. It's just a call!" Agina said with pouting eyes.

"Honey. You're the only one who thinks it's just a call. This is your OT. Come! Let's get you ready." Adede put her arm around Agina's arm as they walked together.

"You all talk too much." She leaned over slightly, gently shoving Adede with her weight.

"We all love you." Adede leaned over slightly, gently shoving Agina with her weight.

"I love you all too. You all still talk too much."

"No harm intended," Adede said, patting Agina's arm with the other arm.

"I know honey. But I can't always talk freely in front of you all. Unless I spell out all the boundaries that I expect. And even then you all just break boundaries!" Agina rolled her eyes.

"Sorry. We are open books." Adede held out her palm as she shrugged her shoulders; pretending like she had no clue about Agina's concern.

"No. No. Don't apologise. I don't know how you are more like them than I am. Uncle Oduor must have passed on genes from Dana that I missed. This place is yours more than it's mine." Though it had been long since Adede's father, who was also Agot's brother had passed, he still sometimes came up in conversations. Adede's mother was not brought up as often.

"But we have already said we won't talk about it, and I am bringing it up. Onto other things! Who got here already?" As they walked, Agina turned to face Adede looking at her expectantly for an answer.

Adede stayed looking ahead, eyes focused but distant. "We bring this up often. Even before you got matched. I can't help but bring it up too. So, first I must say, this is your place too Agina.

It's mostly just the aunts, uncles and little ones who are here every week. If anything they are late in comparison to other Sundays. They couldn't come any earlier before the portals were connected or else it would have been bad luck to have guests over before that ritual was completed. The kids are in the playroom as always."

"Let's stop by the playroom! Before I drown in today's events," Agina begged, shaking Adede's hand.

"Okay. But we can't stay long."

They took a different turn and walked into the playroom.

"Aunty Agina!" came a chorus of little voices the instant they stepped in.

"Hi! I'm so happy to see all of you! You all look so pretty and handsome!" Agina waved, using a higher pitch as she spoke loudly and clearly to the children.

"Auntie's getting married today!" said a little girl who looked like she was about 3 years old as she hugged Agina's legs.

Her dress had the same pattern as the bridesmaids. It was green, orange and white and had the same circular intricate patterns as Agina's tattoos.

"Hera, Aunty is not getting married yet. It's an engagement," she said, squatting down to be at eye level with Hera.

"What does that mean?"

"It means we're letting people know who our future partner is; the one we'll marry later. So, it looks like we're getting married, but we're not actually getting married yet."

"How is it not the same?" Hera looked at her with round expectant eyes.

"Hmm. It's sort of like... let's take a look at our plants and animals. How do they know when it's time to mate or fruit? It's not a date on the calendar. But a farmer like Uncle Obuo can choose a date when these things happen. Once he decides, it changes the things that he does before this date comes. Do you remember what he does to help the animals and plants get ready?"

She nodded a yes.

"We have decided we will get married three years from now, so these are the things we are doing to be ready for that day. Today's ceremony is how we let everybody know that we are life partners and do other things like unite our families. But it's not the date yet."

She looked thoughtful for a moment. "It's getting ready?"

"Yes! You got it! I am getting ready to be married. Sometimes people might not even have the exact date, but it changes the way they do things."

She hugged Hera.

"Do you remember what we practised?"

"Yes!" said Hera, giving a toothy smile.

"Good. Mom is going to help you if you forget. So don't worry about it."

Agina went around hugging everyone and asking them how they were before Adede rushed her out of the room. They continued to walk arm in arm.

"You are not in a hurry at all!" Adede was trying to move faster but Agina was holding back, her pace unchanging.

"You shouldn't be telling your daughter I am getting married! Can I get even one person who isn't saying I am getting married today?" Agina shook her head like she was exhausted.

"You are in the Innercity. That's a battle you will lose no matter how you frame it. Aiye and marriage go hand in hand. It means you are getting married. Or at least it's your first step. Either way, the words have become interchangeable even if they are not." Adede smiled like she had just presented something she was very proud of.

"You are right about that. Can't teach an old dog new tricks. But why do you all turn a deaf ear to me explaining that there are several other steps? That is also something that you all know. *You are all so biassed with traditions.*" Agina was whining as she spoke the last sentence.

"You are the one who went and planned such an event. It looks like a fairy tale wedding. Who are you trying to convince it's not a wedding? You even have so many initiated elders here. As if you don't have enough council of elders between the three families. I don't think such a thing has ever happened in history."

"You can't know that for sure! And no, I'm not going to check our history."

"Because you know I am right. It's unusual for so many elders to be gathered."

She turned to face Adede, feeling defensive. "Adede, don't you remember what it's like to get married? Give a girl a break. I'm loving this moment. And you're loving it too. I love... I just want to be with OT."

Her heart skipped a beat. She had been so close to saying she loved Otiende. Why did she almost say it? Did she love him?

She had said those words in such a short time when she was with Chloe. She had felt it was love at first sight and was already declaring her love to Chloe in front of everyone a week after she met her. After all she had been through, she felt like she wasn't sure what love was.

"Agina!!" Adede said, stopping them suddenly which startled her. She dramatically turned to face Agina.

"..." Agina stared at her blankly.

"You were about to say it. Weren't you? You were about to say you love him!" Adede pointed a finger at Agina.

Agina was still in shock herself and had not been expecting Adede to have realised what she was going to say. So, she just stood frozen.

"Ahhh!! I can't believe it! This day just got better!" said Adede as she looked like she was going to start jumping up and down in excitement.

Agina finally came out of the trance. "I said no such thing."

"Of course, you didn't say it. You *almost* did." Adede emphasised the almost as she spoke.

"Don't say that. And don't you dare tell a soul. What makes you think that's what I was going to say?"

"The way you said it. And honey, let's be honest, you fall in love fast."

"It's not really love. It's a sexual attraction." Agina turned away in defiance. She was not ready to accept that she loved him, much less discuss it.

"It's different this time for you and you know it. You might be getting married a month after meeting him too, but it's not the same. You can't even let yourself have sex with him. It's different. You love him for real." Adede's eyes gleamed with excitement and warmth.

"Seriously you all need to stop with the: I'm getting married. *Engaged.* Okay. And I really don't know if I love him. So don't say anything! Seriously. Not a word! And do you even know anyone other than me who got married in a month?" She looked at Adede with an eyebrow raised.

"There was... I don't personally know anyone. But isn't that how it works with that True Match app you used?"

"That I cannot argue with. But in all honesty, when I applied, I just wanted to date. Then I gave up on dating and told it to find me what I thought was impossible: someone in the Innercity that I was compatible with, who wanted to get married. Such a person was not supposed to exist. That was years ago." She felt like she sighed with her entire body.

"And now he is here, and you are marrying him. And you actually love him." Adede said, then gave Agina a long hug.

After a while, Agina said, "You really don't listen. Please stop saying I love him." They separated from the hug.

Adede had tears in her eyes and a large smile plastered across her face. "I'm happy for you. Let's go before I make you late."

FAIRY TALE 4

IT TOOK A long time for Agina to get ready. But as long as it took, they were not ready for Agina to be presented yet. Lunch had been served before the discussions as guests had started to arrive.

They served bull, goat, sheep, chicken, beef. All cooked in different ways. There was also tilapia, salmon, mudfish and lungfish. All cooked in two ways; stewed and fried. These were served with sides such as rice, *kuon, chapati, matoke,* sweet potatoes and various vegetables such as: *dek, alot, apoth, mito, osuga, obuolo* and many more native vegetable varieties.

They also had several fruits including wild fruits like *mapera, maembe, ochuoga and etch.* They had several non-alcoholic drinks as well as beer, wine, brandy, whiskey, including traditional brews such as *changa, busaa and otia.*

The food was all artfully spread in a buffet, fashioned in the same theme as the tables. The smell of the food seemed to travel for miles, calling people to feast on the carefully curated food that looked too good to dismantle.

Hired staff dressed in pristine white with tall chef hats, stood by the food ready to serve the guests. Other than the servers, they also hired people to help carry the food and service the tables. They wore white, the vests and collar of their suit jackets were teal, with their bow ties being bold orange. It all looked no different than a high-end fancy restaurant.

Since Agina couldn't leave the room yet, food had been brought to her. The discussions between the families were always unpredictable. You never knew how long it would take. They were not just discussing dowry and family matters. There was also the matter of the three titles that Otiende was unexpectedly going to bring up.

When the elders were discussing matters, it always took a long time. The elders were not all there, but she was sure those who were in attendance would have had their protests or opinions to share. Considering her superiority, people did not speak against Agina even when they did not trust her choices.

If they discussed it now, Otiende could take the time to hear them and ease their doubts. It was Agina and Otiende's hope that the elders would all walk away feeling more at ease with following through with the decision they had made regarding the three titles.

They felt like it was a better strategy than Agina declaring what she wanted like she did when she was ennobled as The Supreme Elder at her initiation. No matter what, they would follow her decisions, so it was the best way to respect their opinions and gain allies, rather than having followers like subjects. She didn't want to be the supreme ruler she was meant to be.

Agina, her bridesmaids, the hair stylist and makeup artist were talking amongst themselves as they waited. They had music playing in the background and light snacks and drinks. If you had not seen the way they had dressed, you would think it was girlfriends getting together and having a good time hanging out; enjoying each other's company as they talked and laughed.

The bridesmaids all had different dresses. Each one was designed to their preference but somewhere on the dress or throughout the dress, the same Ankara fabric was used. It was the same fabric Hera had on, with an intricate circular pattern in white, green and orange.

It looked like they were all out of the same fashion line that was launching new fabric, because of how each one was unique and designed in high fashion. Some had a headpiece, ranging in size, from large to small. Others had hair jewellery or beads in their hair.

Everyone's shoes were all white, but they were also not all the same. They matched individual outfits and were as per their preferences.

They all also had their makeup and hair professionally done and wore different accessories. Considering they had printed the fabric to match Agina's tattoos, they had been put together beautifully in such a short time.

Agina looked stunning in her dress, which featured the colours orange, white, green, and teal, in the same shade as the wedding decor.

The pattern was unique, with large orange stripes and smaller white stripes, decorated with a small black swirling line that formed a beautiful pattern. Teal and green circles were spread evenly across the fabric, giving it a beautiful mandala-like configuration.

The mermaid-style dress hugged her hips and spread out at the bottom, with a tapered slit that showed off her tattoos when she sat cross-legged.

The dress's waist was layered with a long cape that seemed to descend endlessly and filled the room with its presence. The top half of the dress was sleeveless and well-fitting, with an extra-large white fabric decoration that looked like a flower by her arm at the shoulder.

The tattoos on her arms and neck looked like henna, matching the pattern on her bridesmaids fabric. Agina's white stilettos added a touch of sexiness to the outfit, with white lace that matched her dress.

To complete her look, Agina's hair was braided and tied up in a large bun with pure gold beaded jewellery woven into it, while a beaded choker necklace and beaded bracelet respectively adorned her neck and forearm.

Her eye makeup was done in the same teal and green colours as her dress, with large lashes and raspberry lipstick. Her dark skin looked like it was glowing against the white and bright colours of her outfit.

Finally, Agina carried her spear which she got when she was 7 years old, she never missed an opportunity to take it with her.

If you saw her seated there with her spear, laughing and talking with the others, you were more likely to believe she was in the middle of a photoshoot, making a sexy pose that showed her legs. Agina tended to be sensual even when she didn't make much effort, it also helped that she was always elegant.

"Girls, they are ready for you," said Agot, coming into the room.

The relaxed atmosphere suddenly changed as everyone seemed to get up at the same time. Agot walked over to Agina and held her hand.

"Agina. You really threw us a curveball. We were all convinced you were going to denounce your title again... Denounce three titles, and avoid all the responsibility. You have grown so much in the last month," Agot said, looking Agina deeply in the eyes. It was obvious Agot had so much to say.

"Mom! Can we talk about it later?" Agina asked, feeling an awkward embarrassment under Agot's gaze.

"Yes. Now is not the time," Agot said, her demeanour easing.

Agot hugged Agina as she said, "Now is time to present you to the family and your OT. The council of elders decided to go sit with the rest of the guests now that the discussion is done."

"I know you said now is not the time to talk about this. But can I get a short version of what's going on?" asked Adede as she tried to get their attention.

Agot held Agina's hands and looked at Adede as she said, "Now that your sister here has three titles, she will be sharing them with OT. So, the two of them have three titles, rather than it being just her with titles. Technically Agina has four titles because she is also our magician: our Supreme Elder. Since she's initiated, he will join us as an initiated elder without having to be initiated. I will remain an initiated elder. You get to keep the title you have but you can't pass it on since that is now Agina's responsibility."

"And they agreed to that?!" Asked Adede in shock. Titles were never shared between spouses. Initiated elder seats were never added. She could understand Agina changing her own responsibilities regarding the title of Supreme Elder because of the work she wanted to do around the world, but she would have never imagined she would stretch the bounds to such an extreme. Merging the three families was already too much, considering how they usually track the family lineage as the generations pass.

"Yes. OT is quite the talker. I can see why he is popular and practically worshipped by some people," said Agot.

"Mom!!" Agina said, feeling embarrassed.

"You know what I mean. The man is well put together and even your family here who knows you are marrying him are still too excited to see him," Agot said, moving her hand nonchalantly as she spoke.

"Mom!!!" Agina nearly turned into ash from burning with embarrassment, Agot always seemed to have a way of saying things that made her want to hide.

"It's true. You can't have been with him all this time and not know this." Agot looked at her like she was innocent in causing Agina's reaction.

"Mom. Can we just go before I get too worked up giving a defence?" asked Agina, gesturing to the door.

"Yes. Let's get going girls. Who is going first? Let's line up and go," Agot said, shifting her attention to everyone else in the room.

FAIRY TALE 5

AGINA WAS AT the back of the line, her dress trailing behind her, while her bridesmaids were being presented one at a time before Otiende's groomsmen and family; they had to guess which of the people presented was Agina. Otiende's entourage had to correctly identify Agina, distinguishing her from her bridesmaids, so one by one they were sent back whenever they were not recognised as Agina.

"I'm so nervous," whispered Adede to Agina as they waited for their turn.

She whispered back, "I'm nervous too."

They continued to talk in whispers. "But you look so calm."

She had mastered the art of looking extremely calm. "Good. Because I am so nervous. I haven't met so many of them. Now I know what you felt like."

"Yours has to be worse. At least I knew more of Ochola's family when I had my Aiye. The family you are marrying into are both council of elders and his parents are celebrities. I would have kept wondering if they would like me because you are marrying into such high status. But forget about the status because you are at the same level of status, if not higher, as a Supreme Elder; I don't know how you can marry a celebrity. You avoid that a hundred times more than you avoid elder stuff."

"You are not helping at all. You're making me feel worse." She glared at Adede.

"Sorry. At least you love him."

"Hush. Not helping."

"I thought you would be happy to remember why we are all here? OT. You and OT."

Agina remained quiet for a while before she whispered back, "Thanks."

After Adede had gone into the living room, it was Agina's turn. She walked into the living room with her arm in Abura's arm, and their spears in the other hand. Everyone got up and bowed to her. Otiende was at the furthest end at the centre.

He had on a round collar formal shirt that was white. The shirt wasn't all white; a triangle with the same pattern as Agina's dress was on the right side of his shirt. The triangle went straight up the middle of his shirt then turned up beyond his shoulder to cover most of the back.

He wore white pants and white high-top dress shoes. Over the shirt, he wore a long suit jacket that was in the same pattern as Agina's dress. It dropped down to the length of his knees. The jacket had no buttons and a double collar that made it look like he had layered two jackets. The jacket collar stood up around the back of his neck.

Everyone sat back down after Agina told them to rise and get seated. Abura gave a brief introduction along with instructions. She then asked Agina to start by going around to greet everyone. Abura sat down on one of the empty seats. Then Agina started by shaking the hand of the person that sat closest to her.

"Hello," she said, still feeling nervous.

"Hello. This is definitely, Supreme Elder, Our Ler Mahia, Agina Akongo. Is there any doubt!?" he declared, as he turned to look at Abura.

People around the room laughed and clapped, as the bridesmaids returned to the room and found a seat. Agina grinned as she continued to say hello and shake everyone's hands. If she personally knew them, she would greet them with a hug.

When she hugged Otiende he whispered in her ear, "You look beautiful."

It made her stomach flutter, and she was sure she was also blushing no matter how much she tried to fight it. She also noticed his hair was styled differently. He usually maintained the same hairstyle keeping the shaved part looking freshly cut. But this time, the intricate twists and turns his hair did as it perched in braids, plus his open hair, spun differently. She was trying hard not to blush, so she didn't get a chance to tactfully tell him how wonderful he looked.

She continued around the room. Now that she had passed Otiende, she found herself ease, and become fully aware as she looked around the room. She noticed some of the people had an envelope that was green and orange. Did her mother receive an envelope yet?

In the envelopes was probably the gift Otiende gave them for the appreciation of Agina's birth and upbringing. She wondered if it was money, *e-pesa* tokens, or something else. She would never know. What was in those envelopes was traditionally an unspoken secret.

When she got to her father, he gave her a long hug. With the look on his face, she knew the day would not end without them both crying.

When she finally finished circling the room she sat down beside her mother. Everyone took a turn to stand up and introduce themselves, saying how they are related to Agina or Otiende, and gave a few words of advice.

As expected, when Obuo was talking about being Agina's father and wishing her the best, they were both crying. When he finished talking, she went over to hug him. They had always been close.

Agot was the last to speak. Standing proud, with her spear in her hand. When Agot announced that she accepted the marriage proposal everyone cheered or ululated. While the sound of excitement continued, they congratulated Agina and Otiende.

Of course, she mentioned that she was a little sad to let Agina go since they were not following the tradition of moving into the home. There was just no way she would go without talking about broken traditions!

That Morning Abura had already said they shouldn't bring up the matter. Agot usually listened to her mother, especially when she dismissed an important matter. Yet here she was announcing it in front of everyone.

It was like once Agina got matched and gained powers, Agot had expected Agina to suddenly become compliant and stop fighting her. But the daughter Agot had dreamed about having just didn't exist. Agina let the comment go because Agot said she was happy for them nonetheless.

Unexpectedly there was one last message: Agina's aunt Adika made it a point to make it clear that Agina had not been bought. That they had accepted the gifts because they were a sign of appreciation. She made sure to meet everyone's eyes, her eyes firm despite having the same gentle eyes as her sibling Obuo.

With everything concluded that the immediate family did behind closed doors, they left the living room area to go to the tents. The bride, groom, bridesmaids and groomsmen stayed behind to go out last.

FAIRY TALE 6

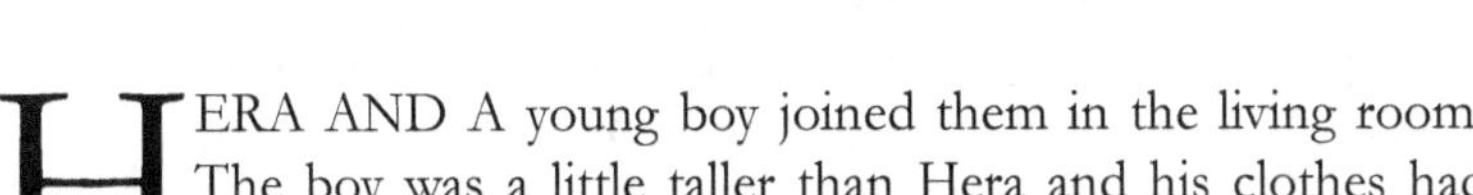

HERA AND A young boy joined them in the living room. The boy was a little taller than Hera and his clothes had the same pattern as that of the groomsmen who, like the bridesmaids, also had different designs and accessories according to their preference, paired with white shoes.

There was a difference with the groomsmen and bridesmaids in their Ankara pattern: the groomsmen's pattern was teal, orange and white with a dynamic triangular pattern that looked like it had futuristic influences. Because of the way the shapes overlapped it looked dynamic.

The complete group had finally come together with their patterns and colours a direct representation of both Agina and Otiende. There was a nervous excitement with everyone in the room like that of a performer about to go on stage. It was time for the fun part to begin.

After they received the go-ahead, the groomsmen formed two queues with the young boy at the front and centre, and Otiende in the back. They proceeded outside as they danced in unison to traditional wedding music that was upbeat with a strong fast beat.

The bridesmaids also lined up in the same way with Hera at the front and centre, and Agina at the back as they waited for the groom's entourage to go ahead. They cheered on the groom's entourage as they left and everyone in the tents got up to dance and cheer as the groom's entourage arrived through the entrance centerpiece. They were received like they were stars meeting their much-awaited fans.

The groom's entourage stopped at the central space surrounded by the tents, and danced a little longer before they all formed a single line and continued to dance as they waited for the bride's entourage.

Agina's entourage proceeded forward, dancing in unison as they followed the same path, with everyone cheering as they arrived. Her entourage also formed a line as they continued to dance. Surprisingly though, while Otiende was the star, Agina's lineup was received with much more vigour.

A large number of the guests and the professional traditional dancers circled both groups and cheered them on. At that moment Agina was glad she had made the choice to have a traditional wedding; being surrounded in that way induced Agina into a state of pure joy, deep down in her spirit.

When the dancing crowd had surrounded them, they formed a square perimeter, with the bridesmaids and groomsmen on either side. The song changed then Agina and Otiende danced a simple dance in unison with everyone, smiles and even laughter on everyone's lips.

They all danced in unison as they cheered and ululated even louder. The group of guests surrounding them got bigger as more family joined them, unable to resist the excitement.

The joy from the crowd was so infectious that it seemed like the birds had happily joined in song as they cheered and ululated. It seemed the flowers growing nearby had bloomed brighter and were dancing in the slight breeze.

When the song and cheers were done, one by one the crowd went to sit back down, the high from the singing and dancing still evident in their faces. Hera and the boy also left. The DJ thanked everyone as they went to sit, and also praised everyone.

As the crowd dissipated, they stepped back, so that there was more space between the two sides. They remained in line, forming a perimeter around an invisible stage.

The DJ announced that the groom's group were going to present a dance. Everyone cheered as a song started playing and Otiende and the groomsmen started dancing in sync.

It was a very energetic dance to a modern song in their ethnic language. Their shoulders and legs moving to the beat, matching the song's rhythm. Their faces were a clear expression of joy and happiness as per the lyrics, as some of them even sang along.

When the song was over, the DJ announced that the bride's group were going to present a dance as well, while Otiende's entourage returned to their line.

When the next song played the bridesmaids and Agina started dancing in unison while the groom's entourage stood in line and cheered them on. The crowd also cheered them on as they danced to a similar type of song, their hips and waists moving smoothly to the beat.

When the song was over the bride's entourage returned to their line. The DJ was an energetic man who ushered in the next part of the performances where they would be dancing in pairs. It was like he was raving up the crowd to watch a dance battle! The people in the crowd shouted out names of those they thought would dance better. Most of them yelled out Agina or OT. By the time the song started, the crowd was in full rave mode. If there was a tool to measure their excitement, it would have been measuring at the top.

The bridesmaids and groomsmen danced in pairs to their chosen song queued by the DJ. The songs were all modern, upbeat and in their ethnic language. Eventually, Agina and Otiende went last, building up the most cheers from the crowd.

All the paired dance routines were unique, as they moved in a synchronised manner that showed their individual talents, rather than following the same choreography.

On the last song in the queue, they all paired up and danced at the same time. Some of the moves were in unison but it was mostly synchronised unique moves, as they all joyfully danced. The dancing was the embodiment of the joy of their families coming together.

The DJ invited the guests and the rest of the crowd to join in and dance freely. For that song, everyone joined back in, with no specific order to where everyone stood, crowding around closely. Somehow, with all the singing and dancing around, the train of Agina's dress managed not to get stepped on.

The dancing crowd got bigger but soon Agina's energy level decreased. Likewise, people in their entourage got tired and started to take breaks in their respective tents. Like the council of elders' tent, their tent had relaxing sofas.

The tent sat their parents, grandparents, bridesmaids and groomsmen who were not all seated there at the same time; they were either still dancing, eating at a separate tent or moving about; they all also had designated dining seats in another tent.

The crowd continued to dance while others ate or drank. In the middle of all that exciting chaos the professional dancers were performing a dance. They were all dressed in matching outfits, with a different costume for women and men. Their outfits had a traditional inspiration, with feathers, sisal skirts, goat skin and ornaments made from shells.

"Excuse me," Otiende said to the others in the tent, shortly after the professional dance started. He leaned in and whispered to Agina, "Find me." Then he stood up and left.

"Where did he go?" asked Adede, as she leaned into Agina's ear.

Agina made up a lie, "To the bathroom."

Agina waited a while until the professional dancers were almost done with their dance performance, then got up to leave. She tried to leave as quietly as she could, holding the train of her dress. Adede gave her a questioning look and Agina put a finger over her mouth as she left.

When Agina got into the house she let the train of her dress go and let it trail behind her. She paused for a second then took a breath. She walked into the hallway and went towards the bedroom suits.

She went into one of the suites, then walked through its living room to its bedroom. She paused at the door then went around the bed. She found Otiende laying on a plush white rug, his white clothes almost blending in with the rug. He had propped himself up on his elbow, looking up at her.

"How long did it take you to look for me?" he asked with a sly smile.

"I just left. This was the first place I looked."

"I changed my hiding spot so many times and you found me at the first place you looked?! Agina, you have to be psychic or something."

He stood up. "Can you tell what I am thinking?" he asked with a grin as he approached her.

"No." Her voice was almost like a whisper. Like it had got stuck in her throat as she spoke.

He was standing right in front of her as she looked up at him. "You might not know what I am thinking but you can sense it. That's why you are like this. You know I want to take that dress off, lay you on the bed and make love to you right now."

"I..." This time her voice didn't even make it out of her mouth. Her heart was racing so fast she had no idea how he couldn't hear it or how it had not exploded yet. When she saw him lying on the rug, she had already been thinking about how she wanted to lay on top of him and forget about waiting to have sex.

"Don't worry. I won't. I can't help but think this way when I just made you my wife."

"Engaged. Not Married."

He burst out laughing. His laughter made her loosen up a little.

"Yes. Engaged. I still haven't done what I came here for. This time, when you found me, I won't ask you to leave. Stay a while with me," he said, piercing her in place with his gaze. Giving her an invitation that meant more.

"I don't know if I can. Right now, I don't want to just kiss you." With all the excitement of the day she felt too lax to hold any boundaries.

"I know. But I think you can only kiss me. Trust yourself."

"Then, come this way."

She picked up her train, slowly taking a step back as he followed, like a magnet drew him to her. She stopped when she stood with her back against the wall. She let her dress go then pulled him to her. There was a desperation in her kiss. She had anticipated this moment since they spoke over the com. Seeing him lay on the rug had spun her desires in another direction.

"Agina?"

"I'm fine."

"Am I making this too hard for you? Do you want me to stop?"

"No." There was almost a panic in her voice as she replied.

"I want you to know that we will not have sex yet. But do you want me to stop?"

"No." Her voice was more stable and confident this time. So, they continued to kiss.

She separated from him.

"OT."

"What is it? Are you okay?"

"Hold my hands above my head."

He stood for a minute looking into her eyes. Then without taking his eyes away, he intertwined her fingers with his on both her hands and slowly raised them till they were over her head.

"Is this what you want?" His voice was so seductive it sent shivers down her spine.

"Yes. Kiss me."

He obliged.

Put in such a position she felt like she didn't have to try so hard to hold herself back. So, she became more relaxed and more giving. She kissed him like she really wanted to. As they kissed, he raised her hands up higher over her head then held both hands with one hand.

With his free hand he cupped her breast and gently squeezed it. She felt her knees go weak as she somehow got the strength to give him more. It was like her body got weaker, but her desire got stronger. She was already in his mouth, so she deepened the kiss. It was like she completely became undone, her emotions and desires unstoppable.

He separated from her lips and leaned down lower to kiss her on her neck. He continued to caress her breast as he kissed her neck. She could only arch herself forward while tilting her head back, and moan as she experienced the pleasure. After a while of exploring her as he kissed her neck, he finally stopped but was still holding her hands.

"I can't help loving you," he said in a strained voice, his eyes closed, their foreheads together. Her heart was fluttering so much she wasn't sure why it hadn't taken flight as she looked at him Somewhere deep inside she knew what she felt, but it was buried too deep to be expressed, obscured by doubt. She gently bit her lip, closing her eyes, their foreheads still together.

Opening his eyes, he lightly kissed her lips then continued to speak, "I wanted to hear you moan. I can't quite hear it when we are kissing. We have to get back, but I don't want to stop." He was searching for her to stop him, looking into her eyes. But she couldn't resist him when he looked like he did. Like he wanted to completely devour her.

"Kiss me one more time." She could hear the pleading in her voice, but she didn't heed the warning logic was giving her for being too entailed.

She saw the hesitation to leave on his face and took it as her cue, closing her eyes and leaning forward. He met her halfway and they charged forward, his hand moving where it dared, to a place right before diving into the deep end.

He finally let go of her hands after kissing her and caressing her for a while.

"I need a few minutes in the bathroom then we can go." He gave her a light kiss on her lips and then went into the adjoining bathroom.

51

FAIRY TALE 7

GINA WAS STILL leaning against the wall in a daze, feeling helplessly weak. She touched her lips, as a smile emerged against her fingers. She stayed this way lost in her thoughts.

"Let's go," Otiende said, as he put on his jacket that he grabbed from a closet, where he had left it.

"Wait. I..."

"..."

"I need to go wash up. My body can only react after being touched in such a way. I don't want to have to stay in wet underwear." She was still too dazed to feel any embarrassment.

Otiende was thrilled. "I pushed it too far. But I have no regrets. I am only sorry I didn't finish what I started."

"No regrets either."

They talked as they walked to the room where Agina had got dressed. She had spent the night there, so she had brought some clothes to change into. She had spare underwear. She continued to talk to him through the closed bathroom door as she cleaned up. By the time she was done with the bathroom, she was talking about her morning.

"I came so close to telling Adede that I love you. I still don't know if I love you. I told her that I didn't know if I love you, but that ship already sailed. I can't convince her to stop talking about how I love you."

She noticed how he froze for a moment. Saying 'I love you' is something she would like to do. However, she didn't want to say it when she wasn't sure.

"Come here," he said as he walked towards her, stretching out his arms.

He gave her a long hug as he said, "I don't say it to you because I don't want to put you in the position of feeling like you need to say it back, or to make an awkward situation. You'll say it when you are ready. Don't say it till you know. I won't pressure you to say it. I have held these feelings for a long time. So, I am sure."

They were still embraced in a hug for some time after he spoke. They later let go of each other. She always felt like he understood her.

"Agina! Your neck. I left a mark," Otiende professed, looking intently at her neck.

"Is it really noticeable?" she asked, instinctively touching the spot where he had been kissing her.

"Do you think you can cover it up?" he asked, as she was looking at herself in a mirror.

"How long have we been gone?" she asked, still touching the spot as she looked at it.

He took out his com and looked at the time. "Over an hour"

"Do you want to stay here for up to another thirty minutes to try and figure it out? I don't use makeup often. This is not my makeup either. First, I'll have to figure out the right makeup shade for my skin but even then I am afraid it might stain the gold necklace, making the makeup look obvious. I'm not very skilled at putting on makeup, I didn't pay attention to how she made my makeup stay. You can tell she did a great job, because I didn't get any makeup on you. I don't think anyone is going to look at my neck, or figure out what it is if they do, with this dark skin. You didn't notice it right away," she said, making up excuses.

"Agina. They'll notice. Your Skin is flawless. We have been gone for a while. They'll know what it is."

"Sigh. I don't want to cover it. You're probably right. But even if they know, it's not a big deal, we just got married."

"Engaged. Not married."

They both burst out laughing.

"Let's just go. They already know we were up to something." Agina said, as she started walking.

Otiende's departure caught the attention of most people right away. However, when Agina left, fewer people noticed, and they didn't immediately make the connection that they were together.

When Agot noticed, she asked the others in the tent. Agina didn't usually leave her spear behind so having seen it on its own meant Agina was up to something. Otiende's mother suggested that they ask Otiende's bodyguards because they always knew where Otiende was.

None of them had even noticed that Otiende had his bodyguards there that day! After they asked the bodyguards whom they could now easily identify because they were standing watch in front of the house, one of the bodyguards simply responded:

"It would be in your best interest to not look for them. They do not wish to be disturbed at this moment."

Those who were slow to make the connection didn't remain in the dark for long either because the person who had been hosting and making announcements jokingly mentioned that the couple had disappeared together to have fun.

It turned out to not be a joke. No one had expected that they would have been gone that long. When they finally returned holding hands and looking like they were in bliss, people were buzzing about it for different reasons.

However, it was like they never noticed anyone, they were in their own world. They just happily went over to their seats as they were talking. Most guests had been dancing while they waited, finding ways to occupy themselves. Others were eating or drinking. Or just socialising.

They were supposed to have moved on to giving well wishes. Those who had complaints about having to wait didn't say anything in the end because the couple looked happy. It was especially heart-warming to see the way they looked together and to see how he helped her organise her dress before she sat down. It was like his world only had her.

The guests had also not complained because they had been enjoying themselves. They liked the non-structured time. It gave them time to bond while they talked, danced, ate and just had a good time. They were actually reluctant to have to quiet down while different family members took the microphone to speak and give gifts.

FAIRY TALE 8

WHEN EVERYONE WAS done giving their blessings and well wishes, and many tears and hugs were shed or shared, they handed the microphone to Otiende. Agina wasn't sure what was going on since Otiende didn't just speak but asked her to come along and stand with him in front of everyone, where they had been dancing earlier.

As he faced her, holding her hand he said, "Agina. I never knew how much I needed the friendship we had, until it was gone. You saw who I was, and you didn't want me to be anything else. I lost that. But now I have a friendship with you again. This time it's better. I don't want to lose it again. I want to spend the rest of my life with you. And I want to have children with you. Be a family. Today we also brought our families together."

He got down on one knee and continued.

"I love you. And I cherish the friendship we have. Will you wear this ring as a symbol of our love and partnership?" Otiende held out a small black jewellery box and opened it, showing her what was inside as the crowd cheered. Agina didn't know what emotions she had. She felt a lot at the same time.

She had already done so much crying, but it did not stop her from crying some more. She couldn't find the words to say either, so she nodded her head. He took the ring and put it on her finger. It looked like a classic gold three stone diamond ring. With a larger diamond in the centre.

What's more, she could feel there was something different about it. It had technology infused in the band. She wanted to see what it could do and ask him about it but now was not the time. He got up and gave her a hug, lifting her up briefly.

She was so overjoyed. She had only known what it's like to propose, and she had not expected him to get down on one knee with a ring in front of everyone; they had not discussed it at any point. Their plan was a traditional engagement. When they separated from the hug, they looked into each other's eyes.

The day felt whole. Complete. Except that, it was not because he completed her. It was because she felt like when she had him, she didn't need anything else. She felt secure when she looked into his eyes. He gave her the space to be her complete self.

Touching her face, he leaned in and kissed her and she put her arms around him as they kissed.

Then Otiende whispered in her ear, "Do you want to wait to put my ring on, so you don't have to do this in front of everyone? Don't feel pressured to say anything."

Often with engagements two rings are presented by the person who proposes, and if the proposal is accepted, they put rings on each other. He said that because he understood that she did not like being the centre of attention.

She didn't want to say she loved him at the moment. Nonetheless, at that moment, she did want to put a ring on him. She looked at him and shook her head. He gave her another jewellery box. She took the ring out and looked at it briefly.

It was also gold but had a single diamond. A wide band of green opal was ingrained around the middle of the band surrounding the rest of the ring. She could tell it had the same technology.

She put it on his finger. Because of the way opals reflect light, it looked like it was electronically lit up. It was the perfect ring for him.

She could have also said something to Otiende before she put the ring on. But all that came to mind was: *I love you too and I want to spend the rest of my life with you. Have a family together. You also make me feel like you accept me for who I am.*

Therefore, she remained silent, not trusting herself. They hugged each other again for a longer time as tears came down her cheeks. A rainbow was suddenly spotted in the sky as people pointed it out in awe, but Agina had not intentionally meant for the rainbow to appear. She was glad that with all the tears she had today, it was a rainbow instead of rain.

"Thank you all for joining us today," said Otiende, then he handed the microphone to Agina.

When Agina took the microphone, everyone got up and bowed. They were all family now. Agina hadn't expected it, so she was taken aback. Otiende also bowed along with everyone.

"Rise... Thank you all for coming today. Feel free to continue to celebrate. This day also celebrates you all and what you have done for us."

She handed the microphone back to Otiende who handed it back to the host who announced that the music and food would go on, and that they would now begin to take pictures.

Agina instinctively held out her palm and her spear came into her hand. Most people didn't know that Agina's spear was a com. The only time her com had clearly shown it had received a message was when she was in the tree receiving the message from True Match.

Otherwise, no matter what came through her com, it always appeared to be from the screen she projected. People don't usually wonder where the projected screen appeared from.

Therefore, people would never have guessed that even before her powers, she could call her spear into her palm by commanding it with words. They certainly would never have been able to guess that thanks to her powers she could telepathically control her spear because it was a com.

No one knew the extent of her powers but in that moment they all knew they were witnessing her use her powers. Agina was modest so she didn't use her power often. What she had just done was out of habit rather than as a display of power.

Holding hands, Agina and Otiende walked over to the props where they would be taking photos. Taking photos took a long time. It felt like every single guest lined up to take a picture, though most of the pictures were taken in groups.

As Agot had mentioned, there were family members who were excited to see Otiende. Consequently, they wanted a picture with Otiende. A group photo was the best they could do without looking like an obsessive stan asking for an autograph. Sadly, those who were excited to see Otiende's parents couldn't come up with an excuse to take a picture with them.

Otiende and his parents were not seen in the Innercity often, so it was a rare occurrence to have all three celebrities there. A lot of people had been lucky enough to get the photos with the three because of group shots. Once the photos were done, they silently waved goodbye and walked to Agina's house.

On cue at the wave, the bodyguards appeared just then to make sure they were not being followed. Similarly, people hadn't noticed the bodyguards were there that day, so they could only reluctantly watch the couple disappear down the path. They usually partied till later in the morning, so they felt Agina and Otiende had left the party too soon.

53

BUILDING TRUST

EVEN THE DEEPEST shadows behind layered juxtaposing leaves and branches seemed to come to light, as Agina and Otiende walked past. Their mood was bright and uplifted while they talked about their rings; their rings monitored several bodily functions like, heart rates, voice tones, sweat, their movement or location, as a more efficient way to read and understand the other person.

It was like having a therapist that could help you at the moment rather than visiting a therapist later, once a week, after things might have already escalated. Studies even showed that it improved relationships.

"It doesn't have to be fully set up. It's up to you what we do with it," said Otiende as they entered her home. Their entourage had been meeting at her family's home for the past two weeks, and he had been walking her home. It felt like the natural end to their day.

"Let's fully set up. After we try it, we can decide what to do moving forward."

She let her spear go and it made its way to where it plugged into the home. They were standing facing each other, as Otiende took her hand. His hands were large, so it made her small hands look even smaller. He held her hand as he looked at the ring then lifted her hand to his lips and kissed her fingers.

"Your fingers are beautiful. The ring looks good on you," he said, looking into her eyes. She liked the way he looked at her, like she was finally his, the weary look that said he couldn't believe she was here and would disappear at any moment, had gone.

"Thank you. I love the rings. You did a really good job with the design. I love how you used your colour on yours." She looked down at the ring and then looked back into his eyes.

"I thought it would be better for us to have something that is more like your way of doing things. Technology that is hidden."

"You're always so thoughtful of me. I should return the favour sometimes," she said with a smirk.

"I enjoy spoiling you and giving you what you need and want. That's enough for me." The smile hadn't left his face since the moment she first laid her eyes on him today.

"Even if it means I am holding back sex, marriage, children?" Though her mood was still uplifted, you could easily tell she had asked a serious question.

"Either way you're still my partner. We'll have time for those later. It shouldn't matter if they happen sooner. It's in your best interest to have them later. So, it's okay."

"If you truly see us as partners, I will need that to be the last time you will bow to me." She suddenly used a directive tone that would make even the most headstrong person bow. It was explicitly different from the gentle loving tone she had been using as she spoke.

Otiende burst out laughing.

"Seriously! I can take a lifetime convincing my family to do otherwise. I shouldn't have to convince you. You already know it bothers me," she demanded, poking him with a finger.

He was still laughing. When he finally stopped laughing, he said, "Okay. I'll stop. I knew it would bother you, but I can't help poking at you when it feels harmless!"

"Thank you!" she said, with a hint of sarcasm in her voice.

They sat down on her sofa, sinking into its supple material.

"Help me set these rings up. Can you connect them to our coms?" he asked as he took her ring off and touched the connect button. He put her ring back on and did the same for his.

"They are connected," she said, without touching their coms.

"Start the set-up."

Agina mentally went through all the prompts in the initial setup, and then tinkered with what it could do. She seemed to be staring into the air. "It's all set up."

"Great. It's wonderful having a wife who can just telepathically do these things at lightning speed."

"Fiancé. Not wife," she corrected. They both burst out laughing.

"I need to get out of these clothes before we have dinner." Having realised what that sounded like she blushed as she hurriedly said, "Change my clothes. I need to change my clothes."

He grinned mischievously as he said, "Go ahead and take them off. I won't look. I'll turn around."

"I'll change in the bathroom. It's fine."

"Agina. I need you to feel more relaxed around me, especially when we are at your home. Take them off here. Do me a favour and trust me." With his change in tone, he didn't seem to be joking around anymore.

She couldn't refuse now that he seemed so serious and had baited her by calling it a favour and asking for her trust. At the same time, it was herself she couldn't trust. "You're asking me for so much constraint."

"You already have so much constraint. I'm just showing it to you, so you won't put so much distance between us."

"But it's a problem that I don't want to have any distance between us. That I want you all the time and that I think about you all the time," she confessed.

"Hush," he said, putting a finger on her lips. Then he continued.

"I do not think it's a problem. We both desire closeness and a very intimate relationship. It's the way we are. It's mutual. You're not going to crash because you're going too fast or be enmeshed with me. Stop imagining a nightmare. We are still taking it slow. We have set clear boundaries. Close the distance between us. Okay."

She nodded her head with his finger still on her lips. He took off his finger.

"Turn around," she said.

She went over to her closet once he turned. She touched a panel, and a screen came on. She selected the clothes she was going to wear on the screen then it was brought to her.

She looked at his back and took a deep breath as she started to take off her accessories. After she was done taking them all off, she took off her dress.

She stood in her lace underwear and strapless bra that didn't match as she put away the clothes she had just taken off. She tried to remember what she did to her other underwear that had matched as she put the dinner dress over her head. She then took off her bra and put it away.

She tied the top of the dress around her back and neck then looked at herself in the mirror. The same pattern she had on earlier was on her dress from her waist down. The top half of her dress was white.

Her heart had been racing since she walked away from him, and she felt like she had been holding her breath. She couldn't imagine what it would feel like to get dressed when he watched. She was too shy to dare.

Yet when she was undressed, she hoped with all her heart that he would turn around and walk over. That they would finish what they started earlier in the day, and he'd take her right there as she leaned against the closet. She had watched him from the mirror as she silently imagined and wished he would turn.

Having her clothes on, she felt like she could relax and dispel the thoughts. However, looking at how the top of the dress looked more like a bathing suit, with her entire back and sides exposed, except for the straps, she wondered why she had thought the dinner dress was a good idea when the clothes were being designed.

The bottom of the dress was long and flowed outward like a maxi dress. It was comfortable. However, she couldn't help but think of how it felt when he touched her earlier. Wasn't she the one who set the boundary, yet she did not want the boundary anymore? She tended to prefer a sexy look, but wasn't she trying not to have sex with the man she knew she would provoke once he turned?

The thought sent a jolt of lightning up her spine and her heart that had calmed started racing again. For the first time since she had hit that phase in pre-teenagehood, she found herself considering not dressing too sexy. She walked up to him and stood in front of him. "Done," she announced, then did a slow spin.

He had his eyes closed so he opened them and looked at her as she spun. He had seen her in a swimsuit before. She knew he had seen more. But he just sat there gaping.

"That dress looks really good on you," he finally said.

She felt his sincerity. She knew he hadn't had any ill intentions when he asked her to feel free to undress. Agina felt bad that she had ruined the moment.

"I am sorry I keep pushing you away. I didn't want to compare you to Chloe or imagine the worst, but I am still making those comparisons. It's affecting how I treat you. I was always texting too much, calling too much, wanting to spend too much time together, wanting to cuddle too much, always wanting to cuddle after sex, wanting to know what she was doing too much, nagging, clinging, possessive. You know this story already #1008 when I confided in you then. We had different intimacy needs. Unfortunately, the sex was damn good. It's why our relationship got better after the divorce. We finally had the distance between us, and we were focused on sex. I know there is a difference between putting people at arm's length. You know, the distance. And taking things slow. But sometimes I can't tell the difference. So, I end up pushing you away."

"I know. Come here," he said, gesturing for her to hug him.

54

TRUE FORM

SHE WALKED OVER to him on the couch, to his outstretched arms, lowering herself into the couch and into his arms. She leaned into him, feeling enveloped by him. She knew she was wrong, yet he was the one making her feel better. As he hugged her he said "Thank you. But you don't have to apologise. This is new for me too."

"How? What about Aliana and Gabriella?" she asked, turning to face him on the sofa. She could still feel the heat from where he had held her when they hugged. She thought again about how her bare skin was a bad idea.

"We were close. You know I still keep in contact with them. I loved them. But I have never felt such a pull to anyone like I do with you. We are compatible in more ways. The two biggest differences are, intellectual. Like I said, you're the smartest person I know. Your intelligence is not just focused on one subject like the other smart people I know. And the other difference is sexual. I have never wanted anyone as much as I want you. I felt it the moment I saw you in that cafe. Just being close to you makes my heart beat faster. My lust for you makes me feel like I have no control. But I love you too much to just ravish you. I love everything about you. I love how you look in that dress... May I take pictures with you?" he asked, changing the topic.

"Yes. Your com?" She was sure she had not fully processed what he said. If she truly thought about it, it would change the way she should treat him as well as change the perception of how she thought he saw her. He had strategically asked that question at the end, giving her an exit from discussing it. Therefore, she shamelessly took the exit and focused where he offered.

He took out his com and gave it to her. "I don't want to pose for the camera though. I have done enough of that today. Can you do the thing where you make it take pictures through the night?"

"Yes. I would like that too. I don't think I have ever posed for so many pictures! I would never be able to make it through a photoshoot." They both laughed.

After they had some of the food from the Aiye for dinner, they were both lying on the cushions in the sunken seating nook under her bed's platform looking at her painting.

"I don't have anything electronic under here. I used to complain about tech dead zones, yet in the end, I built one into my home. Or maybe I have surrounded myself with too much tech, so a place with the lack of it feels different when it's really not. These days, when I lay down this way and just let go of everything. I can feel it all. I feel the connection to everything electronic. I feel a connection to nature. To all beings. I even feel the connection to inanimate objects. I don't know what it is. But here I can truly expand beyond myself and stop limiting myself or compartmentalising everything. I just am. And when I turn off the lights..."

She mentally turned off all the lights. Her painting changed almost entirely. All the mystical creatures and spirits could now be seen glowing in the dark. Some were in the night sky, some in the day part of the painting. They were different varieties, and their sizes were different and inaccurate.

"It's beautiful," he said.

She became very aware of him lying next to her. Her eyes still hadn't adjusted to the dark. They were cradled in opposite directions like celestial bodies in historic art, spread on opposite ends of the canvas, with a narrow space between their ears at the epicentre; she rested on the northern horizon of the sunken nook, while he occupied the southern expanse, their bodies diverging yet their heads converging towards the centre.

She turned to look at him. She could feel his heart beating. Something new she sensed now that she had the ring on. She could smell the faint scent of sandalwood. "I think they are all out there. We just can't see them."

"You've always been attuned to them. I think that's why they have a presence for you." She laughed lightly. Judging from where his voice was coming from, he had also turned to face her.

"So, you don't think it's crazy? I don't tell people these things," she asked, still feeling sceptical.

"You are multidimensional. It's one of the things I love about you. You're not just one thing. All the people who I know that talk about spirits in such a deep sense, run from me. You're the first one who didn't and came to me instead. You didn't have to tell me about believing in spirits. It's in the way you accept the unknown. I can tell when it's not your Science or Maths brain going."

"When I'm here and I've let go of everything, I feel multidimensional," she said, realising it was the first time she declared this part of her, truly owning it.

Her eyes had now adjusted to the dark. There was some moonlight coming from outside. She moved closer to him and kissed him briefly, a meeting of north and south, getting acquainted with the sensation of kissing him while he was upside down. Then they both moved closer together and continued kissing. They both held each other at the back of the head as they kissed, cradling their heads into position.

The kiss was like gentle rain when it was welcomed. They welcomed each other with every drop, gently caressing. Collectively they were like the force of rain gently changing the landscape with time.

After they had kissed for a while, they cuddled together. They had adjusted positions. He lay down beside her and she had her head on his chest while his arm was around her shoulders. He was firm but warm. Somehow, using him like a pillow felt better than her perfectly comfortable pillows.

"When I feel everything, it's like having on lights of different colours. When they mix you can't really see the colours. You just see white. That's how everything related to my powers comes together to create an overall sensation. I don't always feel the specifics, I feel it all together. But today you are here which made me realise... I don't know why I can always find you. I can find you in the midst of all that, where everything is connected. It's like no matter what, I can still distinguish your coloured light from the white light. I feel your presence. Not just here..." she said, placing her hand on his chest.

"I feel it there," she said, gesturing towards her painting.

"And with these rings..." she said, interlacing her fingers with his and continuing.

"I can read what it's picking up and analysing, so it can send information to our coms."

She turned around to face him, propping her body up with her elbow as she held her head in her palm.

She asked, "Is it too much? Don't you need boundaries? I shouldn't feel you all the time."

"Can you stop it all completely?" he thoughtfully asked, caressing her head.

"Not really. I still don't have complete control of my powers. I now know how to block my powers, but I cannot do it for an extended time. Not only is it exhausting to try and stop it, but finally letting it go is like opening a floodgate. You know how it goes when my powers spiral out of control. It's worse when I release the hold. Sigh. Having powers feels like I don't own my headspace anymore. That feeling of overwhelm only goes away when I am here, letting everything go and feeling it all."

She moved back to the previous position, laying her head on his chest.

"It's fine with me. I thought the rings might be that way for you when I got them. Wouldn't it be better to not block any of it? To just feel everything all the time?" He rubbed her arm with the arm that was around her shoulder.

"Do you remember what it was like for me when I first got the power?"

"Yeah. You couldn't control any of it."

"Here, I lay in silence. Almost like I am meditating. No matter what, it's always manageable. When I am in movement going about my day, it gets too complex. There is too much information to process. Sometimes I can't even tell if what I am seeing is in the past, present or future. I'll even sense too much, like what is in other dimensions. Do you remember how I would get lost when I was trying to create portals?"

She continued without waiting for his reply, "When there's too much info coming in at the same time, even though I am trying not to teleport, I'll find myself in a state where I can't properly discern space, causing me to teleport. Maybe I tried to create portals when my power was still too new and unstable. I block my power because I sense too much at once. Also, it gets worse when my emotions are involved." Saying it out loud made it seem worse. She had accepted it without giving it much thought.

"That must be very overwhelming. I didn't know you could see the future. That would make sense considering Gor Mahia was greatly known for his ability to tell the future. Does having the power get any easier over time?" She could feel his chest move as he spoke.

"It doesn't. It gets harder. My powers have been evolving. I have just learned to adjust faster. So as bad as the effects are of releasing the hold, I block it or some parts of it, just so I can get a break from sensing too much at once."

He kissed her forehead and rubbed her arm.

"Will you stay here with me tonight?" she asked, leaning into him.

He squeezed her arm. "Do you want me to leave early tomorrow, or should I send my stuff over so we can leave together?"

"Either one is fine. It's up to you."

"I'll send my stuff over."

GOOD MORNING

WHEN AGINA WOKE up she didn't immediately recall that Otiende had been there the whole night. She became aware of it when she read the report on how she had slept. It also had a report on how he had slept. Reading her sleep report was always the first thing she did when she woke up.

She lay in the middle of her king-size bed, seeming to be drowning under her comforter and pillows, staring at the report. Her mind still seemed to be asleep, not catching up fast enough with what she read.

Her eyelids still felt heavy with sleep. Opening them and closing them when she blinked seemed to be a task. The translucent screen hung over her, patiently waiting to be dismissed as it showed the text, charts and tables.

She slowly sat up, feeling like she was finally waking up. She looked around but she didn't see Otiende. She knew she couldn't see the entirety of the room from where she was, but it was silent enough for her to know he wasn't close.

When she thought back, she didn't remember getting in bed. Plus, she definitely did not remember him getting in or out of bed. She had fallen asleep in the sunken seating nook. She was a deep sleeper, so he must have carried her onto the bed after she fell asleep.

She was still in her dinner dress and her hair had not been covered. She tried to imagine Otiende carrying her up the stairs, but she could only burst out laughing. She couldn't imagine it.

"Someone woke up in a good mood! Good morning."

She leaned over and turned to see Otiende in a towel, standing by the bathroom. He was drying his hair with another towel. She suddenly stopped laughing. She was staring at his bare chest. When they had gone for a swim, the light had not been this good, so she hadn't taken a good look.

She could clearly see why he was a model. He was not only handsome, but he had the kind of perfect body people spent countless hours photo editing or that people used filters in real time to imitate.

"So handsome!" She found herself saying.

He grinned. "Are you coming down? I won't bite. Well unless you want me to bite."

She laughed as she got out of bed, dismissed the sleep report, and started straightening the bedding.

"Do you always wake up so early?"

"Most days I do. I like an early morning run. I got a running trail from your house and went for a run. Today I had ran later than usual because I was looking at the pictures from yesterday."

"Were the pictures any good?" she asked, just as she finished straightening the bedding.

"Any picture with you is great."

She blushed as she came down the stairs and the platform began to rise. By the time she had got down to his level, the steps had disappeared. She walked over to him. "No biting!"

"Can I at least kiss you?" asked Otiende.

"I haven't brushed my teeth yet!" She hugged him.

"Come on. It's like waking up next to you and kissing you before we get out of bed."

"Fine. That's your loss. But you still have no clothes on."

"Yet you still gave me a hug. May I have a kiss?"

She laughed. "Yes."

He planted a playful peck on her lips then put a hand through her braids. "You are beautiful when you sleep and even when you wake up," he said as he continued to put his hand through her braids.

As she felt the sensation, she thought of how he had helped her take the gold out of her hair after dinner. Now that she thought about it, she was glad she also took off her makeup then. If she hadn't, she would have slept with it on.

"I fell asleep. Then when I woke up, I saw..." She couldn't finish the sentence. She just ended up blushing instead.

"I kept thinking I would wake you when I brought you up to the bed, but I don't think I would have woken you up even if I tried."

She nodded, "I sleep like a log. It was a long day. Today should be easier."

"Are you ready for today?"

"I am. But honestly, it's because you are going to be there with me."

"There couldn't have been a better reason for me to come back to the conferences." His lips were curved in a smile.

"Yeah. We both walked away from this, but we still ended up being politicians. Yesterday was our family and people who love you. Today will be different with people who... I don't want them to talk to you how they used to. Is it okay if I stop them? Though honestly, I still can't control what happens when I get upset. I can't promise I won't accidentally strike them with lightning. A thunderstorm can never just disappear once it starts."

Otiende laughed.

"You are actually a little scary when you get upset," he said, raising one eyebrow.

"It scares me too which makes matters worse because I have less control when fear is added. I wouldn't even raise my voice before all this. Now even if I still don't raise my voice, I cause chaos. Will I ever be okay?"

"I don't know. It's like learning to walk. Give yourself time."

"I hear that too often."

"You have got better. Give yourself some credit."

"But I am mentally exhausted. I really need to take the time to figure this power stuff out. Like some training. But I am all alone. What I learned from my Mom and my Dana is like giving someone a book on how to swim. Then expecting them to figure it out when they have never even seen someone swim. I have no one to help. Gor Mahia was granted his powers by his grandfather. He was the first. Others before him did not have power, so he was also alone, but he was still a magician who came from a family of magicians who practised magic. Now it's a lost practice. It even lost its value in our sacred circle; they only focus on the practice of healing herbs as witch doctors."

"I can't help you with your training. But I am here to support you. I can help you track down some practising magicians. If we don't have them in Dala, our tribespeople from other countries might be able to help."

"Thank you," she said, hugging him. She knew he was a person of resources and could find anything.

"I need to go get ready. I'll go take a shower. So you can get dressed," she said, stepping past him and walking towards the bathroom.

56

PASSING IT ON

WHEN AGINA GOT in the bathroom, music started playing. She liked to listen to music while she got ready. Sometimes she danced while she showered, making rhythmic movements out of the process. Other times she sang out loud. It was more about enjoying herself, shamelessly singing off-key, with some performances sung at the top of her lungs. When she had just got in the shower, she heard the alert that her father had come through the portal. There was no chance to sing or dance.

She wondered why Obuo would have come to her home, at this time in the morning. Out of everyone in her family, her father had visited her home the greatest number of times, but he came so rarely that a year could easily pass without him coming.

Instinctively, she wanted to postpone the prompts that she knew would have come up. However, once she focused her attention on the system, she felt that Otiende had already taken care of it. She could feel that the prompts that had come up had been dismissed.

She was so preoccupied with wondering what could have happened that she went through the process of taking her shower without being fully aware of what she was doing. When she was done with her shower, she wasn't sure what to do because she knew her father was still there.

She quickly dried herself off and then put on a robe. It was a plush luxury bathroom robe she never used, that was placed there more for decor, but she knew it would cover more than her towel. Just as she was leaving the bathroom, she heard the audible alert that Obuo had left through the portal. Instead, she found Otiende who had not finished getting dressed.

She wondered what kind of thoughts her father had when he saw Otiende partially dressed. But she was more curious about why it seemed to be an urgent matter that prompted him to visit her early in the morning and leave without saying a word.

"What did you talk about? Is anything wrong?" she anxiously asked, trying to read the expression on his face.

"Everything is fine. He brought this over." Otiende walked over to the dining table and showed her their family shield that had been placed there, then continued speaking.

"He asked if you could carry it today when you went to the conferences. He came early because he wanted to give it to you before you left. He wasn't expecting to talk to me instead."

Agina walked over and took the shield, then sat down with it at the dining table. She observed it closely like she was seeing it for the first time. But she was remembering moments from her childhood.

She remembered how Adede would be so interested in such things and pretend she was an elder, long before she lost her parents and became adopted into their family; Adede had always lived there till she got married and moved out. In contrast, Agina would always complain about how everything the elders did was boring, she was not one to sit still.

She would always ask so many questions and want to change the traditions that didn't make sense to her. Her mother had tried to be patient with her and had Adede attend the lessons as much as possible, to help keep Agina interested.

Though Adede's presence helped Agina not get too bored with the lessons, it never changed anything. She still hated it. It just made Adede happy to be able to learn or participate in things she would never have been able to.

Agina couldn't do anything with technology, which she was interested in. Because she knew what it was like to be shut out of something you are interested in, she could only be happy for Adede and keep giving her that opportunity; it became the only reason she participated.

It was always clear Agina was disinterested; she wouldn't cooperate with participating, she would either be doodling or even fall asleep, often getting into arguments. If Adede didn't show up, Agina would walk away from the lessons or not show up entirely, no matter what the consequences were.

"I can't just pretend I want this now. I still want to be true to myself. This is not me," she said, then put down the shield and pushed it away. At that moment she had deep doubts. What was she doing now? Why had she accepted this path? Why didn't she try to fight it when she had fought it her whole life? Was it too late to escape all that she had taken on?

"I am doing this for us. They should understand that after the discussions yesterday." There was irritation in her voice. She was not entirely sure who she was irritated with.

He stood behind her and massaged her shoulders. "He understands. We talked about it. But the shield still needs to be passed on. So, it's in your hands now."

She sat silently as he massaged her shoulders. She hadn't realised how tense she was. It helped her relax, feeling like the tension was melting away.

They probably chose her father to come over because they were closer, so she would be less likely to get upset and start a raging storm. She somewhat felt cheated: he didn't even face her before he left.

She thought about how the council accepted that her title could be passed on to Adede when she left for the Outercity to get married, so Adede moved back into the house. She had not even had her Supreme Elder status when she made the request.

So, she voiced a thought that came up, "If it needs to be passed on and it's in my hand now... May I pass it on to you?" she asked, looking up at him. He wasn't just family now, sharing her last name. Because of her request at the Aiye, he had the titles that she had, so she thought it shouldn't be a problem.

"Will your conscience be clear, especially when people have an opposing opinion about whether I should have it? I also don't want it to be something you're passing on like a hot potato when you don't want to burn your hands. I want you to pass it on because you think I should have it. Not because you don't want it. I need to know how you feel about this."

She stopped looking at him and turned her head to look forward. He was still massaging her shoulders.

Staring into the distance, she spoke, "This stuff is all symbolism. This one is a symbol of higher status. Elders don't carry them often, especially when they are all going to be there. It's because they don't want one to be higher than others; there is always someone who refuses to carry the shield since it's too troublesome. So, it's been that they all have it, or no one has it. This way, it's an accurate symbol that they all have the same status. Family symbols are on shields. This shield, or should I say symbol, has been carried by Supreme Elders in the past, especially when other elders were not carrying their shields. I know I should logically carry it because I am The Supreme Elder. But I have seen how people are around you. Your fans. No one behaves like that around elders. And it's not just in Dala. It's around the world. People see you as someone special; like you have a higher status. And it's rightfully earned. You have three titles now. Everyone else has one. Even before you gave up your title you still had two titles you should have passed on… You should carry it. It would feel right if you carried the Odero family shield."

She turned to look up at him. "This symbol is yours more than it could ever be mine. So will you carry it and have it be yours in every way?"

"I told your father that it was more likely you would ask me to carry it instead. And that I would accept it if you asked."

"How did you know I would ask!? And why did you make me give that long speech!!" She was not sure if she was more mad or surprised.

He laughed, "I would rather hear you say what you feel even if I think I know what you might feel."

"You know me too well."

"Your father said the same thing. He said he was impressed with how I spoke on your behalf at the discussion. And even today, how I said you wouldn't carry it."

"You are too happy about that."

"I think I can safely say I won over your father's heart. Without even trying! It's even better than taking an oath to protect you with my life. The love between you two is irreplaceable. Also, your whole family. But his good grace is priceless!"

They both laughed.

"You read me like a book. I think I talked too much to you in all those messages #1008." She sometimes called him #1008 as an endearment.

"Shh," he said, putting a finger on his lips, then got back to massaging her as he whispered, "The walls will hear you calling me that."

Returning to speaking regularly, he continued to say, "I couldn't talk about the things that would let people know who I was. But with you it was different. I wasn't playing the person I made up. I was myself. You know things about me too, and you understand me like no one else does."

She looked up into his eyes, then held his arm by his wrist and nudged him to come down. He got on his knees beside her chair. He put his hand on her face, at her jaw and kissed her as he gently held her face.

57

BACK TO THE START

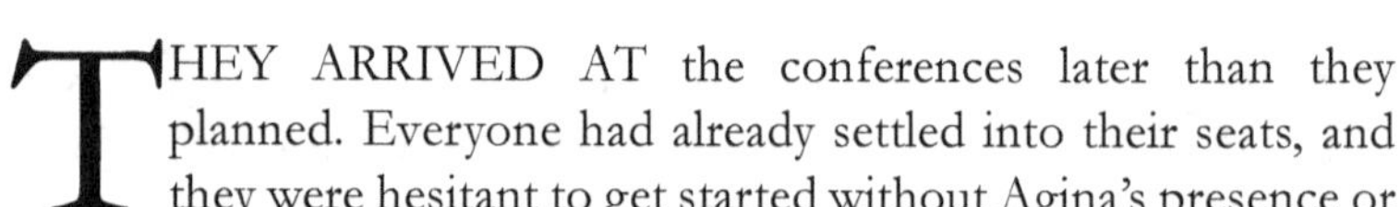

THEY ARRIVED AT the conferences later than they planned. Everyone had already settled into their seats, and they were hesitant to get started without Agina's presence or to decide to do anything alternatively.

Several meetings usually took place at the same time during the conferences. The initiated elders would split up for most meetings. But usually, they stayed together for the meetings on the first and last day.

Some meetings also took place in the Outercity. The meetings in the Outercity would sometimes include leaders from other countries.

The leader of Dala would also show up in at least one or more meetings but he could not enter the Innercity. Not only did he lack access to the Innercity, but he had no authority there. It was self-governed.

The council had authority both in the Innercity and the Outercity, but their execution of authority in the Outercity was not as prominent.

There was a mutual agreement that the council would handle the Innercity because it suited their methods better, and the leader of Dala and his governing body would handle the Outercity. But it wasn't a formal agreement, and it wasn't put into writing.

On this occasion where both sides participated, you couldn't help but notice the residents of the Innercity were the only ones that used the terms Innercity and Outercity. The conferences were the time when the Innercity and Outercity would come together to discuss the plans and well-being of the people of Dala. Major decisions were made at these meetings.

The conferences were usually broadcast so that people could see what was happening if they were not able to physically attend. On the morning of the first day of the conferences, there would only be one meeting everyone attends, similar to an opening ceremony. Then later, they would split up and hold several meetings at once. Then the ending was more like the closing ceremony or concluding summary.

Therefore, everyone was focused on this one meeting and they were waiting in anticipation, whether they were in the room or looking at their screens.

Word of Agina and Otiende had not spread, but no matter what you knew, because of the empty seats and the nature of the wait, you knew they were waiting for two people, one of which was the most important person. So, they waited cluelessly, only knowing about Agina who has recently become their Supreme Elder. Unless they were at the Aiye or an initiated elder, they were not expecting Otiende to show up.

When they arrived, the huge double doors were open wide, and held open on either side, as Agina and Otiende walked in. Everyone's attention suddenly turned to the doors like they would if a bride was walking into her wedding.

She had her hand in Otiende's firm yet gentle hold as they walked, her hand was at the top and his hand was at the bottom. It looked like he had just done the gentleman thing of holding out his hand to ask for a dance and she had agreed, gently placing her hand in his so he could lead her to the dance floor.

It was a large hall that probably sat a thousand people. Everyone simultaneously got up and knelt on one knee, their heads slightly lowered, while the elders seated at the front remained standing but lowered their heads. They held their positions in silence as Agina and Otiende passed, moving from the back where the doors were, to the front of the room.

The first thing anyone would notice was Agina's and Otiende's coordinating outfits, their outfits were a mix of Innercity and Outercity styles. In certain places on their outfit, an interlocking pattern changed colour to a beat that seemed to match their steps.

Agina created a slight gentle breeze that made their clothes gently flutter with the breeze. It was a breeze that only they could feel.

She held her spear in her right hand and Otiende held the shield in his left hand. They were both smiling and would occasionally look at each other as they walked then look forward.

In her usual style, she rocked a cool-looking sleeveless catsuit on the right side, mixed with a long Ankara dress with a hood on the left side. The outfit had a unique diagonal asymmetry.

Completing the ensemble was a black belt with straps, emphasising her narrow waist, along with stiletto boots with an interlocking pattern, that lit up in changing colours.

She added a touch of edgy flair with accessories strapped to her right thigh and upper arm, resembling leather armour. The accessories had an interlocking pattern that matched, lighting up in sync with her boots.

Her braided hair was partially up in a bun, while the rest cascaded down, crowned with a stunning gold intricate piece that stood tall, adorned with small diamonds and a few orange opals, that gave the overall impression of a sparkling diamond crown. The complete look was undeniably spectacular.

Otiende had given her the crown that morning. She had not expected to receive it so it was part of why she was late; she could not decide on how to wear her hair when she had a crown on.

Otiende wore a typical Innercity tailored fit Ankara. Over his right shoulder, and part of his right arm and chest, was what looked like black metal armour. It had the same light-up interlocking pattern as Agina's boots and accessories. It was easy to tell the armour was not made of metal because of how it moved with his body.

He looked like he was not wearing shoes, but rather had on black armour that covered his feet and lower legs. The black metal-looking part was higher on his left leg, rising above his knee and stopping mid-way on his thigh.

He had on a cape that had the same interlocking light-up pattern as Agina's. Part of the cape was fastened at the front, with a standing collar. It was worn under the armour on his shoulder and danced in the wind, in sync with Agina's dress or anything else on them that the breeze could gently flutter.

Because there was an upper floor of seating, it did not take them long to walk through the kneeling crowd of a thousand people to get to the front. It was a room that was carefully designed so the sound panels were beautiful, looking like wings from the upper seating that swooped over them in a protective hug at the walls and ceiling.

At the front of all the seating on a platform were three long tables with modesty panels. Usually, fourteen elders sat on each table, but today there were fourteen seats on the centre table and fifteen seats on the side tables. The two centre seats at the centre table were left empty, waiting for them to arrive.

There was a label on the table in front of each seat that showed who the elders represented. There were three labels with three titles centred between Agina and Otiende's seats. Having forty-two people represent their own families was an ideal situation with a population of about six hundred thousand people in the Innercity.

They stopped in front of the platform and the breeze as well as colour changes stopped. When the light-up colours were off, it looked like a pattern formed by gold interlocking lines. They let go of each other's hands and Agina gestured for everyone to rise as she spoke the words: rise.

When the elders and the crowd had stood up, Agina and Otiende gave the gestured greeting to the initiated elders, who returned the greeting. The sound of their spears touching the ground at the same time seemed to extend through the room.

Then they turned to greet the crowd in the same way. Council elders were scattered in the crowd, so their spears were also heard, seeming to amplify through the room as they returned the greeting.

Agina and Otiende walked up the platform steps and around the table to their seats, as the colours and breeze continued. When they got to their seats, Agina set her spear beside her in the holder at the edge of the table. There were spears set this way beside each elder.

At the same time, Otiende set his shield beside his seat. He then pulled out her seat and held it until she sat down. Then he pushed her chair in as she moved closer to the table. He pulled his chair closer to Agina and then sat right beside her.

58

INTERRUPTED

THEY DIDN'T TALK to each other throughout the meeting, but they subtly touched each other's hands, sometimes stealing looks. They did not speak for long, when it was their turn to speak. They had not been scheduled to make a speech.

Agina simply gave a statement about how she hadn't come up with a plan yet and had the intention to help where she felt she was needed the most. Otiende gave a statement about supporting Agina and extended an open invitation to those who needed help from Agina because they had run out of options. They knew it wasn't their time to speak to their people yet.

Several powerful speeches were delivered that day from people who were not part of the council. They called people to action, stating the situations they brought to awareness and the goals they had. The conferences were always a good time to amplify the voices of the people.

It was the longest meeting of the day. When the meeting was over, they left the room first. The seating in the room they were directed to had been pre-arranged. They were shown where to sit. There were eight seats at each round table and the tables were set up for lunch.

Otiende helped Agina with her chair and like before, pulled his chair and sat closer to her. They were deep in conversation when the elders they were seated with arrived. Instinctively they both stood up, but the elders were not expecting it. The elders all got on one knee.

"No need for that. Please sit," Agina said as she helped up the person closest to her. As she helped her up, Otiende pulled out the seat for the person closest to him as they all stood up.

"Please. Allow me," Otiende said to the elders and went around helping them with their seats.

"I am still not used to this. My work has been in the Outercity, dealing more with technology than with people. My Mother and my Dana did show me these new formalities, but they are not in my nature. It didn't matter that I practised them over and over again," said Agina as she held the hand of the elder she had helped up.

The elder spoke, "It is your nature that we need. Even that of your husband. He wanted to be a part of this but was rejected by the people he wished to serve... He still found a way to serve others. Now he has found a way back to us."

At that point, Otiende had reached the elder's seat Agina was standing beside, so Agina let go of her hand and Otiende helped her with her seat. She was closer to Abura's generation. The other elders they sat with were closer to Agot's generation.

According to custom, only one family member who was an elder was chosen as a representative and initiated. The other family members were members of the council. Those with a title who were eligible to represent the family were elders.

Agina guessed she was still the representative because there was no one to directly pass the responsibility to. Otiende's grandmother was in a similar situation. She was still the family representative. People in Otiende's family tended to prefer other occupations.

Otiende helped Agina with her seat and then sat back down.

"We are glad to have you both. We might have practised these new formalities for a longer duration because of our elder lessons, but it's been over one thousand years since we had a magician from Gor Mahia's descendants. It's new for us too," said another elder.

Their orders were taken, and the food was promptly brought out.

They continued to converse as they ate their food.

"OT, we are leaving now," said Otiende's mother who appeared behind him. Otiende's father was standing beside his mother.

"Please continue," Otiende said to the elders as he stood up. Agina had also stood up as she gestured to the elders to remain seated. They had also started to get up. On account of her gesture, they remained seated.

"We will escort you to the portals," said Agina.

"You don't need to trouble yourselves," said Otiende's mother.

"Mom. We insist," Otiende said as he gestured to the exit.

Hence, the four of them left after excusing themselves. They stood in front of one of the exit portals, Otiende and Agina were holding hands, facing Otiende's parents.

"It will probably be a while before we can see you both again. Please be well and take care of yourselves," Otiende said with a tinge of sadness in his voice.

They gave the parents hugs. Just then Otiende's mother got a message. Auma Agutu Oneko took out her com and looked at it, then she looked at Otiende's father and said, "Something came up. It's going to be another two hours before they can meet."

"We shall meet them later then," he responded to Auma, then nodded to Agina and Otiende. "We took time off for you two anyway. It turns out we interrupted your lunch for no reason."

"No, it's fine," said Agina and Otiende in unison. Then they both burst out laughing. They looked at each other as they laughed.

"I won't even ask why that is so funny. But the more I see the two of you together the less I am convinced you really didn't keep in contact with each other over all those years," said Auma.

They were still laughing. Agina stopped laughing first, "Sorry. It's been a long morning. How about we spend some time together instead?"

"You said it's been a long morning, I know exactly what you need. We could go to our Outercity home. It's more relaxing there. I'll go talk to the bodyguards," said Otiende's father. Oyange Okoth Oneko went off to talk to the bodyguards. All the four of them had been using the same bodyguards that day.

"He just likes to entertain and looks for all the excuses to have people over. *You must see how amazing this or that is. This one is the latest one,*" she said, imitating him, then laughed.

"I think it's nice to have you see where OT grew up," she continued.

"That would be nice," Otiende said putting an arm around Agina's shoulder. They looked each other in the eyes then Agina blushed. Just then, Oyange re-joined them.

Auma looked at them sceptically. "It's totally not my business but I am going to ask, and you don't have to answer. I still see innocence in the way you look at each other. Are you still waiting to have sex?"

"Auma!" Oyange said in surprise, his eyes wide.

"What? I said they didn't have to answer. I know it's a personal question," she said, shrugging her shoulders.

Agina and Otiende looked each other in the eyes again. Then while smiling, Otiende replied, "It's fine. A lot of people seem to have taken an interest in our love life. We are still waiting."

"I think it's cute. You are like high school kids," Auma said.

"They were not even in high school at the same time," protested Oyange, gesturing with his hand.

"You know what I mean. I just wasn't sure after you were gone for so long yesterday, then Agina had a love mark when you reappeared. You both looked too happy to not have had any fun," Auma said, appearing confused.

Otiende burst out laughing again and Agina blushed and turned as if she was trying to hide behind Otiende. Instinctively covering the mark she knew could not be seen, since she had covered it with make-up.

  **STRANGE LIGHT: Ler Mahia**

Oyange laughed then said, "Now I see what you mean. It is cute."

"It's your fault," Agina whispered loudly. Playfully hitting Otiende on the arm.

"Sorry," he said, hugging her while awkwardly holding the shield.

He was still holding onto her when he said, "I just find it funny because you said people might not notice. And now because of it, my mom is asking about our love life." They went back to holding hands. She was sure her face was bright red with embarrassment despite her dark skin colour.

"I am sorry for intruding. I'm not usually nosy. I feel like I made the wrong impression," Auma said, looking distressed.

"That's what is funny about it. I would never have imagined you asking," said Otiende still trying not to laugh.

"It's fine. The question does come up often in my family," said Agina.

"Let's get going then. We are family now after all," said Auma as she began to move towards the portal.

STORIES OF PICTURES

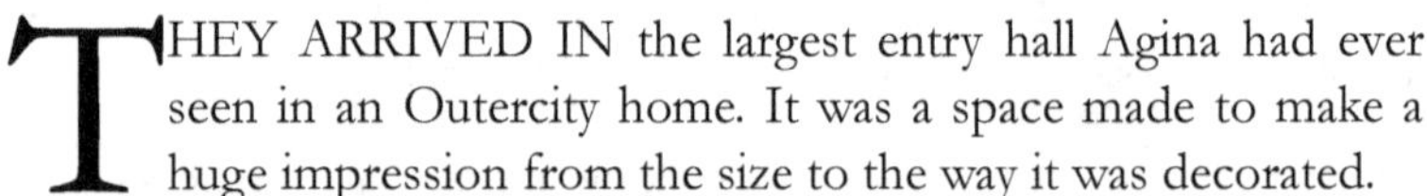

THEY ARRIVED IN the largest entry hall Agina had ever seen in an Outercity home. It was a space made to make a huge impression from the size to the way it was decorated.

Because of the way the Innercity was run, things were often handed down. It was closely based on the model of family; people got allowances that they requested from their representing elders rather than compensation based on what someone thought your work deserved. They did not work for food either. Food was accessible throughout Dala without needing to be paid for.

The rest of Dala was similar, but since it was multicultural, the allowances were more constricted, standardised and provided by the government. Consequently, the houses were usually similar no matter what your occupation was. It was why Agina was surprised to find such a large house.

This system gave people the ability to choose to follow their passions and to do whatever they felt inspired to do without being motivated by compensation. Life was different when you didn't just work to be compensated nor work to feel like you needed to contribute to society. You were valued as a member either way.

But like every system, it had its faults. This system worked more flawlessly in the Innercity because the land people lived on was ancestral land associated with people they knew who had passed it on. Also, they often traded, rather than bought items. Plus, without

     STRANGE LIGHT: Ler Mahia

technology, the wants of the people were simpler.

In the Innercity, fulfilment was easily reached even for the people who liked finer things. A common occurrence was that family members liked similar things. It's a large part of why passing things worked. Agina could see similar things that Otiende liked, starting with large spaces.

When she saw the family portraits on the wall, she understood why the family portraits in Otiende's home were displayed the way they were. The layout of the portraits in his entry hall was done in the same way but was incomplete, showing only one side: his family.

The family portraits on Otiende's wall only looked complete if you were yet to see the full layout; done in full it displayed two sides of the family meeting at the centre. She thought it was a nicer, more intimate way of showing family lineage. Like his, some pictures went back, with some portraits being digital and interactive.

At her family's ancestral home, it was just the names over the portal. The pictures on display were photos of ancient documents, writing their ancestors' names. Now that she thought about it, the emphasis in her family was on titles and magic power. Unlike here where the focus is family. She guessed that the portraits in Otiende's ancestral home were probably similar, but now she wondered what pictures they had and how far back they went, since they were more likely not digital.

"Your home is beautiful," Agina said, still looking at the portraits.

"It's missing your picture," Otiende said leaning in as he spoke, like he was sharing a secret. But he hadn't whispered. He said it out loud. He had been standing behind her. Agina got the impression that he was talking more about the portraits in his home; that he knew she was thinking about the ones in his entry hall.

"Yes, your picture. We should give you a tour, but first, we have had an old picture of you two in our living room for a long time. Come take a look," said Oyange as he dramatically gestured for them to follow, walking towards a door.

Agina looked at Otiende with a curious expression. She thought she saw him either blush, be shy, or be embarrassed. She wasn't sure. She had not yet seen such an expression on his face. It made her more suspicious.

"You have had my picture in your living room all this time?" she asked in disbelief.

"Technically it's my parents' living room. We were still kids when I put it up," he said, leading her through the door.

"Don't be so technical. It's your home too. But this picture was like a mystery to us. So, it made a good story that your father loves to tell," said Auma as she walked into the living room.

It was a large elegantly decorated living room. It was open to the dining room which was also open to the kitchen. Through the tall full-height glass wall with windows, she could see that they were high up in a tall building that stood above skyscrapers. They all walked over to a gallery wall.

At the centre of all the pictures, was a picture of Agina when she was 7 years old and Otiende when he was 12 years old. Judging by the way both her arms were extended you could tell that she took the picture. The young Otiende was standing beside her younger self, almost looking like he had his chin on her shoulder. It was a close shot so part of their heads were not in the picture. They both had a huge grin and had looked directly at the camera. Someone could easily have thought it was a picture of siblings.

Agina quickly looked at the other pictures. They were single or group pictures of Otiende with various trophies, medals, certificates, or other achievements. There were also pictures of his parents' achievements. Agina's picture was clearly the odd one out, larger and centred.

"We could never really figure out why. But when he got back that day, he rearranged his pictures and put this in the centre. When we asked him about it, he said friendship was more important than the other achievements and the reason why he chose the picture was not his story to tell. We suggested taking all the other pictures down and putting pictures of friends instead. But he refused. Your friendship was... people had a lot of opinions about your friendship. It didn't help that OT always said you were different. There are so many achievements on this wall because he doesn't just keep an interest in one thing. He is good at a lot of things. I don't know how else to say this, but you were more consistent in his life then, than all these things he tried," said Auma.

"May I please tell this story? You left out all the good parts about how stubborn he was about it," said Oyange.

"Yes, you may," replied Auma smiling. It was like giving a child candy.

Oyange went into a detailed description of what happened. Agina could see why he liked to tell the story. He was also a great storyteller. They all laughed as he described it. She wasn't just laughing, she had tears in her eyes from laughing. She was also holding her belly because she was laughing so hard it hurt.

"You have too much fun telling this story," said Auma with a large grin.

"It's a good story. And now he's married to her. So, it makes a better story. All these years I have told this story has not gone to waste. Wait till the people who heard this story return! Aaa!! It's too good. Can't wait for them to hear she is now family!" said Oyange cheerfully.

SECRET REVEALED

"**T**HEY DON'T KNOW about the spear. Do they?" Agina asked, turning to look at Otiende.

He shook his head.

Agina raised the spear, holding it horizontally. "We designed this spear together. That picture was taken on the day we were done."

She held the spear down again. "Now that I look back, this project was many firsts and had a lot of ripple effects. But right away, it made us realise we were not just friends, but we made a good team. It started out as a prank because we were supposed to keep the secret that it was actually a com and not a spear. But the moment we started designing it, we took it seriously. It was such a perfect design that I have only modified it through the years. My parents were happy that I had actually taken an interest in elder stuff for a change when I took up my spear. So, they encouraged me to use the spear. After liking the spear lessons and getting exceptionally good at it, and after using the endless supply of tech information to invent more stuff, it wasn't just a secret I had to protect. It was who I am meant to be. It took my parents years to find out it was a com. When I look at how you put up this picture, it has the same spirit. It's a secret, right in front of everyone." She turned to look at Otiende. "For you, it had its purpose no one else needed to know." Then she turned back to face his parents. "So, that's why you couldn't have gotten any information from him no matter what you tried. OT gave me that opportunity to be myself, not just when I was around him."

They had gotten closer as she was speaking. He had an arm around her shoulder, and she had an arm around his waist.

"You challenged how things were done. Even when you were 3 years old! You didn't just try things. You would rather make things better. I learnt just a little of that from you and it changed my life," said Otiende as he looked at her. She was also looking at him as she smiled.

"It made it harder to raise a child that was already stubborn!" said Oyange. And they all laughed.

"So, it started as a prank. This story just got better. But I get the feeling this part of the story is not meant to be shared," said Oyange as he moved closer to the picture and looked at it intently.

"No. Leave it be. It's still a good story. I could never have imagined OT holding such a protest because of a prank. We never mentioned that it had to be a secret. It was just an understanding we had. My family doesn't even know how OT was involved, or that it was a prank," said Agina. It was a secret she didn't trust her family to keep. Even if they had not revealed that her spear was a com. However, she trusted Otiende's family with the secret they had carried.

"Of course. That's the loyalty of a Leo," said Auma.

"Mom. I don't believe in that stuff. If I really was loyal, I wouldn't have said goodbye that day. Or I would have stayed in touch." She rubbed his back in comfort. She was moved by the regret she heard in his voice.

"That's okay. We are here now. Do you remember what you said then?" she asked Otiende as she continued to rub his back.

"If our destinies are meant to align, we will meet by fate," he said and kissed the side of her forehead.

"Fate and destiny in the same sentence! You believe in that stuff even less," said Oyange in surprise.

"She's different," he said, looking at Agina with a large grin.

"There it is again! I can't tell you how many times I heard that Agina was different!" said Oyange.

"She is," insisted Otiende.

"You are right. I would never have believed you when you said you were going to marry someone you love when you told me you are getting married. But it was Agina, so I knew it was different. Plus, she has magic powers!" said Auma, then she walked over to Otiende.

"Why don't you put those down? Our spear and shield holders are there. OT, show Agina Around. We'll bring out drinks and snacks," said Auma pointing beside the door they had come through.

After setting their spear and shield in the holder, Otiende showed Agina around. "This was my room," Otiende said, holding the door open for Agina. She walked through and looked around the large room. It was barely personalised. It looked like a place in an interior design magazine; a place he didn't spend much time in.

"It changed a lot. Sometimes it would only stay the same way for a few months. This was how I left it before I moved out and found a place with Aliana."

"Do you miss the stardom and entertainment creativity, now that you stopped?" Seeing the home that he grew up in made her realise how much it was a part of his life. Everywhere you turned was something about his life of entertainment.

"I was always busy. It took years for some of those contracts to end. I didn't want to go into this phase of my life with any obligations I couldn't easily change. I don't miss that; having a schedule I can't easily move around. But sometimes I do miss the fun parts." He sounded like he was reminiscing about something so far away. She knew he left in phases. She wondered if he had missed it for a while, even though some of the performances were recent.

"I feel like I am making you wait too long to go back with such a long engagement." She was searching for an answer. She wasn't sure what. She looked at his face, trying to see if she'd find it there.

His childhood was a path she had crossed. But it felt different seeing his home. She felt something in her shutter. She knew what she was building the walls for, but what about him and what he was building? He had progressively built the path his life was on.

"I would rather spend time with you," he said, nudging her forward towards the bed.

The bed looked like a strip that flowed out of the wall and flowed into the ground. It made the bed look like it was floating at the headboard. The rest of the furniture in the room also had the same flowing design.

"I would rather not get on the bed," she said, her heart beating faster. With the way he looked at her, she knew she had to be on guard.

"Don't worry. I would love for you to lay on the bed so I could make love to you, but I just want to sit with you and make out," he said, as he kept nudging her.

"Laying or sitting, I'd rather not get on the bed." She should have stood her ground, but she was letting him nudge her forward. Logic had told her to stop, but her feet moved in opposition.

He sat on the bed then before she was fully aware of what he was doing, she was sitting on his lap. "Then you can sit on me instead."

"I can feel your heartbeat. I think this is worse." She was sure those words came from her, though what she really wanted to do was bring him closer and kiss him.

"Good. I like having you close. You know I won't let you go so easily." She was about to speak but he stopped her with a kiss.

Once Agina felt his lips on hers, she forgot about everything else but the feeling of being kissed by Otiende. His lips were soft and gentle. Open slightly, they embraced her lower lip. It made her stomach flutter, and it was as though her body temperature was rising.

She could smell the slight scent of her soap on him. It brought forth the memory of sleeping next to him last night. The thought sent a shiver up her spine that made her body tremble for a slight second.

The subtle sensation of the chill combined with her rising temperature, sparked her reflexes, causing her to wrap her arms around him, pulling him closer as he did the same, rubbing her back.

The sensation of the fabric against her back as he rubbed it seemed to leave a trail of heat on her back. The lights on their clothes were changing colours at such a fast pace that colour would stay on for less than a second.

She loved the way it felt to be kissed by him. She held his face as they kissed. There was a yearning in her kiss for something more. But she didn't want to get lost in the kiss. It was so easy to get lost in the feeling.

As they kissed, his hand moved to her neck and gently brushed the nape of her neck slowly moving lower. Her heart began to race faster, feeling like it was occupying her entire chest. A soft gentle moan was caught in the back of her throat. His hand froze.

She knew she had lost control for a moment and only managed to pull herself out because she needed to breathe. He looked into her eyes as he moved his hand away. He held the back of her head and continued to kiss her. She wrapped her arms around him again, pulling him closer.

"Otiende! You could have closed the door," said Auma as she walked away.

They both stopped and looked but Auma had already disappeared. They both shrunk in embarrassment, looking at each other.

"Wow. That was embarrassing. She hasn't called me by my full name in such a long time," said Otiende, lowering his gaze.

MULTIDIMENSIONAL

SHE STOOD UP first then he followed.

"We should head back," Agina said, hanging her head low.

"Wait. Not yet. Don't worry about Mom. She was more surprised than anything. I want to make sure you are okay first," Otiende said, examining her face.

"I am fine," she said too quickly.

"Agina, you don't look fine," he said, worry furrowing his brows.

She took a deep breath. "I am fine," she repeated slower.

"Okay. So maybe you are fine. But there is something you are not telling me." He knew he had hit the nail on the head when he said it. He was quick to catch her reaction.

She stood in silence. She didn't want to bring it up. But she knew he was going to keep being persistent, now that he had figured it out.

"Can we talk later?" she asked, still trying to divert the conversation.

"We can talk later but you need to tell me what it's about." He wasn't going to budge.

She hesitated then looked him in the eyes. She could not keep looking, so she turned away and spoke, "When we were kissing, I lost control of my powers. I knew when it happened. But I only realised what I had done when we stopped."

He embraced her in a hug. She just stood frozen in his arms before she finally gave in and hugged him back.

"I'm sorry. It's my fault," he said, looking remorseful as he held her face.

"It's not your fault. It's hard to keep it together when holding back." She looked at her feet. She couldn't keep looking at him when he was sorry for her mistake.

"Right. The longer you have to hold it, the harder it gets," he said remembering their conversation.

"I have been trying really hard not to mess up today. I was not made to sit that still for so long. I held on to my energy. I didn't mean to hold on to the magic as well. So, I damaged a lot of devices when I unintentionally let go." Having revealed what happened, she was left feeling extremely vulnerable.

He held her face again and brought her eyes up to meet his. "We are going to have to agree to disagree. It was my fault. We still have meetings ahead of us today. Are you able to take a mind break now? We can go to your place if you need to."

She had not considered taking a break. She analytically thought about what would be best at the moment. Despite all that had happened, intrinsically she still didn't want to be at the conferences. Too many variables had changed, forcing her to make the shift into being a Supreme Elder. Part of her knew she would find it harder to stay on this path if she went home. Once she would retreat to her comfort zone there was no way she would want to come back and attend more meetings or want to be a Supreme Elder all together. She wanted too much with all her being to go into her nook and quit.

"We are already here. It would be too rude to leave, even if I know they will understand. I think I know what to do. It will reverse the damage I have done. I don't like messing with time and space. But the analysis I have done gives this as the best option," she said thinking out loud about what she could do instead and what she needed to fix.

"You can turn back time?" he asked in surprise.

"No. It's like a system restore. But it doesn't just revert software back to a healthy state, it also changes the physical composition of anything or even anyone to an optimal state."

"Alright. It sounds like a plan. Is there anything I can do to help?" he asked, holding her hands in his.

"No. Just... I think it's best not to touch me during the process." She looked in his eyes, hoping he wouldn't get offended, and think she was brushing him off. He nodded. Seeming to have grasped what she needed without any hard feelings.

"Okay." Letting go, she took a few steps back from him then closed her eyes.

The more she tried to follow the analytical path that was the shorter way out, the louder and more out of control the chaos in her mind got. It was like she was being crushed by a dam she forcefully took down.

She suddenly felt an overwhelming pain in her temples. As a result, she cried out in pain and held her temples, while bending over. Panic-stricken, she direly searched for an escape from the pain. It was almost like the pain was so agonising that it was numbing anything else she was feeling. All she could do was try to avoid feeling pulverised by pain. Clasping for release, she desperately tried to escape the pain.

When she finally felt like she had escaped it, she realised it was because she had teleported into a different dimension. She got her senses back. However, just as she arrived, she noticed she had also teleported Otiende with her. When had he closed the distance and held her?!

In shock he let go of her arm. In a reflex driven by adrenaline she grabbed his hand just in time, as she involuntarily teleported into another dimension. She kept shifting from dimension to dimension till she finally stopped when things calmed to a serene stillness in her mind.

She slowly opened her eyes to find that they were high up in the air at what looked like a beach. The sun was setting in the horizon. She looked over at Otiende to see that he was evidently terrified. Without thought, she stepped closer to him in mid-air and put a hand on his forehead. She felt the magic surge through her fingers into his head, as she used her power to help him calm down.

When she felt his anxiety dissipate, she took off her hand. "I always close my eyes in multidimensional travel. So, I don't know what you saw. We are still in this dimension, and I don't know how to get back to your parents' home. My home is a strong enough anchor that I can always find my way there. It's like a homing signal. We'll go there first."

She was about to step away when he embraced her in a tight hug. She still had a grip on his hand, afraid that even if she could find him in any dimension, letting go would mean he would fall to the ground below. It was her magic that let her defy gravity. So, he couldn't fully embrace her because she was holding his hand. However, he partially embraced her tightly in gratitude, before finally letting her go.

"I..." He seemed to be at a loss of words.

"We can talk after we leave. We have to get back. This is already too much exposure," Agina said, letting him know she wasn't cutting him off, but they needed to leave in haste.

COMING BACK DOWN

THEY GOT BACK through the same portal to find Auma and Oyange in the entry hall, looking at them in confusion and shock.

"Sorry. I am still learning how to use my power," said Agina.

"We thought something happened to you when we heard you. I was worried. We came to look for you to find out what happened. But you had both disappeared! Are you okay?" asked Auma, as she focused on Agina.

"I am fine. I have experienced this before. But I didn't expect to drag OT in with me. I know we came to spend time together, but do you mind if I talk to him alone?" asked Agina, as she reluctantly put Otiende on the spot.

They finally took a closer look at Otiende and saw that he did not look okay.

"Baby, what happened? Are you okay?" asked Auma, rushing to his side and holding his shoulder.

"I am fine," said Otiende with a tone that sounded aggressive.

Agina couldn't believe that she just heard him speak that way to his mother. It was the kind of answer he would have given when they were children to the adults who failed to help him when he was being bullied.

She was standing by his side holding his hand, so she gave him a sideways glance, trying not to get caught looking at him.

"Why don't we leave them alone for a bit, we'll be in the family room," said Oyange, taking Auma by the hand and leading her away. Auma followed reluctantly.

Agina let go of Otiende's hand and moved her position to stand in front of Otiende.

"I am sorry I put you through that. If you are not up to it, we don't have to go back to the conferences," she said hesitantly. She felt guilty about the situation and though she was not sure about what he felt now, she couldn't forget the terror she had seen in him and felt how his body had reacted through the ring.

Otiende finally seemed to get out of his daze.

"No. Agina... It was my fault. I couldn't see you in pain and just stand there. I didn't expect that to happen. But even if I knew it would happen, can I just stand there?"

"Sorry. I should have told you why you shouldn't have touched me. But I didn't expect it to hurt."

"Agina, stop apologising. It was my fault. Are you saying that it hasn't hurt like that before?"

Agina paused, realising she had given information she didn't intend to give.

"Agina?"

"No."

He cursed under his breath.

"It doesn't usually hurt. It's the first time I have been hurt because of this power. I was trying to rush something I shouldn't have rushed," she admitted, mostly to herself, like it was something she just realised.

The look on his face changed.

"I am so sorry Agina. I... I had brought up this idea. We should have gone back to your place. We should have taken the time to let you do what you needed to do, so you can use your floor seating area. It's where you typically let everything go and reset yourself. It wasn't my intention to rush you."

"I know you didn't mean to rush me. I was impatient because we had already come here with the intention to spend time with your parents. I am sorry. Leaving here and going home would have been too much," she said, feeling sunk, looking down at her feet.

"Agina, stop apologising!" He hugged her.

They stood in the embrace for a long time. She felt tears start to fall down her eyes onto his clothes. He held her by the shoulder and pulled her away so he could see her face.

"You're crying. Agina, why are you crying?"

Then he embraced her again, rubbing her back. After some time, she looked up at him and asked, "Do you want to talk about what happened to you? I feel really bad about it."

After a pause, he said, "Let's sit."

He sat down on the sofa first, then she sat next to him.

"Come here." He put an arm around her shoulders. "Thank you for helping me calm down before I got worse."

"What frightened you that way?" she asked, looking at him quizzically.

"Sigh. I was already afraid something had happened to you. Then when I held your arm... I didn't expect to teleport with you. These dimensions... We went through many dimensions, and they are all different... And what I saw... I wasn't expecting any of it."

She paused to see if he would continue speaking. After the silence only stretched longer, she broke the silence and spoke.

"There are more worlds in dimensional travel than there are stars. Dimensions are easier to accidentally teleport through because of their proximity. Plus, a large number of them overlap. But I have never seen what is in all the dimensions I have accidentally teleported through. I have only seen the ones I end on. Those are usually calm." She had been thrown into all kinds of situations after she got powers, getting accustomed to chaos, in comparison his life had been relatively simple. She wasn't sure what to say to him; she was unintentionally bringing chaos into his life.

He turned to look at her. "It's better that way. I wouldn't recommend having your eyes open. And thank you for catching me when I let go. I felt gravity start to take me."

"I might not see like you do with your eyes open. But I can still sense with my eyes closed. It's like I see things at a… It's almost like I see things in their truest form."

She leaned over and hugged him from the side after pushing her arm between the sofa and his back. She buried her head in his shirt, cradling herself in his arm. She could smell the scent of the soap more clearly.

"OT?" she called, her voice muffled by the shirt.

"Yes?" He replied. She could feel the vibrations as he spoke.

"Why does this feel so familiar? Being with you instead of being at the conferences." She held him tighter as she said, "I really don't want to go back to the meetings when the afternoon meetings start."

She knew that at that moment she sounded more like a child than an adult. She already didn't like being at the conferences. Though in her childhood, it had been more like age-appropriate instructional coaching, she had escaped the conference meetings then, insisting on finding and meeting with Otiende.

She only attended when she was 11 years old up to the time she was still 15 years old. She had spent so much time complaining and unintentionally disrupting the others, if she was not sleeping.

Everyone was well aware Agina did not want to be an elder.

They had almost wished she wasn't there. She stirred up too much trouble with her ideology. They eventually allowed her to join the traditional dancers who performed at the conferences to keep her partially occupied. Even if she had been too young to officially join their group; she became a member who only performed at the conferences.

She stopped attending altogether when she finally turned 16 and she had the opportunity to opt out. Unfortunately, her mother forbade her from renouncing her title. By then she was fully aware that she was not interested in most of the council activities, especially the meetings. She found it boring.

She had only managed to stay alert in the meetings that morning because Otiende was at her side, keeping her distracted. She maintained the respect and trust of the council through the years because she always helped with the diplomatic needs, in the same way Otiende helped with the technological needs and security. She hoped the council wouldn't lose the trust and respect they had for her if she didn't go. But if that happened she was okay with it; she had never tried to get them on her side.

He kissed her forehead then spoke. "It's probably better if we don't go. I feel you made the choice not to go in your heart and you just need assurance. If you hadn't helped me calm down, I would have been in a terrible state. Even now, I don't think I can honestly focus on people's matters. They deserve to be properly heard. We can always catch up on what happened later. It's different from the entertainment industry where you just go out there and perform no matter what you feel. And... You have been crying. I can act, but I don't know if you can turn your state around that quickly."

Agina looked up at Otiende and said, "My Mother or my Dana would probably still go out there. Definitely Adede. No matter what they experienced. For them, being an elder is everything. Am I being a bad leader? On the day of my first public appearance?"

Otiende sighed, gently rubbed her back then said, "You can't ask me such a question. I know your intentions. This is something you don't want to do in the first place. So, you don't need me to validate you. I am already seeing things from your side, and I know it's valid. I think this is true leadership; when you don't just put on a performance."

"Then I'll allow myself to be at peace. I hate to admit it but a lot of who I am crumbled when I left this place and went back to the Innercity. Perhaps it was going back to live in that house that broke me. It was an identity crisis. I had to get out and build my own place. It was the only way I could save myself. I used to be so sure of myself. Do you remember those days?..." She felt her tears try to resurface again as she trailed off in thought, then she regained her attention to say, "OT. What do you need at this moment to feel at peace?"

"Talking to you is putting me at ease. Let's talk for a bit then I'll go get my parents," he said, gently touching her head.

63

TENTATIVE

O TIENDE NATURALLY WOKE up with his internal clock and slowly opened his eyes. He quickly noticed he was at Agina's place again and smiled to himself. The plain ceiling met the cabinetry on one side and the drapes on the opposite side. The heavy drapes that were covering the large glass retracting doors were still drawn, making it look darker than it was.

A screen suddenly hovered over him. Before he could read it, he felt a wetness on his underwear. He quickly sat straight up and took a look. Confused by the sensation.

Feeling embarrassed, he quickly turned to look at Agina who was sleeping peacefully by his side. She had a playful look and always seemed to be smiling so she looked like she was enjoying a wonderful dream. He wondered what she was dreaming about.

When he looked at the bright side, he was glad he had a sensual dream rather than a nightmare about what he saw in the other dimensions. He couldn't remember any dreams from last night. But in all honesty, since Agina came back into his life, he had been getting aroused too often. At least he didn't have to hold himself back in his dreams.

Otiende's face cringed when he looked at his sleep report that was on the hovering screen. According to the report he had slept well but the report showed that he had a nocturnal emission. So even if he got up and quickly took a shower, she would still know what happened as they slept.

He kissed her on the forehead and went down the stairs, wondering what she would think when she saw the report. What do grown women think of such a thing? It was a common occurrence when he was going through puberty.

This time Agina had been aware she was sleeping next to him. After they got dressed for bed, she led him up the stairs. He loved being with her and longed for the time he did not have to hold back with Agina.

Their day had ended well after they got back to his parents' home. As he expected, Agina connected wonderfully with his parents. When Agina and Otiende found out that it was Odek's parents they planned to meet, they all decided to invite them over instead.

After they arrived, they all stayed at his parents' home till after dinner. Odek, his wife and kids also joined them for dinner. They had such a good time that it felt like an extension of their engagement celebration; like Agina was formally introduced and welcomed to their Outercity family friends, the Omondi family. Their mood had absolutely turned around by the time they went to bed.

After taking a shower he took his morning run. He ran a different route today, so he saw a different view and ran past Agina's family's cattle. They already had a lot of animals that looked well taken care of. He wondered how they would manage after he paid the dowry and they had to care for more animals. Perhaps he should propose a plan to expand the animals' homestead.

When he got back, he took another shower and got dressed. He set up a temporary workstation with his com. Because of the open plan, there wasn't a distinctive place to set up, so he used the same place that Agina used to work while standing in the dining room.

He got the information from the house. Her house was a friendly personality and knew Agina surprisingly well. Because of its friendly personality, it kept making an effort to know him better. It didn't just stay with the information he put in.

He was deep into reading work-related reports when Agina hugged him from behind. He was a little startled because he had not been aware of her presence. He turned and hugged her. It was comforting holding her in his arms. Though his heart was beating faster, he felt more relaxed, like being tense just couldn't exist when she was near.

"Good morning," he said, giving her a light kiss on her forehead and then on her lips. Her body was warm, probably because she was just under the comforter.

"Good morning. Work?" she asked, holding him while she looked up at him.

"Catching up on reports I haven't managed to read daily. We have had too much going on."

"Mmh. We have been distracted with a lot recently. Am I taking too much of your time?" She gently hugged him again while she rubbed his back. His senses seemed to become more alert.

He could smell the scent of peppermint on her breath. Had she already brushed her teeth? Had he been that preoccupied with work?

His thoughts wandered like they always did when she was close. He found himself looking at her lips, thinking about kissing her. He wasn't sure if he imagined it or if she opened her mouth slightly, inviting him to kiss her.

He was drawn to her lips, holding her face as he kissed her. He liked the feeling of her soft lips. It sent a gentle flutter through his body. He forgot about everything else, like the world just had the two of them, but the world felt expanded with so much more. He wondered what it would feel like to touch the rest of her body if just her lips made him feel this way.

But he didn't dare touch her again. He had to keep waiting to make love to her and she awakened a desire in him he wasn't sure he could control. He loved her, so he had to respect her decision.

But this: kissing her. He wanted to kiss her all the time. At least he could manage that.

She put her arms around him and pulled him closer. But her hands didn't just stop there: they wandered around his body as they kissed. She was hungry for more, driven by her sexual desires. His senses were already too sensitive. He was at his limit. The energy in his body was busting, making him feel too hot.

She got her hands under his shirt. Touching him briefly before she started to pull off his shirt. He had to stop her! It was now or never while he still had his thinking capacity.

She didn't want to be pushed away. He tried several times before he finally managed to separate from her. She looked confused like she didn't even realise what she was doing.

"Sorry. I'm so sorry. Sometimes my rational mind gets away from me," she anxiously said, almost in a panic, when she finally found her words. She started to retreat but he caught her and drew her back.

"I know. But I have to be honest with you, there will come a time when I won't have the will to stop you. It's hard for me to hold back. And because of all the times I have stopped you, it feels more like I am the one who wants to wait. Are you going to stop me then when my desire for you overwhelms me?" he asked, beginning to feel frustrated.

She was silent for a long time. She looked like a child that had been scolded. He didn't want to see her like that.

However, Agina was always like this: strength and weakness. Most of the time you knew if she was going to show up strong or weak. But sometimes you just didn't know what you were going to get.

Though Agina felt like she became weaker after abandoning her life in the Outercity and getting divorced, he felt like it was more like a flip. It wasn't just her strengths that became weaknesses, her weakness became a strength. She was just too focused on what went wrong to realise it.

He couldn't stand it anymore. She looked like she was about to start crying. So, he reached down and kissed her. He had thought she might resist a little with how suddenly he satiated his desire, but she responded right away. Did she have that pained expression because she wanted to be kissed? Was it because she wanted him to keep going?

Why did he now feel like the bad guy for pushing her away? Her body language was guilt-tripping him, like it asked: why did you stop me when I just wanted you to kiss me and love me? He got the impression that she wanted to have sex but didn't dare to say what she wanted.

What was he supposed to do with this realisation when he had been lusting for her since he saw her walk up to him in that cafe? He wasn't the kind of a person who often had strong sexual desires. Maybe because he learnt early on that sex that was given so easily came at a price he was not willing to pay.

While his friends were out having sexual experiences, he focused on his work and only had sex when he had dated for some time. But hadn't he known this woman longer than he had known any other woman in his life? Why had she still been a child when he left? Why had he fallen for her when she was still underage? Why did he always have to have so much restraint?

If he had stayed longer, would they have naturally made that transition from friend to falling madly in love with each other? Or would he still see her as a childhood friend, like she had? The sexual pull between them was becoming more intense than he could bear. Keeping himself from her was catching up with him.

He made a promise to himself to do some research and find out what he could do to fulfil her sexual desires without having sex. All these questions were driving him mad. It was clear that they both wanted more than this, but she still wasn't ready for sex.

PLANNING FOR CHANGE

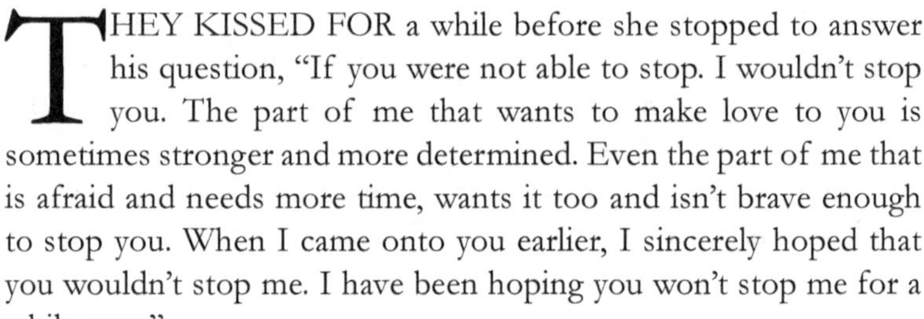

THEY KISSED FOR a while before she stopped to answer his question, "If you were not able to stop. I wouldn't stop you. The part of me that wants to make love to you is sometimes stronger and more determined. Even the part of me that is afraid and needs more time, wants it too and isn't brave enough to stop you. When I came onto you earlier, I sincerely hoped that you wouldn't stop me. I have been hoping you won't stop me for a while now."

"Agina, do you understand how confusing that is for me. Do you want to wait, or do you not want to wait?" he asked feeling distressed. It was one thing to think it's how she felt, but it was another to hear her say it.

"I... I have an internal conflict. I don't know," she hesitantly said, her eyes shifting to avoid his gaze.

"So, you just left it up to me to decide for you? Why would you look so dejected when I give you what I think you want? Just tell me that you want it, and we can forget about the conferences, so I can take you now. I'll make love to you all day. I have already told you I have a very strong desire for you. All I need is a confirmation from you, that you want it. And I will love you till you are senseless, anytime, anywhere. But can you do that? Can you tell me that it's what you want? You can't even decide that, can you?" He became too frustrated to watch his tone. He was more reprimanding than he would like.

She had that scolded look again and was shrinking at his words. He knew she was too conflicted to declare she wanted to be loved. But what was he supposed to do now, knowing that such a decision had been left in his hands.

He gave her a hug. He had to change the topic. The conversation was not leading anywhere. He did not like the mood he had unintentionally put her in. He needed more time to think about what he would do.

"The flowers from the Aiye arrived in our home yesterday. Do you have a plan for how you are going to use them to decorate the home?"

She seemed glad to have the topic changed. "Not really. I haven't walked around the exterior of our house. It's a large home. I'll need to be more strategic. I could probably start by walking around while looking at the plans for the house.

I want to make different levels of gardens, one that is more for relaxation, one that is more like a playground. I don't know how many different types of gardens I would like," She quickly got lost in her imagination as she spoke. He was glad he could redirect her.

He kept her talking about decorating their home. It was a good way to shift her mood, though he didn't know if he needed to make that much effort. Her mood had changed almost instantly, since she was speaking about something she was passionate about.

They had to get their day started so she proceeded by getting in the shower. After he watched her disappear behind the door that appeared to be a part of her floor-to-ceiling cabinetry, he returned to his com workstation.

As she took a shower, he began to research intimacy, trying to find the best way he could solve his dilemma. He also wanted to see what alternative options existed, that they would both be comfortable trying.

Based on what he found, he decided seeing a therapist who specialises in intimacy was a good idea. He scheduled a couple's appointment for both of them. He felt much more at ease knowing there was a possibility he could find a solution.

Soon after, she got out of the shower. Her hair was tucked under an enormous shower cap, and she was cocooned in a fluffy bathrobe. He put away the workstation, putting the com in his pocket. He then sat on the sofa and updated her on what he found out about intimacy as he faced the other way and she got dressed.

"My therapist had referred me to an intimacy coach, years ago when I was trying to date but couldn't get intimate. She thought I had sexual trauma. I didn't go. I told myself I had turned into a Demisexual and there was nothing wrong with me. Later, I didn't tell her about Chloe when that started. Even now I can't tell her I had been meeting Chloe. I feel too much shame. I just let her believe I no longer had any desires. I know lying to a therapist isn't helpful. But this is different now. I will go with you," she sincerely said, just as she was done getting dressed.

He was glad that she had agreed. He wasn't sure if she would think he was making a big deal out of nothing. But she was clearly conflicted. He wasn't sure what would happen if he just went ahead and decided they were no longer going to wait to have sex. Emotions shouldn't just be ignored. They were an indication something needed to be done. There were a lot of emotions surrounding this issue.

"I'm glad you agreed to go with me. I hope it's what is best for us. Let's have breakfast," he said, hugging her and then following her into the kitchen.

As they ate at her dining table facing each other, they talked about the conferences. Once they were on the topic, inevitably, a weighty conversation loomed. It was strangely quiet outside, as if in anticipation of what was to come.

Filled with hope and apprehension, he took a deep breath and began, "Agina, we have received an overwhelming response from people around the world. They are looking for all sorts of help. I was hoping they would mostly be situations we could leave other people to resolve, but unfortunately, I found that most of these people actually need your help. They don't have other options. I have decided to put together a team and set up offices for all of us to work from. We'll need to buy offices outside Dala so foreigners can come into the office. I believe in your vision. I want to support you in this way so you can remain focused on what you love to do while the team lightens your workload. I didn't mean to add all this Supreme Elder work. Thanks to my statement, it seems like you serve the world, not just Dala."

A huge part of Otiende's success stemmed from his ability to effectively manage people; he was really good at delegating tasks to the right people. He already knew what kind of team he would need to set up, and how to go about getting everything done.

"Where could we even set up office? It feels like such a huge undertaking. Can't I just do it all myself. I worry it's too much to take on now. Can't it be a future goal? I don't even know what kind of team you are thinking about or if we will need any of it. Where would we even find a team?" she asked, sounding sceptical and seeming to hate the whole idea.

"Trust me on this. Let me handle it. You know I wouldn't lead you astray. They don't even know you have powers; the overwhelming number of requests are coming in because of the influence I have on people. It hasn't even been twenty four hours. Reading through it all is a task in itself. The messages were filtered before I read them. Let me right it. I have bought places all over the world in the past and I have put several teams together in the past. You don't have to worry about any of it. Just focus on getting through the conferences and it will all be ready for you," he said, taking her hands in his, his touch reassuring.

"Can I at least have a part in this office buying process? I won't just sit back and let you handle everything. I have already let you handle my family responsibilities as an elder by having you share my title. How much of my Supreme Elder responsibilities are you also going to take on?" She seemed to have budged a little. Her voice had softened. He couldn't help but feel like his arrival brought all the chaos in her life. So, he always wanted to help her.

"I am not truly taking it on. I am supporting you. I am getting a team of people to support you, who will help lighten your work. I have people who handle these things. In fact, we need to get on a call with my assistant. I already had him look up some places and reach out to some people," he said, as he took out his com to call him without waiting for her approval.

"You did what?! What about all the responsibilities that will come with it? I don't even feel comfortable letting you spend the money!" She was firmly defensive now, but he had already made the choice. He just needed to have her look at it. He knew she would agree to it once she saw what he had planned.

He moved closer to her and held both her hands, "Agina… I'm doing well financially. People use my money and influence, all the time. It's come to mean nothing to me. But this is different. It matters to me. It's not often I get to do something this helpful for someone I love. This will help you. It's not just my frivolous gesture of love, it really will help you with everything. Just hear what he has to say and keep an open mind. We have planned what is best for you but your input still matters. You won't know till you give it a chance. When you came up with the idea, I didn't think sharing titles would work, but I gave us a chance. Let's share this workspace. Let's also make this ours."

"…" She remained silent for some time.

"You are doing this for us? … It's a big step, OT" she slowly said, letting it sink in.

He nodded before he spoke, "First just hear him out. Okay." He completed making the call before she would have time to object.

In the end they decided on a large office space that had an indoor controlled environment and a large outdoor controlled space. It was easily accessible, and ready for them to start working in. There were only a few changes that they would need to make.

Agina was far more hesitant when she saw the price, but he managed to assure her. He knew it was more likely that she felt backed into a corner by him and his assistant; It was all new to her and they had a good answer to everything she asked, leaving no room for objections.

65

BREACHED

THEY ENDED UP arriving late again, though they were slightly earlier than the previous day. They walked in right when the meeting should have started. This morning it was just the council that was meeting so they were in the council's meeting hall.

He walked in with his arm across Agina's shoulder and Agina had her arm around his waist. Everyone stood as they walked in. Before they arrived, they had been talking about working abroad and he had been telling her a story about working in a different culture.

It was a funny story so when they got into the room, they were both still grinning, looking more like they were in the middle of an exciting date. The mood they arrived with seemed to brighten up the atmosphere that surrounded them.

The room was rectangular with screens on all four sides. The seating had been divided in four sections by walkways. The long sides of the room began with fourteen seats and the short sides began with seven seats. Ever so often, the number of seats increased in the following row, and the following rows stepped up with each concentric row.

Since the seating was fixed with screens and microphones on the tables at each seat, they couldn't just add two seats like they had in the previous room. Everyone was represented under the forty-two families. For that reason, a table had been added in the centre, in front of the row of seven seats.

It put them in the front and centre, in a room that usually read more like it had four sides without a hierarchy. It was a situation Agina would not have liked, but there really wasn't much of a choice. It was where the supreme elder should be seated, if they had one.

They walked down the steps to the centre table. Before they sat down the screens on the walls and tables came on. There were two camera views, one with the leader that represented their country. The other showed a further view of the people in the room with him. It now made sense why they met in the room that had more screens, and was optimised for video conferencing.

Otiende had gotten so preoccupied with securing the office space that he didn't check if the leader would be making an appearance. The leader had not been scheduled to show up by the time they unexpectedly left in the middle of lunch. He wondered if the leader only showed up because the number of people watching the broadcast was abnormally high.

What was especially out of the ordinary was the number of people outside the country who were watching the conference broadcasts. Usually, people outside Dala did not care to watch the conference unless they were citizens of Dala.

Everyone on the screen also stood up as soon as the screen came on. "Supreme Elder Agina Akongo Odero." Announced a voice from within the room on the screen.

All the initiated elders bowed down at the same time. Those who were not initiated elders got down on one knee, all descending at the same time.

Those on the screen were slow to react if not, unsure of what to do. But they all got on one knee eventually. It was only Otiende who was left standing beside Agina. "Rise," said Agina.

In the same way, the council members all reacted at the same time, as soon as they got up, they gave the gestured greeting. It was quite fascinating to watch all the spears move in unison. Otiende also gave the greeting with his shield in hand. He also thought it looked fascinating yesterday, when a larger sea of people reacted at the same time.

Today what was particularly fascinating was the comparison of how the Innercity did it and how the Outercity did it. You could easily tell where the cultural practice mattered.

With the way they perfected it, you wouldn't have been able to tell that they only started the practice after Agina got her powers. They took such practices seriously. So, even the people who did it for the first time were perfectly synchronised.

Some of the people in the Outercity didn't even know what they were supposed to be doing and tried to follow along. As soon as Agina returned the greeting they all sat down after setting their spears beside them. When he thought about it, no council member would fail in etiquette and posture.

Even Agina who had escaped lessons whenever she could get away with it, was always proper. Likewise, Otiende grew up in the Outercity, but he could not escape the constant lessons and reminders from his parents.

He helped her pull up her seat and then sat down. The first meeting of the day was a discussion, so it was at least interactive.

The rest of the meetings in their day were split up by different topics. Next, Otiende and Agina went into the Outercity to attend the meeting that was focused on technology and development.

It was also an interactive discussion, so considering the topic, Agina and Otiende loved the discussions. The hall in the Outercity was designed more adaptively, but Agina still wound up being given the seat at the head of the conference room, where he sat beside her.

It was the seat where she belonged. From the moment she was initiated, she had resisted being set apart for being a Supreme Elder, but he didn't see himself taking up a distinguished seat in her absence. They would have to avoid using such rooms if he attended a meeting without her.

They should have had lunch in the Innercity with everyone else where they were scheduled to go, but they had unexpectedly been invited to have lunch with the leader of Dala.

The residents of the Innercity were the only ones who commonly used the term leader when they referred to the president. Their native term Jatelo was used to mean both leader and president. They were geared toward using the word leader because Jatelo was associated with the meaning leader for a longer period. The term president had been introduced by colonisers.

Surprised by the invitation, they went where they were directed. This lunch break felt different than the previous day because it was being broadcast. Cameras seemed to surround them from all sides like they were being cautious to not miss a single incident. It was hard to tell if the leader and everyone at the table were sincere or if they were putting on a performance to influence people to vote for them.

He was certain Agina hated every moment of it, but no one would have been able to guess. Even if she hated being in the spotlight, she was perfect in it.

In the same way that she never lied about wanting to be a Supreme Elder, she was always truthful while she talked to the people at the table. Despite her realism, she managed to remain diplomatic. There was an elegant charm to her diplomacy.

He didn't usually keep up with the conferences. Most people didn't; even citizens of Dala in the Outercity did not care about the conferences. Yet so many people were watching. As a whole, the council outranked everyone in the country in power and title, but no one usually took an interest in the council.

In fact, before the Innercity was enclosed behind the barriers, it had always been a place that was more underdeveloped than the rest of Dala. Their people had also been isolated from the country's politics. In their multicultural country, people from other tribes usually became leaders.

It wasn't just an agreement based on preservation, creating the barrier officially gave them power over their own people, and their people finally got power in the government. However, it only worked because they chose to peacefully stay behind the barriers and not be publicly visible.

It was easier for the government to give them money and resources to make them disappear behind this barrier which reiterated how they couldn't simply give them the money to develop themselves.

Unexpectedly the Innercity residence ended up happier this way and wanted to stay there and preserve their culture. It was almost like Dala handled their people the same way they were handled when their borders were closed, and they were isolated from the rest of the world.

Ultimately the people of the Innercity valued their traditions and families above everything else. They agreed to it even if they were prideful and were given the power as more of a Public Relations move.

A lot of the matters of the country were decided during the conferences but people tended to assume the matters presented did not pertain to them since the meetings were primarily held in the Innercity. So, for thousands of years, it was held unnoticed, unless people were passionate about politics.

After contemplative thought, Otiende reckoned people had realised they could not save or record any part of the broadcast where Agina was present. It had been part of the program they released to prevent cyberbullying. The program hadn't included his images, but he had consistently been with her.

O_ts had probably tuned in to watch him since it was currently the only way they could see him after he had gone silent about a month ago. Personal devices were not permitted to be used in the meeting rooms, but even if they could record him, they would have been unable to share the recording or pictures, leaving the broadcast as a coveted appearance.

After the lunch break, they went back to the Innercity. They had just started the meeting on the topic of food when Agina leaned over and whispered, "Your com. We should leave now."

He had turned off his sound for notifications and he couldn't check his com while they were still in a meeting. He wondered what was going on. He could tell by her tone that it was important. She also wouldn't have asked him to leave if it wasn't urgent. He nodded at her, and they both got up. The room suddenly became silent as everyone stood up.

They were all not sure what to do after Agina stood unexpectedly. "Proceed without us," she simply said as they both hurriedly left the room. Everyone in the room bowed, with most of them doing the bowing position on one knee, remaining this way till they had left.

Anyone who had been observing them would have easily noticed something had happened. They usually walked hand in hand, but they walked out in a hurry with a serious expression.

As soon as he stepped out of the room, he looked at his com. It was a national security alert. He wanted to step away to make a call but after looking at the expression on Agina's face he changed his mind.

As soon as the call connected, he said, "It's Otiende. I'm with Agina. What is the brief?"

"You'll have to come down and see this." There was a brief pause before the familiar deep and resonant voice continued, "You can bring her too."

He was worried about how she would react to everything, but she already knew something had gone wrong and had started worrying. Now it was a conversation he couldn't escape. He might as well not hide it from her. With her powers, you never knew what she was reading or sensing.

STORM ARRIVED

HE GESTURED TO his bodyguards, and they nodded. They approached them and followed closely to the portals. When he was sure the place was clear and that he was not being recorded he approached a portal.

Because of where he was going, he couldn't just go through. He took out a card and used it on the portal's keypad. After entering information to allow them to use the portal, he scanned his fingers and eyes, then used another card.

"I'll go first," he said to Agina. He went in then she followed him. The bodyguards remained behind. They arrived at a security checkpoint.

"Sorry, we have a lot of security to pass through," he said, directing her to the daunting opening.

There was also a security checkpoint at the building entry to his lab, but he was able to permanently grant her access to his lab, without the checkpoint. The security checkpoint ahead of them was more thorough and could not be bypassed by anyone. It was the only way through.

After they had been fully scanned, probed and sanitised, they were met by the owner of the voice he had just spoken to on the call. He was slightly shorter than Otiende and his Afro hair was in a short tapered haircut. He had on a black tie with a crisp white shirt and black pants.

"Supreme Elder, our Ler Mahia, Agina Akongo," he said in his resonant voice as he gave her a bow and then gave the gestured greeting. Otiende was impressed that he had got that right, addressing her the same way the elders usually addressed her. For some reason that made him happy and proud.

It was the way she should be addressed and greeted. Agina returned the greeting. Otiende wondered if it was the first time she had been forced to do the greeting without her spear, or if she had ever had her spear taken away. She always had her spear.

"I am Agent Joshua Odondi. Sorry for taking your spear. It is quite a powerful weapon. I have never seen anything like it."

Otiende almost burst out laughing. Agina made eye contact with him briefly. He could tell she had the same thought: *Haha weapon? It's a com that was designed by a 7- and 12-year-old child.*

But realistically it was a powerful weapon if you consider its upgrades. Moreover, he heard she was probably the grandmaster at using a spear in the whole country. She had a natural talent and had started training when she was 7 years old. She remained undefeated in all the competitions she took part in. Even when she competed in tournaments outside the country.

"Otiende," said Joshua, giving him the gestured greeting. Otiende returned the greeting. "Please follow me," said Joshua as he started to walk.

They both followed Joshua to a room with several monitors. The monitors in his home had been set up in the same way. Judging by the way Agina looked at him he knew she had noticed the similarity. Other than entertainment, which he started when he was still a child, he had worked in security for a long time. Undoubtedly, it influenced his personal life.

"A clone was cleared through standard portal security and almost entered the Innercity. They were stopped by a second line of defence. We were not aware of this defence system. Take a look," Joshua reported in a flat tone, his hands held behind him like a soldier reporting to his superior.

A video started playing. It showed Otiende approaching the portal he had used after lunch, to enter the Innercity. But instead of going through, he passed through it like it was a doorway and fell unconscious on the other side.

Shortly after, uniformed National Guard soldiers showed up through the portal, picked up the body, put it in a pod then quickly disappeared back through the portal, pushing the pod through.

"Look at that time on the video. Why didn't we see this happen?" asked Agina. She was probably considering when they had left for the portal.

He already knew the answer to the question. Joshua looked at him. He nodded. Joshua searched for another video, then played it as he stood alert with his hands behind him.

The video showed Agina and Otiende walking hand in hand. Then Otiende stopped and kissed Agina. Agina stopped him and looked nervously around then he kissed her again. She eventually stopped him, managing to subdue him after failed attempts to continue.

Otiende grinned and looked at Agina who was blushing and looking embarrassed as she watched the video. Seeing her reaction made him want to kiss her where she stood, despite the presence of Joshua or the severity of what they were discussing. How could she have forgotten what distracted them? It was not that long ago.

They had only just gone to the meeting and sat down before they received the message. He made a mental note to kiss her more in public. Her reaction to watching it was so good. He also liked it better when she was the one stopping him. Unlike the morning, or all the other instances where he put an end to their kisses.

He continued to watch the video as it showed her finally escaping from him with a complaint then hugging him. In the video, he put his arm around her shoulder, then with her hand around his waist, they continued on to the portal. They had just missed the entire incident to the accuracy of a second!

When the video was over, Otiende held Agina on the waist and pulled her close. He rubbed her back, feeling the intensity of the heat where their skin met. Her back was bare under her cape. He contemplated following through with his thoughts of kissing her, right there and then. But he didn't.

Joshua chose not to comment on it and continued as he looked down at a report on a notetab, "It's a really fascinating defence system. It sent us an instructional emergency alert on who to dispatch, and a complete report. I have never seen such a complete auto generated report."

You could tell Joshua was excited like a child talking about a new toy they like. Joshua's tone always gave away his excitement. Anyone could easily distinguish the cheerfulness.

"It gave us all the differences between the clone and Otiende. It says that the most obvious reasons were that he was not with Agina; His ring was not connected to Agina's ring; He had no photos of Agina; His clothes were not exactly the same. Actually, I was surprised most of these differences had something to do with Agina," Joshua said, looking up at the two of them. Otiende knew so much of his life had been wrapped up with Agina, but it was different hearing how entangled he was from a report.

Then Joshua seemed to come to an understanding and looked back at the report.

"It was able to access their mind and tell us where the clone came from and what it intended. These people are persistent in getting to Agina. They send a better attack every day. At least they didn't harm anyone today like they typically do. They might have been successful in getting past our systems, but it seems they chose the wrong person to clone. Otiende's DNA might be easier to access, considering how much he leaves the country, but I imagine all these other things are too difficult to duplicate."

Joshua was too focused on the report to notice anything. But Otiende noticed the drastic temperature drop. He looked at Agina. This couldn't be good. How could he turn this around? He needed her to stay calm.

"I am sure they could never get past. Especially if we keep the systems updated," Otiende said, emphasizing his tone to try and tactfully get Joshua's attention. He was hoping to divert him away from talking about the past attacks. However, Joshua was still stuck in his zone, speaking excitedly.

"Oh. I think they could. Look at this analysis and this full physical report. They could manage if they chose to clone someone who doesn't have attachments. They are getting better. Good thing this report did all the work of getting information. It gave us their intentions, their location, and how many clones they have. It's their whole invasion plan. I know it's accurate because it includes all their past attacks in great detail that we have not released. They are not stopping. But with this, we can finally get a step ahead of them. We have been too easy to get past."

The screens had started flickering but Joshua still had not noticed. Otiende couldn't take it anymore.

"Stop talking," Otiende blasted, clearly sounding like he was upset. Joshua looked up and finally noticed what was going on. It was already too late now; her storm had arrived.

67

AFTER THE STORM

"**H**OW LONG HAS this been going on?" Agina demanded.

Otiende was glad she did not sound upset. What her power manifested, had looked much worse than how she sounded. Maybe he could still get her out before it got worse.

"We should leave," he said, trying to hold her hand and lead her out. But she made a fist instead and didn't budge.

"Just answer me. I am trying to stay calm. I am holding myself back. Why are you not helping? Why won't you answer me?" she asked in a pleading voice while she looked at Joshua.

Joshua opened his mouth like he was about to speak but he seemed to remember he was told not to speak. He looked at Otiende, only to find Otiende glaring at him.

"Agina, let's go somewhere else to talk. The more you try to hold back, the more you are unable to maintain control. Having this conversation can only make you worse. Though, I sincerely hope not to upset you. Let's leave."

"I had not even asked you the question. I'm not leaving. I'm fine. I can handle it," she said to Otiende. Her pleading had disappeared, and she found resolve.

She looked at the screen and said, "Answer me."

Joshua looked half in surprise and fascination as what she wanted to know appeared on the screen. It passed really fast, pouring out information that all seemed to last for less than a second, but she seemed to get it all.

"All this time... You knew... So, you lied to me." She seemed to instinctively back away from Otiende, speaking in a pained voice. The wind and cold had intensified.

"I didn't lie to you. I just can't tell you these things because you worry too much and blame yourself for things that are not your fault. You are already going through so much." He knew he held back information. He hadn't meant to lie to her. Had he really lied to her? He probably had at some point, to keep everything hidden. At the moment, he couldn't seem to think of anything else but how to avoid a disaster. All the equipment that surrounded them was too important to damage. He could probably replace them, but everything needed to run twenty-four-seven.

"No! You lied to me. Since the beginning for over a month. With this much unrest we are much closer to war than you made me believe. People have died because of me. We put up that defence system together. You know what you said to me. If you can still lie to me now, straight to my face, how am I supposed to trust you." The words spilt out, like a large angry swarm of bees. A steady buzz approaching, that meant danger was coming.

As she spoke, lighting showed up in the room. It made the sound of sparking electricity as it lit up the place, doing its winding squiggles as it meandered around the room. It looked more like it had life, a vicious monster creeping around the room with a threatening gaze, ready to pounce at its prey at any second.

"We need to leave now Agina, or I'll get you out of here."

He reached for her hand but before he could reach her, he felt an electric shock. He cried out in pain and looked at his hand, but it looked fine. Luckily, he had not been hit by the lightning. It felt like he was shocked by electricity.

He took a look at Agina and decided his only option was to immediately get her out of there. Moving as fast as he could, he carried her over his shoulder as she fought to be freed. He ignored her kicking legs and pounding on his back, holding her steady.

The lighting moved around more wildly, like wild hungry beats that had been struggling to get free, then to make matters worse, finally finding an escape to easy prey. The lightning's wildness seemed unstoppable. He hurriedly apologised to Joshua and left as fast as he could. She stopped fighting him as he rushed out.

As he left with her, he could hear the lighting follow them and what sounded like something being struck full on by the lightning. It sounded like a small explosion had been set off, along with the sound of sparking electricity that had got louder. The sparks sounded somewhat like an angry hissing snake.

He put her down in front of the portal, then looking at her he said, "I am sorry I lied to you. I just wanted you to feel safe. I brought you here because I was ready to have this conversation. I know you can handle it and make your own choices. We don't need to talk here. I can let you know anything you are unsure about once we leave. I've set the portal location. Go through the portal and wait for me. I am going to get your spear."

He didn't want to look at her anymore. He knew his tone clearly showed he was upset with her. He didn't want to be upset with her. He was the one in the wrong.

"Try not to destroy anything else," he added, nervously looking at the activated portal behind her before running off. He wanted to check the damage she had done but it wouldn't have helped. Plus, he was in a hurry. Instead, he called out loud to Joshua to make sure he wasn't injured. After hearing a verbal confirmation, he got the spear and the shield and ran back.

Bracing himself, he went through the portal. She was facing away, standing at the other side of the portal. She had only taken a step away so he could come in after her.

"Did I hurt you?" she immediately asked in a solemn voice without turning to look at him.

"Yes. But I am fine. Could you at least know your limit? Why didn't you want to leave? I am sorry I lied to you. It felt like the best choice at the time. First it was because they were matters of national security I am obligated not to share. But then I had already broken the rules when I told you about that first attack on you at your studio. Then it was because I didn't want you to worry or feel afraid," he vented as he walked past her and put the spear and shield in the holder, then he turned back to face her.

"You had no right to make that decision for me. I know I can be fragile. But let me be fragile. It's not something you can fix or do anything about. I don't like when you talk to me like that. Like I can't handle things. It's like you are talking to a child." Hearing the stillness in her voice and feeling the serenity in the room confirmed her storm had disappeared.

He walked over to her and gave her a hug as he spoke, "I am sorry Agina. I panic when I see you that way. I feel like I should do something. What am I supposed to do in your storm?"

While he was still holding her, he continued, "I got hurt by you today. Yet I brought this on myself." It was like he spat out bitter words. His tone had shifted again. Why was he frustrated? His reaction towards her when they were there had probably made things worse. He escalated a situation that should have been simple.

"I am sorry," Agina's voice came from below. She seemed to soften in his arms. "I am so sorry," she said, holding him tighter.

He held her in the hug as he spoke gently, "I was at fault. You have become my world. I just wanted you to feel safe. How would you have felt safe if you knew we were getting attacked everyday. I wanted you to keep smiling. Your happiness gives me energy. I was selfish for wanting that sweet illusion and not considering what you would want. I still want you to be happy but now I understand it should be up to you what your happiness looks like. I am sorry." Holding her at the waist, he stepped back to look at her.

He looked down at her and their eyes met. Then she kissed him, catching him off-guard. It was a hungry kiss. It was like all her desires were in that kiss. It roused him too quickly. He moved his hands from her waist. Somehow his hands found her bare back. Being kissed, it woke up thoughts he had about her, like he had been in deep sleep and had been startled into awareness. He hadn't meant to feel her soft, smooth, bare skin that always seemed to be flawless.

Now that he had, he found that he couldn't stop himself from feeling her bare back and just as hungrily returned the kiss. Then his hands moved lower, unable to stop himself from squeezing her. She put her hands in his shirt and felt his firm chest and perked nipple. Whatever sense of control he had was melting away. Their kiss only seemed to intensify.

She pulled off his shirt. They separated for a short while as his shirt went over his head and arms and was discarded somewhere on the floor. He picked her up as they continued to kiss, and she wrapped her legs around him as he carried her to an entry hall side-table.

They couldn't stop kissing. They were feeding wild hunger. He used his hand to push aside what was on the table and then lowered her onto the tabletop. He couldn't bring himself to care about what he had just cleared out of the way as he heard the items crush into each other.

Nothing seemed to matter more than wanting Agina. He was completely driven by his desire. They both were. They continued to kiss as she touched him. He couldn't think. All he knew was that he loved her. He could only feel like he wasn't moving fast enough.

He liked the feeling of being touched by her and he wanted more. He undid her cape and it fell behind her. Then he undid her dress and held her exposed breast in his hand, sensually squeezing it as they kissed. Since he touched her on their Aiye, he had been longing for more.

As he kissed her, he continued to touch her breasts and gently caress her erect nipples with his fingertips. The soft sounds that escaped her lips were driving him mad as he claimed her lips. He could feel her hands moving lower, touching him below his waist with his pants still on.

He parted from her lips and kissed her neck, lowering his head as he kissed, at the nape of her neck, down to her breast. She was about to take off his pants, then he thought about reaching for the condom. Condom? He didn't have a condom.

He suddenly became alert, pulling away. What was he doing? He wasn't on birth control, and he didn't have any condoms with him. Or should he just get her pregnant? No. He couldn't do that. They both already took on positions with great responsibility. Especially Agina.

He thought about all the requests for help she had already received. He couldn't have her mother a child now. Besides what was he doing anyway? Here? To the woman he loved. He had imagined their first moment being romantic. Being a moment, she wouldn't forget. Should he continue then pull out in time? Could he manage that?

"OT," she said, pulling him closer. He didn't think he would ever hear his name sound so seductive, but she had excelled with the tone. "You know how much I want you. I know you want me too. Let me carry your child." She seemed to read his thoughts. The way she spoke was sensual, tagging at him to continue. Or was her tone all in his head?

He looked into her eyes. She was burning with desire. How could he deny such a request in his state? He knew if she got pregnant, they wouldn't regret the choice. But it would be a decision driven by desire.

"I can't appease you at the moment. But I have condoms in my room. Are you sure this is what you want? I need you to tell me."

CROSSING THE BRIDGE

"**Y**ES. IT'S WHAT I want. I really want us to have sex. I don't want to wait anymore," she said, her intention sounding clear and solid.

He held her face then he kissed her as he put his hand under her dress, feeling her upper thighs.

"So, I can take this off?" he asked in her ear, gently biting her earlobe as he grabbed a handful of her dress.

"Yes," she said, like she was out of breath.

He helped her down then took off the dress, throwing it somewhere he did not care about. Then they crashed into each other again, kissing wildly. Somehow, she was back on top of the table, feeling him, and her breast was now back in his mouth, as he flicked her nipple with his tongue.

He wanted to reach for the condom again then remembered he didn't have it. "Agina, let's go to my room. Are you sure it's what you want?" he asked again, wanting her to be certain.

"Yes. I am sure," she said, seeming to look deep into his soul.

He put his arm under her knees and behind her back, and she put her arm around his shoulder. Then he carried her to his room. He lay her in the middle of the queen-sized bed, still kneeling beside her.

She sat up, looking around in confusion, then asked, "Where are we?"

He almost laughed at how long it had taken her to ask. His grandmother's entry hall had a similarity to their home. She was probably looking down when she arrived and never noticed the obvious differences.

"Dana's. It's the only place we could be alone that didn't have electronics to destroy. You can let go here. You don't have to hold back. I would like you to fully feel what I do."

"What if something goes wrong and I can't control what happens?" Her voice sounded heavily engulfed with concern.

"Then at least we'll know what we shouldn't do. Things can always be replaced."

"What if I hurt you?"

"That's a risk I am willing to take."

"What if I teleport?"

"We'll probably teleport together. But I trust you can find your way back."

"What about the conferences?"

"It will be fine if we don't go back."

"What if someone comes in?"

He laughed. "Agina! So many questions! You were just begging me not to stop, without a care for anything, wanting me to get you pregnant." He could see the embarrassment flush on her face. "Do you still want me to?" He used a seductive tone when he asked the question.

She seemed to be holding her breath. He felt the shift in her demeanour.

"Now that you are fully aware of what I want to do. Tell me it's what you want." He had shifted to a serious tone. He needed her confirmation once more.

She seemed too hesitant to answer the question. Maybe she had just decided to have sex at the spur of the moment. He was now even more confused by her.

"I'll g-"

"Yes. I want to," she interrupted him.

He apprehensively went and got the condom. He was not confident about her answer anymore. She looked too nervous. He came back to the bed and lowered himself on top of her, wanting to lean in for a kiss. But he could feel a resistance.

"Agina, you are resisting me. You have a barrier," he stated, more fascinated than surprised.

"I- What?" she asked in shock, her eyes furrowed and her mouth hanging slightly open as she quickly shook her head.

She felt around him and felt herself, then felt the space between them. Her hands didn't seem to be stopped by the barrier, but no matter what body part he tried, he was stopped from reaching her vaginal area by an invisible barrier.

He was looking between them, too fixated on the occurrence to notice how she had reacted to the situation. But he couldn't ignore what he heard. It was the first time he heard her crying. Every single time she cried she had always cried silently. Even when they were younger.

He looked for her face, but she had turned her head to the side, and had her arm over her eyes. It was still a gentle cry. But he could hear so much pain in her cry. It broke his heart to see her that way. Why did she look so broken? He wanted to pick her up and rock her in his arms. He sat by her side, his body facing her, unsure of what to do.

"This isn't... what I want."

He heard so much anguish in that statement. Her cry pulled at him to do something.

"Your body says otherwise, Agina," he said, feeling empathy for her.

"It should shut up. I didn't even ask for this power, but I still got it. What kind of self do I have?" she asked, sounding exasperated, giving into her tears.

"It's just trying to look out for you. It has saved you several times." He leaned in and wiped the tears that had made their way out from under her arm.

"It has also made me miserable. I don't want to be protected. I want you."

"You have me," he said, gently kissing her on the neck, then planting several kisses on her. It slowly stopped the tears. But she still had her face hidden behind her arm. The kissing brought him back on the same path of roaring desires. Maybe he should have just left her alone and ended things there, before he got himself excited again. They had gone down a path that was difficult to come back from.

"Can I offer you something else?" He whispered in her ear.

She removed her arm from her face and looked at him, curiosity in her eyes. When he looked at her face, he saw her hunger more clearly and wondered what he could have done to not drive her down this path.

Or were they just doomed to end up here? Resisting a pull that seemed to draw them closer, strengthening its tug the more they restrained themselves. Was distance between them the only way they could have avoided this? Should they never have kissed in the first place when they were in the park? He now knew the answer to that question. He also knew that he had no intention to stay away from her.

He gently wiped the tears on her eyes and face. "I can help you orgasm, without touching the part your power feels compelled to protect. Whether you want the protection or not, it's a boundary I will not cross. I love you so much. I love and respect all the parts of you. Even the parts that won't let me get to you."

The change on her face was instantaneous. He was already attracted to her as is, but the look of longing, hope and joy that she had, was stirring up desires in the depth of him in places he didn't even know had feelings. He couldn't wait any longer.

RELEASE 1

"I DON'T KNOW that it matters at this point because your powers also speak for you. But I need your consent. Say you want to have an orgasm." He held her with his gaze, daring her to say it without looking away.

She opened her mouth like she was about to say something. But she just blushed and looked away. Was he being too hard on her? He already knew what she wanted by looking in her eyes.

But what was he supposed to do when she was so indecisive and conflicted about sex. How much would forcing her to make choices harm their relationship? She was somewhat already cornered to him and cornered to her powers; these were not things she was looking for when they showed up.

As humans, we are at a low point when we feel like we don't have options. Especially when you have to make a choice and none of the options are ideal.

He had kept asking her, when her indecisiveness was already driving him mad, and he just wanted to make love to her. Did she not want the orgasm or was she just too shy to say such a thing?

He sat beside her at the headboard. She also sat up then he held her face, gently turning her head to face him. "Only if you say it's what you want. We can wait."

Hearing him say they can wait seemed to cause a reaction in her. She

368  **STRANGE LIGHT: Ler Mahia**

shook her head and said, "I want to have an orgasm." There almost seemed to be a plea and desperation in her voice. If it's what she wants, then it's what he is going to give her.

"I am sorry I-"

He kissed her before she could finish what she was about to say. She put her arms around him, pulling him closer. But he pulled away.

Grinning at her he said, "Hands off. Or else I will tie you up. Do you want me to tie you up?"

"Yes."

He was surprised at how fast she had replied to that. He had said it more like a joke. But now that he thought about it, It was probably better for the both of them because he would have a harder time restraining himself if she had free reign over him.

"First you need to let go and relax. I don't want you to be tense or nervous. You need to fully trust me with your body if you are letting me touch you. That way your powers won't step in and keep me even further away. I'll find something to use in this room. Lay down and get comfortable," he said then got up to look for something useful in the dresser after returning the condom.

He was looking through the closet when he felt a chill. He turned around to see Agina had been levitating and was descending back to the bed. Her tattoos were glowing. She had no clothes on and had a sheet covering her lower body.

He was mesmerised by her light. How was his wife so powerful? What would she be like if she harnessed her power? For her, it was still something she didn't want. What would she be like if she didn't have her powers? The Agina he recently got to know has powers. That was the woman he married.

He hesitated to admit he somewhat idolised her when he was younger. She seemed to have such a free spirit. Appearing and disappearing in his life like the wind, when they would attend the conferences. A presence he could feel but never grasp.

Realistically, he had been too intimidated to say he liked her after he figured it out, because he was afraid to be turned down. Also, he had felt free spirits couldn't be tied down. Especially to the lifestyle he had chosen.

She looked peaceful, like she was asleep on the bed. He didn't feel the gentle breeze anymore. He turned back to the closet and removed the belt of a soft plush robe, then he walked over to the bed, sitting beside her.

"Are you ready?" he cautiously asked, like he might interrupt her sense of peace.

She nodded her head. Her eyes were still closed.

"You can keep your eyes closed if you like. I am going to tie your hands. Let me know if it feels uncomfortable," he gently said.

He tied her hands onto the headboard with the plush belt then started faintly touching her like his fingers were a brush, over her arms, her belly, circling his fingers around her belly button. She seemed to shiver with his touch.

He leaned in and whispered in her ear, "Tell me what you want me to do next."

Just his voice had made several girls fall in love with him. It wasn't that he sang so well. Just the way he spoke seemed to mesmerise them. He wondered if she liked his voice too. He hadn't spoken to anyone so seductively before.

"Touch me like before. Kiss me." She spoke like she was breathing heavily. He could tell her heart was beating fast when he passed his fingers over her heart.

He circled her breasts with his fingertips and asked, "Like our engagement or when we came here?" Then he held her breast in his hand and touched her nipples with his fingers.

"Both," she said, sounding like she was out of breath.

He did as she asked, taking her where she wanted to go. He was impressed at how much easier it was than he thought, to get her to moan and look like she was near the end, arching her back and curling her toes.

He knew the moment she got there by the sound she made and how her body seemed to release tension like an arrow being shot out of a bow. She was left completely relaxed, her body spent.

RELEASE 2

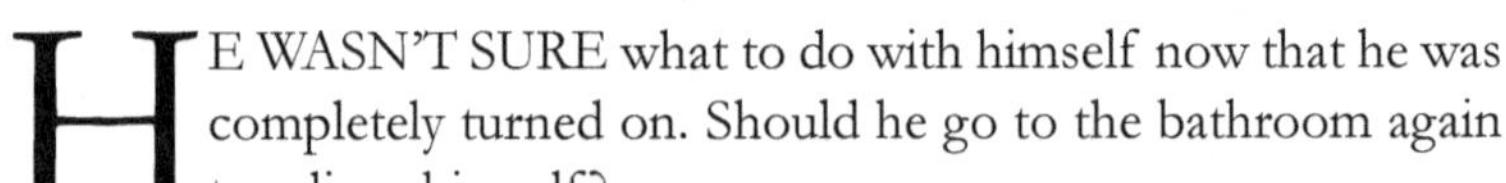

HE WASN'T SURE what to do with himself now that he was completely turned on. Should he go to the bathroom again to relieve himself?

She opened her eyes and looked at him with bliss as she said, "Your turn. Untie me." Her words had caught him off guard.

"Are you sure? Or is this the spur of the moment again? It's not our job to make sure the other person gets their sexual needs met," he said, as he gently touched her face.

"I know. I am sure. I have constantly thought about how you would feel inside me all day. At least let me do this since I can't give you that."

She suddenly seemed to have realised what she said and blushed, looking away. So that was the reason why she had come onto him: since the morning her libido had been high. From the beginning, she didn't have any curiosity about what it felt like to be with a man. But now, her curiosity was genuinely peaked.

"Okay. If it's what you want," he said, touching her head.

She looked at him again, following his movements with her eyes. He untied her hands and then pulled off his pants along with his underwear. She had obviously not expected him to take them off at that moment. She lay there staring at him with wide eyes. "OT?" she said in a shaky voice. "You're never going to fit."

He grinned. He couldn't help but feel proud of himself. He had only experienced virgins when he was younger. He could understand how intimidating it was to see an erect fully grown man when you had not been penetrated before.

"Your body is perfectly capable of taking me in and pushing out a child. Don't worry about it today. You don't need to experience that yet."

He switched places with her. Her body was beautiful. It took a lot of effort to not just gawk at her naked body or pull her towards him.

"Do you want to be tied?"

He almost laughed at how she asked. She was shy when she was not entranced in intimacy, being driven by her desires. She was one or the other extreme. He wondered what she would do to him. Would she be too shy to get anything done?

He wanted to cheat a little and touch her, not letting her do all the work. So, he told her that he didn't want to be tied up.

She started in the same way. Lightly touching his body as he closed his eyes. His heart raced, making it feel like it was so loud, beating in his ear. The slow movement of her fingers lightly touching him seemed to leave behind a live molten stream of hankering.

Then she kissed him as she continued. It felt really good to feel the stimulation of her fingers on his body as he was kissed by her soft lips. Maybe she wouldn't have to try so hard after all.

He could sometimes feel her breasts on him as she leaned over to kiss him. He really wanted to touch them. He had just been touching them, doing whatever he wanted to her breasts, but it still didn't feel like he got enough. Feeling the soft buoyant flesh on his bare skin was a newfound feeling.

She whispered in his ear. "Use your mind. Let your mind take you there too. Think about all the things we are not doing that you want to do."

She explored his upper body with her hands and her mouth. Part of him still couldn't believe she was here. She had been in his digital world of #1008 when he knew he had fallen in love with her. He had loved her from a distance. He didn't know he could have her and fall more deeply in love with her. Yet here she was, her touch real. He got pleasure from being touched in places he didn't even know he could get pleasure from. She kissed him on his lips again. Gently exploring his mouth.

Then she stopped. He could tell she was looking at him, so he opened his eyes. "What is it?" he gently asked. By the look on her face, she wanted to say something, but she had been too shy to say it. He rubbed her back to encourage her.

"Can I get on top of you? I think I am about to have another orgasm." She spoke really fast like she had to get it out in one breath, or she would never be able to say it.

He smiled at her.

"You can have whatever you consciously ask for. Get on top of me," he said, giving her a nod with a grin that couldn't help but take over his lips.

She hesitated for a minute then said, "Keep the sheet on top of you." She put her leg over him, straddling him. She started to gyrate her body, her breasts rubbing on his chest, her eyes closed and her lower lip held between her teeth.

He was holding her waist but chose to let go. It would be too easy for him to pull her where he wanted her to go. The way she humped rubbed against his penis with a gentle pressure that rose the intensity of excitement building up within him.

So instead, he watched her, taking her advice and imagining what he wanted to do. Imagining how he wanted to thrust deeper and deeper into her. Imagining that she was saying how much she loved him.

He knew she loved him just as surely as he knew he loved her. It was always in the way she looked at him. Watching her face of bliss as she humped on top of him, spoke so much of this love.

This time, she cried out louder, her moans filling the room. She raised the speed of her humping.

He could feel that the stimulation had aroused him to a point where he was about to release. The intensity reached its peak, but he held it. Hoping the feeling would last. He watched the look on her face. With the way she tightened her grip on his shoulders, moaned, and the way she moved her body, he knew that she was experiencing an orgasm.

He felt fluid discharging from his penis, but he wasn't there yet. He couldn't tell if she was done yet, she seemed to be having a longer orgasm. She was convulsing, still having a strained grip on him. She took his mouth in hers and kissed him as she continued to grind fast and out of rhythm.

He couldn't hold it anymore. He let out a sound as he finally felt himself release, his mind going blank as it slid down his leg onto the sheet. He could also feel that the sheet between them was wet from what she had discharged. He didn't have to look to know that they had made a mess.

She lay naked on top of him, too exhausted to move. She wasn't heavy but her body was slack, seeming to put more weight than usual on him. They lay this way for a while as they caught their breath and their hearts slowed down to the normal steady rhythm.

"Why does it feel like we just had sex?" she asked, looking at him.

"Because we did too much. It's honestly not that different from having sex," he said, putting an arm around her.

She put her head back down and gently stroking him, she said, "Next time let's just have sex."

"And how long do I have to wait for your barriers to come down?" The words seemed to come out before he had formulated them in his mind. As soon as he heard himself, he wished he hadn't said it.

Her fingers froze. "I don't know. Maybe it's just about having an internal locus of control. I know the barrier wasn't there when I was moving on top of you. Even now I can feel you under the sheet." She replied.

He wondered how she felt about what they had just done. So, he decided to ask.

"Any regrets about what just happened?"

"No regrets."

"Did I please you well today?"

She nodded.

"You are too easy to please. How have you not been with more people?" He was teasing her. Apart from Chloe, she had not been with anyone else since she got married seventeen years ago.

"Being with someone is only easy when I love them."

He wondered if she truly intended to say that.

"Do you love me Agina?"

She remained silent. She probably didn't mean to say it.

"It's ok. You don't have to answer. I love you," he said, gently rubbing her head.

She had already brought the topic up so he might as well have asked.

"We should wash up. Do you want to get in the bathroom together? We have already seen each other naked." He was teasing her again.

He couldn't help but make fun of the situation. He didn't think it was possible, but he could feel that she was blushing by the way her face felt on his chest.

"I'll go first," she said, taking the sheet with her and leaving him naked on the bed. He laughed silently to himself as he watched her disappear into the bathroom like she was being chased. She didn't dare to look at him.

CHOOSE BOTH

SHE STOOD NEXT to the freight containing flowers, looking intensely at a plan of their house on her com. A large screen was ahead of her, showing the blueprints. Occasionally, she would zoom in and out, using her fingers to resize the images.

"This place looks so much larger on the plan. It looks more like the plan of a resort. I didn't even realise you have a pool. We didn't tour the whole house. Right?" asked Agina, looking up at Otiende.

"Yeah. I didn't show you some of the suits, the outside, or the pool. For now, other than the master suit, the suits are furnished exactly the same. To see one is to see all of them," replied Otiende.

She looked back down at the plan.

"What about this place? What is this?" She looked up again.

"I'll show you when you are done," he said, with a mischievous grin.

She looked at the plan even more intensely, formulating a plan.

"I know where I am going to start! It's going to be great! Definitely all along here. This deck has become my favourite place. The view of the lake is already breathtaking. So, positively there! And also, here. And here is a perfect place for a playground. And I can't neglect the entrance! Here too." She was beaming when she looked up at him.

"When I looked at this plan, my idea got bigger! I'll need more flowers. Is it too much? I-"

He suddenly kissed her.

She was surprised by the sudden kiss, but she still found herself melting into his kiss. She felt her knees get weak. How could he still kiss her in this way? After what they had done yesterday, she was afraid she would be too tense and awkward or that kissing him would make her insanely want to have sex with him. She feared she would always feel out of control. But thankfully, she felt more in control.

Since then, they had spent time cuddling more than anything else. She was glad to find kissing him still had the same effect. Since the intimacy happened, she had avoided kissing him. They had gone to her home after they showered, and after sleeping in the same bed, attended the conferences for several hours. They came there soon after.

Maybe she had spent too much time overanalysing what her relationship with Otiende was going to be like. Especially worrying about what sex would do to their relationship.

They stood there kissing. None of them seemed to want to stop. He finally pulled away, grinning at her.

"I like to see you happy. It's your place. You can do whatever you like. I'll get you more," he said to her, looking at her with adoration.

"Okay! Thank you! Let's start then," she said, putting away the screen.

They walked around as she happily used her powers to plant the flowers, sometimes accelerating their growth. She had set the freight to navigate on its own and follow them.

She always went into her happy world when she was creating. She hadn't created landscape architecture before. So, she was enjoying giving the new experience a go.

She would occasionally step back to see what she had created and ask Otiende what he thought. But he would just praise her no matter what she did.

She asked, "Which side do you like better?"

"I like both."

"OT! You are not being helpful. I need your opinion on this," Agina said, pouting at him.

"If you want to choose one you can evaluate what you like about them then decide," he said, shrugging his shoulders.

She took a look at the way she had arranged the flowers and then asked, "Are you afraid of heights?"

"No."

"Close your eyes."

He cooperatively closed his eyes.

She held his hand.

"Do you remember that feeling of being in mid-air? Are you comfortable with that?" she asked, wanting to gauge what he felt.

"I don't know. After it all happened, I was under the influence of your power. Even now if I try and think about what terrified me, I shift to the gentle calmness you had created in my mind. Then it's like the thought vanishes. It's like my mind won't allow me to feel that terror again."

"Why didn't you tell me this? It sounds like I drastically changed your neuro pathways." She was concerned she had transgressed the limits therapy didn't even dare to cross when she helped him. It was something she didn't even know she could do. Her instincts had led her. She might not have seen what he saw, but she had felt what was there through other ways, sensing the fundamental nature.

"It's not a big deal. I think it was for the better. I like that you messed with my mind. Mind shifts can also naturally happen when you love someone. It messes with your mind; the decisions we make because we love someone: our family, our friends. They become choices we are okay with even if we know our reasoning is altered. But love is also a choice. It starts with a choice."

They had been ascending into the air as they spoke. They were now suspended in mid-air. Agina thought about what he said. Choices. It sounded like he was talking about something different, needing her to read between the lines. Rather than speaking directly.

She looked down at the two designs she had just created. Was he talking about choosing to love him? Or was he talking about choosing not to wait to have sex? It could be her indecision about a number of things, like the details regarding their new office. There were so many other decisions she had a hard time making.

Too many times she found herself wishing she knew what to do. She thought about the decision he made. Both. He always seemed to be comfortable with both, with the grey areas of life.

Why did she have to choose? She thought about how she chose women as her type even if she liked more than that. Eventually, she ended up with Otiende. She constantly struggled over doing things as naturally as possible or using technology. Otiende reminded her that she didn't have to choose.

"Agina?"

Was there truly a reason why she had to choose? Was choosing both also a choice? She looked at him. She wanted to see his reaction. But more importantly, she wanted to feel how he reacted through the ring, to ensure he would be okay.

"Open your eyes."

When he opened his eyes, he looked surprised. Then he looked down. She was glad that he didn't feel afraid.

"I wanted us to look at the design from a different view."

"I like this perspective," he said, grinning at her.

Again, she got the feeling that he was talking about something else.

"You are beautiful," he said, smiling at her.

"Would you look at the different designs?!" she asked, trying to direct him to look at the landscape below rather than her.

His gaze lingered on her face for a while before he finally looked down. She thought about how often she heard him say she was beautiful. She didn't hear it from other people. When she heard it, it was because she had changed something about her look, or she had on an outfit that complimented her. He was the only one who randomly said it.

There was nothing out of the ordinary about her beauty. Because of the way he was, she knew he was being sincere when he said she was beautiful. It was not just exaggerated flattery.

Agina asked, "What do you think?"

"I think it looks great."

"Do you prefer one over the other?"

"No. I like both."

"Okay. Then both it is. I am taking us back down."

They started to slowly descend.

"You are getting better at using your powers."

"Thank you. When I think back to how much influence you have had on me... I have a lot to appreciate you for."

"I appreciate you too."

When their feet were back on the ground, he said, "Come. Let's go inside. I'll show you what you were asking about earlier."

72

TAKING A SPIN

S HE FOLLOWED HIM back into the house through the door at the deck, then followed him into the entry hall.

"Stand still," he said, then scanned his hand on what appeared to be no different than the wall. She could only tell it had scanned his hand because of the light that moved across his palm.

A circular strip began to rise from the floor, forming a ring around them. Agina thought it would keep rising and form a wall around them, but it stopped after a few seconds. Then the floor inside the circle started to slowly descend.

It was like a hidden elevator. She suddenly had the feeling she was about to witness something extraordinary. The lights had come on as they were on the way down. She seemed to be facing the back of the room.

"You can move now," he said when they stopped moving and were at the same level as the lower level floor.

First, she looked up, tilting her head to see where they had just come from. The hole they came in from was already covered, leaving no trace of where they had just gone through. She turned around and gasped. She had never expected that she would see what was in front of her.

"OT!! This is so cool! … Wow. Saying that reminds me of old times. We were kids when I used that word all the time. Remember... you used to be cool guy," she said, bursting out laughing.

"I am still cool guy," he said, striking a pose like he was about to have his picture taken.

She laughed even louder.

"And you were cool gal."

"Eh. Don't remind me. It was self-proclaimed. You always had the cool stuff. I was just pretending to keep up," she said, cringing her face.

"Now it's your stuff too."

"I wouldn't dare call them my stuff. You were too quick to sign stuff over to me without asking."

"That was a personal choice. What good is having these things that I know you would also like to use if I can't share them with you?"

When they had just started the prep for their engagement, he gave her a foreign card with her name so she could buy what they needed where money was accepted. It had triggered a conversation about their finances. But by then it was too late. He had already added her name to everything he possibly could, and he was not willing to reverse any of it. He even declared that he would keep going till everything that wasn't done was taken care of.

She looked at how gentle his eyes were as he looked at her. In all honesty, she did understand why. She had always chosen not to have much, but what she had, especially her space, she had enjoyed sharing with him. It made her glad to see him get comfortable in her space.

He just had so much. As much as she would love to share all his spaces, it would take her a long time to visit his residences around the world, leave alone, spend time there.

Unfortunately for her, from what she heard from him, she now also shared a large number of his fans because they had a couple fan base. This had happened over the past few days as people tuned into the conferences. Sharing aspects of his life was inevitable.

Nevertheless, she still didn't see the need to have her name added. Sharing could happen without all the formal procedures.

What could she do but accept what he wanted to share when he looked at her like that with love in his eyes and spoke from heartfelt emotion. It was the same eyes that had convinced her to spend money in sums she didn't even know were possible. Has this truly become her life?

"You can go and take a look around and try any that you like," he said, nodding at his collection.

"Can I really?" she asked like a little child allowed to touch something fun but forbidden, taking off before she waited for an answer.

The room looked more like a superhero's hideout or lair with different means of transportation, outfits and strange objects on display. Agina ran to the one closest to her.

"What is this?" she asked with beaming eyes.

"It's a hoverbike. It looks different because it's made to be more lightweight. But it has just as much power. Do you want to take it for a spin?"

"Yes! I want to try it," she said, almost jumping onto him.

She couldn't contain her excitement. It's not that she had never seen such things. But these things were here in their house. Right in front of her and always available. Somehow it was different than having seen one of the transportation methods or having already ridden one.

Agina always got excited about technology when she interacted with it for the first time. Plus, she had never seen most of the transportation that he had. Not because they were all new, a large number of them were vintage.

He got two helmets and gave her one. She followed his lead and put it on. She could feel the helmet build a layer of protection over her skin. He got onto the hoverbike with such ease then held out his hand. She put her hand in his, and he helped her get on.

"Closer. Hold on tight," he said looking back at her.

She had not thought about how she would need to ride the hoverbike while holding on to him. But now that she was seated behind him, it felt like such an intimate thing to do. She moved closer but still left some space between them, then leaned in and held him around his belly.

She couldn't help but be aware of how solid he was under his shirt. They were still in their outfits from the conference. The shirt he wore was loose and the fabric wasn't heavy. She could practically feel his skin underneath the fabric.

"Ready?" he asked, but before she even replied they were moving.

She was surprised by how quiet it ran. He seemed to have ridden it countless times. He effortlessly zoomed past everything in the room to what looked like a large portal that was not only quickly activated, but showed what was on the other side.

Larger portals for transportation appeared and disappeared based on whether they needed to be used. However, for privacy reasons, portals didn't usually show what was on the other side.

She could tell right away that they were not in Dala after they went through the portal. They were moving so fast that she almost didn't catch their surroundings. She opted to use her powers to take in the view. She found his comfort with speed intriguing, considering she could process things that moved at a faster pace, and he couldn't. He finally brought them to a stop after some time.

73

SYMBOLS

"**Y**OU SHOULD TRY it. I'll help you from behind," he said, getting down.

"But I don't-"

He didn't give her a chance to protest. She found that she had been lifted and moved forward then he swiftly got behind her. She didn't even fully realise what was going on till it was too late.

He took her hand and placed it on the handlebar and explained the basic controls, moving her hand in his. She could not hear what he said. Her heart was beating fast. She wasn't sure if it was because she thought driving it was a bad idea, or that he was pressed right against her back as he reached forward to explain the controls. Because he was leaning over from behind, he had his head beside her.

She could feel his chest vibrating as he spoke, his deep gentle voice coming from beside her. The clothes she wore were also loose and thin, barely leaving a boundary between them.

"Ready?" he asked. Like before he didn't wait for her response, he moved her hand to start the hoverbike. It started to ascend. He let her hands go and held her. Somehow, he seemed to have moved even closer. Her heart beat even faster. She couldn't focus on what she should be doing. They stayed this way for some time.

"Agina, it's electronic. You can make it do whatever you want." She could hear the amusement in his voice.

Whatever I want? She thought to herself. She had to stop herself from thinking about him so she could think about what to do. They started to move forward but she hadn't touched any of the controls.

She had noticed some people as she was looking at their surroundings, but she still couldn't figure out where they were. "Where are we?" she asked, as they moved forward at a slower pace.

"The city of Steam. In Ruglua. I come here when I need to go for a ride. Here they don't make a big deal about what you drive or how you drive it."

"I haven't been here before. It's got terrible laws." Anyone could hear the disgust in her voice.

He laughed. For some reason his laughter helped her relax.

"Yes. But it's because of those terrible laws that I can do this. I've learnt how to navigate the world outside Dala. Push beyond limits without getting myself into trouble."

She thought about how he had hacked their system when he was 5 years old and how he was always ambitious. It was probably a good thing the core of his nature was good and that he had a moral compass. Especially considering how much money he had. Such power could easily be used to oppress others.

"What have you always wanted to do on this? I can push its limits with my power," she asked, wanting to please him.

He seemed to be thinking before he answered, "Honestly, I just want to kiss you, but we can't take these helmets off here. It doesn't just have terrible laws; it's got terrible air quality. Being here with you is enough. I know you could come up with something. It's your first time trying it. You can't just want to move it forward."

She gave it a thought. She had been thinking about what he would want. But what she really wanted to do was... She didn't need to ask him to hold on. He was already holding her so closely that they couldn't have made more contact.

They began to move around in different ways as they did aerobatics. She didn't even spare taking them around in loops because she knew how to defy gravity.

"Do you trust me?" she asked when she was done with the stunts, looking back towards him.

"With my life and soul," he said expressively without any hesitation.

"Take off your helmet," she said, blushing as she took hers off.

He took off his helmet. She didn't need to say anything to him. As soon as his helmet came off, he heartfeltly kissed her. She earnestly kissed him back. He was a giving person, it made her want to give him what she could.

She had her head turned back towards him. She couldn't hold the position for long, so she pulled away from him after they kissed for some time.

She also didn't want to get carried away. She needed to maintain their protective barrier, using her power.

"We should get back. We have more toys to play with," he said, smiling and putting his helmet back on.

"How can you call them toys?!" she asked in disbelief, putting her helmet back on. They had still been on the move. Luckily there was barely any traffic in the airspace.

"I got them because they are fun." She heard him say.

She thought about how she enjoyed the ride. All his rides were probably a lot of fun. They did not look like they were bought for necessity. But even if she had never attempted to buy any, she knew they had to have been expensive. Toys were not expensive!

"Could you make a portal back home?" he asked.

She gave it a thought then said, "I could get us back home. But if I use our house coordinates, it's going to take us outside to your outer portal, where all vehicles enter from. I'm not sure how to get us into your toy room."

"If you lower the coordinates by twelve and a half metres you could get us in. If you don't want to try that, we could just head back to where we came from and use the return function."

She had spent a lot of time practising how to create portals when she first got her powers, and they were taking down the surveillance system. Because of that, she now knew a lot about creating portals. She knew she would be able to do it.

"I'll give it a try."

She followed what she had done when practising, keeping her eyes open and maintaining their forward movement, while she focused on the location. A portal opened in front of them, and they went through.

Agina wasn't sure how to make the portal show what was on the other side. It felt like she was driving into darkness. As soon as they got to the other side, she stopped. Afraid she would crash into something. Thankfully she had managed to come back safely into the room.

They were still hovering, so she got a better view of everything in the room. It was a really impressive collection. He even had some that were docked in water, looking like they could only be used in water or something similar.

"Take a look around. I'll take it back," he said.

She nodded and brought down the hoverbike so she could get off. Once she dismounted, he pushed the controls and took off. She wondered how he could control it at such high speeds without crashing into anything. He sped the short distance to its original position.

She had been looking at one of the vehicles when Otiende hugged her from behind.

"This is the first one I ever got. I don't usually take it for a ride. It's got so many weapons it's ridiculous. If I took it anywhere it would look like I am declaring war!"

But Agina was focused on something else entirely.

"What is that symbol? I have seen it somewhere before," she asked, staring intently.

"Symbol?... Oh, that symbol," he said as Agina pointed it out.

"I was still a kid when I came up with the symbol. It's my symbol. A symbol of the letters OT and number 1 because I always win," he said smiling proudly.

"But my team never liked it because the OT doesn't read clearly. And people do not know me as OT. So, it was never officially used. I sort of kept it as a personal symbol."

Agina examined the O that was created using diagonal edges and straight lines. The T was split up in two, with the horizontal line appearing to unravel from the O. The vertical part of the T also formed the number 1.

"It's bothering me. I am sure it's something more significant," she said in a hushed tone as she scrutinised the symbol.

He was still holding her from the back, so she looked up at him with questioning eyes.

"Take a closer look. Maybe it will help you remember," he said.

Earlier, she had approached the vehicle as she walked past, and it reacted to her. It drew her curiosity, so she changed her direction and walked towards it. It was like it was alive, reading its surroundings. The low-lying vehicle looked more like a cross between a jet and a solar sportscar.

Without realising it, she had somewhat of a conversation with it. Telling it she was Otiende's wife and that she was just looking around. It was like it relaxed. The change made her realise it had been trying to decipher whether she was or wasn't a threat. It was weird how she felt connected to it, like her house.

It opened its door, like it was inviting her to take a closer look or take it for a spin. Almost the entire body of the vehicle had lifted up like a lid, revealing two seats. Likewise, the symbol was revealed at the seats and several other places on the control panel, catching her attention. She had been staring at the symbol when Otiende held her from the back.

She got halfway into the vehicle and touched the closest symbol that was upholstered on the seat, moving her hand slowly over the letters.

"OT!!!" She exclaimed, her eyes flying off the symbol to look at Otiende in surprise. She hurriedly got out of the vehicle and faced him fully with her body.

74

DECIPHERING SYMBOLS

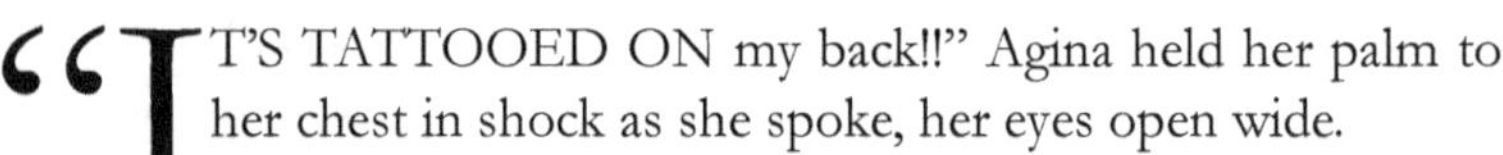

"IT'S TATTOOED ON my back!!" Agina held her palm to her chest in shock as she spoke, her eyes open wide.

Otiende looked at her with a blank expression, then a grin spread across his face. "I have been tattooed on your back by magical powers, in an ancient ritual, blessed by ancestors, the powers beyond, and the creator of all." He seemed to have been possessed by a sense of pride.

Agina relaxed and smiled at him. "You could brag less, and it will still be too much."

He came closer and held her hand as he said. "I will show it to all the people who think we shouldn't be together. Rub it in their faces." He laughed cockily before he continued, "What are they going to say then?!"

"OT. First, I thought other people's opinions don't bother you. And second, we are not showing anybody anything."

"But you do show the tattoos on your back. I just want to tell them what it means," he said, protesting.

"For ancestors' sake! I show them because I like them, and I think they are beautiful."

He looked dejected. How could he be stubborn about this? It was her body after all. Only the elders understood ancient text, and even they couldn't decipher all the symbols because they were not all in ancient text, like the symbol she just discovered was Otiende's symbol. She would rather people didn't know what they all meant.

"You didn't even notice it anyway. How did you not notice your own symbol?" She was curious if anyone else who knows what it means might spot it.

"I don't know. The patterns are very intricate. The most noticeable is the Ler Mahia in ancient text. When we were getting the dresses done, we used the patterns on your arms and legs. They are easier to copy into a repetitive pattern. Those are the patterns I look at more often. When I look at your bare back, I... get too distracted to read the symbols. You constantly distract me. Sigh. It would have been nice to silence them all."

"OT. I never would have thought you wanted to say anything to them. You make it seem like this stuff doesn't bother you."

"I have dealt with this stuff for a long time. It's not easy. I got tougher. But occasionally I still get knocked down by things people say. I just get up and keep going. It's tougher when it's about us and especially if it is about you. I haven't developed any kind of immunity for that. It bothers me more than I would like to admit. You are perfect, we are perfect together. I want everyone to see that."

She gave Otiende a hug.

"No one is perfect. We all have flaws," she said, as she kept him wrapped in her arms. She wanted to keep him in a bubble where he would be safe from it all. But he wouldn't let her stop all the negative comments. She only did that for herself. She knew that he couldn't have gone his entire life unscathed by all he experienced. But the way he said it made it sound like it had really affected him deep inside.

"My Agina is perfect. Your flaws, they make you perfect." He kissed her on the forehead.

"Not everyone sees me the way you do," she said rubbing her thumb on his cheek as she gently held his face in her hand.

"Sigh. I know. Right now O_ts are all over the place. I haven't posted anything since the day I went to meet you at the cafe, and I haven't publicly talked to O_ts in an even longer time. Sometimes I feel like I should say something. But then what do I say? What do you think?" he asked, looking at her with expectation.

"Have you gone this long without saying something before?" She gently rubbed his back, consoling him.

"Not really. My team always posted something for me. Especially when I was a kid. More so when I was inactive between projects, so I could truly get a break. The longest I would go silent was a week; which were rare occasions. But I told my team to put everything on hold until further notice. They advised against it. They don't understand us.

The confusion makes sense. No one understands why I am silent unless they hear the whole story. I hesitate to share the whole story because it's not just my story. It involves you and our whole community.

I don't know what to explain about how we met. Just giving them the ninety eight percent match story would feel like a lie. As a celebrity too much of your life is exposed. This part of my life in the Innercity managed to stay hidden for so long.

Now that our Innercity people know I am an elder, I am still not ready to talk about such things like why I gave up being an elder. It's somewhat a dark past. Our Innercity people who witnessed this darkness helped make things easier in my transition back because they already understand. But they would never talk. Especially to outsiders.

Not a single person in the Innercity has asked an inappropriate question that I do not want to answer. Those involved know I was a part of them, and they know why I was rejected. Those who were not involved know some things should not be talked about. It's a weird thing in our culture, but secrets stop the chaos we see in modern culture. Since our people like to stay silent, why should I speak?

Even worse, no one outside the Innercity will understand. They don't even know what an elder is. Leave alone that most people didn't even realise I am a citizen of Dala because of my multiple citizenship.

The conferences were the perfect place to make our first public appearance. They all have an understanding. Even if they don't know the story. They received us well. The rest..."

"Then just leave it be for now." He probably had more to say before she interjected when he paused. Their story was complicated. She just didn't know how to help him.

"Can I see the tattoo?"

"Only if you don't touch me. I would rather you don't stir anything. Will you be good?"

"Yes."

She highly doubted his answer. His eyes always gave him away. But she turned around anyway. She felt him slowly unzip her jumpsuit. Her heart raced faster as the zipper steadily came down. The fabric loosened around her upper body.

She held down her clothes to her chest with her forearms crossed in an x. She felt him slowly drop the left side off her shoulder, then the right side off her shoulder.

"Let it drop so I can see."

She knew it wasn't a good idea because of the way his deep gentle voice sounded, it was almost hypnotising. She let go, putting her hands to the side. But it still hadn't gone down all the way.

She took her arms out of the clothes then it dropped, leaving her standing in her bra and the bottom half of her jumpsuit. What possessed her to listen to him? She felt like she was holding her breath as he looked.

Then she felt his hands unhook her bra. She felt it come loose but she didn't do or say anything. He slowly took the strap off her right shoulder, then off her left shoulder. She felt as though she had gotten hotter despite the cool air she was aware of on her skin.

She felt him hold both sides of the strap and slowly pull them down, till they came off her hands, dropping to the floor. Did he need to take off her bra? She didn't stop him even though she had doubts, still feeling the lingering sensation where his hands had trailed when he removed her bra. She stood there feeling a tingle on the back of her neck, waiting.

Then he gently touched her, running his fingers down her spine as he gently asked, "When will you let me inside you? When can I have you Agina?"

She remained silent. She didn't dare say a word. She could only close her eyes from the intense experience of his fingers brushing down her spine.

"Tell me when Agina," he said, speaking softly by her ear. She also felt his breath as he spoke. It left trickling sensations all over her body. Because she was intentionally standing still, she was hyper aware of every single movement he made.

It didn't help that she could feel how wildly his heart was racing thanks to the ring. The ring read that his body was tense, and his body temperature had changed. She had never been focused enough in the moment to realise when the ring was reading the signs of his arousal. However, thanks to her hyper awareness, it was like it was shouting what he felt to her.

As much as she would like to respond, he was too aroused that anything she did would take things too far. She didn't dare move. She remained silent. She felt like she was using all her strength to resist him.

He sighed and picked up the bra. He held it open while she put in her arms, then he hooked it at the back. She put her arms back in her jumpsuit, then he zipped it up. She turned back around to face him.

He clenched his fists. If you didn't understand the moment, it would have been easy to think he clenched his fist in frustration; perhaps he was easy to misread because of his face that looked like it was made of porcelain, or a face that was sculpted art.

His face gave the impression that it was a cold smooth surface, that didn't curve up into a smile. It was pleasantly surprising to see it when he smiled and laughed, remitting warmth. It was always easy to tell how he felt by looking at his eyes.

Currently, he had clenched his fist because he had been holding back. Not because he was upset. She didn't even want to admit to herself how aware she usually was, that he wanted her. Especially now that the ring was clearly spelling out his arousal, she couldn't dare admit she knew exactly what he felt.

"Keep looking. I'll be back," he said in a strained voice, walking off.

75

MY INNOCENCE

THEY HAD BEEN walking around the room for a while before they stopped in front of a body suit.

"Can you really fly in this suit? I want to see!" She turned to look at him in excitement. Because of her abilities, she had been able to read some information about the suit as she approached it.

"I'll only hover for a little bit. It would be more fun to go flying with you," he replied with a grin.

Otiende quickly took off his shirt and pants. Agina had not expected it, so she blushed and turned away. Her heart was beating fast as she waited. She really wanted to look but she couldn't dare bring herself to. She knew he had done it on purpose to catch her off guard. He had a growing interest in catching her off-guard. He enjoyed seeing her get flustered.

"Afraid to look. And afraid to touch. What am I going to do with you?" he asked when he was done, coming into her view. He rubbed her hair then touched her crown.

The suit had been custom fit for his body. It fits perfectly.

"I am... not afraid." But her voice was so shaky and timid that it wouldn't even have convinced a naive child.

He laughed then he said, "You are right. Most times I have to keep stopping you from going too far. I look forward to being devoured by you."

He gave a salute, stepped back, and then hovered up. The suit he wore was now lit up. He quickly flew around the room and then came back down. That was not a hover! He was the same way with the hoverbike. How was he not afraid of speed in such an enclosed space?!

She had telepathically read its warning to him about his speed. So, she knew she wasn't just being paranoid. Warnings from electronics were much harder to ignore and let fade into the background unlike everything else her powers picked up on.

She thought about flying with him. Wondering what he would dare in the open air, seeing herself hold his hand and spin around with him. Lost in thoughts about flying, she stared at him in marvel, not being aware he was taking off the suit. Her mind was more in her thoughts than in what was ahead of her.

"I want one!" she found herself saying out loud, not fully conscious of her words.

She watched him walking in his underwear like she was hypnotised. First, he returned the suit, then walked back. She watched the way he moved, staring at his crotch. He stopped and bent down to pick up his clothes.

It broke her off from her trance. She was so absent minded that she forgot to turn away! She suddenly closed her eyes, covered her face and looked away. She was blushing and embarrassed for having looked at him.

"I am enjoying stealing your innocence," she heard him say. She was still too flushed to look or take away her hands. How could she just gape at him?

"You speak so lightly about these things," she said, feeling upset with herself.

"We are engaged already. I'm just playing with you."

"OT, legally we are considered married. And we have already played around too much. But I'm still like this."

"Have I been teasing you too much and coming on too strong?" She heard his voice shift to concern.

"No. You are fine. I am already holding you back too much. It's... I don't like that it will sound like I am making a comparison but..." She wasn't sure if she should continue.

"It's fine."

"...One day my virginity was there. Then it wasn't. It happened fast. There really wasn't any innocence to be taken. It's more accurate to say I threw out my innocence. I just went for what I wanted. Maybe it feels different because I always initiated, and I was persistently in pursuit. I think it's more in my nature to hunt and be dominant. But now I am fighting against this nature. Which in turn is making me hide from it all and constantly feel embarrassed. Because I don't know how to do anything else but seduce and attack and conquer. Forgive me for being like this. I want to wait but I don't know how to wait."

He tried to take her hands off her face, but she didn't budge. She could still feel that she was blushing and was too embarrassed.

"No need to apologise," he said, hugging her.

He was being considerate. Shouldn't he be mad at her for still trying to hide or hold him back when she had told him she didn't want to wait? After some time, she took her hands off her face and hugged him tight, burying her face in his shirt. She felt comfortable and secure in his arms. She needed to stop fighting it. He put his fingers under her chin and lifted her head so she could face him.

"You okay?" He was looking at her with concern.

"Yeah. Fine."

"Good. I'll buy you a suit while you finish looking around," he said, kissing her. She watched him walk off to an open area that had three sofas. He sat on one of the sofas and took out his com.

Why had she told him to get a suit? She needed to watch her compulsive behaviour. She didn't want to start a conversation on how he shouldn't spend the money. She didn't feel like having a heavy conversation when she was carrying guilt for holding him back.

She was doing the opposite of everything she would normally do. She recognised herself less and less every day. She turned and continued looking at his collection.

76

SLEPT IN

S HE FELT HEAVY with sleep as she turned over.

"Agina. Wake up," she faintly heard.

She mumbled something that couldn't be understood but she wasn't sure what she said either. She was too sleepy to put words together.

"Agina! Wake up!"

She mumbled again. She meant to ask what time it was. But it was not audible.

"Agina!"

She pulled the blanket over her head and continued to sleep.

She woke up to Otiende kissing her. His lips, moving against hers, were stirring her into something she wanted to be awake for. Her eyes barely opened, she smiled at him and then said, "How blessed am I to wake up to your handsome face."

She still felt sleepy, so she wanted to pull the blanket over her head and sleep a little longer. But she didn't find a blanket.

"Did we go to bed without a blanket?" she heavily mumbled as she yawned and then closed her eyes.

"Agina! Do not go back to sleep!!"

"Just for a few more minutes," she said, sounding like she was already going back to sleep.

"Agina! Wake up! We are already late!"

"What time is it?" she asked, yawning again, her eyes still closed.

"It's 6.45."

Agina sat up, suddenly wide awake. As if listing her thoughts, she spewed, "It starts at 7.00! We were supposed to be there at 6.30 to be briefed. I am on my period! That's not enough time to shower and be there by 7.00!"

She looked like she was about to start crying.

"Why didn't you wake me up earlier?" She looked questioningly at Otiende, finally really noticing him. As she was speaking, he had sat up at the edge of the bed. He was already fully dressed.

"I have been trying to wake you up for an hour and fifteen minutes." He sounded irritated.

She dismissed her sleep report without looking at it, even though she could read it at super speed. She climbed out of bed and didn't even bother to take the stairs. She stepped off the platform and descended as she walked closer and closer to the bathroom. She moved abnormally fast and ignored the warning that sounded as she stepped off the edge.

"Why did I go to bed late?" she asked herself out loud. Then she remembered that yesterday, they had gone to see the intimacy therapist after all the conference meetings. She was slowly starting to piece together what happened before she went to bed.

After they got back from the therapist, they had a lot to talk about. Agina had been the one who insisted they stay up and keep talking after it had got late. She was also the one who fell asleep on the sofa.

> OT. Don't be mad at me. I'm sorry. It was my fault. Okay. What can I do to make it up to you? Sticker attached.

As she got it out of the bathroom, she slowed down when she saw Otiende standing with his arms crossed.

"Sending your com to apologise for you?" asked Otiende, with his eyebrow raised. She had telepathically sent him the message as she was in the shower.

"Turn. No time," she said, ignoring his question.

She continued to get ready at super speed. As soon as Agina was done getting dressed they left.

Her morning was a blur. Why on earth was such an important confidential meeting held so early? Agina thought to herself as she dragged herself forward. She wondered, even though she realised it was best because it was before most peoples' regular work hours. It gave people a chance to do other things later in the day. The meeting they were headed to was held in the Outercity.

"Here eat this. It will help with your energy, and you will not feel hungry till later," said Otiende as he held up Agina's palm and put a small chewable tablet in her hand.

She didn't hesitate or ask what it was, she just ate it; she had looked at herself before she left. She looked terrible. It was also helpful because she had skipped breakfast.

She was grateful she felt the difference right away. "Thanks, OT," she said, then she tiptoed to kiss him on his cheek.

There were two bodyguards on either side of the door they approached. They stood frighteningly still like they were unmoving. Otiende opened the door, and they went through the doors.

"Supreme Elder, our Ler Mahia, Agina Akongo," said Joshua, bowing and giving the gestured greeting.

She silently returned the greeting. She had not expected to meet Joshua so soon.

He greeted Otiende with the same gesture. Once Otiende returned the greeting, Joshua started to walk down the hallway as he spoke, "There is no time to brief you on what to expect. But I do want to say that you will be opening the meeting. It's a discussion anyone can direct. The others that were briefed can lead it."

It was a wide hallway with seats lined on one side and several doors on the other side. The doors were widely spread because they led to different meeting rooms.

"I understand. Do you have the meeting brief on file?" she asked Joshua, still feeling slightly embarrassed from the last time they met.

"No, it's in the internal system where we are meeting. Please scan your right hand and eyes to be let in. I will be escorting you in and listening from the back," Joshua said as they stopped at a door.

There was a security keypad with a scanner for the eyes and hand by the door. Beyond it was a doorway-sized scanner that looked like it searched for weapons. The door into the room was behind it.

"Joshua? I'm... I'm sorry about the other day. I have never hurt anyone before. I was truly out of character." She glanced at Otiende remembering how she hurt him, then continued, "I can't say the same for electronics. I have damaged them too often since getting this power."

"It's all right. It was an honour to watch something that had been completely fried and left so physically damaged, fix itself. The best part was how it works even better than before." He seemed to be getting excited again.

Otiende was glaring at him. He seemed to understand some hidden message and gestured to the scanner, waiting silently. He had on what looked like the same clothes she had seen him in and stood at attention with his hands behind him.

Otiende walked over and lifted his hand to start the scan, but was interrupted by Agina.

"Wait. OT..." Since she couldn't seem to finish her sentence, he walked back to her. "You're nervous?" he asked as he stroked the side of her face.

THEIR SITUATION 1

THE HALLWAY WAS a secure threshold. It was lit so brightly that there probably wasn't a single shadow in the hallway. She looked up at his illuminated face, contemplating what to say as she felt the affirmation in his soothing hand, as he stroked her cheek.

He dropped his hand from her face and held her hand.

"You know that feeling like everything is going wrong? Like you woke up on the wrong side of the bed?" Agina asked hesitantly.

"Yeah," Otiende replied, waiting for her to continue as he searched her eyes.

"That nagging feeling is making me lose my confidence," she said eventually.

"Some things just can't be controlled. You are all you need to be at this moment. Trust yourself." He squeezed her hand.

"Okay." She took a deep breath and then hugged him as she said, "Hold me under the table."

"I always hold you under the table. I was going to do so even if you didn't ask," he said, raising the corner of his mouth as he gave a slight grin.

She heard Joshua suddenly cough when Otiende spoke.

"Yes. I like how it feels. Don't let go." She smiled, putting her arms around his neck.

"What if I want to stroke you instead?" he slowly and provocatively asked, raising an eyebrow as he still smiled.

"That's okay. I just need the calm your touch gives me. In a lot of ways your touch makes me lose myself. But the assurance it gives me is more important at the moment."

He nodded. "You ready?"

"Yes."

They walked to the scanner together, holding hands. Otiende scanned himself then Agina was processed as scanned before she even got close enough. She froze and then glanced back at Joshua. She hadn't meant to do that. She had just thought of what she was supposed to do as she approached it.

"Let's go," Otiende said as he started to walk, holding her arm in his.

She decided it was okay if Otiende didn't make a big deal out of it. She didn't know what Otiende's position was in security but from what she observed he had more of a say than Joshua. His position there was one of those secrets elders kept so well. Otiende had only mentioned that he worked there.

It was the first time that Agina saw a meeting room where the initiated elders were not all at the same level. Their seating was stepped up in three arches in the front of the room. They were all already seated with their spears set beside them.

The rest of the seating was at the level of the door they just walked through, three arches curved to complete a circle. Agina suddenly came to the understanding that the elders have always had a bigger role in the country, but it was done in secret. It was almost like as long as they remained silent and hidden, they kept their power.

Some things were only known once you became an initiated elder. Like this room. She had only heard a small fraction from her mother and grandmother after she became the Supreme Elder. She still didn't have the patience to listen to it. Elder's lives and customs were so much more complicated than everyone else in the Innercity.

She decided she wasn't going to let them down in the meeting. Feeling a renewed sense of honour. She found the resolve to give everything her best despite her lack of sleep.

Before making her way to her seat, she turned to Joshua. "Joshua. I am going to remotely access the internal system. What is the name of the file you used to brief everyone?"

He looked a bit confused.

"Give her the file name. Never wonder about how," Otiende said. He always seemed to know how to handle Joshua. They must have worked together for a long time.

"110.38.437," said Joshua, still looking confused.

"Thank you for your help," she said to Joshua. She turned to look at Otiende, "I am done going through the entire file. Help me open this meeting by joining me in an intro."

"Okay. I'll follow your lead," he said, giving her a nod.

Otiende was the perfect person to be walking into this meeting without being briefed. He had more security secrets and international secrets than she would ever be able to grasp.

She nodded to Joshua whose expression was hilarious for someone who had just watched someone remotely access and run through a file in two seconds. She could tell Joshua had questions, but they would have to wait. Agina and Otiende proceeded to their seats as they held hands.

After the greeting formalities, she began. "We are a nation of family and community. We have never had a large military. We currently don't have an active military. Our police force almost disappeared after our borders were closed."

At the pace that she spoke, she projected a large three-dimensional projection in the centre of the room that occupied most of the vacant central area that their seats surrounded. It was like watching a show as she spoke, the light from the projection reflecting onto them.

The visual she started with was evocative, showing how they helped each other like a community, living like brothers and sisters. The images were realistic in colour and highly detailed, drawing you into the emotion. Their sounds were hushed but audible.

"They enforced a no military zone at the border in all countries that surround us, and at our coast. That helped. But there is nothing stopping anyone from matching in or firing at us with weapons. Most of our ancestors never thought we would survive when the border was closed, and we suddenly couldn't bring in food or medicine."

The visual changed as she spoke, showing depictions of the vulnerable borders, to people dying because of a lack of food or medicine. The images were a background video to her words.

"Things only shifted when we started thinking about how we could build a civilization. As if we were starting over on another planet with all that we already had. We have come a long way. But we still don't have forces we can organise. Our focus in development has been in survival and preserving who we are."

As she spoke, the projection changed to show how they progressed as a country, showing the different stages they experienced as a nation to date.

"There are a lot of reasons why we were left alone in isolation through all these millennia. Even though our circumstances are now different, our borders have not been opened to others. With what is happening recently, it's clear that one of the reasons we were left in isolation was because we were never a threat that would fight back."

As she spoke, her projection showed how over the years, they remained isolated. No matter what happened to them. They were never mentioned. No one seemed to care. It was like they didn't exist.

"Now that I have power, we have been seen as a threat. We went from a country that did not exist to being the most searched and researched. Broadcasting our conferences magnified the attention on us, raising our vulnerability. Our current defences and our attack are not enough to withstand an attack."

As she spoke, she replayed how people were worrying that the citizens of Dala were going to retaliate for being left behind when the world turned its backs on them. She also showed the reality of how they couldn't launch an attack or defend against one.

"Talks can help. But because of the way things were put into writing when we closed our borders, countries will hesitate to have open conversations. Opening conversation voids agreements that were created to stop war. It's unfortunate that it was part of the world peace contract."

She continued to project the consequences these countries were going to face if they tried to step in, and how voiding this contract could potentially trigger a full-on world war. She felt Otiende let go of her hand and then rub and massage her thighs repeatedly. It helped her relax. She didn't realise how much she had tensed up. She intentionally paused for a few seconds before she continued to speak.

"We have been consistently getting sneak attacks since I gained power. These attacks are not from people who recently made their way here. Its people who stayed hidden among us as spies through all these years, since before the border was closed, managing to stay hidden and organised."

In the same way, as she spoke, she projected how they recruited people into the country and stayed hidden. She showed how they managed to maintain their secret organisations through several generations.

"If their sneak attacks continue to be unsuccessful, that is when we will have to worry. They have every intention to launch a devastating attack if they can't successfully capture me quietly or kill me. It will be a massacre. We have received Intel on exactly how they will do this. It is not speculation."

78

THEIR SITUATION 2

AGINA NODDED TO Otiende, and he continued from where she left off. He took over the rest of the introduction. Just like she projected what she was saying, she did the same for Otiende's speech. Like they were a team; he spoke, and her projection was the visual.

"Even if we try to develop our weapons further, we will be like our ancestors who fought against guns with spears and shields."

She projected the gap in technology between the weapons that existed then and the gap that exists now. Giving a visual of what Otiende said.

"Since we have no trading with all the countries, people have always smuggled in foreign items, and there has always been a black market. So, we could secretly bring in advanced weapons. But we still don't have people we can mobilise. If that time comes, it will be our brothers and sisters making sacrifices to save each other."

While he spoke, she projected people emotionally saying goodbye and leaving their families to train with the weapons they would smuggle.

"Bringing in weapons and letting foreign military in, will be against what our ancestors wished when we closed our borders. They wanted to maintain complete independence, so we wouldn't be manipulated. More importantly, they wished we would help ourselves, valuing each other rather than having our resources be more valuable than our lives. Otherwise, all the people that died in the process while we adjusted, will have died for no reason."

To support what he said, she projected the ceremonies they regularly hold to honour all the people they have lost to the senseless pursuit of power and control. Their communities gathered in large numbers, moaning their dead and celebrating life.

"We are peaceful people. We don't want to wage war against anyone. We have never had a war within these borders. But unfortunately, it's a momentum we cannot stop. They are only comfortable when we have less power."

As he spoke, she projected their people dancing and getting together, truly living the philosophy of *Hakuna Matata*. People who wanted to enjoy life and live joyfully with no regrets.

"Right now, Straei is the most persistent country, which strikes every day. The other countries that have been targeting us are Grela, Plaria, Ecrestan, Spana Trouqua, and Labrialand."

Hearing what he said, she projected their attacks, showing how they were genuinely afraid of the power shift. They had even managed to convince others that the people of Dala were a threat that could devastate even the most powerful countries.

"These countries have unconfirmed secret bases in Dala. We confirmed one of Straei's bases and shut it down on Tuesday. But they still have other bases. Once these spies shifted to attacking, they exposed their location."

To illustrate what he said, she showed the suspected hideouts and the hideout they recently took out.

"Agina and I have stayed in Animal Realm Park most of the time. It's safer because they have no access there. But that has put the park in danger. It was created for conservation, it's not a bunker. They have tried to infiltrate it several times and almost succeeded by creating my clone."

To supplement what Otiende said, Agina continued with the visual display, showing the attackers trying to get into the Innercity for over a month. All the images she had shown from the start of the meeting, were actual events that happened in history, if not predictions. She was able to pull them up and reconstruct them with her powers.

The visual reflected what Otiende was saying till he was done with the introduction. She also proceeded to visualise what the other guests and elders said, as the discussion continued around the room.

Additionally, Agina would analyse any solutions they came up with. It helped them see the advantages and disadvantages of their solutions, as if the suggestion happened in real time, so they could observe the outcome. It enabled them to find loopholes. She continued the visual, non-stop throughout the meeting even if she was not the one speaking.

They had representatives of several organisations present that were not afraid to bend the rules to help others. They were not just people who made executive decisions. They were change-makers.

Of all the meetings they had, Agina was content with the outcome of the meeting. Although they were small organisations and they couldn't have other countries aid them, it was the first time Agina felt hope.

Dala was not a member of Peaceful Missions. It was an organisation that was intergovernmental and maintained international peace and security. Because they couldn't receive the organisation's help, the people at the meeting were their only hope.

She had been carrying guilt and fear for having put Dala in such a position. If push comes to shove, she has the power to stop most of their weapons and could bring disaster to them. But she was not a person of violence and didn't want to see it come to that. She had no desire to become anyone's enemy.

Instead of two hours, the meeting had gone on for a little over three and a half hours. Since the next meeting didn't start till eleven o'clock, some people stayed behind to chat and didn't leave right away.

Otiende had been waiting for her lead on what to do next after the meeting ended. She had not got enough sleep so he didn't want to push her to exhaustion.

Since Agina didn't know the initiated elders at a personal level, she would have conversed with her mother, Otiende's grandmother or Otiende's uncle but they had all left right away, so she decided to leave rather than stay behind to socialise.

As people trickled out, someone beside them spoke. "Hi, I'm Sandy. I really liked the presentation. I've never seen anything like that before. I heard the technology here is different, but I didn't expect it to be more advanced."

Agina turned to find one of the quests. They were dressed in bright colours. "Hi, Sandy. I'm Agina. It's actually part of my power. We have some more advanced tech, but this is not one of them."

She unwrapped her arm from Otiende's arm and held out her palm. She made a small three-dimensional projection of a kitten in her palm. The projection looked even more realistic when it was smaller because it barely gave off light.

Its soft brown fur looked real as the kitten moved its head, looking at them in curiosity with blue eyes. Its ears moved from side to side as it picked up sounds.

"Sooo cute!!" Sandy beamed, leaning into Agina for a closer look as they walked.

"I know! So cute!!" Agina said, putting her arm around Sandy so that her spear in her hand was not between them.

"Do you want to touch it? It has density," Agina offered.

"Really?!! I love cats. I have eight cats," said Sandy, then petted the kitten on the head. The kitten followed Sandy's hand with its eyes, then allowed her to touch its head. Its ears continued to move around. It would occasionally reach for her hand with its paw.

"How is it so soft?! You're amazing!" Sandy said, then turned her head to face Agina.

Sandy had a large smile on her face with perfect rows of white teeth.

"I love your energy. Combined with a smile that beautiful, I imagine you're a wonderful cat mom," mesmerised, Agina spoke as she looked at Sandy.

Otiende suddenly stopped. So Agina also stopped. Agina's arm was still around Sandy, so Sandy also stopped. Agina and Sandy had been leaning over to see the kitten and they were facing each other so their faces had been close. After they stopped, they stood more upright and alert, which caused more distance between them.

"If you want, we can keep in touch. I would love to show you, my eight babies," said Sandy, sensing their interaction come to a close. She had started by speaking excitedly then spoke more tentatively.

"No." Otiende's voice came from Agina's other side.

They both looked at Otiende in surprise.

"Um. It was nice meeting you. Maybe we will meet some other time if you come to Luschein," said Sandy as she moved from under Agina's arm. Trying to tactfully step away after failing with her first attempt to end the conversation.

Sensing the awkwardness that just descended upon them like heavy fog, Agina stopped the projection then said, "It was nice meeting you too. I just exchanged our contacts. I have a new office in Luschein. I'll keep in touch."

Sandy didn't say anything else. She half-heartedly gave a wave and then took off like she was in a rush to go somewhere. When Agina thought Sandy was out of earshot she turned to Otiende.

"I think you just scared her off. What is going on with you? What got you upset? You were fine a moment ago." Agina asked in a reproachful tone.

Otiende remained silent. He turned to face the side. She could swear he was a child again, stubbornly pouting and refusing to talk about what he was feeling.

"OT, right now I have no patience for this. Speak now. Why are you like this?"

He was still silent. She held his chin with her fingers and turned his head. His eyes were raging.

"What happened?" she asked again, looking concerned.

"You were flirting with her," he finally said.

"I did what?! I did not flirt with her. I'll admit she was really beautiful, and I loved her energy. It was so cute how she petted the kitten. And her smile was gorgeous."

Otiende seemed to get even more upset.

"She was obviously blushing," he spewed out.

"Why would she blush, all I said was..."

Agina finally realised what he was upset about and started laughing. But she stopped herself from laughing.

"Ow! Ow. I don't know why, laughing seems to make my head hurt… It must be instant karma," she said, rubbing her temples, and looking distressed as she looked down.

"Now I understand that you got jealous. Sorry. But that is not flirting. I haven't even flirted with you yet," she said in a playful tone, kissing him on his cheek.

"I need an apology that is a better kiss than that," he said seeming to finally soften up.

She looked around to see the people that were still lingering around, and then she pulled him down and gave him a deep passionate kiss.

They remained kissing for a while before she gently held his face and said, "OT, I suddenly feel like energy has drained out of me. I want some quiet and rest. I need to use the bathroom first. Then let's go back to the Innercity. We can wait in the next room for the meeting to start."

She yawned as she turned and began to walk. He quickly glanced at her and noticed that she did suddenly looked tired.

79

MORE THAN FRIENDS

THEY WALKED IN silence to the restroom. Otiende waited outside the restroom door for Agina in the hallway, while the bodyguards hung back. He had been thinking about their trip to the therapist yesterday, and their talk last night. Their situation had ended up being more complicated than he thought.

It first stemmed from her fear of engulfment. She had grown up in a close-knit family that sometimes just didn't have boundaries. So, she did not want to feel controlled and have them tell her what she should do.

Then her divorce from Chloe was the breaking point, causing a fear of abandonment. She didn't trust that love could keep people together. After she remained entangled with Chloe for so long, she stopped believing in love altogether.

In her own way, she was looking for something else other than sex and love that would keep them together. The resulting fear of intimacy caused the push and pull, wanting someone to be close, but also pushing them away.

He had also formed unhealthy behaviour considering all the things he experienced in his life, particularly in childhood. He had formed insecurities which made him believe people didn't want to be in his life because of the real him; they either had a delusion about who he was, or wanted something from him.

He knew the friendship he had with Agina was different, but there was so much he feared. Nothing else in his life had been that terrifying. Things only started to change when he realised she would stay with him; it was not about money and there was no delusion about who he was. He had received therapy consistently throughout his life, but having someone who could help them as a couple was paramount.

Luckily, what they were experiencing could easily be solved with time, if they followed the therapist's guidance. He had got into quite a journey after meeting Agina. He hoped it would be solved. Now that he had her, he didn't want anyone else in his life.

Why did love have to be so undefined, and relationships be not just unique to every individual, but be forever shape-shifting?

She got out of the restroom looking like she did this morning, like she was sleep-deprived. Since the most important meeting was done, he felt that she should go to sleep at home.

He was not upset with her anymore, so he had the capacity to mention that she should get some sleep. But considering the non-verbal cues, he did not think it was a good time to tell her what to do. They continued to walk in silence.

The elders that had left right away were gathered in the hallway, deep in conversation, standing by the doors to the room they were meeting in next. The elders tended to arrive and leave in groups. Because of the nature of their practices, they know each other very well, often having been friends throughout their lives. Few of them noticed her arrival.

"Let's go in. I want to rest," she said heading straight for the door without giving anyone her attention. She clearly looked too tired.

They were the first ones in the room. She set down her spear. Otiende set down his shield and then helped her pull out her seat.

"If I fall asleep, will you wake me up? Your com has been complaining about something. You should check it." She sounded like she had no energy at all.

"Agina? Why do you look even more tired than you looked this morning?" he asked when he saw her yawning, as he took out his com. He looked at her in concern, it looked like she was having a hard time keeping her eyes open.

She yawned again, she seemed to have opened her mouth even wider, squeezing her eyes shut as the yawn continued. She had her hand over her mouth. It was like watching her quickly slip away. It was how she faded to sleep at the end of the day. The chewable tablet he gave her must not have worked the way it should.

He looked down at the com in his hand. It showed a notification from the application that connected their rings. His com's form was the size and shape of a regular credit card. Curious, he extended the size of his com, from its portable small rectangle to the size of his palm. He opened the warning and read the message.

"You have been having heart palpitations since this morning. However, your condition is quickly worsening. Your ring has been keeping track of your vitals. It suggests not taking energy boosters because you are reacting adversely to it, you are not just crushing," he said, after reading it, giving her a worried look.

"How do you feel?" he asked, feeling guilty for what happened.

"I know my body well. I am fine. I'm just really tired. I was tired this morning too. But that tablet helped, so I was not tired for some time. Now I feel even more tired than I did this morning," she said, sounding drained.

"Sigh. I think the tablet wasn't suitable for you. I didn't give you an energy booster. It's not caffeinated. Nor is it something similar. It's supposed to be safe. You're not even supposed to crash," he said, moving closer to her and hugging her from the side.

She put her head on his shoulder.

He waited for her to say something. She never responded so he continued speaking.

"I'm sorry. I didn't know what else to do and I wanted to help." He turned to look at her. She had already fallen asleep. He sighed.

"How can you fall asleep so easily? Will I be able to wake you up?"

Now that her eyes were closed, she didn't look tired anymore. He wondered why her energy suddenly declined. She had been alert and focused throughout the entire meeting. He looked at the rest of the notifications on his com then put it away.

He smiled as he looked at her sleeping face. He recalled a time she had randomly fallen asleep when they were young:

Twenty-eight years ago…

"I am feeling tired," said Agina.

"You used too much energy showing off," replied Otiende.

They sat on the ground, seated back-to-back, leaning against each other. They had a lot of clear space in the room, so Agina had just been showing Otiende what she had learned.

Her serious expression was rarely seen. But she had a serious expression the entire time she showed her spear skill, moving quickly, light on her feet and flexible with her movements. With her balance, posture and stability, it almost looked like a dance, but her lunge was powerful.

She seemed to stay on the balls of her feet even when she made sudden movements. The serious expression made you believe she would not hesitate to attack any opponent despite her age.

"Was I cooler than you today?" she asked.

"Way cooler than me today. You got the crown that rules all cool guys and gals."

She laughed. "Not that cool. Cooler than you is enough."

"Wasn't that my point. I already think you are cooler than everyone I know. Today you've elevated above that."

"OT!?" she called, turning her head to the side and grabbing his upper arm with her hand. "Does that mean you already claimed the crown?"

"Shh. People already think I am too cocky. Don't say it. I don't want to lose the people who still think I am humble."

They both laughed.

"You are humble. You're just too good at too many things."

"Thank you."

She laughed again. "OT. Let's always be friends."

"Okay."

There was a brief silence.

"Is there anything better than being friends?" she asked.

He thought about it for some time.

"I don't know. Family?"

"Hm. I think you're better than a friend. But now that I have a sister, I think you're different from a brother."

After a brief silence, he asked in hesitation, "How is it different?"

But she didn't reply. He turned to look at her.

"How did you fall asleep already? I thought you don't take naps anymore."

He held her back and turned his body, so he was sitting beside her, then he put her head on his lap. The question lingered in his mind, but he didn't get a chance to bring it up again.

By the time they had to go, she was still asleep, but he couldn't wake her up, so he just carried her on his back. He found his uncle Osano before he found her mother Agot, so Osano took Agina from him and carried her, waiting to meet Agot.

"You couldn't wake her up again? Isn't she too big for you to carry?" Osano asked, adjusting Agina's weight so he could carry her more comfortably.

"Uncle Osano, just let it be. I also got bigger. She has always been this big to carry. We are growing at the same pace," Otiende said, looking to the side.

"Will you keep refusing to meet with her properly? We spend time in my place with Uncle Odongo before I take you to Dana's. I wouldn't mind giving up that time. Dana also wouldn't mind having Agina over when it's her time."

Otiende found a chair to sit in and slouched into the chair.

"Too complicated," he said nonchalantly.

"Watch your posture," Osano warned.

Otiende looked like he was about to protest but changed his mind and sat in perfect posture.

They chatted about other things for a while before Agot finally showed up.

"How did she fall asleep?! She is always impossible to wake up. I thought she didn't take naps anymore," said Agot in defeat.

"Hello Agot."

"Hello Osano. Hello OT."

"Hello Mama Agina."

Osano handed Agina over to Agot.

"Sorry for your trouble," apologised Agot.

"It's not much trouble," said Osano, waving off.

"Both of you are too stubborn," Agot said to Otiende, referring to him and Agina.

Agot and Osano chat for a short while before they decided to part.

"See you tomorrow," said Agot, adjusting Agina's weight.

Osano and Otiende gave the gestured greeting then they left.

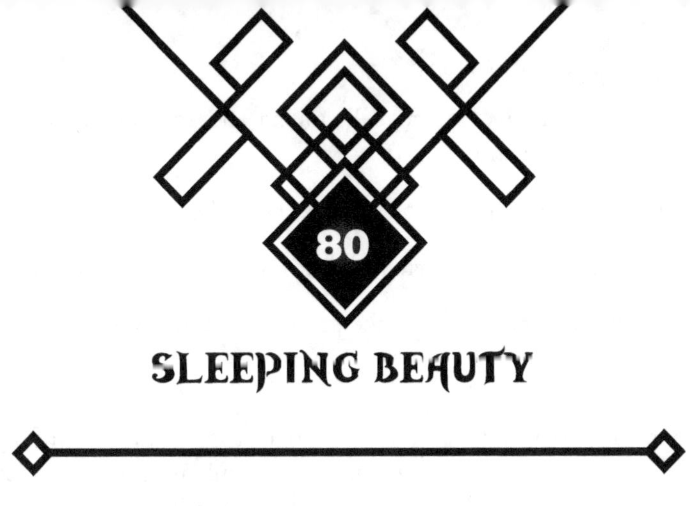

SLEEPING BEAUTY

Back to the present time…

"I NEVER DID find out why you said I was better than a friend but different from a brother. Did you like me back then? You were too innocent. When I think about it now, you are the one who planted that seed. I wondered about it."

He quietly laughed then continued, "I was wondering by myself! It was too easy to misunderstand. But it was also too weird to bring it back up. And I didn't understand my feelings. I could only walk away without saying anything."

He was speaking very softly and gently as he stroked her face and hair. He thought of the day he last saw her as a child. She silently cried, not saying a word, yet looked directly at him like he might disappear if she looked away. He never said he wasn't coming back or that he was giving up being an elder. They just understood it was the end.

Despite knowing they might never see each other again; they parted without promising to keep in touch. They left it up to fate. They never talked about parting. They had been too stubborn. It was his fault for having left her with that statement about fate.

He looked down at her and thought about their future. Thinking about how he would have to care for their child when she was asleep. He doubted she would be able to wake up in the middle of the night to care for a child. He was still smiling and showing affection to Agina when Agot showed up.

"Is she okay?" She had a look of concern on her face.

"She is fine. It's my fault that she's burnt out. She is just sleeping."

"Isn't she still impossible to wake up? It's about to start."

"Yes. I'll carry her out."

Osano showed up at that moment. "No. Just stay. I think even for you it might be too much to get her home. We could use your perspective in this meeting. I heard you say she is still impossible to wake up. You are both already here. And she will still be able to rest."

Agot agreed with him.

Otiende looked at Agina's peaceful face. What would she want? She had asked him to wake her up. He looked around at the elders who were starting to walk in.

"Excuse me while I try to wake her up first," he said, making his choice.

He held her face in his hand and kissed her. At first, he didn't get a response, then he felt her reaction. He slowly pulled back and looked at her. Holding her face close.

"More kisses," she said in a sleepy voice with her eyes still closed.

"Agina, wake up. The meeting is about to start."

She slowly opened her eyes and looked at him.

"I really can't stay up now," she worriedly said. Her eyes were barely open, and they seemed to involuntarily close every time she slowly opened them.

"I can try and carry you home, or we can stay here while you keep resting on my shoulder."

"Stay," she said, finally giving in and going back to sleep.

He gently lay her head back on his shoulder.

"I am impressed she managed to hold a conversation... Will you stay then?" asked Agot.

"Yes," he replied.

Agot and Osano went to their seats. Otiende carefully took off his long suit jacket, even though he knew he wouldn't wake her, and covered Agina like it was a blanket.

His grandmother also came up to them. "Is Agina okay?" asked Aero Akinyi Oneko.

"Yes, Dana. She is just asleep," replied Otiende.

"Okay. We will talk later," Aero said leaving to go to her seat, still looking concerned.

With the way everyone looked at Agina, they seemed to be concerned about her, rather than being judgmental. He wondered if it would be any better if they saw him carry her out of the room. He couldn't help but feel like he created the mess, which was going to be broadcast.

But if he carried her out, he would be making a selfish choice because he didn't want people to think she was sleeping on the job; it would be because of his insecurities as a public figure. But her public image was different from his public image. They were fairly content after confirming she was okay, because this was the Agina everyone knew who often fell asleep at elder activities. It was somewhat already part of her image.

Besides, she had already told him to stay. Carrying her whilst she looks unconscious was an issue, just as sleeping was not an issue. It was not just those who knew her well who seemed to be more concerned about her health than upset about her sleeping. Her being in good health was more important. So, he couldn't cause unnecessary alarm.

It was quite different from the entertainment industry where your image to the audience was important, if not more important than your health. Especially if it wasn't a major health issue. He needed to stop worrying and let her manage her image. The world of the elders just functioned differently. Plus Agina's world functioned at its own level, different from everyone else's.

To help or not to help; was a question he was asking too often. He was starting to see their relationship was never truly going to be easy to figure out. Where should or shouldn't he step in? Especially after finding out from the therapist that he needed to be careful about making her feel like he was trying to control her.

The meeting started awkwardly. They were not sure about how to proceed with Agina asleep. Should they acknowledge her in some way? Or should they ignore her presence? Time seemed to pass slowly though it was a shorter meeting because they needed to break for lunch.

He kept looking at her throughout the meeting to see how she was doing. She remained in peaceful sleep, looking more like she had been put under a sleep spell. When the meeting ended, everyone left for lunch walking out more quietly than they usually do, none of them lingering behind.

"Here is your lunch," said Osano, putting two packaged meals on the table. "Look how nicely they packaged it when I said it was for you and Agina. Pretty nice. Huh? I didn't even know they had such fancy packaging. They even wanted to deliver it themselves, but I insisted.

She makes the right sort of leader because she inspires people to go the extra mile for her, without even doing anything directly or indirectly. People see her sincerity; they know it's not just a performance or a job."

Otiende had already shifted Agina's position when everyone left, she had her head in his lap and her body was lying across two seats.

"Mhh," he said as he continued to rub her arms. He was deep in thought about when he should wake her to eat or if he should just take her away.

"OT?" Osano probed, placing a hand on Otiende's shoulder.

"You need anything else?" Otiende asked, looking up at his uncle.

As usual, he wore a lot of expensive traditional accessories over ordinary clothes. His brother Oyange was the same way. It was not a wonder his mother's and father's families came together. Both their families liked to present themselves in this way. It was quite the opposite of Agina's family.

When he thought about how he met Agina and how his parents fell in love, he wondered how more elders did not marry each other. Elders not dating each other was one of those unspoken ways of the elder. Elders lived quite a constricted life; there was a long never-ending list of do's and don'ts.

"No. You did good today. I'll take my leave," he said, turning and leaving.

Because they remained still in this way, the motion detector light ended up turning off. It couldn't sense any movement in the room.

The lunch break was always long because they typically had entertainment after meals were cleared, to help pick up people's moods. It was a boost before they got back to meetings.

Otiende finally woke Agina up thirty minutes before their meeting.

He lifted her slumped body to sit on his lap and then kissed her. This time she was a little slower to react. He didn't stop right after she became responsive, wanting to keep kissing her. She shifted her body slightly and held his face as they continued to kiss.

"Tell me I am dreaming, so I can make love to you," she said, stopping to take a breath and leaning her forehead against his.

"I just woke you up. Our meeting starts in less than thirty minutes," he replied, with his forehead still on hers, looking closely at her closed eyes. Her lashes moved slightly, letting him know she was still awake.

She opened her eyes and looked at him. "That's the wrong answer. That was an opening for you to seduce me and take advantage of me."

He grinned, loving the thought of seducing her. "Patience my love. After all that talking, we agreed to wait a few days. You can wait three more days to make love. We need the birth control I took to work."

She snuggled in his arms, somehow making herself smaller.

"Are you going back to sleep?" he asked, wondering if she would eat. However, he was more interested in keeping her close. He liked how she had made herself fit in his arms.

"I want to. I think I can manage to stay awake now if I push myself. But even that won't last long. If I fall asleep again, lend me your shoulder," she said, keeping her eyes closed.

"I am sorry I-"

She covered his mouth with her hands. In a soothing way, she said, "What are you apologising for? Keep your apology. I won't accept it."

He wanted to say something else, but she kept his mouth covered with her palm. He could only make a muffled noise. He kept trying but she wouldn't move her hand. Even when he tried to move it with his fingers, she resisted.

She leaned over to face him.

81

CAUGHT

"**I** AM TIRED. My patience is at its limit. Let me sleep," she said, suddenly sounding awake, giving a straight face. She wanted to fold back into his arms then noticed the food on the table. She gave what sounded like a wicked laugh.

"Oh, this couldn't get any better. This must be the joke of my life. Chloe would have loved that," she said offhandedly, pointing at the food. "We used to eat out all the time, because she loved food that was packaged like that. Even in this light, I can tell the box is her favourite colour and style. I saw it so many times that I know what it looks like in this light. She always shows up just when I am starting to forget her. It's really pissing me off," she said, her sarcasm evident.

He attempted to say something but she still had his mouth covered. She turned to face him, looking like the attempt had got her more upset. "I already lost sleep. I already chewed the tablet. I don't want to be here, and I don't want to go home by myself either. And no, I won't let you leave with me either. This place is you." She gestured with her arm, swinging her hand in a huge arch.

"These conferences are you. You made that choice to keep coming back when we were kids because you wanted to be here. Even when they treated you like crap," she impatiently said, poking him slightly with a finger.

She squinted her eyes as she continued, "But me," she poked herself then said, "I have been escaping these things since I could turn away.

I know you didn't ask me to, but I am genuinely doing this for you... And I'm also doing this for kids we haven't had yet. I am doing this for us. These past days at these conferences, the only thing I love is being beside you."

She seemed to calm down a little after having vented her frustrations, gently placing her hand on his chest, she gently spoke, "When people fall, they don't always need help getting up. Sometimes they just need someone who can stay close enough because they are too damn exhausted to do anything else.

They get up on their own when they are ready. At that point, they choose how they get up, whether it's a slow crawl or a leap up.

Lastly, they choose how to interact with this person who stayed close enough waiting patiently. They are no longer too exhausted and are now self-driven. They still somewhat need this person; it's important to stay beside them. They just don't need to be picked up," she said, sounding sullen.

It was like she unloaded everything at once; she looked more at ease. She snuggled back in his arms, her warm body touching the depths of him, making him want to cocoon her in his arms. So, he held her close.

"Just hold me. And be silent. I am thankful, but you don't have to worry about helping me. We can talk later," she said, falling back into a gentle, soothing tone, and then she slowly removed her palm from his mouth.

He didn't want to push it. He didn't get a chance to ask her about the food. Maybe he shouldn't have woken her up. He found his thoughts wondering as he listened to the silence, feeling her warmth in his hands. He could only try and listen to what she asked.

After a while of being deep in thought, he was startled by her voice, "Damn it OT!!... I can't even sleep. I can only think about kissing you and being touched by you." The words fired out. She was shaking like she was laughing silently.

He had to unload what he was thinking, he couldn't just be silent anymore. Speaking rather fast like he wanted to let it all out before she stopped him, he spoke, "What do you want, Agina? You shouldn't have to make these sacrifices. I never put pressure on you. You keep making these decisions like you have no choice. It was all your idea. You don't have to forget who you are. This role, you already publicly said it was going to be inactive. You don't have to be here. Yet even in these circumstances you said we should stay... In fact, it applies all around; you don't have to forget Chloe. Those memories can still bring you happiness. You talked to me when I was #1008. I don't think anyone else understands more deeply than I do, how happy you were when you were together."

She paused, remaining in silence. He knew what she wanted. She had already said it. He knew it was not the right time, but he didn't care. After hearing her say it, it was now what he wished. When she had need, she was his weakness, he knew he would indulge her if she asked. But he thought she wouldn't ask, so he anticipated what she would say, as he thought of what he wished. His heart was beating fast. If she asked, all he would need to do was give her a few minutes before the meeting started. Right? It could work. They were still alone. He wanted so much to touch her, hoping she would ask.

"Right now, I only want one thing… I need you to touch me."

He came undone after he heard her. She said it in that tone! He thought he wouldn't hear it so soon, much less here. Yet, she had managed to sound so seductive once more. Did she really know what she was asking for at this time? She had really gone ahead and asked. What's more, he hadn't expected to hear it that way. Why did it feel like he had decided to give her what she wanted? Even before he heard it? Like it was his lucky day and he was simply being granted his wish.

It was fairly dark in the room, but everything was still visible since they had both adjusted to the dark. He looked down at her, searching in her eyes. He could tell she looked into his eyes briefly, like she had seen her answer.

Before he said anything, she shifted her body and started kissing his neck. The sensation of her soft lips gently kissing his skin sent shivers down his spine.

How did she find such a sensitive spot or was he just sensitive to her touch? Then he felt her tongue slowly slide against his skin as she continued to kiss him. He was awakened somewhere else as he felt her teeth gently slide and release, as she sucked on his skin and caressed with her tongue. It was like his whole body was being caressed.

How could teeth be so gentle? The sensation was too much to bear. He reached into her dress and held her breast, caressing it and fondling her nipple with his fingers. She intensified the kiss on his neck. He could hear a gentle sound of pleasure that couldn't escape her mouth.

He doubted she would ever be able to be silent while they made love.

"Is this what you wanted?... I don't think so. You're always looking for more," he said, somewhat teasing her and also seriously wanting to know. He continued to touch her.

She stopped kissing his neck and sat facing him with her legs on either side of him. Her dress had rid up all the way so she could properly straddle him.

"Then give me more," she said as she leaned down to kiss him. Now that both of his hands were free, he nestled both of her breasts, showing love. She untucked his shirt after a bit of a struggle then put her hands in his shirt, feeling him as they kissed.

She found his nipples. Gently touching them with her fingers. The way she touched him was pulling at his instinctual primitive yearning to impregnate her. He wanted so much to take the woman he loved, thrusting deeper and deeper into her. The innocence of wanting to just touch her was long gone.

He stopped kissing her for a short while and planted kisses all over her skin, hearing her gentle soft moan. He flicked her nipple with his tongue, immersed in the sound of her moan as she gripped him tightly.

He brought his head up and looked at her face which looked like she was filled with elation and pleasure, finding a deep sense of joy for being the reason why she looked like that. She continued to touch him, sending a surge of heat through his body. He felt like he was filled up but everything just seemed to keep pouring in, even his emotions felt like they were heightened.

"I love you," he whispered in her ear. The more she touched him, the more the words wanted to slip out. It was like the words were on a slippery slope, falling to the edge with nothing to hold on to. All they could do was slip out, even if he knew she wasn't ready to say it back.

She held his face with both hands and found his lips again, kissing him gently with her tongue in his mouth. His body was reared as he continued to touch her breasts, hearing a moan manage to escape her.

"OT!"

They both stopped and opened their eyes.

He hadn't heard that sharp voice Aero used to call him when he was in trouble, for years. His eyes needed to adjust to the bright light. They were in the front of the room and Agina had her back against the room.

Agina moved backwards, sliding off his lap and crouching at his feet. She continued to back away until she was under the table. She looked down and fixed her dress.

It was a turtleneck, but it had an opening that showed a little bit of cleavage, enhancing the contrast of the leather-and-lace bodice against her skin. Since she put on that dress, that opening that showed her cleavage had been like an invitation to him.

He sat frozen, so he couldn't even think to cover her breasts which looked like they had accidentally spilt out of a corset in a wardrobe malfunction.

He hoped no one had seen her breasts. Now he wondered why he thought such an outfit was innocent. Agina's clothes were always like this, elegant and stylish, but never completely innocent. Even now that she had fixed it, he still had the desire to undo what she fixed.

She suddenly covered her mouth. Like she found something surprising. Then she took off her hand and exaggeratedly mouthed something to him while she pointed. It looked like she was saying: fix your pants.

He looked down and saw his very obvious erection pushing up against his pants. Of all the clothes he could wear, he had on pants with fabric that would never hide an erection no matter how hard he tried.

He finally reacted, remembering to be embarrassed. He wasn't frozen anymore. Agina appeared to be amused by his reaction. He tried to adjust his pants with little success and tucked his shirt back in without daring to stand up.

"Agina!!"

He wasn't sure if he should feel better for attention being taken off him or worse because of how Agina was called. Agot sounded absolutely fierce when she called Agina.

But the sound of her voice just seemed to trigger Agina's rebellious quirk. Instantly washing away the embarrassment on her face. She emerged from under the table straightening her dress as she reached for his suit jacket and threw it on his lap.

She hurriedly sat in her seat and they both pulled their seats up to the table. She leaned in and whispered, "Sorry."

"Sorry," he whispered back.

Time had passed faster than he thought. People who had stalled at the back of the room finally continued onto their seats. They had somehow piled up in numbers at the back of the room. His uncle Osano looked amused. Otiende was sure he was going to tell his father Oyange as soon as he got the chance. They both loved a good story.

He was also sure his grandmother Aero was going to complain to his mother Auma. He didn't think anyone else would dare share the story. Elders were the kind of people who carried secrets to their graves without needing to be told. Gossip was never worth it. If anyone had dared to broadcast anything, he was sure Agina would have their head; no one would dare.

He wondered what he would hear from his parents. He was more worried about what Agina would hear from her mother. Agina spoke like her mother was always watching, hanging back so she could find something to complain about.

But Agina didn't seem bothered. Considering how much she butted heads with her mother for no other reason other than sharing different perspectives, she probably got used to being reproached.

It had almost looked like she had rolled her eyes when she heard Agot, and she had not only been instantly cured of embarrassment, but she had been possessed by a daring spirit to face off the world.

The meeting started even more awkwardly than the last. Agina and Otiende didn't stand up like they should have and Agina was not in a pleasant mood. She would glare at people whom she felt she needed to put in their place. Being that Agina had powers, a glare from her wasn't just a glare, it made you want to hide; it was an unnatural overbearing pressure.

Everyone in the room was her subordinates after all, even if she had chosen to have them acknowledged at their level as her equals. She even glared at the person who had tried to take away the lunch they left abandoned on the table. They scurried off, almost tripping as they left, leaving the food behind.

Other than that, she spoke blandly, and the meeting went well. Everyone just let it be. He would say she had great acting skills, but it wasn't that, she was just really good at holding back emotions.

Maybe that's why her powers were sporadic when emotions were involved; she tended not to show her true emotions. You could only know how she felt by conversing with her.

"Let them leave first. I need a break," she whispered in his ear on cue as soon as the meeting was over, lifting his jacket, laying on his lap, and covering her head with it. The movement was so swift he didn't instantly realise what she had done.

He put an arm on her, reassuring her with a rub of his hand. Luckily no one approached them, and everyone left. He did not feel like explaining himself. Once everyone left, he lifted the jacket and was surprised to find that once again she had fallen asleep.

Agot returned to the room, looking like she was still upset. "Agina!!"

"She's asleep. Don't give her a hard time. She's had a hard day. If you are looking for someone to blame, I was at fault," he said, feeling protective of her.

"Are you sure nothing is wrong with her?" Agot asked, clearly appearing displeased, not quite ready to let it go.

"I am not certain," he replied honestly. Her libido was high again. She hadn't eaten. She didn't get enough sleep. She sometimes had mood swings during her period. It was also clear something had gone wrong with the chewable tablet, taking her day off the rails.

"I think you know the woman you have married. She is a handful. She has a pure sense of justice. It's good, but it also means that she doesn't follow the rules while in pursuit of this justice, and she cares the least about social standards. She just follows what she thinks is right.

You can't always take the blame for her actions. Eventually, she will end up doing something you are against. That's just the way she is. She will not make sure to align herself with your side. Be careful," Agot cautioned.

She turned as if she was also spinning the air around her and started to leave. Then without turning, she stopped to add, "I expect you to do better moving forward. Take proper care of her." Then she left the room like she had left a cloud of dust in her wake.

He sombrely looked down at Agina and said, "Something I am against?... What could I possibly be against? She is already doing so much for me even if I tell her she shouldn't. Maybe you can say I am against her sacrificing so much. Everyone is problematic in one way or another. Only time will tell. I can only live in the present. I love these moments we are having. I have come too far to heed caution."

82

UNEASINESS

AS SHE SLOWLY awakened, Agina was surprised to find that she was in Otiende's arms. Usually, he got up before her, so she had continued to wake up in the solitude she had, before he started sleeping over.

She could feel his warm body against hers and his arm was around her. She turned around and they hugged each other, holding the embrace for a while.

"Why are you still in bed? What time is it?" Agina asked Otiende when her face was still buried in his chest.

"It's 8.00. I just came into the bed two minutes ago so you could wake up in my arms. I knew you would wake up now because you always wake up at the same time."

"I'm a creature of habit," she said, dismissing her sleep report. She moved in closer and asked, "Did you want to cuddle?"

"Yes."

"Move lower. Let me hold you." When he shuffled lower, she held his head on her chest and she wrapped her legs around him.

"Is this good? Are you comfortable?" she asked, wondering how he felt about the way she entwined herself around him. She had liked to be held like this.

"Yes. I could stay here all day," he said, sounding content.

"You want to skip the festival with me!? Technically the conferences are over," she said, sounding too excited.

"I thought you would like today's itinerary better," he said, attempting to look up at her, then giving up on the straining angle and looking back down.

"I do. I would rather not go if it meant I get to have a lazy day with you, cuddling in your arms. We would do nothing but make our food together, and then eat together. Just the two of us. We haven't had a day with just the two of us in a while. And with all that's been going on, we haven't been on a date recently. But don't misunderstand my gratitude for the time we have had together," she said, rubbing his head.

"I can't believe my ears. Do you remember how I had to make a deal with you to spend more time with you? Have I converted you to the other side?" he asked with a laugh.

As she rubbed his head, she looked down at the design of his hair. It looked better from the top. Part of the hair was open showing his long hair that seemed to behave better than hers, plus some of it was braided close to the scalp in raised lines, in an elaborate curvilinear design. The parts that were shaved, had a pattern shaved, making it look like a continuation of the cornrow and open hair pattern. She liked the style that he chose for their Aiye. He had been wearing it since.

"Seriously? Part of me still feels like I am moving too fast and is afraid I am plunging into another dark abyss where I'll keep falling. You should pay attention to that part. It's the part that will ruin whatever happy future you have imagined," she warned.

"I love all of you. I can only try my best," he said then kissed her arm.

"Where did you find such words about love? No one ever accepts a person fully. It's a lie." She had construed this belief about love based on her experiences.

"It's the truth about how I feel about you. Don't tell me it's a lie when you accepted me the way I am from the first day I met you. That's other people's perceptions. You have always seen me for who

I am and accepted it. Don't throw that out now. Don't let fear and hurt stop you from accepting my love," he said, sounding like he was sincerely speaking from the heart.

"OT, don't make me cry in the morning. I think I am too broken. You have known me in the past. The current me can't be what you expected." She felt tears in her eyes. She felt defeated.

"Yes. You are different. I am too. But I love you all the same. Not just who you used to be or what I expected. I love who you are now. Give me a chance to earn your trust in my love."

She was silent before she spoke, "…I'm trying. It's not coming to me easy. I want to love with my whole heart like I did before. But not exactly like I did. I was too naïve."

"I know. I just need to remind you more often that I love you the way you are and that I am not asking you to change. I just want you to be free to love and to accept my love. Most importantly, know that I don't want control."

After silence she said, "…Thank you."

He rolled over while still holding her so that he was now on top of her body, supporting his weight with his hands. He looked at her with such gentleness and sincerity in his eyes.

When he looked at her like that, she felt warm and solid. Like an egg taking shape, starting off runny, then becoming a solidified form after being heated up. She felt like no matter what shape she took; she was warm and solid.

The tears escaped her eyes. She quickly closed her eyes, wanting to avoid his gaze. He shifted his position so that he was holding her and had a free hand, wiping away her tears.

"You cry so silently." She heard him say in his deep soothing voice. "I am here for you." He said, gently rubbing her arm.

They stood in an alcove, in front of a bench with flowers seeming to surround them. "I hate such crowds. You can never truly control them. It makes me nervous. What if someone tries to attack you?" asked Otiende, interlocking his fingers with hers. It was later in the day. He had started the day's event feeling uneasy and his uneasiness was starting to put her on edge.

Judging from what he had told her, he had dealt with tough crowds in the past and handled them well. There was obviously danger then. There was no obvious danger here. Yet, it was clear he was struggling with feeling at ease.

In fact, to her, it looked like the crowd was more excited to see him than her. On top of the uneasiness brought on by Otiende's uneasiness, their enthusiasm for him made her uneasy. She felt like they were not even pretending to fawn over him. It made her uncomfortable because the event had been planned for her. She felt unworthy.

Her uneasiness was expected but this was not normal for Otiende. He was a performer. He was too focused on what could go wrong. She didn't want to say anything because she didn't want to minimise how he felt.

However, she could no longer just be silent, "We take care of our own. I'll be fine. I won't get attacked." She tried to assure him.

"There are always anti-fans. And our own have been even more terrible towards me than the so-called outsiders. Our own refused to acknowledge me as one of them," he snapped back.

"Sorry. I shouldn't have spoken to you that way. I haven't been myself today. However, it's not an excuse to take out my frustrations on you," he said looking at her apologetically, quickly realising he had stepped out of line.

She looked at him. He had a stern look. She found that the hard expression didn't put her off. His face had a familiarity deep within her. It was welcoming like a cool breeze on a warm day. A breeze that might even make you shiver slightly but it was welcoming.

"I am here for you too," she said, holding his face in her hands. Reflecting words she had heard from him often. Wanting him to know he wasn't the only one who was supportive.

He hugged her.

That morning they had promenaded through the town. Every resident of the Innercity seemed to have gathered into every spot they could fill. Each person was trying to get a view, as they looked past each other in the crowd.

Those in the front reached out their hands, if they were brave enough to try and touch her, or tucked their hands to their side and pushed their palms upward, a gesture to give her blessings. Together the crowd sang and ululated. Their voices were loud enough to drown out the instruments that were being played as they processed.

They were cheerful and in awe: It was a historical moment for all the eager onlookers. They had come here for one purpose, to celebrate Agina gaining the ancient power given by the ancestors. Yet it was Otiende that stole their hearts.

They were talking after the promenade was over, during a transition before the next event. They hadn't found a place to escape all the people but with the help of the bodyguards, they had found enough privacy to pause in an alcove within a garden, isolated from the crowd but still in their view.

They remained hugging each other for a while before they finally let go.

"I'm sorry. I didn't consider that we have different experiences with our people. Is it really me you're worried about?" she asked worriedly, looking at him, searching his eyes.

"Honestly, I don't know why I am like this. It could be because of my past. Or maybe it's because there are too many O_ts in that crowd. And things don't always go well with them," he said, sounding genuinely perplexed.

Agina still wasn't sure about how she felt about being engaged to a celebrity. Everyone seemed to know him at a deeper level and often had an opinion on how he should behave. People declared they loved him so often. Others seemed obsessed with him. People constantly tried to talk to him, touch him, or take pictures with him. If Otiende hadn't always insisted on bodyguards, it would have been unbearable. Not to mention how she was now experiencing the same things, particularly their scrutiny, just for being with him. She had never contemplated O_ts would become her fans.

FEELING DECEPTIVE

ORGANISING THE CROWD took quite some time. It was like herding cats. It didn't help that they took a diversion and spoke in the alcove. The detour was outside of the well-organised plan that assumed people would just follow directions like robots. The council had left no room for variance because they were used to being well-organised and following directions.

Add that to how people were too excited to comply with directions, and it was havoc. Slowly but surely, they made their way to the next event that was held in their stadium. It had a capacity of twenty thousand people and was mostly used for football matches.

Everyone had been vivaciously waiting for them to arrive. Agina had a realisation that she was glad to have the elders in her presence again. She didn't want the spotlight. Even if she had accepted the role of Supreme Elder in the hierarchical way it was intended, the elders would have been like her team, where every one of them mattered and accompanied her to events.

Earlier, it had felt lonesome as she processed through the town with Otiende, in what felt like his crowd. She had felt strangely exposed. She didn't dare admit she was jealous, but she had been so uncomfortable with how people reacted to his presence. The feeling in her body was so strange that she was certain admitting it would be of no help because jealousy didn't define what she felt. She felt more than that.

While carrying those feelings, she was even more uncomfortable with everyone bowing to her. It was the most unnatural thing she had to endure since she got powers. She was sure her discomfort showed, or at least those who knew her well would have noticed the irregularity in her countenance.

The stage created for them was raised within the field, surrounded by stadium seating. There was a small area for performances on the stage, though most of the performances were held off the stage in view of the three section tables, where the initiated elders sat, side by side. Other than the stage and this performance area, the rest of the field was packed with seating. So, a surprisingly coordinated large crowd of over twenty thousand people bowed at the same time, unnerving Agina.

Different performances were done in honour of Agina. She especially loved what the children did; some with songs, others with a skit. It moved her to tears. She didn't feel like she deserved any of it. She was a Supreme Elder because she was born in her family. It wasn't because of any work or effort she put in. What's worse, she didn't want the position.

She silently vowed that the next time anything like this would happen, she would have done something worthy of recognition. But deep in her heart, she knew that she probably would never have such a large event organised in her name.

Her initiation had already been a trade-off with the council of elders. They protected traditions, and Agina had begun her reign by ripping apart tradition.

From the moment she was born, they all knew who she had the potential to become. Unfortunately, she also happened to be a free spirit who didn't want elder responsibilities, right from the beginning.

She had been forced to face her destiny. Consequently, it was destiny itself she was seeking to rewrite.

When all the performances were over, they took pictures. The picture that became an iconic historical reference was the picture where

Agina was seated on a backless seat, her back standing tall as her dress seemed to flow over her seat, whereas Otiende was seated to her left on the floor. All the initiated elders stood behind them. Including Agina, they all held spears, except for Otiende who held a shield.

The rest of the day was loosely structured. The activities were held both in the Innercity and Outercity. There were temporary stalls where people could shop; temporary places where people could dance, learn traditional dances, learn how to play traditional instruments, and crafts, play games, do group cultural activities and eat a variety of foods that included traditional foods.

The atmosphere of the town was intoxicating with excitement; people were laughing, and dancing and joyful outbursts were heard repeatedly. It was like a cultural festival. But because they were concerned about security, Agina and Otiende remained in the Innercity.

Not only did all the attacks happen in the Outercity, but the crowds of people in the Outercity were much larger and too hard to control. The Outercity simply had a much greater population and too many people who didn't have a heartfelt understanding of the importance of following the security measures; it was a multicultural place that didn't see the council as their leaders.

Agina and Otiende walked lazily around, as they held hands, stopping every now and then to take part in one of the festivities. The bodyguards helped clear a path around them as they walked. Thankfully people made way for them. It was an easy crowd. So, they didn't require a wall of bodyguards around them.

Having clear space around them, made it seem like they were in their world enclosed in an invisible bubble. As they moved their bubble moved with them. Keeping them separated but in view.

Agina loved the way Otiende looked at her lovingly, like she was the most important person in the world. The way he was focused on her and didn't react to the crowd, made it easy to bear the crowd of people who were swooned by his presence.

It was like he could only see her. He had been in the entertainment industry for a long time, so she had assumed he had learnt how to control his verbal and body expressions. It especially made him a good actor.

But when it came to how he was around Agina, it seemed like he had never learnt how to control his feelings of love. Nor did he seem to have any interest in trying to hide his love for her. Even when all he did was stand still you could still see the love in his eyes. At that moment, she loved that about him. He was so sure of his love. One day she hoped to have the same confidence.

If it hadn't been for Otiende, she probably would have stayed at the festival for a short time. She only enjoyed such events when she was with her friends. She was comfortable with staying longer at the festival because it felt more like she was on a date with him. Even though they occasionally interacted with people for any activity that required more than two people.

Agina looked to her left. In the distance, she noticed brightly coloured braids that had been held up in an intricate way. Below the clever twists and tangles was a short narrow head. Her big cat-like eyes, were shadowed in colourful makeup. The eyes were looking directly at her. She had a large familiar grin on her face.

"Cathy!!!" Agina yelled out in excitement before dashing towards her.

If Agina could list her top skills, escaping would be one of them. Before anyone even realised what was going on, Agina disappeared into the crowd after swiftly swinging up her spear and shrinking the spear into its smaller form, subsequently wearing it concealed on her back.

The movement was so fast that to most people, it looked like her spear disappeared in mid-air before she slithered into the crowd, disappearing without a trace. A lot of Agina's spear training was like martial arts, so she quickly made it through the crowd without people realising she was passing through.

Cathy hadn't noticed Agina emerging from the crowd. She was searching the crowd in the distance, the smile on her face having grown with excitement.

"Cathy!!" she called out again, shifting Cathy's attention. Agina held her hands open for a hug as she continued towards Cathy. Cathy finally saw Agina, opening her arms just as Agina jumped onto the stage, into Cathy's arms.

84

OLD FRIEND

"I MISSED YOU!" Cathy pulled her in tight as she longingly spoke.

"I missed you too!" Agina expressed, as she hugged Cathy tight.

"I thought you forgot all about me. Did you really miss me?" Cathy asked, making an exaggerated pout.

They stood close, Agina feeling a tinge of guilt as she thought about how silent she had been and how they would have gone to such an event together with their other friends. She had not intended to stay away; she had just directed most of her attention to Otiende. Chloe had always been persistent about Agina spending time with her friends, so it had not happened in the past.

"It's been too long since I saw you. Of course, I miss you," said Agina, touching her face to try and console her.

"Of course, you forgot me. I wasn't even invited to your Aiye. It hasn't even been too long since I last saw you, but I keep hearing about you. The you I keep hearing about has changed so much. So, I thought you left me behind with your old life," Cathy said, gloominess pulling down her face, as she was no longer joking.

"Honey, what do you mean old life? I'm still the same person. And you know those kinds of ceremonies are more about family than about inviting the people you care about," Agina said, but she barely believed it herself, feeling the guilt sink deeper.

"Sweetheart, you married a man who was your friend. It was heartbreaking enough when you chose another woman you didn't know over me. But I was shattered when you chose him over me. We were both your friends," said Cathy, her words piercing her. She had not thought of how Cathy would feel. It made her realise how little she had thought of her friends.

Without thought, Agina gave Cathy a kiss on the cheek. "See. This is why I avoid you and can only meet you when I meet with the girls. You shouldn't be stuck to someone who doesn't love you back. You will find someone else who will love you the way you deserve. And, who falls in love with their best friend?" After Agina asked, she remembered how Otiende fell in love with her, then quickly brushed away the thought.

"You knew I was in love with you, but it didn't bother you to hang around me before you fell in love with Chloe. I know you love me," Cathy insisted.

"I love you in a different way. And I have known you since we were kids. I-"

"Agina!!" She hadn't heard Otiende being this angry before but there was no mistaking his voice nor the anger in his voice. She completely forgot what she was saying.

She turned to look at him. He was standing in front of the stage, glaring and looking impatient. He said something but she couldn't hear it over all the noise and music. She had been able to hear Cathy clearly because she was standing close to her. If any of them took a step closer their bodies would come in contact.

She turned back to look at Cathy. "Come. Let me introduce you," said Agina.

"I don't know about that. He looks more like he wants to murder me and lock you up in a love chamber for the rest of your life! I think you finally met someone as possessive as you," said Cathy, as she cautiously glanced at him.

"Ugh. When you say it like that you make it sound like I used to be a creep. No wonder she left me," Agina said as she furrowed her eyebrows and wrinkled her nose.

"No. It was cute. She left you because she was a jerk," Cathy stated, smiling again.

Agina looked at Otiende again, He looked like he was hanging on by a thread.

"Come. I am not taking no for an answer," Agina said, taking Cathy's hand and leading her toward Otiende.

They stopped and stood at the edge of the stage. When Agina looked down, it looked like a long distance.

She wasn't sure how she had made the jump so effortlessly with her short tight dress. It had two layers below her waist with the second layer being loose, long, and only covering her back and sides.

Cathy was tall with a small curvy body. She had tucked a white t-shirt into Ankara shorts that made her legs look even longer.

Agina found herself wondering what their bare legs looked like from Otiende's angle. Cathy was like Otiende in the sense that most people found her extraordinarily beautiful.

But even so, Agina had never felt intimidated by her friend's looks because she knew she had a body that was just as beautiful, and she was confident with her beauty.

Otiende held out his hands to help Agina down. But Agina offered Cathy to go instead, moving her closer to his hand. He still insisted on taking her so Agina impatiently said, "If you don't help her I will."

He reluctantly chose to help Cathy first, then helped Agina down. Once Agina was down he didn't let go of her waist. She stood there looking at his flaming eyes, waiting for him to let go. But he did not. So, they just stood there. They were looking at each other.

"Uhhmm… So… This is Cathy," she said awkwardly as she nervously pointed to the side.

The situation couldn't have been more awkward, but it was her fault for setting it up this way. She could only move forward with the introduction.

She continued, "We have been friends since childhood."

After some time of silently looking into her eyes, he finally let her go and tightly put an arm around Agina, turning to look at Cathy.

"I'm Otiende, her husband. We have been friends since childhood."

The way he said it sounded more like he had just issued a threat. Especially considering his body language and how he tilted his head slightly as he spoke.

Feeling tense, she tiptoed, leaned into his ears and quietly spoke, "Calm down. I meant to properly introduce her later. I also have other friends in the same circle I would like you to meet. We usually all hang out together. I haven't seen them in a while. We don't meet up when she is touring. I was just happy to see her because I wasn't expecting her to be there."

She could tell he was jealous. His mood had already been dysregulated since the morning. She knew he couldn't help it. She gave him a hug and a light kiss on his lip, keeping him in her arms. At first, it seemed like he would pull away with the way he resisted her. She felt him start to relax as she rubbed his back.

When he had calmed down enough, they turned to look at Cathy again, his arm firmly wrapped around her waist. Cathy looked like she was ready to sprint away. Agina reached out to touch Cathy's hand but changed her mind mid-way.

"I'll set up a time for us all to have dinner. Okay. I'll get back to you. I have really missed you and the girls."

She tried to apologise with her eyes. Agina didn't want to admit it, but she had changed a lot since she met Otiende and got her powers.

She used to spend more time with her friends, even though they always met spontaneously. They were all free-spirited and did things spontaneously. They wouldn't have scheduled dinner; it had felt so awkward to say that.

They usually just thought of something and acted. The behaviour that was more in Agina's nature was to go and gather the rest of her friends and then spend the rest of the day together. They lived in the present, always acting in the now.

She had been truthful about not usually meeting the girls when Cathy was on tour. However, she had only brought it up as an excuse. Usually, they didn't like to leave one person out. Hence, they avoided meeting when Cathy toured.

Cathy was a free-spirited musician who rarely toured. She preferred to perform for family and friends. Her tour was more like a road trip with unscheduled performances, her spirit leading her where she was feeling called to perform. The spontaneous locations made her hard to find.

Like most Innercity people, her friends all rarely used coms to communicate. Agina was the best person at knowing where they were. She would have to personally find them all, to schedule the dinner.

Cathy nodded and quickly took off before Agina could say anything else.

"You scared away my friend," Agina protested.

"You can't just take off like that to kiss your *friends* when I have been worrying about you all day and not expect me to get upset. Something could have happened to you in that crowd." She could still hear the anger in his voice.

"I'm fine. Okay. Don't get yourself worked up again," she gently said, rubbing his back. she honestly hadn't thought about what she was doin, she just reacted.

85

CHANGED

"I WOULDN'T BELIEVE it was real if I didn't see it with my own eyes," said Cathy out loud to herself, looking at the sea of people; their differences in skin shade, hair and height defining the surface-tension of the crowd and making it look like a single entity you could lift, just by pulling up on one side with something large enough.

There were people everywhere. It had to have been impossible to see beyond the people around you if you were standing in the crowd.

It wasn't a very dense crowd. It was more like the crowd you would see in large highly populated cities, with some people walking, some people standing more so around stalls, people taking pictures, people rushing past.

There was no organisation to how the people gathered. Some places had more people than others. But there were no empty spaces. In all the history Cathy experienced, she didn't think there was ever a time when everyone came out to celebrate.

She liked parties, celebrations, these kinds of things. Whether she was performing or not. Unlike Agina who avoided these things. Agina only went to socialise with her friends. Agina had taken part in the dance performances during the conferences when she was younger because it was more fun than 'boring elder stuff'. Otherwise, Agina avoided crowds, parties, and performances.

Yet there was Agina, at the centre of it all. To top it all off, Agina wasn't just an elder, she was the leader of the elders. Agina had bodyguards clearing a path for her. Moreover, Agina was in the arms of a celebrity known in all countries.

If she had not seen the smile on Agina's face and how they looked at each other, she would have thought someone had forced Agina to marry him and accept the fate she always ran from. But there it was in Agina's eyes.

It was like Agina was mesmerised by gazing at the stars, looking at something infinite. It wasn't like Agina was looking at the person in front of her. It was clear Agina wasn't seeing what the rest of us were seeing.

She had never seen Agina look at Chloe in that way. Though Agina had looked at Chloe with love. Naturally, Agina often pushed the boundaries between flirting and being nice, between sensual and graceful. Agina unintentionally misled a lot of people.

But there was no mistaking Agina's current facial expression. Even Otiende, whose performances she has followed for a long time in respect to another musician, never had that look. It didn't show up when he was in his past relationships either.

Looking at them together warmed you and made you want to take a picture, just so you can capture what love looks like. Instantaneously she just realised that seeing them had shed away all the feelings she had against their relationship.

Now all that was left was a pain somewhere deep inside that she had carried for a long time. She was now at ease enough to feel joy for Agina.

Unexpectedly Agina looked straight at her. Agina's facial expression suddenly changed. Then even faster than Cathy could comprehend, Agina ran into the crowd. Cathy couldn't follow her movement; it looked more like the crowd was a living entity that had swallowed her whole!

"Are you really headed this way? I didn't think you would be happy to see me," said Cathy as she looked around trying to find where Agina had disappeared to.

"Cathy!!!" she heard over the loud music.

How loud did she have to be to be heard over the speakers Cathy was standing next to? She followed the sound to find Agina running towards her. She had been friends with Agina long enough to know that she was going to make the jump.

Just as she opened her arms, Agina arrived in her embrace. Days like this Cathy wished she could get rid of her feelings for Agina. But after all these years of trying and almost succeeding, she had not managed to get over her. She kept falling in love with her. Her heart still beat harder whenever she was this close to her.

Later, Cathy walked back to the stage. Amused and slightly irritated, she spoke out loud, "Fool. Don't you know you were the first one to break her heart? Now you want to hold on to her like she is yours."

She recently pieced it together. That day she had run into Agina in the town as Agina walked in a daze. Agina was so lost in thought that she did not notice her even when Cathy tried to get her attention.

When she thought she finally got her attention, Agina said, "OT is back. He came back. I have to go meet him." Agina continued in her daze to the point where Cathy couldn't tell if she had actually been noticed or if Agina was just speaking out loud while she was in some kind of trance or sleepwalking.

She watched her walk away in confusion, but she couldn't stop wondering who OT was. Later it came back to her who OT was. One memory about that time stuck with her:

She went down to play at the lake that day. Agina was usually there but she didn't see her that day. So, she played alone. She picked up some small pebbles and leaned low as she threw a pebble on the surface of the lake.

It bounced on the surface of the water a few times before being overcome by gravity and disappearing to the bottom. The surface of the water rippled as the impact of the pebble disrupted it.

She decided to do something else, then that was when she noticed someone sitting at the foot of a tree. Their feet were bare, and they were wearing a white dress. If she had kept playing without looking in that direction, she probably would have left without noticing the person.

She began to approach then she realised it was Agina. Why had she come this far without her shoes?

"Hi, Agina. Why didn't you say anything when I was looking for you? Didn't you hear me calling you?" she cautiously questioned. Even from a distance, she could see there was something strange about Agina.

Agina didn't respond.

As she got closer, she realised that Agina was crying. She looked more like she was lifeless than sad. Her eyes looked empty, as if she was looking at nothing. Tears were silently flowing down from her face.

She hesitated to approach. She looked more like a zombie with life still in their body. The way her arms were positioned beside her body made her arms look lifeless with a cold stillness. It was painful to watch.

"A- Agina, what is wrong? Are you hurt?" she hesitantly asked in concern.

But no matter what she did or said, she did not respond.

Finally, Agina painfully said, "Fate is cruel."

But that was all she would ever get out of her.

In the following days, she would find her like that. She got nothing else out of her. Even when she tried shaking her. She refused to respond.

At the present time, she managed to piece it together. She figured it out because she previously ran into Agina walking past in a daze, and started wondering who OT was.

It was looking back at that time that made her realise, that that was when Agina stopped talking about OT and that it was also the last time Agina saw OT.

Now that she looked back again, Agina had done a great job of hiding her sadness from everyone else. She would only run into her by mistake. Cathy had been too young to do anything or to understand what happened. When Agina had come with Adede, she would be okay, like nothing happened. Her young mind could only assume Agina was okay, because most times, Agina came with Adede.

Eventually, she stopped crying when she came alone. Her young mind could only imagine something had upset Agina, and that it most likely had to do with the pressures her family put on her; that was usually what upset Agina.

She also remembered their conversation just before Agina contacted Otiende through True Match.

Agina had gathered the girls. They all either sat or lay on the floor in a circle. When you looked around, they all appeared nonchalant despite the conversation; a book held, a sunhat covering a face, a cup of tea in hand, a slim vape dispenser held loosely between fingers, a glass of wine swirling around, quiet humming with drumming fingers, toenails being painted, incense burning somewhere along with candles. They were an offbeat bunch of people that never seemed to fit together.

You could only tell they were taking the conversation seriously by their responses to the conversation. Agina's main concern had been the differences between being with a man or a woman, and more importantly, the lifestyle of a celebrity.

Agina was considering turning Otiende down. Nothing in her words or body expression suggested she wanted to be married again. She spoke about marriage like it was a business transaction. She wanted to have nothing to do with a celebrity.

At that time, she must not have realised that OT was Otiende. She left, deciding she was going to give it a shot, but she had no hesitation to end things if there was a single thing she couldn't get past about him being a celebrity. She knew she wouldn't get past it so it was only a matter of when she would reject him. She was certain she wouldn't marry a celebrity.

Though some of them knew who Otiende was, no one had pieced together that OT was Otiende. Other than Cathy, they all became friends with Agina after Otiende left. By the time she met the others, Agina had stopped talking about OT. Moreover, because he lived in the Outercity, hid and gave up his title, not many people knew OT's face back then.

Would she have hesitated so much if she knew from the beginning that it was OT? Would she have waited a week to contact him? She had spent almost two weeks in resistance, between the time she got the message and the time she met him at the cafe. How did a broken heart feel when you gave it a second chance? Seeing how happy Agina was today sealed the door she left open to Agina's heart; it was time to finally get over her. She had always been his.

86

OLD ENEMY

AGINA AND OTIENDE continued to walk in awkward silence. The festival was scheduled to continue late into the night, ending with a night street party. Parties like that often continued into the early morning. They did not have to stay for it all; their presence among the people was appreciated but not a necessity.

Agina suddenly felt like she had enough and decided to make a quick exit. Otiende's mood had been off, and it had worsened significantly after she ran into Cathy. The longer she stayed the more she felt exposed for becoming a stranger to herself.

"I have had enough of this. Let's get out of here," she impatiently said, holding Otiende's hand and pulling him into the crowd. He started to protest trying to hold her back and slow their pace, but she resisted, insisting on rushing out.

Because of the sudden change in direction and because they were no longer patiently waiting for a path to be cleared, the crowd was much tighter as they went through.

Being fed up, Agina was not patient enough to wait for the bodyguards to clear a path. Realistically, she didn't expect them to start pushing people out of the way to keep up with her pace. She dismissed the bodyguards as they tried their best to quickly disperse the crowd, but they ignored the dismissal and kept trying to keep up.

 STRANGE LIGHT: Ler Mahia

This irritated her, causing her to move faster, like she was trying to get away from the bodyguards. If she wasn't struggling to tow Otiende along, who was being uncooperative and trying to slow her down, she would have made it just fine.

As they went through the crowd, she suddenly became aware and alert, sensing someone's malicious intent. She quickly took out her spear from where it was stowed concealed on her back, as she extended it, shifting her position to stand further ahead of Otiende. She faced the direction of the person as they quickly came into view.

Before she could even register who it was, she shifted her feet, firmly planting her feet as she rotated her spear above her head to gain momentum. She powerfully struck forward with the bottom of her spear bringing the person down by striking their legs. Their body momentarily flung into the air as they were struck.

She quickly spun her spear around and thrust forward with the intention of driving the spearhead through the bottom of their chin.

When she was in the middle of the motion, she recognised the person and stopped herself just as the spear made contact with his skin, drawing blood at the point of contact. He stared up at her in surprise, caught off guard and too stunned to move.

Hovering her spear above him, she shifted from her survival instinct to anger and tased him with electricity, rendering him unconscious. It looked like her spear was channelling bright white lighting that left Agina's hands unaffected.

"Damn it Peter, I almost killed you. Why would you approach him with such intent when there is someone beside him armed with a spear?" Agina thundered in anger.

Blood had dripped down his neck from where the spear had made contact with his skin. But it had stopped bleeding. The cut was shallow.

Just then, she noticed a knife that had dropped from his unclenched fist. By the looks of it, she had deduced through analysis that he had grabbed it from a nearby stall. The scent of the barbequed meat from the nyama choma stall was strong, and the grease from the beef's fat was clearly visible on the knife.

He was one of the people in Otiende's group when they used to go to the conferences; she only found out later that he was one of the people who used to bully Otiende. She met him when he had approached her with some nonsense about how her work was evil, trying to convert her.

"Why do you even have such a foreign name when you can't see past your damn beliefs?" she asked in rage, directing her spear towards him and giving him another shock; his unconscious body shaking lifelessly as the electricity passed through his body.

"Agina, that's enough," she heard Otiende say as he pulled her back. She struggled in his arms till he let her go.

"No. I've had enough. He should be grateful the culture that turned him into a monster is also mine. And that I'll let you stop me from taking his life," she slowly hailed, looking at Otiende's startled face, before she walked off, not bothering to see what would unfold next.

She had a lot of anger in her body, so she redirected it to making people move out of her way. As she walked, people scurried out of the way, even before they knew why they were moving out of the way.

They just had a sense they should move out of the way, so they moved just in time for Agina to storm past. After some hesitation, Otiende followed behind Agina, not sure as to what he should do.

She knew it looked like she was out of control, but it was the first time Agina felt like she was directing her storm. She had intentionally called that lightning and intentionally electrocuted him. She knew he was going to be fine based on how much voltage she used.

In all honesty, it was probably good that Otiende stopped her. The more she thought about what Otiende had to experience in his childhood, or the things Peter had said to her, the more she wanted to keep harming him.

She hadn't cared about what others thought as they watched it happen. They would probably never find out why she did it. That was not something she would tell.

There was also a possibility that they would cover up what just happened, and no one would ever hear a word about it. However, she didn't care if others found out. He was a bully. Let them know what kind of a person he was.

Some of the bodyguards had also followed them, but they honestly were not needed at this point. The crowd was parting just as fast as Agina's quick steps. The rest of the bodyguards had probably stayed behind to clear up the situation.

87

MISSING HIM

e-bot... Project the call.

~Hi Mom.

~*Hi OT. I don't see Agina. Is she there? Is she busy? I hope I am not interfering.*

~No. She went ahead to her family. I'll meet her there later. I didn't want her to keep her family waiting. With the time difference, I knew you wouldn't be able to call earlier.

~*Sigh. Too bad. I was really looking forward to talking to her. She is such a sweetheart! Since I missed her on this call, let's meet for dinner soon this week. We can spend time together again. Okay?*

~She would love that. We always have this call but why do I feel like you only called to talk to her? Give her a call too. Don't just message her. She also wanted to talk to you.

~*Okay. I will call her later. I've had you all your life. I just got a daughter, so I am still excited about it.*

~It seems you have done more than welcome her into the family. Don't make her your favourite child! Thought, honestly... I'm glad she has someone else who can support her. She needs the support.

~She has told me she is having a hard time adjusting. Of course, I'll do what I can to offer support. It's not easy to be in a supporting role, is it? There are times when all I did was support your father. And there are times when all he did was support me.

~It's been a challenge so far. I can't say I thought it was going to be easy, but I really was not expecting to do all these mental exercises. I don't know what to do with her moods. I mean- Don't mind what I just said. Maybe I am too dysregulated as I adjust to birth control. It usually puts me out of sorts. Or maybe things have been piling up without properly getting solved. I don't mean to sound like I have endless excuses. I get the feeling I am always going to be facing unpredictable situations.

~It's expected. She is a Gemini. So, she has a versatile nature. This horoscope also indicates that there will be times when she will lack focus when it's most needed, be prone to nervousness, and take flight halfway through a job.

~Mom, I don't believe in that stuff. However, there is a bit of truth in there. I am seeing more and more that it's not that she can't do it. It's not a fear either. She can handle things fine. She just chooses to hold back. Sometimes we get those brief moments when she isn't holding back, and they are... frighteningly powerful. Her power is a god-like strength. Anyway, I am speculating too much at this point. And I have said too much about Agina without her being present. It feels like I am talking about her behind her back. How are you doing?

~My First Flight project is being paused. They have decided to rewrite the script. It's really frustrating because it's going to mess up my schedule if they pause it for too long. I only planned to live with my co-stars till next month, when we wrap up the project. Maybe that's why it was too easy to get those days off. But when I look at the good that will come from it: I should get to spend more time with you both. In fact, let's not just do one day of dinner this week.

~Okay. Sometimes I miss such moments where it's just work that's causing tension. Work-related problems are easier to fix. Maybe I have been out of a relationship too long. Or maybe I just miss entertainment. I am sorry to envy you. I do look forward to seeing you more now that you have the free time.

~*Don't forget it was your choice to step away from the entertainment industry. You can always come back when you get tired of your computers. These past years, O_ts have patiently waited and supported you as you have rolled back. But I wonder... you started both at such a young age. I don't know if any of them were really your first love. They happened simultaneously.*

~I don't know which came first either. I'll come back to entertainment eventually. I love it too much to just let it go. But right now, I'm happy being focused on what I love most. O_ts are even more entertained by my love life. It's not the first time but it still feels so strange. I think it's the mystery that is getting them. They are so used to knowing everything about me. This turn in my life is tipping the scales where their hate is turning to love, and their love is turning to hate.

~*I know you are happy to focus on her. You and Agina coming together is a whole other story in itself. I wonder what legends they will write of it. Even I find myself too curious about you two. I'm rooting for the two of you.*

~Hahaha. I haven't seen your number-one fan dance in a while. Thank you… When I look at how long it took me to get out of my contracts without breaking them, and see the path I set, it still feels more like it was fate. I never would have planned such a life in the role of an elder. It was something I genuinely gave up. She gave that to me. She gave me my title; I didn't even ask, and she insisted when I refused.

~*Yes. We can only plan so much. Give yourself a break for all the emotions you both have to deal with. You're doing well. Your hormones will balance soon when the birth control becomes effective. I'll leave you to go to her.*

~Thank you. You have been really supportive of us through this. We'll speak again some other time. I'll let you know when we'll meet for dinner. Tell Dad I said hello.

~*Okay. I'll let him know. Goodbye.*

~Goodbye.

-End of call-

AGINA WALKED WITH Adede in her arms, glad to have the familiar feeling. It felt like it had been a while since she was in her family home without being there because she was preparing for the Aiye or attending the Aiye. Everything was exactly the same. Sundays were always a day when her family gathered.

She had only stopped attending during the time she was married to Chloe. With the way things ended, that period in her life is now more like a black hole. Even if she had genuinely felt happiness at the time.

She looked at the door for the fifth time in a minute, feeling on edge with anticipation. Then she looked at the clock, feeling empty. When had she grown so attached to him? She didn't think about him so much when they were together.

Now that he was away, why did she keep looking for him? How could she miss him? Is this what living with him for a week did to her? They had just got an office together, so they would keep spending a lot of time together. What would all that time together do to her? She had not spent that much time with Chloe; Chloe had liked her personal space.

It's his fault for not telling me when he was coming, she thought to herself. She hadn't wanted to arrive by herself, but Otiende had insisted that she go by herself and that he follow later, because he had business matters he needed to wrap up, and his mom was likely to call that morning.

But hadn't he known she wanted to talk to Mom too? She smiled to herself. She found it easy to call her: Mom. They were getting along well. She had told him, but it didn't change his mind. He insisted time alone with her family would be good.

She wondered what business it was. He had so many business ventures that she couldn't have guessed what it was. He had someone who had helped manage everything since he was a child, and several people who managed the individual businesses. Thankfully Otiende was not constantly running his businesses.

They stopped walking and stood in the living room. She found herself remembering how he sat across from her at the Aiye when she was being presented after the discussions. There might have been a distance between them in the large living room, but she had kept looking at him and finding him looking at her.

She tried to shake away the thoughts, but she couldn't seem to stop thinking of him. She forced herself to look around. Her family members were scattered all over the sofas and dining seating. Some were standing like them.

"Agina, did you hear anything I said?" Adede asked in disbelief.

"Huh?" asked Agina, looking clueless and still finding herself glancing at the door.

"You keep spacing out and you won't take your eyes off that door," Adede reproached.

"What did you say? Sorry. I'll listen this time," asked Agina, feeling guilty, then apologising. She had been trying not to think of him which made her think of him more.

Agina chose to turn away from the door. She had to actively practise awareness to remain present as Adede was talking. It took effort but she was able to manage; they were finally having a back-and-forth conversation.

After a long while, because Agina had been highly focused on Adede, she noticed a change in Adede's body language. She seemed distracted by something. But she ignored the change, thinking Adede would speak up about it. She gave up when Adede just remained distracted.

"Earth to Adede. Have you taken over being inattentive as revenge? I already said I was sorry because I couldn't remain focused even if it was to save my life!" said Agina as she waved her hand in front of Adede's face.

"Mtchew," Adede made a sound sucking her teeth in protest then hesitantly said, "It's just that..."

Agina waited for Adede to continue.

"Just that what?" she asked, curiosity taking over her.

Adede nodded her head to point in a direction behind Agina. Agina looked in the direction Adede had shown her.

She turned to see Otiende looking at her, a smile spreading across his face.

"OT!!" Agina burst out, giving into the impulse to spring to him.

MEET THE SOUL

S HE FELT LIKE she was filled with excitement as she rushed to him. Somewhere in the back of her mind, she registered that he had not come straight to her because he had been hijacked by her family who had surrounded him.

When she arrived in his arms, he lifted her in a hug and turned her around. He had the largest grin on his face. She felt great joy to be in his arms again. Everything she had been worrying about seemed to disappear. She liked the feeling of joy.

"Why did you take so long?" she asked in wonder, touching his hair.

"I'm sorry. I had a lot to do. I did try to rush," he said, kissing her on her forehead.

"No. Don't apologise. You didn't have to push yourself," she said looking in his eyes with a tinge of guilt.

"It's fine. I wanted to be by your side," he said, wrapping his arms tighter around her body.

"I'm glad you're here now," she said, burying herself in him and pulling him in tighter.

"Me too," she heard him reply.

"Okay love birds. It's like you didn't see each other this morning. We all know where he slept," her aunt playfully taunted.

She heard some light laughter as she pulled away from Otiende, she just remembered they were not alone.

Agina looked at her eager relatives that had surrounded Otiende, like baby chicks chirping excitedly when their mother had returned with food.

At that moment she understood. To connect with someone is to get to know them at a deeper level. To meet their soul. A person's soul doesn't lie about who it is. But what we see, what we observe when we look at someone, is what a person creates to interact with others; How they choose to show up.

Right from the beginning, she had met his soul. Otiende doesn't connect with most people because people cannot get past what they observe to meet his soul. People become too invested in the image.

They went about the day socialising. Being that she traded Adede's arm for Otiende's arm and closeness, it didn't feel the same as any other Sunday anymore. Despite not truly connecting with others, it was like Otiende had a natural gift to socialise. It made it easier to interact with everyone; being an introvert, she usually spent most of her time with Adede.

At some point, Agina went to help get the food ready for dinner. She needed a break from all the people. He was like a magnet for people.

Everything might have been the same, but it was different. Agina thought as she smiled at Otiende and worked in the kitchen.

At times like this, she felt like she didn't just have another chance at love, but she felt like she might have found something better. There were so many compromises she had to make, but she was happy. Looking back, Chloe couldn't enter the Innercity, and most people never left the Innercity; unintentionally Chloe had remained separated from her family. Otiende integrated with her family seamlessly.

She knew she was not going to be able to fully enjoy being with Otiende till she forgave herself for letting go of the future she had created for herself; a creative free spirit with no partner or children, going where she may. Her spirit finally free and unburdened. That was the life she was supposed to have.

Where she had felt free and not burdened by the world, she now felt tied down and bound to the fate of the world, especially shackled to her bloodline. It was something she still needed to work through.

There were a lot of hands in the kitchen, so dinner was soon ready. When they had lunch, it was more informal with people serving themselves from the kitchen and seating where they liked. Otiende had arrived after they had lunch.

Dinner was more formal with people seated together around the dining table. The place settings were also formal, with the head of the table clearly being Abura. Since they couldn't all fit at the table, others sat in the living room and at the kitchen island. There was a sense they all sat together, centred around the dining table.

As always with dinner, the food was served formally, and everyone began to eat at the same time after Abura blessed the food. On cue, they began to eat as soon as Abura blessed the food and gave her gesture, like silence erupted by noise.

After dinner, while everyone was still seated, Agina silently got up and went outside. She was looking up at the night sky and listening to the music of nature after dark, when she was surprised to see Otiende had followed her.

"Did you really manage to get away? I don't know how you do it. Adede keeps me going; I can't handle people for long. Or any of this new life if I am being honest," she said like she was distant, staring back up at the stars.

Otiende hugged her from the back, looking up at the night sky. She felt his warmth wrap around her, feeling protected.

"You are doing great. I have been handling people my whole life. Well... except for the Peters of this world. Even with your powers, I never imagined you would be the one to protect me. But you also managed that well," he said rubbing his face against hers. His skin was smooth and soft. He took great care of his face.

"Sigh. I'm tired," she said, turning and burying herself in his arms.

"I am tired of it all," she said as she pulled him closer, feeling defeated and wanting to stay wrapped in his embrace.

"Let's get some rest now. I already excused us. We can go home," he said as he encouraged her by rubbing her head.

"Mmm. OT," she whined. "My legs are tired too. I just want to stay in your arms."

He burst out laughing and then said, "Get on my back then. I'll carry you home."

"Will you really?" she excitedly said, silently calling her spear to her and wearing it concealed on her back.

"Yes. Let's go home," he said as he turned then carried her on his back.

Agina liked the feeling of his warm back. It was comforting. She always had a feeling of safety around him. It felt like being by his side was something she was supposed to be doing. She was so comfortable that she felt like she might fall asleep.

"Do you remember it?" She heard Otiende's deep soothing voice ask.

His voice made her alert, pulling her back from the slow drowsiness she was falling into.

"Remember what?" she asked, the tiredness slowing her speech.

"I used to carry you on my back when you would fall asleep," he said, sounding deep in thought.

Is that why this feeling is so familiar and comforting? She thought to herself. But most of what she felt about him felt familiar. Even loving him. Though she was sure she didn't love him in a romantic way back then. The sexual attraction was new.

"I don't remember. You said it like I was already asleep when you carried me," she said, trying to recall what happened.

"Yeah. I am sorry it took me this long to come back to you." She heard the regret in his voice. He sounded sincerely sorry.

She knew she should say something back. But the statement had drawn her into the memory of the past. She felt a tear drip down her cheek before she realised she was crying.

"Agina?" He sounded surprised and concerned.

"Sorry. I haven't cried about you leaving since then," she said, struggling to hold back her tears, then giving in to the stream. She felt ridiculous for crying now but she just let it out, looking to the side like it would help avoid his attention. She was genuinely tired, she couldn't fight the tears anymore.

He suddenly stopped walking.

She suddenly realised what she said, "I mean..." She didn't fully intend to say that, and now she couldn't think of what she should say instead. She leaned in and held him tighter as her tears continued to fall.

He continued to stand in place and they both remained silent.

He turned back towards her.

"I am sorry. I was figuring myself out. I never thought about what it meant for you." She felt guilty for hearing the deep remorse in his voice.

She hadn't meant to make him feel that way. She could only blame her tears that didn't seem to want to end.

"No. Don't. Don't apologise. It's already passed. I had put it behind me. You just brought up the past so suddenly. It pulled out this pain I buried and forgot. It was hard for me when you left. I had to keep moving forward with your memory in my spear. I could never fully forget. I could only bury the pain so deep that it would never surface. I didn't think it would show up so easily." The hurt in her forlorn voice was evident.

"I cried when no one was around. It was hard for me to put it behind me because you were the only true friend I had. It hurt so much more than anything I had experienced. I don't know why I felt leaving you and leaving my title had to go together. I became a coward for not even being able to admit my regret. Leave alone admit my mistake. I foolishly convinced myself it was the right choice. I was afraid to face you after knowing I made you cry. And like the coward I had become, I took advantage of my anonymity as #1008, so I could selfishly stay by your side," Otiende said, his entire demeanour changing. He was beating himself up about it.

"OT. It's fine. We were kids. Those emotions were too complex to process. Even for adults, it would have been hard to process such feelings... Let's go home. I think it's time to revisit the past," she gently said, noting that she was still crying yet it had not started raining. When she faced her feelings honestly, she didn't seem to affect the weather.

REVISITING THE PAST

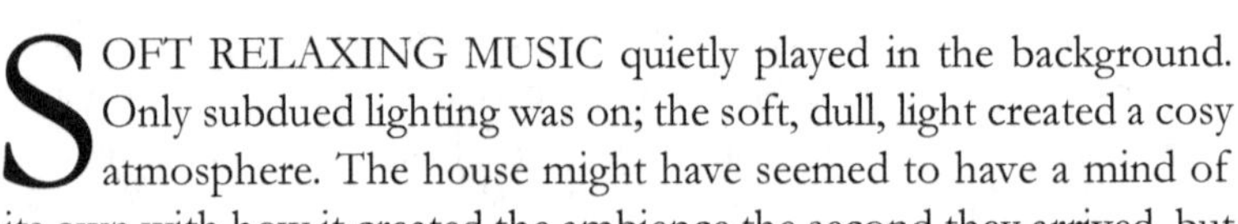

SOFT RELAXING MUSIC quietly played in the background. Only subdued lighting was on; the soft, dull, light created a cosy atmosphere. The house might have seemed to have a mind of its own with how it created the ambience the second they arrived, but it was the way it was set to react to their emotions.

Otiende sat on the sofa, leaning against the arm of the seat with his bare feet up on the sofa. Agina was seated between his legs, leaning against his chest, also barefooted. His arms were wrapped around her at her belly. They idly played with each other's fingers as they looked around at the photos they both just took out.

"We have so many photos," Agina said as she telepathically brought both photos together and then arranged them chronologically.

The digitally projected images were all hovering in the room, moving where she directed them. They seemed to fill up the room as most of them hovered behind the other, taking up their own space.

"You always loved to take photos," Otiende idly said as he looked at the photos.

"Are you really going to put that on me when you even have seventeen years worth of photos you took of me as #1008!" she accused, glancing back at him.

When she was a child, she had been fascinated by his com and especially loved to take pictures. Nonetheless, he had also taken pictures of her. So, the pictures they both took had started from the day they met.

He laughed. She felt him shake with laughter behind her.

"Some things are hard to get rid of," he said, rubbing her head.

They went through the pictures from the start, talking and laughing as they reminisced about the past.

"OT. Some of these pictures are not that different from the pictures we are taking now. But how did we get away with taking such a photo?" she slowly said, her thoughts elsewhere, then looked back at him. He was staring at the picture lost in thought. When he remained silent, she looked back at the photo.

They were looking at a photo of Otiende holding Agina at the waist and Agina kissing Otiende on his cheek. They were standing side by side, but Agina was on a platform that brought her up to his height. In the photo, Otiende had a large grin on his face.

Agina often hugged and kissed people when she met them as a greeting, even if she was meeting them for the first time. This photo did not look like one of those kisses.

She had been innocent in her childhood. Almost too innocent in comparison to others her age. She had played in the trees, sometimes in the rivers and lake. Most of the time she played alone, preferring solitude. Nature was her playground she never quite grew out of. Hence, her social habits were always different.

Being that she constantly tried to escape council activities, she had unintentionally isolated herself. More so when she got her spear that no one knew was a com. If she wasn't learning how to yield her spear, she was secretly using her com.

As far as romance went, she always felt confused. She found that she liked girls, and not only girls. It didn't help that it caused a rift between her and her mother who adamantly reminded her of her responsibility to continue the Supreme Elder's bloodline.

The rift was created because her mother knew she didn't just like girls. So, Agot concluded that Agina only chooses girls out of spite; that she was being rebellious. Hence, Agina intentionally avoided relationships for a long time.

So, even when she got tired of being called cute and boyish and changed her style, she looked like she was just seeking attention since she was not quick to get into relationships or experience romance. Her elusiveness pulled more people to her, but she remained focused on discovering and expressing who she was.

She wondered what her mother would think if she saw the photo they had taken. They were younger; she was 5 years old in the photo. What they shared was obviously innocent. She remembered that she had kissed him because she was feeling grateful.

If they had been siblings, the photo would have been cute; It gave that feeling of a deep love shared between a brother and a sister. It only became questionable because they were not siblings and had ended up together.

"Do you think we loved each other back then? I used to say I loved you all the time. Even if I meant it as a friend. Now I can't even say it," she said, feeling like she was sinking. She felt her feelings for him grow. If she was asked, she would say she loved him. But she couldn't bring herself to tell him the words.

"That's okay," he said, kissing her on her forehead. "People say they love each other all the time and they don't mean the same thing. I trust how you feel about me. I don't need you to call it love," he said, holding her tighter.

She held his arms, holding them in place around her, though he probably wasn't going to let go of her. "OT. Why do you say such cute mushy things?" she jokingly asked, looking up at him and smiling.

They looked into each other's eyes. He was smiling. The trust genuinely showed on his face. She felt drawn by his certainty. She suddenly felt her heart beat faster as she looked up at him, his face close. Then she closed her eyes and angled her lips towards him.

He slowly and gently kissed her, holding her face with his hand. Their kiss forged an understanding of who they were as their tongues met.

After some time of getting lost in each other, they returned to looking at the pictures, remembering the past they shared.

Agina looked back at Otiende and said, "We should put some of these pictures up in our home. Especially the one that is in our parents' house. It belongs in the living room. Too bad it won't have the same story."

"It will have its own story to tell. We should also get pictures for our entry hall. When you get a chance to go back, see what pictures of your family and ancestors you can find," Otiende said, interlacing her fingers with his.

"I will. Did you always know you were going to start a family?" she asked in interest. The way he did things seemed to point his life in that direction. It was the opposite for her, who seemed to move as far as she could from where she was constantly told she must go.

"Yeah. It was wishful thinking that it could happen here in the Innercity. That app was my way of facing reality. I told it I would go anywhere in the world to find love. I made this choice because our people, no matter how open their personalities are, have a fear of advanced technology. You have felt this. Haven't you? The fear when they see it in action," he asked, like he was holding his breath, looking for confirmation that he was not the only one who had experienced the mania.

"That fear is real. Even in the people I love. It makes it hard to truly connect with them when you have to hide. My father was the only one I didn't see have that fear. But he couldn't care less for it. Plants and animals are his world," said Agina, suddenly becoming aware of her reclusive life.

"My family was easier in that regard. But I grew up in the Outercity. I grew up like an outsider. It didn't help that I always had to stay covered. The Innercity was where I should have belonged, but somewhere in the beginning, it wasn't just my technology or what I was doing that was evil. I was seen as evil. Have you seen what even the most righteous person will do when they face evil?" he asked, pain in his voice.

"Throughout history, people have done the most inhumane things because they were allegedly facing something evil, wrong, or whatever they chose to call it. It's the most devastating human weak point that gets exploited too often." She rubbed his arm and kissed him on the cheek.

"We have come a long way with acceptance of diversity. But this weakness is innate. Other than my family, you were the only one who fully accepted me. Even the people in the Outercity had their own biases. I missed you terribly after I left. But I couldn't bring myself to come back for you," he said apologetically, kissing her hand.

"I understand. I didn't reach out to you either. Why were we so determined to leave it up to fate?" she asked, more so to herself.

"I generally don't believe in destiny. I don't know what overcame me to say that. I asked myself too often what would have happened if I didn't say that. Even later when I knew I loved you, I held too much guilt, shame and fear to say anything. Looking at these pictures with you really reminded me of what we had and why I felt so broken for giving it up," he said, holding her tight and pressing the side of his face against the side of her face.

She also had a deeper understanding of why it hurt when he left. They had formed such a strong bond at that time that couldn't compare to anything. Not even Adede or Cathy could offer the friendship they had.

She had worked hard at forgetting him. She already did not see him that often. But she took his memory everywhere along with her com. For a long time, most of the pictures in her com were of him. It couldn't be helped that she didn't photograph others, when the com was kept a secret. No matter what, she could never truly forget him, because the spear was birthed with him.

"Let's put together the photos we are going to send to Pierre. I'll send them to him tomorrow," he said after they had put away all their old photos.

They looked through all the pictures they took every morning before they left for the conferences and picked the ones they wanted.

"There are none of the last day. It's a miracle we made it there by seven o'clock. I'll get those from the broadcast. Then we'll have a complete set," she said, looking back at him.

They picked some more pictures and videos out of the footage from the broadcast; Otiende accessed it effortlessly. They compiled the conference photos and video and Otiende kept the files so he could send them later.

90

THE FAINT SIGNAL

IT FELT TOO quiet and empty. It felt like Otiende's presence lingered in the room. The emptiness was worse than yesterday because it was like he was everywhere. Everything reminded her of him. She kept finding herself drifting off to thoughts of him.

"What kind of a life did you live if you have already stepped away from so much?" she asked out loud to no one in particular. He always woke up early so he often spent the morning occupied with something.

She wondered if a workaholic could truly make time for their family. If Otiende was like this when he was on a break from entertainment and she had been called a workaholic herself because she got lost in her inventions, going too long without eating or sleeping, what would their family be like?

Could they raise a family together? They would soon be working together. The office had already been set up. Otiende was surprisingly efficient in setting it up. At least they would see each other often despite having a large workload.

She was glad to finish distractedly getting ready and being in time to her studio. She felt a sense of grief as she looked around the large room. In comparison to Otiende's lab, it looked like a cluttered mess. There was equipment all over the place.

It looked more like her team worked on top of each other, but they had come to this conclusion after having to keep moving things around. It saved them time which they could use to focus on other things.

She wasn't sure how often she would come back since she planned to start her new projects in the new office. There was so much in this studio she would be leaving behind, including her team. After getting powers all the projects she was working on had quickly come to a close. Being able to magically influence her equipment had a great advantage that shortened the product creation time.

Otiende had sent someone to catalogue her studio the same day that they bought the office. Otiende was able to get her all that she needed and more. She might have the status and magic powers, but Otiende had the resources. He was like a bottomless pit of money and connections. If she hadn't seen the figures of all the money he had already spent, she would have never believed such money existed. Leave alone that he still had plenty left. It had eased her into accepting all the things he had insisted on buying for her.

She recently discovered that at some point in his life, he had shown up in the list of the world's richest. He dismissed the list saying that he never stays in such lists because he spends a lot of money, especially when it comes to helping others and helping his country. He vouched that he only made so much money so he could help more people. She had wanted transparency in his financial matters but she had not expected to see what she saw.

He was a huge money spender. He didn't spend money too often, but he spent large sums at a time. She couldn't just stop him because she was the kind of person who would be content to live in the wild with nature's resources, as long as she had her spear.

The office was the first thing they had bought together after their relationship legally became official. Her life felt surreal. She didn't recognise herself.

Agina didn't usually take off her ring, but she took it off for the first time since she set it up. The ring made her too aware of Otiende's presence. Usually, it was an awareness she held in the background like her own breathing. But today she found herself being fully aware of him. It was like she was focusing on him in a meditative state, feeling his heartbeat and subtle body sensations.

With the ring off, she managed to get through her morning. When lunchtime arrived, she stopped to go meet Otiende. She was looking forward to seeing him again.

The moment she got to his lab, she had a sinking feeling. There seemed to be some kind of chaos. No one noticed she had arrived. There was a warning blaring on the screen, and everyone was focused on a computer, typing at what seemed to be impossible speed.

There was a portal that was now inactive, set up in the middle of the room. She wondered what they had been working on. It was just one portal, but it was similar to the setup they had when Tony disappeared. The sinking feeling got worse.

"Where is OT?" she finally asked, noticing the bodyguards were still there but Otiende was nowhere to be seen.

"Supreme Elder," said the person who was closest to her in a timid voice, startled by her presence. He hurriedly got down on one knee, clearly looking anxious.

Agina found herself getting irritated. She had not taken the time to get to know the staff when she had been working with Otiende, but she knew their faces and names. She had spent most of the time with Otiende and he was the one who addressed his staff. Otiende must have told them not to bow when she had worked there before.

"There is no need for formality here. Get up," she snapped at Amani.

She was fully aware that she sounded harsh, but the bow had got on her nerves. She knew he was probably feeling overwhelmed by her gaze that was influenced by her power, but she was too irritated to control her power. He must have been feeling crushed under her gaze.

"Yes. Sorry," he said, stumbling up and looking like he was looking for an escape.

"Where is OT? Otiende. Where is Otiende?" she asked, trying to change her tone.

"He... We found a faint signal from Tony. Otiende went into the portal to get him. Then they both disappeared," he said, looking like he was wishing he was anywhere else in the world but in front of Agina.

"Wh- What?!" she uttered in disbelief, falling to her knees, all the strength in her gone.

Agina felt like her world was spinning. Did she just also lose Otiende? Where had he disappeared to? Was there nothing she could do? Was she just supposed to sit around and wait like she did when Tony went missing? No. It wasn't the same as losing Tony. The Otiende who was sleeping in her bed last night? Who she married in a traditional wedding that they had not yet completed. How could she live with herself?

Her breathing was not steady anymore. It was like she was starting to panic. She was aware the atmosphere in the room was changing and she briefly felt a tremor as the ground slightly shook. She needed to control herself, but she couldn't bring herself to do anything. Was she now also able to cause earthquakes? But she didn't care if the place crumbled; he wasn't there.

How could he just leave her? He must have known what it meant to go after Tony. Did he think that she would be okay without him? Why does he always just think she will be okay when he walks out of her life? What did he feel? Then she suddenly remembered the ring and put it on.

"He went in a minute or two before you arrived. But we can't locate him. He took a portable portal with him, but it was corrupted once he went through. We were not sure if it was Tony, but Otiende didn't want to take any chances, since it's the only signal we got, and the signal was on the move. He didn't want to lose the signal," she heard someone else say as they continued to intensely type at the computer without looking at her.

Now that she had the ring on, she could feel his heart rate. He was alive. But something was wrong with his breathing and the way his heart was beating.

"He knew I was coming. Why didn't he wait for me?" she spoke blankly, asking no one in particular. She felt like she had frozen in place. She couldn't think of anything other than how he was missing and wondered when she would see him again. Her mind couldn't move past the thought unless she was wondering what was wrong with him, imagining all sorts of terrifying possibilities.

"He left you a note," said a third voice from behind as they walked over and expanded the small device into a notetab.

Negasu handed it to her. It was briefly transparent before it took form and showed a page with familiar handwriting.

> Sorry if I didn't manage to make it back. I trust you will always be able to find me.

Otiende had also drawn an illustration of wings. Agina smiled when she saw the wings, feeling like she finally got her thought process back. She had been too stunned to think of what to do next. Unfortunately, even when confounded, she still affected the atmosphere of the room. She felt herself stabilise and the atmosphere also changed, stabilising to how it had been before she panicked.

She stood up. Now she knew what to do.

"Tell me everything," she commanded, speaking to both technology and nature, the forces she was able to control.

She was vaguely aware that she had moved forward, toward the screen, without moving her feet. The equipment in the room responded to her, giving her the information. She also picked up information from her surroundings.

"What's the best way to retrieve him?" she asked without saying out loud.

As she received the information, she raised both arms, her spear still in her hand. Like she was a magnet, she quickly gathered some equipment, materials and tools.

The things she collected levitated towards her and spun around her in a circle. They orbited her continuously at a rapid speed.

She felt like her power was steadily surging since she had fully used her power with complete confidence. She had never felt more in control. Her power seemed to be growing infinitely.

Having gathered everything she needed, she teleported to the lake, disappearing from the place she stood.

CREATING WITH MAGIC

THE WATER IN the lake stretched far and wide. Its colour was brown like someone had kicked water in a puddle and the mud had subsided, but hadn't quite settled. The island on the horizon couldn't quite be distinguished, looking like a blue cloud sitting across the water. The water slowly moved, swelling in tiny waves. The lake didn't have a shore that stretched wide; the water met the earth, then vegetation grew soon after.

She appeared at the shore, on the water's edge, the items still orbiting around her. She put her outstretched arms down and looked out into the water that seemed to touch the sky on the horizon. There was no turning back now.

Even if there were other ways to save him, she knew in her core this was what she was going to do to get him back as soon as possible. For the first time since she got her powers, she had a high sense of confidence. She could still feel her powers increase which raised her confidence, which in turn raised her power. She loved the feeling of power. For the first time, she had more reason to want it than to be afraid of it.

She did not have any fear or doubt; she felt no need to hold herself back. In the past, she hadn't realised when she had subconsciously crossed into the spirit world. She hadn't realised she had gone there or that she had returned, until now that she was fully in command. Now that her choice was clear, she could see things clearly; she knew exactly how to return to the spirit world.

She crossed into the spirit world. She could see spirits wondering about. The spirit world was a dimension that shared the physical part of our world. It's why spirits could sometimes influence our world or be seen. Their world looked almost the same but, had so much more that she could fully sense with her powers.

The one she came to meet stood before her, seaming to be standing on the water. It was as though it had known this moment was coming and had stood waiting. Throughout time it had been most commonly known as Nandi Bear, but its true name was ancient and silent like the language it spoke.

"We meet again. I knew you would one day return when you listen to your inner wisdom," it said, looking at her with eyes that looked like they could simply kill someone by accidentally spotting them.

Its mouth did not move but she understood the words it said. She knew it was not just simply speaking telepathically but it was its ancient language born before words.

It rose, standing on two paws. It was already a large creature close in height when on four paws. So, it towered above her when on its hind legs. It was more impressive than any image of it she had ever seen.

Using her spear, she did the gestured greeting and acknowledged, "My apologies. I do not come before you today to visit or to seek advice."

"The clarity in your eyes suggests so. It is why I can now stand before you and speak to you on this level. You have earned my respect. You may now speak to me freely," it said, its imposing presence seeming to give it more height.

"I ask that you walk amongst us again, to assist me, with your form bound to a machine," she stated in confidence, her path clear.

"Spirits cannot be truly bound. You understand this quite clearly because your spirit struggles to create its freedom. To bring me into your world in such a way is to unleash something you will never be able to control," it warned.

"It is not control I seek. But your intelligence and wisdom as you fight beside me," Agina stated, sure that the world already held chaos and would always have some form of chaos, no matter where it came from.

"What shall become of the day we stand on opposite sides?" it asked, knowing but testing, making its force fiercer.

It was a highly imposing energy. If her power made people feel overwhelming pressure when she was not even trying to force them to concede, a power like this would have made people instantly pulverise from the pressure, actually physically turning to nothing but dust.

"The moment we choose to have an ideology is the moment we are bound to have someone oppose us. Considering the world we live in, we cannot all be the same. It is a fate for us all who make choices. When that moment comes, let us face it with wisdom. For now, I need a machine that thinks independently and is not artificial intelligence."

"I shall join you. Long has passed since time and space could be manipulated by your kin. You have this ability because it's what your destiny calls for. For spirits, then is now. Time does not have a boundary. My return has long been spoken of in our world. It leads to success in this fight that affects us all," it said, withdrawing its pressure.

"You have my gratitude. I have created a spell specifically for you. It will give you an original form I create, but you can change into any form you desire," she said, her confidence surging and with it, her powers increasing.

It was time.

"I am ready," it said, resigning to the path she had created.

Agina raised her spear and started chanting.

"Bind in spirit and technology. Maintain spirit and mind at the core," she said out loud then kept chanting, stringing words together that she had deciphered would work. Saying the words she had thought of, in the same way she had thought the words on the night she gained

her powers. Switching to the ancient silent language as the words pieced together.

The objects that had been orbiting around her spun faster and faster, such that it looked like a solid ring. The spinning ring left her, passing over her head and going over to the Nandi Bear spirit. It spun like a tornado making contact with earth as they fused and merged. The objects lost their form and integrated with the Nandi Bear spirit.

Her chosen form slowly took shape from the top of its head to its claws. The last part to form were the wings, spanning several metres wide and somewhat looking like the wings of a bat. The Nandi Bear never had wings, but this chosen form had the majestic wings Agina always pictured.

It made a loud roar revealing sharp teeth that looked too frightening, like they were not even worthy to be on the deadliest bear on earth. But the Nandi Bear never quite looked like a bear but something more ferocious, so it was quite frightening to see such teeth that looked more like a giant hyena's teeth.

The creature that stood before her was more like the one she always pictured as a child. So, she didn't fear it. Its fur was colourful, resembling the soft colourful pallet of the Lilac Breasted Roller. But because it had a synthetic body, its fur glistened in the light, making it look more like it had the gleaming reptilian skin of a Panther Chameleon.

That, combined with the wings, gave it an overall look that was more like that of a dragon. That was the reason why in flight it became commonly confused with a dragon.

"Welcome back. We must leave now. OT needs us," she said, having returned them to her world. She touched its fur heartwarmingly and was surprised by how soft and warm it felt.

The story continues in...

SILENT SHADOW
Ler Mahia

ACKNOWLEDGEMENTS

As always, a special thanks to my kids for bringing adventure into my life and keeping my life interesting. I am especially grateful for their understanding, all the times I said, "Not now, I'm writing."

Thanks, to my family who are supportive even when they don't understand exactly what I am doing with my life! I don't understand either. I just live, and love my life.

This journey started with my One Short Book family, who I wrote together with. I learnt so much about writing and grew so much there. Thank you, for your love and support.

And thanks, to my Trauma of Money family who were with me when I was writing this book and lifted me up at a very crucial time.

Thank you, to my team at Spinkly Creations who were a part of the book even if it was just for a short while. Thank you, Sylvia, for your beautiful cover art and all the things that are too much to mention. Thanks, Nzisa, for your part in editing the book and thank you, Beryl, for your edits.

Thanks, to all the music that kept me inspired to write this book as I heard their music on repeat, especially Deep Disco Records music.

Thank you, to all the writers of Black Speculative Fiction out there. Especially the Africans. I loved all the stories and being immersed in the culture. We need more people like you all!

Sincere gratitude to everyone who helped me understand my culture better and all the random cultural sources that inspired me.

ABOUT THE AUTHOR

Yvette Oloo is a soulpreneur who is helping others grow their soul. She is on a passionate quest to live a life filled with joy and purpose, all while inspiring others to do the same. For her joy can be simple like her love for the colour blue or how the simple pleasure of watching a mesmerising sunset brings her immense joy.

She graduated with a Bachelor of Architecture degree and is a life coach. Other than writing, she serves others as a Space Transformation Coach. Her focus is to help BIPOC cycle breakers design a mindful home that elevates them in mind, body and spirit. Through decolonising their home, they develop a sense of belonging, where they can feel connected to their true selves in a way in which they can deeply relate.

Her website is yvetteslight.com